KT-491-752

NA

05128048

A LITTLE DEATH

A LITTLE DEATH

A.J. Cross

This first world edition published 2017
in Great Britain and the USA by
SEVERN HOUSE PUBLISHERS LTD of
19 Cedar Road, Sutton, Surrey, England, SM2 5DA.
Trade paperback edition first published
in Great Britain and the USA 2017 by
SEVERN HOUSE PUBLISHERS LTD

British Library Cataloguing in Publication Data
A CIP catalogue record for this title is available from the British Library.

ISBN-13: 978-0-7278-8700-9 (cased)
ISBN-13: 978-1-84751-777-7 (trade paper)
ISBN-13: 978-1-78010-845-2 (e-book)

All Severn House titles are printed on acid-free paper.

Severn House Publishers support the Forest Stewardship Council™ [FSC™],
the leading international forest certification organisation.
All our titles that are printed on FSC certified paper carry the FSC logo.

MIX
Paper from
responsible sources
FSC® C013056

Typeset by Palimpsest Book Production Ltd.,
Falkirk, Stirlingshire, Scotland.
Printed and bound in Great Britain by
TJ International, Padstow, Cornwall.

ONE

The insistent buzz dragged Dr Kate Hanson's head from her pillow, the rest of her body still in the grip of sleep. Scrabbling for the phone edging its way across the bedside table, she pulled herself upright, squinting at the time then at her caller's ID: Detective Sergeant Bernard Watts, one of her colleagues in the Unsolved Crime Unit. 1.23 a.m. Whatever he had to tell her was not good news.

'That you, doc?'

She pushed her dark auburn hair from her face, glad her thirteen-year-old daughter wasn't here. 'What's happened?'

'A tragedy, I'd call it.'

'Who?'

'Go back twelve months to the disappearance of child-hero-turned-student . . .'

'Elizabeth Williams,' said Hanson, throwing back the duvet.

'Got it in one. We think we've found her. Chong's being tight-lipped as usual but the age estimate and measurements fit.'

His reference to Rose Road headquarters' pathologist Connie Chong told Hanson that somewhere in the slumbering city the examination of a body had begun.

'Where is it?'

'Just three-quarters of a mile from Williams's college in Genners Lane. There's some undeveloped land off a lane there with all that's left of a cricket ground and an old pavilion from years back. She's in the field next to it.'

Hanson was out of bed, pulling on the jeans she'd worn the day before. She lowered her head to speak into the phone. 'Give me the postcode.'

'No need. Look out your window.'

Pulling back the curtains she gazed out at the slumbering avenue, its houses dark and self-contained behind their low garden walls in the early June, night-time chill. The glossy Range Rover was on her drive, its rich bronze subdued in the meagre light of a newish moon.

'Shall I request a female constable for the brainbox?' he asked
– referring to Hanson's thirteen-year-old.

'Maisie's at Kevin's. Give me two minutes.'

Hanson was in the Range Rover's warmth, its engine running.

'What else do you know?' she asked.

She waited as Watts reversed, then accelerated away from the
house. Fifty-plus and looking every year of it in the dashboard's
reflected light, gruff to the point of rudeness, she anticipated that
any information he had was pivotal. He'd already visited the site.

'A bunch of local kids playing rounders in the field found the
body at around eight o'clock.'

Aghast, she studied him, images of bone-breaks and raw, torn
flesh crowding her head. 'Tell me they didn't come across it lying
there.'

On a series of indicator clicks he turned on to the main road.
'Trust you to knit up a horror scenario. She's been missing twelve
months and buried for God knows how long.' He glanced at her.
'One of the kids tripped, looked to see why and wished she hadn't.'

'What was it?' she asked, reaching up to wind her thick dark red
hair into a restraining band.

'Shredded tarpaulin and the remains of fingers.'

She looked away from him. 'Sounds like a "horror scenario"
to me.'

After several minutes of silence the massive, modern buildings
of the college campus appeared on their right, mostly in darkness
except for lights along its pathways. Passing it they turned left off
Genners Lane into darkness, the road narrow, their headlights
sweeping over compact hedges and the press of trees on both sides.
A pleasant enough setting, thought Hanson, depending on the time
you came here and your purpose.

Watts slowed and pulled in behind several police vehicles and
Chong's black estate car with its dark-tinted windows.

Hanson looked from the black estate to the field beyond the
hedge. Away to the left a large white forensic tent was a concentrated
light source. Getting out of the Range Rover she picked up voices
rolling towards them on the still air. She scanned the area to either
side, getting her first sighting of the old cricket pavilion. Watts
arrived at her side.

'What time did you first get here?' she asked.

'Around nine. Whittaker and Jones were the first response at eight thirty. They called it in and preserved the scene.' He nodded to the fresh-faced officer standing at a narrow gap in the hedge marked by crime scene tape.

'Whittaker's on guard so getting in will be like negotiating access to Fort Knox.'

She gave Watts a reproving glance. 'You should encourage the young.'

'Yeah, right.' He said, his two-decade or so start on her reflected in his voice. 'I've put a rush on the DNA but we're confident it's Elizabeth Williams.'

'How so?'

'The measurements from Chong fit, plus a scarf and a ring believed to belong to Williams.'

More muted voices reached them on a sudden breeze cool enough to be coming straight off the nearby reservoir. Hanson zipped her jacket and they headed for Whittaker who lifted the blue-and-white tape for them.

'Back again, sarge? Names and details, please.' He waited, pen poised over a pad turned silvery by moonlight.

Watts' eyes rolled. 'Detective Sergeant Bernard Watts, Unsolved Crime Unit, police headquarters. Dr Kate Hanson, Forensic Psychologist, UCU and University of Birmingham.'

They waited, Hanson's attention fixed on the field ahead, pulse rate climbing. Watts shifted on his large feet as Whittaker wrote neatly, peered at his watch and added the time.

'Good work, son,' she heard Watts say.

'Welcome, sarge. Here. Take these.'

They took face masks and protective coveralls, silently shrugging their way into them as Whittaker watched.

'You'll be glad of the mask Dr Hanson, take my word for it.'

She gave an absent nod, her attention still on the field which had held on to Elizabeth Williams in death for a year and was now giving up its secret.

Coveralls swishing, they passed the pavilion, long and low, ravaged by time and wilful destruction, tiles ripped from its roof, the remains of its veranda fence snapped at angles like dirty broken bones, blue and black graffiti scarring its wooden walls and 'Keep Out!' notices, its windows boarded and sightless, the wide door angled like a loose tooth.

Watts jabbed a thumb. 'See that? A well-known meeting point for local types who'll need checking out.'

Types. Hanson recognised his word for the delinquent and the deviant which policing brought to him. He wasn't finished.

'Years ago when I'd just started on the job and this was a cricket pitch, I played here and that pavilion was full of sandwiches and tea.' He sniffed. 'Like everything, it's gone to the dogs.'

'The new college we just past cost millions to build.'

He gave her a sideways glance. 'You've only lived in Birmingham five minutes—'

'Fourteen-plus years actually.'

'And that kind of place is your terra firma, not mine. I don't connect to it.' He frowned at the pavilion as they passed beyond it. 'I don't connect here any longer.'

Recognising the morose tone, she said nothing. They walked on in silence, a whooshing sound sending Hanson's tension spiralling as a sudden white light bathed the field in a shimmering glow as the white clad SOCOs formed a line to move over the bright grass in search of evidence. Reaching the forensic tent Hanson got that feeling of being inside a bubble. She recognised it: a self-protective device for whatever she was about to see.

Another officer appeared, clipboard in hand. She gave her name despite the fact that he saw her almost every time she went to police headquarters. By-the-book police work. Security of the crime scene.

Standing in the diffuse light from the tent, Hanson picked up a familiar voice punctuated by clicks. Chong was recording her findings. Bright light hit their faces as the officer guarding the mouth of the tent held back the flap for them to enter, his eyes resolutely fixed on the horizon. Chong's voice drifted out to them.

'. . . found buried in a shallow grave.' Hanson absorbed the few words. *Aren't they always? Easier for the killer. Digging deep took time. Even in early June last year when Elizabeth Williams disappeared.*

The stench hit Hanson, stopping her thinking and her breath. It slid around her mask, so dense, so pungent she could almost taste it. Her stomach rippled. In her haste to leave her house she'd forgotten the mentholated cream. She glanced at Chong's face through the Perspex face shield. There was no cream on her upper lip. Chong was toughing it out. Hanson watched and listened as she spoke into the handheld recorder.

'Zero evidence of clothing, save for the scarf looped loosely around the area of the neck, fitting description of victim's own. Ring, possibly gold, found in the vicinity of one of the hands, fitting description of one belonging to victim at the time she disappeared. Remains wrapped in large grey-green tarpaulin which has sustained significant damage from animal predation whilst buried. No labels or other identification on tarpaulin visible at this time.'

Watts stood, his eyes on the pathologist, his bulldog face impassive, arms hanging at his sides. Hanson forced her focus from the diminutive pathologist to the oozing green-black remains lying on the open tarpaulin in the makeshift grave. They were a sludgy, discoloured hammer blow to the senses. Face flushed, Chong looked up at them, then directly at Watts as he opened his mouth. She clicked off the recorder and pushed up the face shield, fixing him with a look.

'Do *not* ask. The answer's the same as when you last asked me. I can't give you a cause of death. Hi, Hanson.'

'No inkling at all?' he pressed

She looked exasperated. 'How long have we worked together? You should know by now. I don't do "inklings". I can offer you a "probably". Judging by what I'm seeing so far, she was probably buried here close to the time she disappeared.'

He kept his eyes on her face, his own showing none of its usual ruddiness.

She gestured at the remains. 'Just one look should tell you why it's still a "no" on cause of death.' He kept his eyes averted.

'I've told the lab to get a move on,' he said. 'Forensics will ring the DNA result direct to you.'

He left the tent and Hanson knelt at the grave-edge, pressing her mask against her face. A futile gesture but it felt like she was doing something to halt the foulness seeping around it. When people she met socially asked about her work as a forensic psychologist she invariably kept her responses to a minimum yet even those were often enough to turn initial thrill to grimaced distaste. Her eyes travelled over the remains. The reality of her work was light years from most people's experience. Right now she was looking at yet another reality she could never, would never, divulge.

The general shape of the remains was discernible. They looked tall. Long limbed. She watched Chong move around them, peering and recording. They were much alike; she and Chong in the way they dealt with what their work brought them: collect the data, analyse and hypothesize. *Keep it theoretical. Keep it distant.*

Watts was back, displacing odour-heavy air, causing a rush of saliva to Hanson's mouth. Swallowing, she took the photographs he was handing her. She knew which ones they were. For most people in this city, possibly the country, these images had become iconic during the previous year following their inclusion in media reports of Elizabeth Williams' disappearance.

The one uppermost showed Elizabeth as a competitor in the Great Birmingham Run, dressed in shorts and sleeveless top bearing the city's red-and-blue logo, her tanned face smiling broadly as she ran towards the camera, dark hair drawn back in a ponytail, frozen in its sideways flip. Hanson lingered on the details. A delaying tactic. Monitoring her breathing, she drew the second photograph from beneath it.

Elizabeth Williams at age twelve, a year younger than Hanson's daughter, her large, clear eyes gazing upwards as a city dignitary raised his arms above her head, his hands holding the red-blue striped ribbon with its small, round medal as he conferred on her the title 'Birmingham Child Hero'.

Hanson lowered the photographs, forehead slick, heart pounding. She looked again at scraped-away earth, discolouration and putrescence, senses sharpened, an odour like no other filling her nose, her mouth. Anger engulfed her. Whoever did this, how *dare* they? How dare they reduce a vital young woman, anyone to this?

She wondered if the perpetrator had known that Elizabeth Williams was her disabled mother's carer from when she was only nine years old. That despite those responsibilities, she had excelled at school and secured a place at the nearby college to do a sports science degree? Had her killer known any of it? Hanson knew why killers did what they did. It was her job to know. It didn't make the selfish destruction of the act any easier to bear.

A distant memory thrashed and surfaced inside her head, triggering years-old fear and confusion. Instinctively she dragged foul air into her chest.

Chong looked up, giving a sympathetic nod. 'I know. This is about as bad as it gets.'

Chong hadn't understood. There was no reason why she should. The ghastliness in front of them, the photograph of twelve-year-old Elizabeth Williams had stirred a personal memory for Hanson, one known to only one other person, with the exception of the man himself: Hanson aged six, playing with her friend Celia inside a park, surrounded by the fresh scent of roses and the bogus safety of glossy black railings. The man had beckoned. Hanson had gone to him, felt his grab at her hair. The oozing stickiness of his hand had caused it to slip from his grasp. She closed her eyes. At six years old she had lost a vestige of innocence, but she'd been lucky. Elizabeth Williams had had her whole life stolen from her.

Eyes fixed on the remains, she burned their image into her head for the coming days and weeks she and her colleagues would work the investigation.

'Found anything useful?' she asked, her voice steady.

Chong carefully straightened the tarpaulin and gave it a close examination. 'Joseph used those exact words earlier.'

Lieutenant Joe Corrigan. Polite, personable, on secondment to headquarters as a firearms trainer from Boston, Connecticut, also a colleague in the Unsolved Crime Unit.

'Not much so far.'

Chong pointed at various parts of the remains. 'What may be fibres under the fingernails there, bits of tree bark caught within the hair, plus a fine specimen of a stag beetle trapped inside a fold of this.' She pulled the tarpaulin taut, giving it careful scrutiny.

'I have my doubts she was killed here. Relay that to Sergeant Nightmare while I finish up.'

Activating the recording device she repeated the details she'd given Hanson, adding, 'Initial examination terminated at . . . 2.23 a.m.'

She stood, stretched, and called to her pathology technician in conversation with Watts beyond the tent's entrance.

'When we get back to headquarters I want her straight to a refrigerated body store. I'm going home for a couple of hours' sleep before I start her post at seven thirty. If you arrive first, set the ventilation system to max. You can bring the body bag now.'

Hanson left the tent and stood, her eyes drifting around the brightly lit field, pulling sharp night air into her chest. She glanced to Watts, his arms folded.

'OK?'

He avoided her eye. 'Bloody awful, that.'

She nodded. It wasn't only the sight of such horror that jolted even veterans like him. Like everybody here, he had a life beyond policing. His adult daughter had been nineteen once. They stood together, Hanson looking straight ahead, listening to the low rumble of SOCO voices as they went about their tasks.

A small movement some metres away at the perimeter of the field snagged her attention. She struggled with the contrast of scene lights and darkness beyond. A fox? Her eyes focused on the spot, straining against distance, she saw it was neither. It was human. Crouched in shadows, watching them. As if aware of her attention it stood and retreated a few steps towards tree cover. Hanson did not move.

'Did you see that?'

Watts had. He hissed to a couple of nearby officers. 'Get over there. *Now*.'

The distant figure had all but disappeared. One of the officers shouted a warning and both broke into a run, covering the ground at speed before they also disappeared from view. Watts and Hanson waited. Within a couple of minutes the two officers reappeared holding an unresisting figure by the arms, one officer bending to retrieve his hat which he'd lost during the pursuit.

They came into the white light and Hanson saw that their captive was a heavy-set male, forty-plus, in jogging pants and a T-shirt despite the chill night, his face stubble-dark, breath laboured, his forehead shiny with sweat.

'Got him, sarge.' said one of the officers as they neared.

Watts glared at the dishevelled man. 'Who are you?'

Silence.

'Why'd you run?'

Getting no response, Watts unzipped the forensic coverall, reached inside and pulled out his notebook.

'Name!' he barked.

The man was still wheezing from exertion and possible shock. His two-word response was enough for Hanson to pick up the local accent.

'Michael Myers.'

Watts's eyes were fixed on the man's face. 'Search him.'

One of the officers held on to Myers as the other started a series of minimal but efficient pats from shoulders to ankles, then sprang upright.

'Nothing, sarge.'

Watts subjected the man's face to close scrutiny. 'Tell us what you're up to out here in the middle of the night.'

Myers straightened and squared his shoulders. 'Running. Part of my SAS training.'

Their eyes went to the paunch pushing against the soiled T-shirt and hanging over the waistband of the scruffy joggers.

'Where do you live?'

'No comment.'

Tired, out of patience, Watts turned to the officers. 'Stick him in a car and give him a ride to headquarters.'

Brows rising, Myers looked at him. 'Why? I'm a responsible citizen.'

'Then answer the question!'

Myers' eyes darted around the field. 'I haven't done anything but if The Sanctuary gets to hear that I've been arrested, they'll bar me.'

Hearing the name of the local community support facility, Hanson said, 'Mr Myers, no one has mentioned arrest but you need to answer the officer's questions.'

He stared at her then nodded, giving Watts a speculative look.

'Address,' said Watts, pen poised.

'Flat 1A, 24 Abbey Road, Bartley Green,' he recited in a monotone.

'Anybody there we can contact?'

Myers merely gazed at him.

'Do you live with anyone, Mr Myers?' Hanson asked.

'No. Just me. And the other people that live there.'

Watts fixed him with a look. 'I'll ask you again. This time I want a sensible answer: what are you doing out here at this time of night?'

'I come here most nights.'

'For what?'

'I'm a wildlife expert. I need funding.' He swept a tattooed arm in the general direction of Genners Lane. 'I've sent a research proposal to the college over there.'

Watts heaved a sigh. 'Yeah, yeah, 'course you have.' He considered Myers.

'Any idea why we're out here?'

Myers pursed his thick lips, his facial expression thoughtful. 'Looking for me?'

Hanson intervened. 'Mr Myers, as a regular visitor to this area you may have information about an incident the police are investigating which occurred here this time last year.'

He drew himself up. 'I think I can help you there.' He pointed to the dilapidated pavilion. 'I've had that place under surveillance for—'

'Hey!' Watts raised a warning finger. 'Stop messing about. If you were out here in this immediate area last June and you remember anything then tell us.'

Myers looked from him to Hanson then scratched his head.

'Last June . . . I got out of hospital on the twenty-eighth of May. I was in for a week because . . .' He caught Watts's frown and hurried on. 'I started coming down here straight after.' He patted the paunch. 'For my exercise regime.'

Watts turned away from him to the two officers. 'Get him out of my sight and into a car.'

Myers pulled against the young officers' grip. 'Wait! That's probably around the time I heard it.'

Silent, they looked at him.

'What did you hear, Mr Myers?' prompted Hanson.

'A voice.'

Watts shot her a look then back to Myers. 'You heard voices.'

'Just the one.'

'Male or female?'

Myers pursed his lips again. 'Hard to say.'

'*Try.*'

'Youngish male – or it could have been an older male. Or a woman.'

Hanson studied him. He'd given scant details about himself but her impression was of a vulnerable individual. This didn't mean he had no useful information. 'What did the voice say?'

Myers raised his arms and his facc to the darkened sky. '"I'm *here*! Look me in the eye. Lo-*ok* at me-*ee*."'

In the bright field surrounded by the press of trees, the distant outlines of firs, needle-clustered branches stabbing the black sky, Hanson's shoulders tingled.

Myers was looking at her. 'Or something like that.' He started at Watts's voice.

'*Right*. We've got your details. We'll be in touch. These officers will drop you home.'

The officers walked Myers to one of the patrol cars and they followed towards the Range Rover. Hanson reached for the passenger door then turned to Watts.

'Michael Myers.'

'What about him?'

'It might not be his real name.'

He eyed her across the vehicle's bonnet. 'What makes you say that?'

'When he said it, it struck a chord. For the last four years or so, as we approach the thirty-first of October Maisie and I have a difference of opinion. She wants to watch the film. I say no.'

Inside the vehicle, he said, 'Care to give me the merest *hint* as to what you're on about?'

'The date. The film. *Halloween*. Michael Myers is the name of the killer in it.'

He stared at her. 'You're saying I just wasted valuable time listening to a bloke who's head is in la-la land and styles himself on some crazed killer in a horror film?'

Face set, he started the engine.

In her low-lit kitchen, Hanson washed her hands then reached into a cupboard for cups, aware of a series of loud sniffs. She glanced at Watts holding his sleeve close to his face, then did the same to her own sleeve. Death odours cling to clothes and everything else.

'What would you like?' she asked.

'I'm gasping for a cup o' tea. Make mine a mug. Three sugars, ta.'

She swapped one of the cups as he flicked open his notebook.

'Michael-bloody-Myers. What're the chances of running into the local nutter out there in the middle of the night?' He gazed towards the tall glass doors at the end of the kitchen. 'Although, having said it, it makes a kind of weird sense.'

Waiting for the water to boil she watched him read his notes. 'Who originally investigated the Williams disappearance?'

'Officers local to that area,' he said. 'They did the usual checks with family, friends, appealed for eyewitnesses. Nothing. They searched where she was living for leads. Again, nothing. They boxed up her belongings and took them away. When the investigation wound down, they sent it all to headquarters for storage. I've requested the lot but I'm not getting excited that it'll give us anything.' He dropped the notebook onto the table.

'What did the local children who found the remains have to say?' she asked.

He reached for the notebook again. 'Not a lot. That field's one of the places they play because of the space and the grass. They

got there at about six. Didn't notice anything or see anything until
the girl tripped. When they saw the fingers sticking up, they legged
it home, which is Genners Lane for most of them. I've got their
contact details if we need them.'

A hint of a new day had appeared beyond the glass doors.

'Without knowing where Elizabeth Williams was killed and no
cause of death, we've got the worst job possible,' he said. 'We
need to know both and soon or we'll be scrabbling for a way
forward.'

Hanson poured boiling water onto teabags then glanced at his
slumped shoulders. 'We'll find one,' she said.

He broke the brief silence. 'Myers doesn't sound too swift to
me. What's your take on him?'

'The Sanctuary he mentioned is a couple of miles from where
the remains were found. It's a drop-in centre for people with learning
disabilities and difficulties with daily living. A lot of what he said
suggests he's also something of a fantasist.'

She brought the tea and a plate of biscuits to the table. He took
two and gulped the tea. 'You'll be seeing him again,' she said.

'Yes, but before I do I'll check if he's got form.' He looked at
her. 'For all we know, hearing voices might be his thing.'

She shook her head. 'I didn't pick up any indication that he's
psychotic.'

He shrugged. 'I want you there when I talk to him.'

'Let me know when.'

He closed the notebook and slipped it into an inside pocket. 'Seen
anything of Corrigan recently?'

She pictured Joe Corrigan here in her kitchen, the dark hair and
ready smile, his long legs crossed at the ankle as he leant against
the nearby worktop.

'He dropped in a couple of weeks ago to tell me that Roger
Furman has gone,' she said of the inspector who had managed the
Unsolved Crime Unit since she'd become involved with it. Furman
had done all he could to make her time in UCU difficult.

'Good riddance,' murmured Watts. 'His replacement has arrived
from Thames Valley. I know a couple of people at Thames who
know Trevor Nuttall and they don't rate him as an investigator.'

'In which case, he's likely to leave us alone to get on with the
case.'

'Don't count on it. I reckon Rose Road Headquarters and UCU

are his swansong to retirement, which means he'll want quick results.'

She studied his heavy face, the greying hair. She didn't know his exact age but guessed he was in his early fifties, possibly a little more. Many officers were gone from the force by that age. She knew his views on retirement because it was one of the very few personal issues he occasionally chose to talk about. Watts wasn't big on talk about personal matters although not averse to intruding on hers at times. His phone buzzed, interrupting her thoughts. He took it from his pocket, read words on the screen.

'Chong's got the DNA results: a match for Elizabeth Williams.'

He gulped his tea and stood. 'I'm heading straight to Rose Road to read through what we've got from the original investigation.'

She frowned. 'No offence, but you – we – smell of death. Before you do that I'd advise a shower.'

He sniffed his jacket again and nodded.

She followed him to the door, knowing that he was going home to an empty house. His wife had died very suddenly five or so years before.

At the door he turned to look down at her. 'You're young, doc. Don't be alone all your life.'

His words took her by surprise. 'I'm not alone. I've got Maisie.'

Hanson's eyes followed his to the folders and school textbooks on the hall chest, clear evidence if she needed it of change in the making. She suppressed the line of thinking.

Stepping outside he said, 'I'm hoping Chong will give us a cause of death and there's the next of kin to visit pronto, before the news gets out. Will you have some time today?'

'I usually find some.' She thought of the member of Elizabeth Williams' family who would soon be receiving the worst news.

'Her mother?'

'No. She died. It's a paternal aunt.'

Hanson watched him walk to his vehicle then closed her door. Double locking it and switching off the lights, she went upstairs and turned the shower to full force. Stepping out of her clothes she stood under the torrent, Watts's observation on her life still in her head. Married for two years, now divorced, her life suited her. Being a single parent wasn't easy for anybody but she knew she had it easier than many. She had full-time work, which was demanding but she loved it, and Maisie had never known what it was to have a stay-at-home mother.

Taking a lavish palm-full of body wash she spread it over herself with vigorous strokes then took a similar amount of shampoo, applied it to her hair, then stood as soapy water coursed downwards and swirled around her feet, carrying away the stench of death. Watts and Corrigan were experienced police officers but they would soon want her psychological expertise and insight to help them establish the identity of Elizabeth Williams' destroyer. She watched the last of the water disappear. It wasn't that simple for her. Yes, she wanted the 'who' but it was the 'why' which drove her.

She thought back to the field and her sudden rage at what they were seeing. *Violence happens to men but most happens to women, females of all ages. Fact. Many murders remained unresolved if they weren't clearly domestic-related 'self-solvers'. Fact.*

From now, everything she did as part of the investigation would focus on the search for the 'why'.

TWO

Gazing out on the crowded auditorium, Hanson drew her third lecture of the morning, 'Profiling: Does It Work?', to a close. Rows of mute faces gazed back at her.

'I repeat: profiling does *not* apprehend rapists and killers. Sound policing in collaboration with forensic science does that.' The silence was palpable.

'OK, that wraps it up for today.'

She came into her room at the university, dumped an armful of folders on her desk, then went to the window, pushing it open onto the early-summer campus. Cool air on her face, she looked at the Chamberlain Tower clock, feeling the lack of sleep catching up with her.

A young woman with spiky blonde hair and lavish mascara emerged from the adjoining office. 'I'm making coffee. How were they?'

Hanson smiled at her assistant. 'Their problem, Crystal, is that they picture themselves as forensic psychology Lone Rangers after they graduate, single-handedly profiling murderers at the humble request of the police. They weren't thrilled to hear the reality.'

'In the mood for some good news? You've just had this from the VC.' Crystal grinned as she handed a printout to her.

Hanson took the printed-out email and read it, brows rising. The vice chancellor had somehow heard about the Elizabeth Williams case and the Unsolved Crime Unit's involvement in it and had transferred four hours of lecture time from her to the head of school. She looked up at her assistant.

'A whole *four* hours of extra time per week so I can continue to assist the police with their inquiries.'

Laughing, Crystal shook her head. 'Bet you feel totally spoilt.'

'Positively bratty. After coffee I'll start on the admin you've been chasing me for—'

Her phone rang and she reached for it. Seeing her caller's name, she instinctively turned away. 'Hi, Watts. What do you know?'

'Chong will have the post-mortem results at two. How are you fixed?'

She looked at her watch. 'I'll come now.'

Entering the stark white reception area of police headquarters, Hanson saw Lieutenant Joe Corrigan standing at the desk. His arrival at headquarters two years before had caused a stir among its female employees. Judging by the look he was getting from the civilian worker sitting behind the desk, that hadn't changed much. If he was dating anyone, as far as Hanson knew it was no one here. Right now, his face was serious, his arms folded high on his chest as he listened intently to an officer she recognised from the field the previous night.

He turned and Hanson was momentarily stopped by the intense blue of his eyes. She nodded at him.

'Watts tells me Chong's got information for us.'

He smiled down at her. 'Straight to business as always. How about a little to-and-fro? Hi, Red. How's it going?'

She gave another quick nod, ignoring the use of his name for her. 'Good, thanks.' They walked the corridor together. She felt his eyes still on her.

'Chong is expecting us in twenty minutes which gives you just enough time to get acquainted with the Williams case file,' he said. She picked up subtle aromas of soap and cologne as he opened the door leading to UCU for her.

Julian Devenish, Hanson's PhD student was sitting cross-legged on the carpet. Tall, rail-thin, his quick wits and technological expertise had led her to choose him of all her undergraduates to join UCU at the same time she did two years before. He'd proved to be the right choice. As she entered he was totally focused on a massive electronic board she'd never seen now fixed to the wall, a laptop supported on his knees, a projector some distance behind him.

She came to a stop in front of it. 'When did all this arrive?'

'A month ago but this is the first time I've seen it. Like it?'

Dropping her belongings on the big worktable she stared at it. 'I don't know what to say except that I want one for the psychology department. What does it do?'

'It's a Smartboard, so pretty much anything you ask.'

Imagining Watts's response to this, she watched as Julian put the laptop on the floor, stood and went to the board to raise both hands, moving basic details of the Williams case around using his index finger and thumb. He tapped one of the icons to one side of the board. A map of the Genners Lane area appeared and next to it the field where Elizabeth Williams' body had been found. Hanson's mouth formed a perfect 'O'.

He grinned. 'That's nothing. Watch *this*.'

On a single hand-gesture the field filled the board. Following another, she was seeing its surface detail, its hedges and trees in 3D. She watched his hand move again and the 3D image disappeared, replaced by two large, full colour reproductions of Elizabeth Williams' photographs. She stared at them as Corrigan came and stood beside her.

'Tragic,' he said quietly.

'Yes. It is.'

The door opened and she turned, expecting to see Watts. Standing there was a shortish man who looked to be in his late fifties dressed in a brown three-piece suit. He looked at Hanson then at Corrigan.

'Who's this?' he asked.

Corrigan made introductions. 'Dr Kate Hanson, Forensic Psychologist from the University of Birmingham. Dr Hanson, this is Inspector Nuttall, Thames Valley Police.'

Nuttall came inside with a squeak of polished shoes, eyes on her. 'I've heard about you from the chief.' He looked back to Corrigan.

'Where's the pathologist?'

'PM suite. We're going down in a couple of minutes.'

Nuttall glanced at Julian, gave the screen a dismissive look then back to Corrigan. 'I've got a meeting with Chief Superintendent Gander so I'll leave you to it. I don't need to see the PM. You'll learn that I operate with a light management hand but keep in mind that most murder cases are straightforward and obvious and that's exactly how we work them.'

Hanson watched him go through the door and out. 'What was that about?' she asked.

Corrigan shook his head. 'If he was in Thames Valley, he'd be an amusing irrelevance.'

The door flew open and Watts leant into the room. 'Chong's ready for us.

They followed him, Hanson thinking that the case file would have to wait. She'd get it copied and take the information home.

Inside the post-mortem suite Hanson was feeling edgy. It made no difference that she'd already seen the remains. It didn't help that she'd seen bad sights on other cases she'd worked on here and for other police forces. Each post-mortem produced that same mix of edginess and shocked recognition of the harm done purposely by one person to another: lover, relative, friend, stranger.

The extract system hummed as Chong approached one end of the steel table and lifted the green sheet, quietly folding it back on itself until all of the remains were exposed. They stood in silence around the table, their clothes, heads and faces covered. The garb was mandatory. To Hanson it was a final rejection, distancing her and her colleagues from what had been a living, breathing individual. Months ago, she'd said as much to Watts. His response had been, 'When you're dead, you're dead, doc, and when you're alive in this game you don't want to leave hairs or pick up something nasty and take it with you.'

She looked down at all there was of Elizabeth Williams. It had been awful when viewed at its illicit burial site. It was no better under stark post-mortem lights although the odour was slightly less potent.

'OK, UCU,' said Chong quietly. 'This won't take long.'

They watched her stretch her arms to encompass the remains. 'Elizabeth Williams. Nineteen years old. Dental records confirm the DNA identification.' She walked slowly towards the head then back to the feet to reach for a manila file on a nearby work surface.

'I can tell you that she was not stabbed, not beaten and not shot. The X-rays I took rule out all three.'

She removed a single A4 sheet from the file. 'Toxicology indicates she wasn't poisoned. There is no indication of ingestion of alcohol or other substance at around the time she died.' Hanson picked up restlessness from Watts.

'OK. Let's have it,' he said. 'What did kill her?'

She gave him a direct look. 'I don't know.'

He stared at her. 'We've got three weeks max on this and the one thing worse than investigating a MISPER is a murder without a cause of death.'

Chong pointed to the remains. 'Last June was warm and wet. Add to that the damage to the tarpaulin caused by animal predation which allowed moisture to seep inside and you'll understand why the body is in such a poor state. That, plus insect and rodent activity and proliferation of her gut bacteria . . .' She stopped.

'I've spent eight hours on her and I've told you what didn't happen. That's useful, although I understand it's not what you want. There's no indication that she had consensual sex or was raped prior to death but given the state of the body I can't rule them out. She wasn't subjected to a severe beating which damaged her skeletal structure, but there's little of her soft tissue in a good enough state of preservation to indicate what might have happened to her. Elizabeth Williams is a riddle wrapped in a mystery, or however the saying goes.'

Hanson gazed over her mask at Watts, guessing he was choosing his words because he didn't want to get on Chong's wrong side.

'The cases I've worked over the years where the victim was a young female, strangulation was often the cause of death.'

He glanced at her to judge how she was taking this line of reasoning. 'In that kind of situation the hyoid bone in the neck gets broken, plus there was a scarf.'

She shook her head. 'The scarf wasn't a tool of strangulation. The hyoid is intact. Remember the X-rays? As I said there's no indication of trauma to her skeletal structure but like I've also said, there's no tissue in a condition which might provide evidence of bruising or petechial haemorrhage.'

'What about the trace evidence?' asked Hanson.

Chong gave her a quick nod. 'Thanks for moving us on to the good news. I've removed the fibres from under her fingernails. They look to me to be wool, pale in colour, possibly from domestic carpeting. Forensics will confirm or otherwise when they've tested them.'

She walked to the head of the remains. 'I've also given Forensics the fragments of tree bark caught in the head hair which appear to have come from a range of trees, plus slivers of wood, a very deceased stag beetle and a range of other insect remains. Forensics have it all. They've estimated an absolute minimum of several days for a report back.'

'Are you going to tell me where we're going?' Hanson asked Watts as they left headquarters and headed towards the High Street.

She gazed out of the window. Out here, normal life was continuing. The Range Rover slowed and she watched two teenage girls cross in front of them in short skirts and sandals, their demeanour light and bubbly. She felt an urgent need to call to them: *Please – stay aware. Never doubt that there are people capable of doing you harm.*

Lips pressed together, she shielded her eyes with her hand. Since having Maisie, every young person seemed to be vulnerable. Love for her daughter plus the kind of work she did made it unlikely that that view would change.

'To that Sanctuary place Myers goes to. They're expecting us,' he said.

She was surprised. Her initial assessment of Myers hadn't suggested a need to see him again so soon. He was a fantasist, which in Watts's terms made him appear odd, but there had been nothing in his general demeanour at the field which suggested to her that he might have had direct involvement in a murder committed many months before. She doubted Watts was taking seriously what Myers had said about a voice he'd claimed to have heard. She wasn't convinced about it herself if it came to it.

'You're interested in him?'

'I am now.' He gave her a quick glance. 'I've done some checking. You were right. Michael Myers isn't his real name. He changed it from Terry Higgins by deed poll three years back.'

Seeing Hanson's mouth open he said, 'Want to know something else? He's got form.'

'For what?'

'Disturbing the peace times two. He's a peeping Tom.'

'Voyeur,' she corrected.

'Whatever.'

'What do you know about his offences?' she asked.

'They're the usual. Watching women who can't be bothered to close their curtains.'

She chose not to debate this. 'When and where?'

'Both offences date back to 1996 in the Bartley Green area. According to the file it was around the time his mother died, which was given as a mitigating factor in court. There were no aggravating factors so he got a non-custodial sentence.'

She recalled what Myers had told them about himself. 'Did you establish if he's had any army experience?'

'He's got that all right but don't get excited about all that SAS stuff he was on about. He managed to get accepted by the army back in 1987.' He huffed. 'They must have been desperate.'

'So his references to being a soldier have some foundation?'

'Yeah. Three weeks at Catterick before they twigged him and slung him out.'

THREE

'**M**iss Williams? Joy Williams?'

The fiftyish woman nodded to the tall, dark-haired man with the American accent, then gazed at the identification he was holding towards her.

'Lieutenant Corrigan, Unsolved Crime Unit, police headquarters, Rose Road. I rang earlier.'

He hadn't been specific on the phone but it was evident that she had an idea why he was here. The female victim support officer he'd requested should arrive in about an hour. Looking at the woman, thinking of the news he was about to give her, he wished that Hanson was here.

Getting no response he said, 'May I come inside, ma'am?'

She let him into the small hallway and Corrigan closed the door behind him. He'd delivered bad news many times, here and back home. It never got easier but the focus was always the person about to get the bad news. He watched her walk into the room immediately ahead and followed. It was a pleasant room, all pale carpet and soft furnishings and he regretted having to bring the horror of violent death into it.

Inside the sitting room she turned to him, waiting. He wanted her sitting.

'How about we sit down?' he said.

'Sorry. I'm not thinking.'

She waved him towards an armchair then sat on the edge of a sofa, hands fluttering at her hair, then at the collar of her cotton shirt like restless birds. She gripped them together and looked directly at him.

'You've got news. About Elizabeth.'

'I have, ma'am.' A clock above the fireplace ticked on. 'I'm sorry. There's no easy way to say this. Elizabeth has been found.'

Her knuckles showed white. 'Found where? Where is she?'

Suspecting that Joy Williams wasn't yet equating 'found' with 'dead', he said, 'A victim support officer is on her way but in the meantime is there someone you'd like to have with you? Someone nearby? A relative or a friend? Maybe a good neighbour?'

He saw the shock of realisation reach her face. 'She's dead, isn't she? Elizabeth is dead.'

He met her gaze. 'I'm truly sorry, ma'am. She is.' He stood. 'If you tell me where the kitchen is, I'll make you a hot drink.'

Miss Williams gazed up at him 'No, no. I'm . . . fine.'

'You're sure?'

Joy Williams nodded then bowed her head.

A couple of minutes passed until he spoke again, his voice low. 'I'm sorry we have to give you such bad news.'

She straightened, hands clasped tight. 'Every day since she went I've waited for somebody like you to come here.' She looked up at him. He saw hope in her eyes.

'There was nothing on the news this morning. If you've found her, why wasn't it reported?'

'We delayed confirmation until you were informed. It will be reported on later today.'

'There's no mistake?' The question sounded like a plea.

He shook his head. 'No. DNA taken by the previous investigation confirms it is Elizabeth.'

She sat in silence for some seconds then gave him a direct look. 'Tell me where she's been these last twelve months.'

Editing out words like 'body' and 'remains', he kept to the meagre facts. 'She was concealed in a field not far from her college.'

Her hand flew to her mouth. 'So close. She's been there all this time?'

He wouldn't get into more details. It was unlikely that she was capable of absorbing them right now. 'Possibly.'

She looked him in the eye. 'I can't see her, can I?'

He shook his head. 'I'm sorry. No.'

She gazed towards the window. 'This is what I've been dreading since she went but I can tell you, Lieutenant Corrigan, I've learned in this last year that there's something much, much worse and that's not knowing what happened to her. You've found her and there's something I can do for her now. When do you think her . . . she'll be released?'

'I'm afraid I can't confirm that but I promise we'll keep you informed as to when that's likely.'

Her eyes still on Corrigan, she said, 'I'm sorry but I have another question.'

'That's not a problem, ma'am. Please ask whatever you want. If I can give you an answer, I will.'

'What happened to her?'

It was the question he'd hoped wouldn't arise, the one to which he had no definite answer. 'That's uncertain right now.'

He leant towards her. 'The victim support officer I mentioned earlier will be available for as long as you need her. She can give you practical help and advice but also listen when you want to talk. If you have questions she'll relay them to us. I promise we'll get back to you.'

She looked down at her hands, tears falling unchecked onto the cotton shirt.

He waited. Right now there was no way he could put this woman through any more trauma. 'Miss Williams, I'll stay with you until that officer arrives but I'll come back another day to ask you some questions about Elizabeth if you're OK with that?'

'Ask them now.'

He paused. 'You're sure about that, ma'am?'

She squared her shoulders, her mouth trembling. 'Yes. I'll feel I'm doing something for her. Something useful.'

He kept his eyes on her as he spoke. 'The police came here when you reported Elizabeth missing?'

'Yes. I answered all their questions, gave them photographs . . .' She pressed her fingers to her mouth. 'I explained to them that I was Elizabeth's paternal aunt. My brother and Elizabeth's mother divorced when Elizabeth was very small. He died a couple of years later and I had very little contact with Elizabeth or her mother. I was living in Dorset. I was a teacher. But when I heard that her mother had died and there weren't any other relatives I knew Elizabeth faced being taken into care. I couldn't allow that to happen. I had to give her a home. Not in Dorset, of course. Birmingham was where Elizabeth's life was, her friends, her school. She was barely fifteen and I wanted to keep everything the same for her as much as possible. So I sold my house and moved up here. Bought this house for us.'

'When did you last see Elizabeth, ma'am?'

'The weekend she vanished. She came here on the Sunday for tea.'

Corrigan had seen this information in the file. 'Is there anything you recall of that visit, anything you've thought about since that you think might help us in our search for whoever harmed her?'

She thought for some seconds then shook her head. 'Nothing comes to mind.'

Corrigan asked, 'Elizabeth moved into her own accommodation when she went to college?'

'Yes, but not straight away.' She looked at him. 'After a while I could see that she needed to spread her wings. She shared a tiny house with another student. I was a bit worried when she went but I thought I must have done something right to get her to that point.'

'Elizabeth visited with you often after that?'

'Yes. She came a couple of times a week. I'd make dinner for her and sometimes for the friend she shared the house with.'

'Can you confirm that friend's full name?' he asked, with his pen poised.

'Jess –' she put a hand to her forehead, flustered – 'how stupid. I can't think of her second name.' Her lips trembled. 'I'm sorry.'

'That's OK, ma'am. It's not a problem. What about other friends? One's that maybe Elizabeth talked about to you?'

'I think Jess was the main one. Elizabeth was a friendly, outgoing girl but she was also very private. She mentioned some other names in passing but none that stuck in my head. You know she had a boyfriend?'

Corrigan nodded. 'Can you confirm his name?'

'Chris Turner.'

'Did you ever meet him?'

'A couple of times. She seemed to become more independent of me once she and Chris got together. I suppose it was inevitable. When she first came to live with me she soaked up the care I gave her like blotting paper. It was a real pleasure to do things for her.' Miss Williams struggled for control. 'She hadn't had that for a long time, you see. Not since her mother became ill.' She looked directly at Corrigan.

'Don't get the idea I'm some kind of saint. It was hard work at times but I never married so I relished the chance to care for somebody. For Elizabeth.'

'What can you tell us about Chris Turner?' asked Corrigan.

She thought about it. 'He seemed very nice although I didn't see him often enough to get to know him. I thought how well suited they were because they were both sports mad.'

'Was there anyone else, any other male in Elizabeth's life? Anyone she mentioned around the time she disappeared?'

Joy Williams frowned. 'Not that I recall. During that last week she came here twice and I thought she seemed quiet, a little preoccupied. I wondered if maybe she and Chris had fallen out but then I put it down to the pressure of end-of-year exams. Elizabeth was very punctilious about that kind of thing.'

'You said earlier that the last time you saw her was when she came here for Sunday tea.'

'Yes. The twenty-third of June.'

'She came alone?'

'Yes. She arrived at around half three and stayed till about six and then she went off to see Chris.'

Corrigan looked up at her. 'Is that what she told you she was going to do?'

She looked uncertain. 'I can't recall whether she actually said that's where she was going. I might have assumed it.'

Corrigan paused, knowing that Elizabeth's mobile phone had not been recovered from her belongings. UCU had no social media information relating to the young woman about which he might question Ms Williams. A laptop had been recovered but so far there was no forensic report on it.

Monitoring Miss Williams' face, Corrigan asked, 'Can you tell me about her general mood on that Sunday?'

'She was a bit quiet, like I said.' She frowned. 'But now that I think about it, I got the impression she was excited about something. No, wait. That's putting it too strongly. It was like she had something she had to do.' She shook her head. 'That makes no sense, does it? I'm not explaining it very well.'

'You're doing fine, ma'am. You have no idea what that might have been?'

'No.'

'How did she travel from her college to see you that weekend?'

'By bus. At least, that's what I assumed.' She looked up, unsettled.

'When she moved in with Jess, I asked her not to walk here. I said it was too far but she laughed. She said it was an easy walk. She was very fit as you probably know. But that wasn't why I didn't want her walking.' She looked down at her hands folded in her lap. 'I didn't want her out there when it was getting dark.' She wept again.

Corrigan knew he needed to finish but he had one more question. He kept it simple. 'Was Elizabeth wearing any jewellery when you last saw her?'

'Yes. A small gold ring on her right hand.'

'Was the ring a gift from someone, do you know?'

'Yes. Me.' After a few seconds she said, 'Can I show you something if you've got time? It won't take long.'

She stood, went to a small stack of CDs, removed one and inserted it into the player. They sat in silence as the five-minute-long recording played. It showed twelve-year-old Elizabeth Williams in a slightly-too-big dress, her hair in bunches being honoured by her city, her small face glowing as she received her medal, then gazing out at the applauding audience. The recording ended. Miss Williams broke the silence.

'I didn't know about the award at the time. I'd been here about six months when Elizabeth mentioned it.' She pointed to a framed photograph nearby, one Corrigan recognised as now on UCU's board.

'I requested that from one of the newspapers and then I got in touch with the council and they sent me the CD. My view was that what she'd done as a child needed commemorating in this house. Elizabeth was casual about it but I think she was pleased. What she did for her mother was wonderful and I told her so. All she said was that she loved her mother and there was no one else to do it.'

Corrigan broke the silence. 'Do you have any belongings of Elizabeth's still?'

'No. I was going to ask you about that. The police went to where she was living and took everything from it. They told me they wanted to examine it. She'd left a few items of clothing and cosmetics here after she moved out and they took those as well.' She looked at him. 'You've got your job to do but do you think I can have her things back some time?'

'I'll make sure it happens, including her ring. I'm real sorry you don't have them but they would have been retained in the event of a development in the case.'

She gave him an uncertain look. 'There's a small plastic bag upstairs. It's got some oddments relating to Elizabeth's college course. I showed it to the police who came here and they looked through it. It's upstairs. Would you like to see it?'

'Please.' He stood. 'How about you tell me where it is and I'll get it?'

'No, I'll go. I know exactly where it is.'

Listening to her footsteps on the stairs, Corrigan looked around the room, stopping at the photograph of Elizabeth at twelve, her eyes glowing.

He looked away.

FOUR

The door of The Sanctuary was opened by a pleasant-looking woman wearing a pink, short-sleeved polyester dress with white piping and a name badge: Ellen. Watts showed identification, introduced Hanson and the woman led them inside the functional building, which Hanson knew of but had never been inside before. Voices filtering to them from various directions as they followed her gave an initial impression of a busy environment run with calm efficiency.

'I probably know Michael better than anybody else here.' Ellen tutted then shook her head. 'I'm supposed to call him Mr Myers.'

Watts sent Hanson a meaningful look. 'Is that what he tells you?'

'No. It's what the people who fund this place have told us.'

She took them into a large room furnished with several easy chairs and a few low tables. 'It's in the guidelines we've got. Apparently, we're "service providers" and he's a "service user" and we have to show service users respect. I don't see how calling somebody a service user is respectful. Michael and everybody who comes here is a person and that's how we treat them.'

She sat, tugging at the polyester dress. 'This is their idea as well. Some of the people who come here don't like uniforms. They're wary of them.'

'What can you tell us about Michael Myers?' asked Watts.

She grinned. 'He's a character, is what he is. He's been coming to us most days since I started here, which is five years now.'

'What's he like when he's here?' Watts asked, making quick notes.

She hesitated. 'Is Michael in trouble?' Watts looked up at her and she continued. 'He's quiet. He doesn't make a fuss. If he's got a problem he'll come and find me. I tend to be the one he looks to. Don't ask me why.'

Looking at Ellen's round, open face, Hanson had an idea why: Myers probably gravitated to Ellen because he perceived her as genuinely caring.

'And you're happy about that?' Hanson asked.

'Of course. It's my job and Michael doesn't cause any problems.' Hanson watched comprehension dawn. 'If you're asking whether he bothers me in any way, the answer's no. There's one or two who come here I'm not so keen on and I keep my eye on them but not Michael. He's harmless.'

'What do you actually do here for people like Myers?' asked Watts.

Ellen shrugged. 'We help them fill in forms, applications for benefits, that kind of thing, but mostly it's about giving them a place where they can be with other people and chat if they want to. Or just hear a voice that isn't coming out of a television or a radio. We offer tea and biscuits on a Friday afternoon.' She grinned. 'Michael's always here for that.'

Watts made more quick notes. 'What do you know about him?'

She mused briefly. 'Not that much. Mostly what I've pieced together from what he's said. He told me once he was at boarding school. *I* think he was in care. He's a sort of fixture here. If he didn't turn up some time during the week it would be unusual. I'd be worried.'

Watts gave her a direct look. 'We've talked to Mr Myers. He tells us he had some health problems last June.'

Ellen frowned then shook her head. 'I don't recall anything like that.'

Watts' eyes went to Hanson. 'Was anything particular going on in his life around that time? We're interested in the whole of last June.'

Ellen gave this some thought. 'I think it was around the middle of the month he had to move out of his accommodation because the landlord was selling the house. Effectively, he was being made homeless. It was a nightmare finding somewhere for him to go because it was the start of the holiday season, but due to his having a disability we managed to get him a new housing association place for all-male tenants.'

Watts stopped writing. 'His disability being?'

'He's got some learning difficulties and he's classed as vulnerable because of how he presents to people. He doesn't seem to get how to do it. I think he was evaluated by somebody but that was before my time here. I never saw any details. All I cared about last year was finding him somewhere so that he wasn't on the streets.'

'Did you visit him at his new place?' he asked. Hanson watched as Ellen responded, her face relaxed.

'Several times. When he first moved in, me and a couple of other staff went and cleaned it for him, arranged for his few bits of furniture to be moved there, did basic shopping and got him some ready meals he could do in the microwave. With Michael, if he's in a place that's neat and tidy, he's more or less OK, but if he's somewhere that's already disorganised he soon goes downhill. Now that I think about it, it was the middle of June. That whole business really stressed him out.'

'Ever have any problems with him when you were at his flat?' asked Watts.

Ellen gave him a direct look. 'If you mean personal problems with Michael himself, no. None of us have. He's a fairly independent person, actually, but he's always grateful for any help we give him and he's polite. He just likes to talk.'

Having followed the unspoken drift of Watts's questions, Hanson guessed that his interest in Michael Myers was growing. She recalled what Myers had told them back at the field.

'Would you describe Mr Myers as reliable?' she asked.

Ellen laughed. 'I'll say! He comes here regular as clockwork.'

Hanson reframed her question. 'You said he likes to talk. In your experience is he reliable in what he says?' She watched Ellen's search for words.

'Well – according to him, he's been in the SAS and rescued two children from drowning in the reservoir. That's another of his haunts – and he's met most of the royal family.' She paused, her kindly face concerned. 'There's no harm in him but given the things he says – I suppose the answer is no.'

'You know him well, Ellen. What do you make of the stories he tells?'

Ellen thought about this then looked at Hanson. 'You're a psychologist so you'll probably have your own ideas, but I think he says those things because he's very lonely and he wants to keep you listening.'

'He likes to be out and about at night,' said Watts.

'Yes. I've told him to pack that in.'

He frowned. 'Why?'

She sighed. 'Not because of anything *he* might get up to. He's not a threat to anybody. *He's* the one that's vulnerable. I know he still wanders about because he's told me. According to him, he's "on manoeuvres".' She shook her head. 'Like I said, he's lonely. In the five years I've been here I've never heard him mention any family apart from his mother, nor any friends.' She looked at Hanson. 'What's this about? Is he in trouble?'

'Not as far as we know,' said Hanson, ignoring Watts' set face.

Ellen wasn't about to let it go. 'There's a rumour going around about a body being found over by the reservoir.' She looked at them, eyes widening. 'You can't think that Michael had anything to do with that!'

Watts gave her a direct look. 'You know about his police record?'

'Yes. What about it?'

'You know what it's for?'

'Yes.' She shook her head. 'That was years ago. Around the time his mum died. She was all he had. He's talked to me about her and about getting into trouble. He told me he was looking into people's houses because he wanted to see people, families together. If you ask me, he was pining for his mother. I don't think he fully understood what the police said he'd done. In the years he's been coming here, I've never noticed anything about him that tells me he's got that sort of problem.'

'His record is a fact,' said Watts. 'We operate on the facts as we know them.' Hanson silently acknowledged that he had a point. 'Maybe he's good at hiding that side of himself?' he suggested.

Ellen reddened. 'Maybe when the police arrested him back then he just agreed he'd done hell-and-all because he's naïve and easily influenced!'

Seeing Watts's mouth clamp shut, Hanson said, 'Is there anything else you'd like to say about Mr Myers?'

Ellen looked at her, then back to Watts. 'Sorry. I know you've got a job to do but Michael's not what he seems from how he looks and what he says. He's nice, a bit sad and I think he probably had a bad upbringing. He's desperate for anybody to take an interest in him.' She paused. 'Do you want to see him?'

They exchanged glances.

'He's here?' asked Hanson.

'He arrived about half an hour before you did. I was busy so one of the other workers helped him with a form and then I saw him go out the back.'

She caught their questioning looks. 'He's taken over a little patch of what we loosely call the garden here. The soil is rubbish but he's managed to coax a handful of petunias from it. Shall I fetch him?'

Ellen left and the door closed behind her.

Watts tapped his pen against his notebook. 'You'd better watch it, doc. Sounds like she's got a way of working with these types. She'll have your job off you before you know where you are.'

'I'll bear it in mind. What's your plan for Myers?'

'I want to hear him go through what he said last night.' He yawned widely. 'Make that this morning.' He blinked at her. 'So far, he's given us a dodgy-sounding story about something he says he heard in that field and from what this worker's just told us, he lied to us about what was happening to him this time last year.' He sighed heavily. 'Doc, you can look at me like that all you want but it's a fact and like I said it's the facts we're interested in. To me, he's on his way to being our first person of interest in this investigation. What do you think of what she said about his record?'

'She's clearly not convinced about the voyeurism. She and the other staff probably have to deal with some very challenging individuals at times. By comparison Myers probably seems harmless.'

'Which doesn't make them right about him.'

The door swung open and the man from the field came into the room, a paper bag clasped in one hand.

Watts stood. 'Come on in, Mr Myers. Thanks for your time. Have a seat.'

Myers was wearing the same jogging trousers and T-shirt they'd seen the previous night. Opening the bag he held it out to Hanson.

'Want one?' She smiled, shook her head.

Watts's lips compressed as he eyed him. 'You were in a field off Genners Lane in the early hours of this morning. I spoke to you, remember?'

Myers conveyed several cold-looking chips to his mouth. 'Corr-*ect*. I never forget a face.'

'Tell us again what you say you heard in that field last June.'

Placing the greasy bag on the table, Myers wiped his fingers on his jogging pants, swallowed and leant his head back.

Watts pointed a quick index finger. '*No*. Spare us the dramatics. Just tell us the words you say you heard.'

'What I *did* hear,' said Myers, looking miffed.

'Let's have it.'

'It was like a sing-song voice. "Hello. I can see you. How are you?"' They regarded him across the table.

'That's different to what you told us last night,' Watts snapped.

'Is it?' said Myers, selecting another chip.

Watts sent Hanson a weary glance. 'Did you *see* anything?'

Myers stopped chewing. 'No. Nothing.' He swallowed. 'I don't look at anything these days. If I do see anything – which I don't, I keep on moving. "Keep on the move, Michael."'

Watts regarded him with renewed interest. 'Who says that to you?'

'Me. It's my motto. You can give yourself good advice, you know.'

Seeing Hanson's slight smile, Watts pressed on. 'You changed your name to Michael Myers. Why?'

He shrugged. 'We had a party here a few years back. It was great, that party.' He looked at Hanson.

'You'd have enjoyed it. We had sausage rolls and pumpkins with lights inside 'em and a film. Great night, it was. Afterwards, I tried to remember the names of the people in that film but I couldn't. One of the regulars here said "Michael Myers" and I thought, "Yeah. I like that". He said it was the name of the sheriff in the film.'

'Can you tell us anything else about the night in the field when you heard the voice?' asked Hanson.

He nodded. 'I just thought. There was a car.'

Watts and Hanson exchanged quick glances.

'Where?' demanded Watts.

'Parked on the road next to the field.'

'And?'

'He went to it.'

Watts's colour rose. '*Who* did?'

'Whoever was in the field saying the words I just told you.'

'What did he look like?'

Myers shrugged. 'Dunno. Too dark.'

'Tell us about the car.'

Myers pushed lank hair from his face, looking avid. 'Now *that's* something I can help you on. I know about cars. I've had a few in my time, I can tell you: a Beamer, a Porsche—'

'Tell us about the car at the field,' said Watts, enunciating each word.

Myers gazed at him. 'You want to watch that, you know. Stress is a killer for the over-sixties.'

Hanson cut in. 'Can you describe the car please, Mr Myers?'

Myers looking at the ceiling. 'No. I didn't get a good look at it.'

Anticipating that Watts was near to losing whatever cool he still possessed, she gave Myers an encouraging look. 'Nothing at all that you remember?'

'I can tell you what it sounded like: throaty, big. *Bbbrrrmm*!'

'What kind of car do you think it was?'

'One of them big jobs. Four-by-four. I had one of them once.'

Ellen showed them out. 'Was he any help?'

'Possibly,' said Hanson in the absence of a response from Watts. For all Ellen's championing of Myers she came across as a truthful person.

'Since you've known him has he ever been suspected of harassing or following women?' she asked, feeling Watts's interest rise.

Ellen looked irritated. 'Who's been talking? That was all a misunderstanding by a couple of women who live around here. They said as much at the time.' She looked from Hanson to Watts and back.

'It was about eighteen months ago. They came in to say that Michael had followed and pestered them the day before.' She had Watts's full attention.

'What happened?' he asked.

Ellen shrugged. 'The manager here phoned the local police. They came and spoke to Michael. He told them he was trying to talk to the women about a newspaper article he had with him about whales or dolphins or something. The two women confirmed that he kept trying to show it to them.'

She looked at Watts. 'I can see it from their point of view. He probably *was* being a pest but that's all there was to it. They and the police went away happy and that was the end of it. In fact, one of the women dropped off a book on sea animals here for him. He was all for calling round to her house to thank her but I talked him out of it and helped him write a thank you note instead. Sea life was one of his passing fads. He never mentions it now.'

Inside his vehicle, Watts looked up from his note-taking. 'There's nothing in the information we've got about him following women. How did you know?'

'I didn't. I thought it was possible. He's clearly very lonely, very naïve and not very aware of how he comes across. It's easy to see how that might lead to misunderstandings.' She gave him a searching look. 'Can you really see Myers abducting a strong, healthy, young woman like Elizabeth Williams, murdering her, then moving her body to that field? He doesn't even have his own transport.'

'Does your opinion of him being harmless carry a guarantee?' He gave her a close look. 'No. I didn't think so. I hear what you're saying, doc but the fact is he lied to us about being in hospital last June and he's got that worker right where he wants her so she won't hear a word against him. You know as well as me how devious some types can be.'

Right now, she couldn't endorse his view of Myers but neither could she say he was totally wrong about him. She knew of cases where the revelation of a murderer's identity was met with utter incredulity.

'So, what's your plan for him?' she asked.

'Like I said, he's our first person of interest. Nuttall's all for getting him in under caution.'

She pulled at her seatbelt as he started the engine. 'We're looking for a killer. To me, he's merely inadequate.'

Watts grinned. 'I know he is but what about Myers?'

They drove back to headquarters, Hanson conceding to herself that Myers probably did merit further interest. She thought of various research studies on non-contact offenders such as voyeurs and exhibitionists which indicated that a proportion progressed to committing direct, 'hands-on' sexual offences. Workers at The Sanctuary were free to choose what they believed but the police couldn't do the same. Watts had said it himself: convictions were facts. Those had to be UCU's starting point.

FIVE

Still discussing Myers, they walked into the hubbub of headquarters reception and on to the Unsolved Crime Unit. Inside it was warm and deserted. Dumping her bag and jacket on the big worktable, Hanson opened a couple of windows then looked at the photographs of Elizabeth Williams on the Smartboard, tiredness now stealing up on her. It wasn't necessary to be young and attractive to become a victim but they were an added vulnerability. The murderous offenders she'd met in the course of her work came into her head. She could hear their words, their attempted rationalisations for their actions: 'They all had nice hair.' 'It was obvious she wanted me to do it.' 'She was there.' 'It was the way they looked at me, you know.' And even: 'Search me.' 'It just happened.' 'I just did it.' She put a hand over her eyes. Depravity and risk.

The violent men she'd known included one who had worked in this very building. One of their own who had slain several young women and who'd managed to fool them for longer than he should have. Her eyes strayed to the quote in black, scripted letters above one of the windows which she and her colleagues had requested at the end of that case: Let Justice Roll Down.

Watts was at the Smartboard, adding the words 'Person of Interest' next to Myers' name. He turned to her.

'I know what you're thinking, doc, but he has to be considered.'

'I know. What I don't want to happen is for Myers to tick all the boxes and be on a fast track to guilty before we know what this case is about.'

'Come on, doc. Give us some credit.'

She looked at him, then away. 'Sorry, but in my experience it happens.'

'Not here.'

'No.'

He shook his head. 'The way Myers acts, I realise he could be a complete time-waster but we can't gamble on it. Plus, there's his record. If he's a person of interest, we can focus on him a bit more.'

He pointed to one of several names he had taken from the case file. 'We'll be visiting this lot, starting with tomorrow with Lawrence Vickers. He was one of Elizabeth Williams' tutors.'

The door opened and Corrigan came inside. He looked at each of them. 'This a face-off or can anybody join in?' He came to the board and read what was there.

'How did it go with the aunt?' asked Watts.

'Difficult,' he said – starting to add the information he'd obtained. Hanson absorbed it all, including that Elizabeth had had a boyfriend named Chris Turner and had appeared distracted in the few days preceding her disappearance. The aunt had confirmed that she last saw Elizabeth on Sunday, the twenty-third of June when she left at six, possibly to see Turner.

I'll take a copy of the case file home tonight. Get the background of the original investigation into my head.

She saw Corrigan place a small plastic bag on the work table. 'This is all the aunt has of Elizabeth's belongings. I told her we'd get whatever else we have returned to her as soon as we can.'

As Watts related the details of their visit to The Sanctuary, Hanson reached inside the bag, drew out the few items and laid them on the table: a single, close-printed sheet of lecture notes entitled 'BSc Year 2 Sports Technology: Biomechanics of Sport'. She skimmed it and put it to one side. There were two cash register receipts, one from a supermarket itemising bread and a few other staples, the other from a dry-cleaners, both dated 22 June the previous year. The last item was an application form. It was headed 'Internship Placement'. It hadn't been completed. She reached for the laptop and entered the meagre details onto the screen.

Checking her watch she pushed the laptop to one side and picked up her jacket. 'Let me know if Vickers has anything interesting to offer.'

Inside her warm kitchen, Hanson passed the plate across the table. 'I thought you had an after-school club today? What time did you get home?'

Maisie took the plate and slathered mayonnaise over the salad. 'Chelsey's mum dropped me here at four. Mr Hornbeam our biology teacher came into double maths this afternoon to tell us that science club was cancelled. He's having a baby any minute so he's like *really* jumpy and disorganised.'

Hanson kept her tone light. 'You should have texted me. I need to know about any changes to your school day.'

Maisie rolled cornflower blue eyes. 'I was here, like less than an hour and then you arrived. I'm *thirteen*. It's not a big deal, Mum.'

It was a 'big deal' for Hanson. Like any mother, her child's safety was all, but intensified by her professional knowledge and experience. Maisie was wrong. It was a massive deal.

She pushed food around her plate. 'Text me next time there's any change, please.'

'Soz.'

'In fact, ring me and I'll organise things so that I can pick you up.'

Maisie's well-defined brows lowered. 'Hashtag boring, Mum. I *get* it.'

Hanson chose to ignore the attitude. Her hyper-vigilance wasn't Maisie's problem. Unless she herself made it one. It came with the work she did and what she knew about depravity as well as risk.

Maisie was eyeing her. 'Shall I stack the dishwasher?'

Recognising a verbal olive branch when she heard one, Hanson nodded. 'Please. Did you have a good time at your father's?' She got an enthusiastic nod.

'We went to see *Epic*. Stella came with us.'

'Did you enjoy it?'

'It was *brilliant*. It's about this girl who has to save the world. Stella thought it was great but Daddy just scoffed until she told him to zip it.'

Hearing a steady tapping on one of the ceiling to floor glass doors at the end of the kitchen, Hanson said, 'Let Mugger in please while I clear the table.'

Maisie scooted across the kitchen, unlocked the door and pushed them wide. The small black and white cat bounded inside.

She swooped on him, lifting him in her arms. 'Hey, Muggsie Malone. What have you been doing? Chasing cute little meece and ambushing birds? You're misnamed. You're not a mugger. You're a *killer* kitty!'

Hanson flinched. 'He's probably hungry. That's the main reason he comes home.'

'Me, too.' Maisie laughed as she headed for the dishwasher. 'Can we play cards again later?'

Maths-savvy Maisie with a memory like a steel trap had recently taught Hanson the basics of poker. They played for M&Ms. Maisie had won every game to date.

Hanson cleared the table, her thoughts on the Williams case. *Myers knows the area where Elizabeth was buried. He appears to come and go as he pleases. He has two non-contact sexual offences against females. Watts has a point where he's concerned. Am I taking a gamble in doubting his involvement in her murder?*

She looked up and smiled. 'Yes, after you've finished your homework.'

Hanson was in her study reading the copy case file, an image of the lonely field inside her head. Despite the shallow burial, she regarded the field as a 'dump site'. She'd first heard the term during a training course in London she'd attended on repeat offenders run by visiting FBI investigators. She disliked the term but it exactly described what that lonely field represented to Elizabeth Williams' killer. He'd wanted rid of her. He'd wanted to stay rid.

She turned file pages, skimming the shorthand hieroglyphics she'd written so far, two basic questions firing inside her head: was Elizabeth's killer someone she knew? Or was he totally unknown to her? To have a chance of identifying him they had to know what motivated him. The reason he'd killed her. The why. She looked at the list of possible causes of male anger towards females she'd written down: Jealousy. Sexual frustration. The need to silence. She crossed out the word 'causes'. It conveyed justification. She read the words again. Jealousy suggested an acquaintanceship with Elizabeth. She blinked, shook her head. Not necessarily. Dropping her pen on the desk she massaged her eyes, wanting sleep.

The study door opened and Maisie came in. 'I've finished, Mum.'

Pushing file and notebook inside her briefcase, Hanson left her desk. Putting her arm around Maisie's shoulders they walked into the sitting room. *Is it my imagination or is she taller than she was a month or so ago? She's catching up with me fast.*

In the sitting room Maisie swiftly and expertly dealt the cards.

'Come on, Mum. Remember what I told you about keeping a "poker face" and go for it.'

Hanson adopted an inscrutable expression as she examined her cards, not spotting anything promising. 'Ooo-*k*, honey-bun. Prepare to say bye-bye to every single M&M you own.'

'Ha!' said Maisie. 'As if.'

SIX

Watts eyed the students already waiting for their morning lecture and those now coming out of the office followed by an adult male. He stood.

'Dr Vickers? I phoned you yesterday afternoon. Detective Sergeant Watts,' he said to the man ushering them out. He glanced at Watts's identification.

'Come in, come in. Laurie's the name. How can I help?'

Taking out his notebook, Watts gave Vickers a covert once-over: hair to his collar, probably late thirties, soft around the middle, looking like he could do with some exercise. He tensed his own midsection. He'd keep it brief.

'You've heard about Elizabeth Williams' remains being found?'

Vickers looked subdued. 'Yes. Sad business.'

'You were her tutor.'

He nodded. 'Yes, I was. Not the only one, of course.'

Watts felt his usual unease whenever he was inside places like this. He didn't know how they worked. He'd never really felt at home at his daughter's Oxford college. Before she started there he'd assumed there was only one.

'Of course,' he echoed. 'When did you last see her?'

'I was asked the same question by police at the time but it's a while ago so I'd better check.'

Vickers opened a desk drawer, took out a stiff-bound desk-diary and leafed through it to around its mid-point. He tapped the page. 'Found it. It was the Friday prior to the weekend she went missing.' He held out the diary to Watts, pointing. 'There, see? The twenty-first of June.'

Watts examined what was written under the date but didn't see Williams's name. 'Why did you see her?'

Vickers looked momentarily fazed. Sudden understanding arrived on his face. 'Oh, I see what you mean. She didn't come here to my office. She attended my lecture.' He tapped the diary again and pointed. 'Two thirty: Fitness Science.'

Watts made a note. 'Did you see her after that?'

'No.' Vickers dropped the diary back into the drawer then turned to him. 'What a shocking business. Gone for a whole year and then she's found in that lonely place.' He shook his head.

Hearing a knock on the door, Vickers stood with an apologetic look. 'My next tutorial. Should I tell the student to wait?'

Watts also stood. He'd seen Vickers face-to-face, got the basic information he'd wanted confirmed. 'No. Thanks for your time, Dr Vickers. We'll be in touch if we need to check anything else with you.'

Sitting on the edge of her desk Hanson eyed the semi-circle of first year students. 'How would you go about identifying possible linkage between murder cases?'

She waited out the silence then stood and crossed the room to push the window wide. Cool air on her face, her eyes skimmed the terracotta grotesque straining from the outside wall into second-floor space, its dragon-wings folded, horns curved, fangs exposed. She gave its head a light pat. *You think you've got problems?*

She turned back into the room. 'Come on. Being hot and tired doesn't preclude thinking and I'm at the point where any ideas are welcome.' She saw a tentative hand rise.

'Yes?'

'Find a link?'

A few of the students laughed as Hanson considered the suggestion in a parody of thoughtfulness.

'I *think* that's been established as the general idea under discussion. The question is how?'

Another student spoke. 'See if there's any connection between the victims. Look for anything which connects the victims to a potential suspect. Look for similarities of MO and physical evidence.'

'Glad you came,' she said dryly.

She gave them each a direct look, tapping her hand against her palm. 'Links between victims. Links between victims and killer. Links between MO and physical evidence.'

She flicked pages of her diary, hearing a faint knock on the door.

'Next tutorial, each of you brings details of two cases. One where linkage provided the solution and another where it failed. Be prepared to explain both to the rest of the group. In the meantime, cut down the end-of-year partying.'

She watched as they gathered their belongings and headed out of the door, passing Watts on his way inside. She waited until the last of the students had gone before addressing him.

'Tell me what's brought you here and do it in an erudite way. Amusing would be a bonus.'

'I was passing. What's up with you now?'

She reached for some papers on her desk. 'Absolutely nothing. What have you been doing?'

'I've been to see Laurence "Call-me-Laurie" Vickers.' He caught her frown. 'Elizabeth Williams' tutor. According to him, he last saw her on Friday twenty-first of June in one of his lectures. I'll run a check on him.'

'The college would have done that when he was first employed, surely?'

He looked dismissive. 'I'll still do another. If we can establish that that Friday was the last time he saw her and she was at her aunt's place, alive and well on the Sunday, he slips down the list. Hang on.' He searched his pockets.

'I've got a phone message somewhere from the aunt. She's remembered the full name of Elizabeth's friend at the college and her housemate.' He held it out to her. 'Here it is: Jessica Simmonds. There's a phone number as well. Will you ring her and see what she's got to say?'

Hanson took the slip from him as he headed for the door, talking as he went.

'If she's still at that college she could be a useful source of information about staff, including Vickers, plus she'd be in the know about the boyfriend. Boyfriends, husbands – they always get my attention as potential persons of interest.'

'Where are you off to now?' she asked.

'I've got a meeting with Nuttall. He wants an initial progress report.'

She was surprised. 'We've hardly started. Is this an example of the managerial "light hand" he mentioned?'

'As far as I'm concerned, he's a mushroom. The way we play it, we keep him in the dark about what we're doing. People like Nuttall are all right so long as they've got nothing to think about and plenty of time to do it.'

He was gone.

She reached for the phone, dialled the number he'd given her and waited as the call rang out. A male voice answered, followed by a short wait. A female voice came into her ear. It sounded breathless.

'Yes?'

Getting confirmation that this was Jessica Simmonds, Hanson briefly outlined the reopening of the Williams investigation and her own involvement in it. There was a lengthy pause. Hanson was about to speak when Simmonds' voice came again. Now it sounded apprehensive.

'I thought I heard something on the news about a murder case being opened. I didn't realise it was about Elizabeth.'

'You and Elizabeth Williams were friends,' said Hanson.

'Yes.'

'You and she spent a lot of time together?'

'No. Not so much.'

This wasn't what Hanson had expected, given what Corrigan had told them of the friendship between the two young women and the fact that they'd shared a house. 'Did you know Elizabeth's boyfriend at the time, Chris Turner?'

'Yes, why?'

'We're interested in learning about everyone who knew Elizabeth well at the time she disappeared.'

'I can't tell you anything about him. He was keen on her and she was keen on him. That's all I know.'

Hanson frowned. 'Are you still at the college?'

'I dropped out. I was working here part-time as a gym instructor and they offered me a full-time job. I took it. I was fed up of college.'

Hanson held the phone against her chest. *Either my earlier experience with my students was right on the money: everybody under twenty-five has had their mental energy drained by aliens – or you really don't want to talk to me.*

'Where can I see you if I need to?'

She got a reluctant response. 'I'm here every weekday. Billesley Fitness Centre. It's just off Broad Street.'

Hanson recalled seeing the huge steel and glass building close to the Five Ways intersection. 'You were on the same course as Elizabeth?'

'Yes.'

'You had the same tutors?'

'Yes.'

In the ensuing silence Hanson thought of the few papers in the plastic bag given to Corrigan by Elizabeth's aunt. 'Did you sign up for an internship during your second year?'

'That's how I got this job. It started as an internship and like I said they offered me a permanent place.' Hanson picked up loud music and shouted instructions. 'Look, I have to go.'

'When and where did you last see Elizabeth?'

'On the Saturday of the weekend she disappeared. We'd arranged to go shopping that morning but she remembered she had a tutorial so we went later. I left her in Northfield and that was it.'

'Do you recall anything else?'

'She was going on about getting to the dry-cleaners before it closed.'

Hanson absorbed the limited details. 'What time did you separate?'

'I'm not sure. Around half four, quarter to five. Sorry, I have to go.'

Hanson replaced the phone, studying the verbatim words she'd written, as spoken by the alleged best friend of a murdered girl. She looked at the phone.

'I'll definitely be seeing you, Jess Simmonds. I'm interested in all the things you might have said to me but didn't.'

SEVEN

W atts cut the call and looked at his watch. It was nearly midnight. There was nothing to do but wait.

Turning from the low building still several metres away, he went back to his unlocked vehicle parked in shadow at the roadside. With minimal sound he climbed inside it and sat, glad of the warmth. So far this month it was all warm days and chilly nights. His eyes were on the pavilion visible through the hedge. Enough to see who left and who arrived. He'd watched somebody go inside fifteen minutes before. Somebody he knew by his walk. Problem was, he didn't know if anyone was inside prior to that. He hadn't seen anybody else arrive or leave but the light wasn't good and the kind of people who came here wouldn't advertise their presence. He gazed around at the dense trees then at the field, the events of the other night still fresh in his mind. He'd give it another fifteen minutes. The element of surprise would be on his side, plus a low risk of resistance.

He sat well back in his seat, eyes fixed on the low building. Gut instinct had brought him back. That was something Hanson had no time for. With the doc, it was all about 'data', which he'd learnt since working with her included going over every word anybody said and comparing it with everything everybody else said. He understood. He did a bit of that himself. Alibis had to be checked and compared. Basic policing. Where he and the doc parted company was when she started throwing theory into the mix. With her it was all about personality and behaviour, theories and hypotheses and she didn't let up until, according to her, 'the shadow of a suspect has some clear edges'.

She'd joined him and Corrigan in UCU a couple of years before. A bit rocky to start with, at least for him but all right now. More than all right. He knew the stresses of investigation and she felt them as much as he and Corrigan did. On top of it she had her job and other pressures. That ex of hers was about as much use as a chocolate fireguard. It had to be tough for her but that's how it was. She was good at what she did, the best as far as he was concerned and they needed her in UCU. His eyes roamed over the scene beyond his window.

His thoughts went back to the quick exchange they'd had about the single life when he was at her house the other night. During the time he'd known her, she'd been on her own. It made no sense to him. She was still young. Young enough to be his daughter at a push. When she'd first arrived at headquarters some of the officers had made the odd comment to him, trying to find out if she was available. He'd told them nothing. He knew Corrigan was keen. Not that he'd said anything to Watts. Corrigan was the close-lipped type. But he'd picked up on it. He wasn't so sure the doc had. If she had, she wasn't letting on or doing anything to encourage it. For all that thinking and analysing and searching of details that she did, for all her degrees, her training and her experience, he sometimes got the idea she didn't know herself all that well. His eyes were back on the pavilion. Gut instinct was what worked for him. Like now.

He got out into dark chill, pushing the door almost closed. Nearby a fox's bark spiralled into a high-pitched whine which faded away into the night. At the gap in the hedge he waited in the shadows, listening. Another few seconds' pause and he moved in the direction of the faint sliver of light around the edges of the pavilion's crooked door. No sound from within. No sounds from behind him either, worse luck. He knew the rule from his long-gone rookie days: 'Do not enter a situation where you think you might be outnumbered. Wait for backup.'

He wished he was home. If something didn't happen in the next few seconds there was only one way to find out how many types were inside. He'd still have the elements of surprise and threat on his side and he'd get what he was after without wasting days tracking it down.

Reaching the door he leant close to it. Two voices. One he recognised, one he didn't. Both had the lazy, pot-headed delivery he'd anticipated. He reached out, tested the door. It gave slightly. Picking up muted sounds from behind him he stepped back, raised one hefty leg and drove it at the door. It fell away, followed by hoarse shouts and scrabbling.

He stepped inside, a lighted torch rolling towards him. He stopped it with his foot, his eyes on Endo-Tony. 'How's the weed trade, Endo?'

Watts felt rather than saw the other man coming at him as

Whittaker and another officer piled inside and brought the man to the floor, handcuffed him and hauled him to his feet. Watts raised tentative fingers to his forehead, jabbing a thumb at Endo.

'Cuff this one as well.'

He followed all four to the patrol car, Endo moving with his distinctive roll. If you got on the wrong side of somebody in Endo's business, you got a knock on the door from somebody with a piece of two-by-four and a keen interest in your kneecaps.

'Stick that one inside the car and stay with him. I want a word with Endo.' He turned to him. 'Yours, I think.' He held up the two small plastic bags between thumb and index finger.

'Give us a break, Mr Watts,' said Endo, eyes looking anywhere but at him.

'I'll think about it if you've got something for me.'

Endo's eyes narrowed. 'How'd you mean?'

'You're a regular here.' He pointed at his face. '*Don't* deny it. It could make you a very valuable witness.'

Endo looked unhappy at that last word. 'You've got me all wrong, Mr Watts. I'm one of the bottom-feeders in this game. I don't do nothing heavy and I don't know nothing.'

'Course you don't and right now I'm not interested in what you get up to. I want to know if you saw anything going on here a while back.'

'Like what? When?'

'I'm thinking of an incident a year ago this month.'

'A *year*? You're having a laugh—'

'Shut up and listen. This involved somebody who brought something to this field and left it here.'

Endo avoided his eye. 'That don't mean nothing to me.' He gave Watts a calculating look. 'What's in it for me?'

'Who knows? Depends on what you've got.'

Endo licked his dry-looking lips. 'It was sometime last summer.'

'Day and time.'

'Day? Get real,' he said, adding quickly, 'it was night-time. Late, like now. I didn't see nothing, but I heard a voice, the odd noise. You get all sorts out here.'

Watts ran his eyes over him. 'Yeah. I know. What I'm talking about, even somebody like you with dope for brains would have gone and had a look to see what was happening.'

'I never. Then it all went quiet.'

'And?'

'I seen this figure walking away,' said Endo.

'Man? Woman? Young? Not?'

'Ask me another.' He shrugged.

'Carrying anything?'

'Too dark to see but it got into a car.'

'What sort of car?' demanded Watts.

'I didn't see it. I just heard it start up.'

'Hear anything else?'

'Like what?'

'Did you or didn't you!'

'No.'

Watts stared down at Endo who squirmed. 'What did this car sound like? Small? Bag of bolts? Smooth? Boy-racer?'

'I'd say big. A serious motor.'

Watts nodded at the pinched face. 'Thanks for that, Endo.' Clearing his throat he intoned, 'Anthony Miles, I'm arresting you—'

Endo's head dropped back. 'Oh, come on, Mr Watts. Leave it out. It's just a bit of weed.'

Watts watched as Endo was put into the squad car and driven away.

'I don't care about that. It's the rest of the crap you push that I don't like.'

Watts examined his forehead in his rear-view mirror. There was little indication as yet of the glancing blow from the piece of wood Endo-Tony's customer had wielded. He considered the snippets of information he'd gained. Somebody had come to that field in darkness. That somebody had left in a large vehicle. He recalled what Myers had said he'd heard around the same time. He shook his head. As far as he was concerned, Myers was either a suspect or a nutter. That was something else he and the doc weren't on the same page about. And then there was Endo-Tony. About as trustworthy as a ferret with an ID card. Two potential witnesses with issues. But there was similarity in what each had said. It was better than nothing. Maybe.

EIGHT

Barely six steps inside UCU, Hanson stopped.

'What happened to *you*?'

Watts got busy with papers. 'Don't you start. I've already had the same question from the lads here and from Chong early this morning.'

'Oh, yes?' she said, aware as were most at headquarters of his liking for the diminutive pathologist.

His shoulder sagged and he rolled his eyes. 'It's like trying to have a conversation with Sherlock-bloody-Holmes. Her car's in for a service so I gave her a lift this morning. Satisfied?'

'Marginally.'

She eyed the reddened area on his forehead as he walked past her on his way to the 'refreshment centre' in the corner. 'You still haven't told me what happened.'

'It's on the board. Put there by me.'

She read it. 'Good work. Except for the head. This Endo-Tony confirmed he heard somebody at the field, somebody with a large vehicle. Did he mention hearing a voice?'

'He did but no details. He probably had what's left of his mind on his "business interests" at the time so I'm not getting excited about anything he had to say.'

She reached into her bag, drew out a small buff-coloured slip of paper and waved it as Corrigan came through the door.

'I've also got something.'

Corrigan sat next to her. 'Like I've said, *that* is indisputable, Red.'

She looked up at him. 'It was in that bag of bits and pieces Elizabeth's aunt gave you. A dry-cleaning receipt. I went to the shop in Northfield earlier. They told me that it was for a woman's suit. I think Elizabeth had plans the weekend she disappeared.'

Watts looked up at her. 'How'd you work that out? Students wear all sorts of stuff at any old time: trousers, shorts, short dresses, long dresses. A cleaner's ticket is no guarantee she wore it.'

'I phoned Jess Simmonds. She told me that Elizabeth was insistent

on collecting something from the dry-cleaners that Saturday afternoon. Now we know what it was. It tells me that she was motivated
to spend what would have been a significant amount of money for
a student to have it cleaned and she wanted it that day. Ergo: she
was going somewhere special.'

'*Ergo,* she was going out with her mates or she had a date,' he said.

Hanson looked doubtful. 'The choice of a suit suggests that
whatever she had planned, it was something she considered important, formal.' She reached for the laptop and entered the information
from the Simmonds phone call. Corrigan turned to her.

'I've arranged to see Turner, the boyfriend, at midday. He's still
at the college. If you come you can check out the aunt's impression
of him and we'll follow up her assumption that Elizabeth was seeing
him later on the Sunday. He might know something about this outing
you think she was planning.'

Putting down the laptop she reached for her bag. 'That fits with
my day. My last student contact is at twelve.'

'Wish I had a part-time job,' said Watts.

'I'll see you at the college, Corrigan.' She pointed at Watts. 'Have
you seen what's happened to him?'

Corrigan grinned. 'Yep. I've also seen the guys he arrested. They
don't look half as cheerful.'

They were inside the college's light, airy student common room.
Hanson's attention was on Chris Turner, her eyes drifting over his
face. At twenty-one it had lost the softness still evident in many
students. Below the fair hair, beneath the smooth, light tan there
was a good bone structure. Chris Turner was handsome and from
the way he smiled and held his head, he knew it. She looked at his
clothes. Well-fitting, meticulous, probably expensive. The initial
impression was of a man with a big investment in his physical
appearance and possibly a family who indulged him. He was giving
Corrigan an open, pleasant look.

'The police asked me that after Elizabeth disappeared. The
answer's still the same: I last saw her on the Saturday morning.'

'June twenty-second,' said Corrigan.

'If that was the Saturday, yes.'

'What time?'

'I'd say it was about ten thirty or around then. She was heading
onto the campus as I was coming out.'

'Had you spoken with each other or spent time together prior to that?' asked Hanson.

He sent her a brief glance. 'If you're asking whether Elizabeth and I spent the night together, the answer is no.'

She saw Corrigan's jaw muscles ripple. 'I also asked if you'd spoken with her prior to ten thirty,' she said.

'No.'

'What did Elizabeth say to you?' asked Corrigan.

Turner was looking bored now. 'The police asked me that as well.' Looking at the ceiling, he delivered his answer like a litany. 'No, I didn't. She was late. She had a tutorial. She said she'd ring me. She never rang and I never saw her again.'

'Who was the tutorial with?' she asked.

He looked towards the wide windows. 'I couldn't say. Vickers was her main tutor but she had others.'

'You didn't ring her later?'

He turned his gaze back on her. 'No. She said she'd ring me. When she didn't I left it.'

'Had you and Elizabeth argued?'

He looked surprised. 'Not at all. We got on really well.'

Hanson kept her eyes on him. 'How long had you and Elizabeth been in a relationship?'

'A few months.'

She watched him get up, stroll to the window and look outside. 'All of this will be in police files. The officers who came to see me took notes.'

'We've seen them,' said Corrigan. 'This is a reinvestigation. Everything requires a second look.'

Hanson was in silent agreement. The fact that information was written down didn't convey a seal of truth. Asking a person to repeat what they'd said previously often produced anomalies. It was why they were here.

'Did you and Elizabeth have anything special planned for later that Saturday or maybe the Sunday?' she asked, wanting a reason why Elizabeth might have chosen to wear her suit some time that weekend.

'No, nothing. Why?'

'Were you and Elizabeth in an exclusive relationship?'

'Meaning?'

'Were you and she dating only each other?' she asked.

'Yes.'

'So, you have no knowledge of Elizabeth planning some kind of outing?'

Turner's eyes narrowed. 'If she was she didn't tell me,' he said coldly.

As Hanson wrote, Corrigan asked, 'All the students here take up an internship, yes?'

Turner checked his watch. 'Yes, but not Elizabeth. She didn't want what was on offer so she was told to find her own. Will this take much longer?'

Hanson recalled her telephone conversation with Jessica Simmonds. There had been a noticeable absence of interest in the reinvestigation from Simmonds who had been Elizabeth's closest friend, according to what her aunt had said. Now, here was her lover conveying a similar stance.

'Had she anything in mind?' she asked.

Turner shrugged. 'She took all that saving-the-planet stuff seriously so she was looking for something in that line.'

'Did she find it?' asked Corrigan.

He gave another shrug. 'Not as far as I know.'

'Anything you'd like to add?' asked Corrigan, his eyes on Turner's face.

Turner gave the question minimal consideration. 'No. Is that it? I've got a squash game booked and I've seen the other player arrive.'

They left the college building and Hanson gazed across the road towards the narrow lane and the field many metres away where Elizabeth Williams had lain for months, ruined and cold. Lawrence Vickers her tutor had told Watts that he'd last seen Elizabeth at his lecture on the Friday. According to Turner, she'd had a tutorial on the Saturday morning. Who was that tutorial with? She turned to Corrigan.

'Have you got Lawrence Vickers' number?'

'Yep.'

He took out his phone. She guessed he knew what she was thinking. He listened then ended the call.

'Voicemail says he's not available until tomorrow. What did you make of Turner?'

'Very cool. Self-possessed. From his responses it's hard to picture him having the close relationship he says he had with Elizabeth Williams.'

Corrigan nodded. 'Add arrogant and we've got him covered. Where you going now, Red?'

'Back to the university.'

'How about I make dinner for us at my place later? I'll give you the guided tour,' he said lightly.

She thought of the dilapidated terraced house he'd bought and showed her many months before. A 'fixer-upper' he'd called it. She hadn't seen much of him since their last case ended but she'd passed by the house and seen builders hard at work. He'd moved into it back in April. The last time she'd driven past a couple of weeks ago, both house and the wisteria around its front door looked stunning.

'Thanks, Corrigan but Maisie's friend Chelsey is eating with us. You've settled in?' she asked.

'Sure. I like the neighbourhood. It's cute. I get why seniors call it "the Village".'

She grinned at his version of a British accent and his oblique reference to her eighty-year-old next-door neighbour then glanced back at the college.

'I know it's a year since Elizabeth Williams disappeared but Turner's responses weren't what I expected.'

'Impersonal to the point of belittling, I thought. Maybe his life's moved on,' he said.

'I suppose. When I spoke with Jess Simmonds yesterday I got a similar impression from her. There was no emotional content in her responses, no upset or expression of regret. Not even curiosity about our investigation and the hopefulness we usually get that the police will find an answer as to what happened. I found her actual responses odd.'

Corrigan was looking in the direction of the field. 'That doesn't sound like moving on. It sounds like callousness.' He looked at her. 'But she and Turner are young. Both in their early twenties. They haven't had a lot of practice in how to respond to bad situations.'

'Probably true, but I still want to know more about both of them.'

Back at the university Hanson took the few papers which had once belonged to Elizabeth Williams from their plastic bag and placed them on her desk: lecture notes, the cash receipt for basic foods and the internship placement form. Not much to gain a sense of a busy young life. She picked up the receipt from a Northfield supermarket, checked the items again for any hint they might hold of Elizabeth's last weekend: wholemeal bread, chicken, low-fat milk, rice, sweet potatoes. She replaced it on the desk. It merely reflected what they knew of Elizabeth Williams' interest in health and fitness.

Hanson pulled the internship form towards her, all of its dotted response lines blank. If information from Chris Turner and Jess Simmonds could be relied on, Elizabeth had refused the sports-related placements offered by the college which would explain why she'd never completed the form. She recalled Turner's dismissive tone when he mentioned her interest in saving the planet. Hanson's impression was that he was equally dismissive of Elizabeth herself. She recalled her phone conversation with Jess Simmonds. Whilst not dismissive, her responses to Hanson's questions had been curiously spare and disinterested.

She swung her chair to the window and gazed out. Was there something between Turner and Simmonds, either now or at the time Elizabeth disappeared? She heard the Joseph Chamberlain Tower's bells strike the mid-afternoon hour.

Hanson straightened, refolded the internship form, had it halfway into the plastic bag when she stopped, her eyes fixed on its reverse side. There were indistinct marks on it. Taking it to the window, she gazed at it in the strong light. She couldn't make anything of them. Returning to her desk, she took a lens from the drawer and placed it over them. Still too faint.

Collecting her coat and bag she leant into the adjoining office on her way to the door.

'Crystal, I'm going to headquarters.'

Hanson was inside the lab on headquarters' first floor, having given the internship form to Adam, the departmental head of Forensic Science. She waited as he scrutinized the small marks on its reverse side.

'It's not much but I wanted you to have a look.'

He mused over the markings. 'Obviously someone wrote on a sheet lying on top of this one and the writing imprinted itself. You're right, it isn't much. Come on. Let's get it on to the ESDA.'

She followed him as he headed across the lab. They stopped at the boxy Electrostatic Detection Apparatus. She watched as he placed the sheet on to its platform, then drew a single layer of cling film across it, his hands deft as he pulled it taut then tucked in the edges.

She wondered if his painstaking attention to detail extended to other areas of his life. She looked at his ultra-neat hair. Probably. The machine started to hum.

Picking up a long, slender object he said, 'I'll pass this wand over your sample to charge it.' She watched as he did so then put down the wand and raised one end of the platform.

'Now for the key step.'

Hanson pressed nearer as he picked up a small metal container and held it above the film-covered sheet, watching as fine black powder poured from it and flowed over the film. It gathered in the small area of the indentations.

Removing the film from the platform, he attached it to a plain sheet of paper and held it out to Hanson.

She took it, eyes on the indentations now amplified by the powder.

'It's not much,' said Adam. 'But I hope it's useful. Here's your original.'

She took it from him. 'Thanks a lot. So do I.'

He watched her head for the door, calling after her, 'I'll be bringing UCU the results of the trace evidence found with the body pretty soon.'

Hanson came into UCU. 'I'm glad you're both here.' She placed the internship form face down on the work table in front of Watts and Corrigan.

'Take a look at this.' They peered at it.

'See these marks? Someone wrote on something that was over it. See the small indentations?'

Watts frowned at it. 'I'll take your word for it.'

'I see them,' said Corrigan.

Hanson placed Adam's handiwork beside it. 'Now take a look at what Forensics got from it.'

Watts put on his glasses and gave it close scrutiny. Corrigan looked up at her. 'Two words.' He pointed at them. '"Bill" and "Ren".'

'Means nothing to me,' said Watts. 'They look like names. What do you think, doc?'

Hanson considered them. 'Nothing, beyond what you've just said.'

She sat back, looking at Corrigan. 'I've thought about Chris Turner and his responses to our questions earlier.'

'His offhand manner. Thought you might,' he said.

'Remember what I said about Jess Simmonds' responses on the phone? I'm going to see her face-to-face. It's occurred to me that there might have been something between those two last year. Or since.'

Corrigan nodded. 'In which case, I'll arrange another visit to the college to see Turner. We'll synchronise the times. If there is something with these two we don't want to give them the opportunity to warn each other or collude.'

Hanson looked at her watch. 'Let's say four this afternoon if they're available?'

'I'll ring Turner,' said Corrigan.

Watts said, 'I'm going to see Vickers again and sort out this tutorial business.'

Hanson and Corrigan each picked up a phone.

The manager of the fitness centre had offered Hanson the use of his office. She had gotten as far as asking Jessica Simmonds how close she and Elizabeth were prior to Elizabeth's disappearance and was now waiting for a response from the tanned blonde in black leggings and white zipped top sitting across the desk from her. It looked as though she was in for a long wait.

Hanson changed her approach. 'Miss Simmonds, Jess, when we first spoke on the phone the other day I thought there were aspects of our conversation which were . . . unusual.'

Simmonds' eyes stayed fixed on the desk. She made no response.

Hanson continued, 'We'd been told that you were Elizabeth Williams' closest friend. I didn't get that impression when we spoke. That's why I'm here. So we can talk about it.'

She left it there and waited some more, following the young woman's glance out of the window to Broad Street snaking its way to the Five Ways island. She turned at Simmonds' voice.

'I don't know what you want me to say. I've told you all I know. We went shopping that Saturday and I never saw her again.' Hanson saw her gaze return to the window.

'I know that's what you said.' Getting no response, Hanson leant forward, keeping her tone even. 'Let me explain what's confusing me, Jess. Yes, you told me about that Saturday, but there was no emotion in it. There still isn't.'

Simmonds kept her eyes averted as Hanson continued. 'Elizabeth disappeared sometime that weekend, after you last saw her. Now you know what happened to her but I still can't see any impact on you.' Simmonds still did not speak, did not look at her.

Hanson pressed on. 'That doesn't make any sense to me. I'm guessing that by now you'll have seen reports in the newspapers, on television, maybe online, of her body being found.' She was getting nothing.

'Have you been in contact with the other students at the college who knew you and Elizabeth?'

Simmonds turned from the window to look at Hanson. 'No. I haven't been back to that place in over a year.'

Hanson gave her a close look. 'Do you know that area off Genners Lane where she was found?'

She shook her head.

Glancing at the clock on the wall, convinced now that there was something Simmonds didn't want to get into, Hanson raised the emotional tempo. 'I was there when her body was recovered.' She watched Simmonds' hands clench each other, saw the quick flinch.

'I don't need to tell you that it wasn't pleasant. I never knew Elizabeth but I'll admit that what I saw affected me, as it did my police colleague, an officer with more than twenty-five years' experience.'

Hanson looked up at the soft knock at the door. A close-cropped head appeared round it. It was the gym's manager she'd met earlier.

'Excuse me. Sorry to interrupt but I need something from my desk—'

Explosive sobs from Simmonds hit the walls of the small office, startling him into silence and causing Hanson to rise from her chair, eyes wide. Simmonds' upper body was bent low, her head almost on her knees, her hands clasped to her mouth, shoulders heaving.

'Never mind. I'll leave you to it,' he said, quickly withdrawing and closing the door.

Hanson heard more fierce sobs. 'What's wrong, Jess? Are you unwell? Can I get you something?'

The racking sobs continuing unabated, Hanson took several tissues from a nearby box, went around the desk, pressed them into Jess's hand and waited.

The sobs gradually lessened. Hanson lowered her head to look into the young woman's face. 'Tell me if you need something and I'll get it.'

Jess blotted tears with a shaky hand. 'I don't want to talk any more about this.'

'Why not?'

'Because I feel bad. Guilty.' The sobs started up again.

Hanson recognised the first spontaneous words she'd heard so far. 'Jess, if you know something about what happened to Elizabeth you must tell me right now.'

Simmonds straightened, the tissues a sodden mass on her lap, her face flushed and shiny. She looked wiped out.

'It was my fault,' she whispered, staring straight ahead, her eyes red and empty.

Hanson reached forward and took her gently by the shoulders. 'Whatever happened you must tell me about it.' She frowned. 'Was there a problem between you and Elizabeth prior to her disappearance?'

'Yes.' More tears fell.

'Was it anything to do with Chris Turner?'

Simmonds nodded. 'He dumped me. For her.'

Feeling her way forward, Hanson asked, 'Were you angry with Elizabeth because of that?'

The blonde head shot up. 'No *way*. She was my friend. This is about Chris Turner. I feel guilty because I knew what he was like as a boyfriend. He was a complete nightmare but I didn't tell her. I didn't warn her.'

'Tell me,' said Hanson.

One hand to her mouth, her breath catching, Simmonds stared out of the window. 'I got with him towards the end of my first year at the college.' She shook her head. 'I didn't have many friends there and I was feeling lonely and suddenly here was this good-looking, second year student taking notice of me. I thought he was great. He *was* great, for the first few weeks. Some of the students on my course said we looked right together. One or two described us as a golden couple. I was having the time of my life with him. I couldn't believe he wanted me. Then it all changed. *He* changed.'

Hanson had spoken to many women about their traumatic relationships. From what Simmonds had told her so far, she had a few ideas about what was coming.

Simmonds pressed tissues to her eyes. 'It was nothing obvious. I didn't even notice to begin with. But then it really started. The jealousy, the constant questioning: "Where are you going? Where were you last night? Why are you wearing that? Why have you changed your hair?"' She slumped against her chair, her hands lying on her lap. 'He was constantly picking at me, asking the same questions. He never let up.'

'How long did that carry on?'

'A few weeks. When I started my two-month internship here it got worse.' She looked up at Hanson, words rushing from her mouth.

'I'm not stupid. I started to work out what his behaviour was about. I've known girls with possessive boyfriends and thought they were idiots to stick with them but that's exactly what I did. He hated me being here because he didn't know the place. Clyde, that's the manager who came in earlier, he offered me a job. I took it. I think I was trying to get away from Chris but I couldn't seem to make the actual break. If anything it got worse then. He couldn't see what I was doing here, who I was meeting, who I was talking to. He told me I had to leave the job. He went on and on.' She stopped, out of breath.

Hanson put a hand on her shoulder. 'Slowly.'

After a few seconds Simmonds continued, 'I arranged to meet him. He'd worn me out. I couldn't keep up with what I had to do here and all I could think was, "OK, you win. I'll do what you want. I'll leave".'

'You told him that?' said Hanson.

'Yes. I told him I'd given in my notice here. He went, "Oh, that's great, babe".' She looked up at Hanson. 'Guess what he did then, that *same* week.'

'He began seeing Elizabeth.'

Simmonds stared at her. 'Who told you?' She shook her head. 'I couldn't believe it. The next time I saw him, it was like I didn't exist. Like he didn't know who I was.'

Hanson pictured Turner harassing the young woman until he had her doing exactly what he wanted, then promptly losing interest. As far as he was concerned he'd got her. He'd won.

'What happened?'

'All I could think about was getting my job back. Clyde's a good man. He said not to worry about it. He gave me my job back and I tried to forget what had happened.'

'You said you felt guilty about Elizabeth because you didn't tell her about Chris Turner.'

'I should have warned her! I didn't.'

'Did you and Elizabeth ever become friends again?'

Simmonds stared out of the window. 'Yes, but it wasn't the same. How could it be? I was holding something back from her.' She looked at Hanson and Hanson saw the still ongoing struggle to understand.

'But she seemed happy and I thought, Maybe he's different with her. Maybe it was *me* that made him act the way he did.'

Hanson had lost count of the times she'd heard this sentiment. 'Did you see Chris Turner again?'

Simmonds' face darkened. 'You're joking. As soon as he cut me dead I realised that I'd got my life back, that I'd had a lucky escape. He's not the person he seems. He's got a really low opinion of women. He used to say things like, "All your girlfriends are slags." Stuff like that. I started to hate that college because he was part of it, which is why I came here in the first place.' She covered her face with both hands then let them drop, looking exhausted.

'I should have warned her. I should have told her what he was like and to stay clear of him.'

Hanson shook her head. 'You're not responsible for the choices Elizabeth made.'

She knew her next question wouldn't improve how Simmonds was feeling but she had to ask it. 'Did you ever suspect that Chris Turner might have had something to do with her disappearance?'

Her head shot up. 'Is that what the police think?'

'They're exploring all the possibilities.'

Simmonds shook her head, looking uneasy. 'He's a pig but . . . He's got a vile temper. Maybe they had a row.' She looked at Hanson. 'But I never saw Elizabeth upset. Not once. Ever.'

'So what did you think had happened to Elizabeth at the time she disappeared?'

Simmonds bit her lip. 'I just assumed somebody weird had abducted her or something, like it said in the newspapers.'

Hanson glanced at the questions she'd brought with her. 'What was Elizabeth like? What kind of person was she?'

'She was nice. Friendly. Happy. Always willing to help if you needed something. I used to think sometimes that she was a bit too nice.'

Hanson kept her tone easy. 'What do you mean?'

'She was too quick to do whatever people asked. You know, lend them her stuff or money. I don't mean a lot. She didn't have it. Just small amounts and when I realised what she was doing I told her not to because I knew she wasn't getting some of it back, that one or two people "forgot" to repay her. She just laughed, said it wasn't a problem.'

'But you thought it was?'

'Yes.' She looked up at Hanson. 'Do you know about her childhood?'

'Yes. Some.'

'Then you probably know she was her mother's carer from when she was really young. I think she missed out on having somebody caring for her as she was growing up.' Jess's face registered quick concern. 'Don't get me wrong. I don't mean that her mother didn't love her but she was in a lot of pain at times and most of the care went one way: from Elizabeth to her mum. After her mum died, her aunt was really good to her but I don't think it was enough to make up for those years. I think Elizabeth had a big need to feel cared for. Her parents split up when she was young so maybe she needed that from a man. Like a boyfriend.'

Hanson absorbed this, hoping that knowledge and experience would be enough to show Simmonds that she needed to be smart on her own behalf and not allow people to take advantage of her in the future.

Simmonds wrapped her arms around herself, looking drained. 'Your questions have got me wondering if Chris Turner did do something to her, perhaps when he was angry.' A single tear slid down one cheek.

Hanson carefully drew the ESDA result from an envelope and placed it on the desk between them but gave no explanation. 'Do you see these marks, here and here?' Simmonds pressed a tissue to her face and looked to where Hanson was pointing.

'Do you have any idea who Bill and Ren might be?'

She looked at the two small words then up at Hanson. 'I think that's Elizabeth's handwriting but I don't have a clue what "Ren" means. Never heard of it. I know Bill.'

Hanon's breathing turned shallow. 'Who is he?'

'It's not a person,' said Simmonds. She raised her hands. 'It's this place. Billesley Fitness Centre. Elizabeth was under pressure to choose an internship. I tried to persuade her to apply here. I'd checked it out with Clyde and he said he could use another intern. She wasn't interested. She said she wanted something that was a change from sport. I kept saying to her, "Come, on. Come to Bill with me!".'

Seeing Hanson's frown she said, 'It was a joke between us. In my case it was also a bit of a snipe at Chris Turner because I knew how jealous he was of Elizabeth knowing other men. She still said no. She wanted to do something different for a few weeks.'

'And did she?' asked Hanson.

Simmonds shrugged. 'I don't know. She never mentioned anything to me and then . . . she was gone.'

NINE

H anson came into UCU early next morning to find Corrigan at the board, Watts sitting facing it.

'Good timing, doc. Corrigan's telling me what Turner had to say.'

Corrigan pointed to a list. 'Chris Turner. One of those guys who talks like every word is costing him ten bucks. I wanted to get him in here and apply some pressure but I kept it light and he could see I wasn't about to leave without some answers. When I asked if there was some kind of situation between him and Jess Simmonds he reluctantly admitted to a relationship with her prior to the one he had with Elizabeth. He was very derogatory about Simmonds. Described her as neurotic and demanding and that he got increasingly worn out by her. According to him, he finished the relationship.' His hand moved down the written information.

'I asked Turner to verify his whereabouts on the weekend Elizabeth Williams went missing. He repeated what he already told us. He saw her on the Saturday morning. She was in a rush because she had a tutorial. She didn't say who that tutorial was with but now he says he thinks it might have been Vickers. As she left, she promised to ring Turner. She didn't. He didn't ring her. I told him we understood that Elizabeth left her aunt's house on the Sunday saying she was going to see him. He stuck by his story: he didn't see Elizabeth again that Saturday or any other day.'

Corrigan pointed to the last item which was underlined. 'He told me that on both the Saturday and the Sunday he didn't go anywhere.

He stayed in alone, watched box sets and slept a lot.' He turned to them. 'Which means he's got no alibi for the time we believe she disappeared.'

'I like it,' said Watts, rubbing his big hands together.

Hanson looked from the listed items to Corrigan. 'Jess Simmonds' description of Turner suggests he's an archetypal abusive personality: jealous, possessive, somebody who exerts control in a relationship through criticism, manipulation and constant demands. Remember when we saw him? I've gone through my notes of that meeting. He referred to Elizabeth not ringing him and that he didn't ring her. There's a self-centred pettiness and a punishing element in that. It seemed not to have occurred to him that she might have had some kind of problem. He was dismissive about Elizabeth's interest in "saving the planet". It fits with what Jess Simmonds said about him.'

'You rate her as trustworthy?' asked Watts.

Hanson nodded. 'I do. What she said sounded sincere. It also made psychological sense. She's not exactly naïve but neither is she worldly. I don't think she could have described the kind of behaviour she attributed to Turner without experiencing it first-hand.' She took a breath, pointed at his name. 'Hardly into his twenties and he's already a well-developed misogynist.'

She looked at Corrigan. 'What do you think of him?'

Corrigan moved his finger over the board, leaving three large letters glowing red on its surface: POI.

'Right now, he's my main person of interest.'

She nodded. 'I agree.'

Watts eyed the names they had so far. 'He's got to be considered along with Myers and Vickers. I'm undecided about Myers and there's a question mark over Vickers because we've got no confirmation who that Saturday tutorial was with.' He pointed at Corrigan's notes. 'Consider who it is who's dropped Vickers into this. Is he trying to throw us off? All we've got on Vickers is that he last saw Elizabeth on the Friday. I'm still trying to get hold of him to fix up another visit. A longer one this time.'

'Jess Simmonds clarified the word "Bill" imprinted on the back of the internship form,' said Hanson. 'According to her it isn't a person, it's the Billesley Fitness Centre where she works.'

'What about the other one, this "Ren"? asked Watts.

'She didn't recognise it.'

The door opened and Nuttall came inside. His eyes drifted over the information on the board. 'What about the sex offender with the alias who was hanging around the field where the body was buried?'

'We've talked to him,' said Watts. 'He's still one of our POIs but he's got mental health problems and there's nothing else to tie him to the Williams murder.'

'Has he been formally interviewed yet?'

'There're insufficient grounds for us to do that yet,' said Corrigan.

'He's a fantasist,' added Hanson. 'He finds it difficult at times to give a clear account of himself.'

He gazed at her. 'A sex offender-fantasist? Sounds like the markers of somebody capable of killing that girl. What more do you need to get him in?'

Hanson got the point he was making but there was something else about Myers which raised queries for her. 'His involvement in this case so far is tied specifically to the field where she was found. We don't know where she was killed. Until we do, I doubt we can make any constructive link between him and Elizabeth Williams.'

Nuttall frowned. 'That field is enough for me. Get him in here and you might find that link. Let me know what you get.' The door swung closed after him.

She looked at her colleagues. 'What are you going to do?'

'What he says,' answered Watts with a shrug. 'But not for the reason he's got in mind. I want to put a few more questions to Myers and see if there's anything else he remembers about that night last year when he was in that field.'

They turned as the door opened again. It was Adam, the forensics specialist. Seeing their faces, he stopped.

'Not a good time?'

'Come on in,' said Watts. 'Got something for us?'

They gathered round as Adam placed several items on the table. He pointed to a glass slide with what looked like fine, pale hairs suspended within it.

'The fibres recovered from under the victim's fingernails. Pure wool. The kind used in domestic carpeting and rugs. Expensive. I checked the dye charts. Probably pale yellow or a heavy cream colour.'

He moved on to several small items in clear plastic boxes. They peered at them and Hanson saw fragments of tree bark and small pieces of old-looking wood. She looked at the contents of another clear plastic box: the stag beetle Chong had referred to.

Adam pointed. 'The bark is from a range of different trees: silver birch, oak, willow plus two or three others. Quite a mix. These bits of wood are from much larger pieces, long dead.' He pointed again. 'Hence, the fine example of the stag. They like rotting wood. The other insects found within the remains are more varied than those contained in the sample I took from the field, although my sampling wasn't exactly scientific.'

Hanson caught Watts's heavy frown. Whatever he'd been anticipating, he wasn't getting it. 'What's all this mean for us?' he asked.

'I've sent pictures to your new toy.' Adam walked to the board, tapped an icon and several full-colour photographs of the field appeared, taken from different points in daylight. Adam pointed at each of them.

'See? Hawthorne hedging. Oak trees over here. More oaks and a sycamore this side.' He faced them. 'The trace evidence suggests that she was killed inside a domestic environment. The fingernails were in bad shape but the number of wool fibres retrieved suggests that she gripped them, rather than caught a fibre incidentally. She was then moved to another environment where the wood and insect samples I've shown you were deposited on her remains.'

'You're saying she wasn't exposed to these items in that field?' asked Hanson.

'That's right. After being murdered at an indoor location she was kept elsewhere then taken to the field.'

He indicated the stag beetle in its plastic box. 'It'll probably take a while but I'll send it to an entomology expert I know at Cambridge. See what he makes of it.'

'I could take it to our biology school at the university,' Hanson suggested. 'It might be quicker.'

'One less job for us.' He went to the door.

'We're going through the Williams' clothing and effects starting tomorrow. I'll let you have them and details of anything we find.'

She looked up at him. 'You're examining it all?'

'Yes. They've merely been stored here since we took initial custody. There's no mobile phone listed. We've got her laptop but there's no paperwork confirming a search of it at the time of the original investigation. Give us a few days and you'll have all of her effects and anything we get from the laptop.'

Adam left, taking the samples but leaving the stag beetle in Hanson's charge.

Watts lifted the phone. Hanson listened to his half of the conversation. He was talking to The Sanctuary. He hung up.

'Myers is coming in here later this afternoon.'

Hands in pockets he stared at the board, then at the trace evidence details they'd been given. 'According to Forensics, once Williams was dead she was moved twice. I do not like the sound of that.'

'It does increase the potential deviance factor,' said Hanson.

He glanced at her. 'Spare me the psychological whys and wherefores of killers keeping bodies and moving them around.'

She gave a faint smile. 'You already know the whys and wherefores.'

Corrigan nodded. 'When you first told him about them, he skipped lunch.'

Watts shook his head. 'And I can do without hearing them again, thanks.'

Hanson headed for the door. 'I'll be back for the Myers' interview.'

TEN

Watts put down the phone.

'Myers has arrived. He's brought an appropriate adult because of his vulnerable witness status. The duty solicitor's waiting as well. Let's get this done and have Nuttall off our backs.'

On headquarters' first floor he and Corrigan disappeared into Interview Room 1. Hanson pushed open the door of the observation room next to it. Nuttall was already inside.

She looked through one-way glass at Myers, his thick lips pressed together, hands restless, his eyes fastened on a woman seated near him. Hanson recognised Ellen, the worker from The Sanctuary. She watched Ellen lean towards Myers, her face expressive, her hand on his arm. She was trying to soothe him. Still keyed-up, he subsided onto his chair next to a sparely built duty solicitor who was fussily arranging his pens and notebook just so on the table. Hanson flicked a wall switch and sounds from the next-door room became audible.

Her two colleagues were sitting opposite Myers whose mouth was now clamped shut. She listened as Watts went through the required preamble, including introductions.

'Thank you for coming in today, Mr Myers.'

Myers nodded, looking guarded. 'Thanks for the sandwich and the tea.'

'You were a witness to something which happened in a field close to Bartley Green reservoir twelve months ago. We want to take you through that and record what you say. This is a voluntary interview, Mr Myers, and you're not in trouble. Do you understand?' Myers nodded energetically.

Watts indicated the duty solicitor. 'This is Mr Dabney. He's here to listen to what everybody says and give advice if needed.' Dabney gave a prim nod.

Hanson's attention was on Myers. Effort had been made with his appearance. His hair was centre-parted and lying flat on either side of his head and he was wearing a clean, white shirt, open at the neck, tight around his middle. She suspected The Sanctuary had provided it. Below it were jogging bottoms which looked freshly laundered. Ellen had been busy on Myers' behalf.

Watts looked at his notes then across the table at him. 'Mr Myers, you were watching police activity during the recovery of the body of Elizabeth Williams on the—'

'I wasn't watching.'

Watts ploughed on. 'When I spoke to you at that time, you weren't able to give us a satisfactory explanation as to why you were there. This is your chance to do that.'

Myers looked at him, then at Corrigan. 'I was on manoeuvres.'

Ellen leant forward, her voice firm. 'Listen to what the police officer is saying, Michael. He's asking for the *real* reason you were there.'

Hanson saw a frown settle on Nuttall's face.

Myers folded his arms above his paunch. 'I'd like to help you but I'm bound by the Official Secrets Act, Section Five, Paragraph One. If I give you that information I'm placing you at risk.'

Watts gave him a long stare then glanced at Corrigan with a brief nod. 'Sir, we need your help,' said Corrigan. 'We're investigating the murder of a young woman.'

With a sage nod, Myers straightened on his chair but said nothing.

'We need you to tell us everything you remember.'

Again Myers nodded but still said nothing.

'Why were you in the field watching the police that night?'

'I wasn't.'

'You were seen, sir.'

'I know I was.'

In the silence Hanson watched Ellen lean towards Myers again. 'You have to be straight with the officers. Tell them exactly what you were doing.'

Nuttall's voice startled Hanson. 'She the appropriate adult?'

'Yes.'

'Where's she from?'

'She's one of the workers from the mental health drop-in centre Myers attends.'

Nuttall's eyes were back on Ellen. 'Not having much success with him, is she?'

Hanson's own confidence in the process was slipping. 'Without her, I doubt we'll get anything useful.'

Myers looked from Corrigan to Watts, then at Ellen who nodded encouragement.

'I wasn't watching the police,' he said. 'I take long walks at night. It calms my head. It helps me sleep. My personal physician has informed me that I'm suffering from acute, chronic insomnia. It's terminal but I'm dealing with it.'

Nuttall turned to Hanson. 'Is this what you meant when you described him as a fantasist?'

She nodded. 'It's very likely that his self-concept is unstable and his self-esteem poor, possibly as a result of neglect in his early years, although there's no information on his early history. What we're hearing is his way of shoring up his view of himself. I think he's operated like that for so many years, it's probably ingrained behaviour.'

Nuttall's eyes were on Myers. 'I'm guessing he's not too bright.'

Hanson gazed through the glass. 'Staff at the centre regard him as having learning difficulties.' She turned Nuttall's words over in her mind. 'But without formal testing it's relatively easy to jump to a conclusion about an individual's capabilities. You've heard him speak: his vocabulary is good. He can be quite eloquent.'

She heard Nuttall's tut, sensed his headshake. 'He's totally unreliable from what I've heard so far.'

'In some ways he is but that's no reason to doubt everything he says.'

'I didn't say it was but if this case goes to court and he's one of our witnesses we'll be throwing him to the sharks.'

She understood what he was saying about the criminal justice system. 'We have to work with Myers so he can tell us what he knows, as well as he's able.'

Nuttall's head turned quickly to her. 'Watch that. The sharks are always on the lookout for weak witnesses and overzealous professionals.'

'Whatever he knows, we have to hear it.'

Nuttall's eyes were back on the glass. 'I admire your determination but it doesn't always win the day.'

She looked through the glass at Watts, picked up his almost imperceptible nod to Corrigan who resumed the questioning.

'Detective Sergeant Watts spoke to you at the field off Genners Lane a few nights ago. Do you recall that?'

'My memory's A1.'

The duty solicitor placed his pen down and leant away from the table, the expression on his narrow face indicating that he had his doubts.

'That's good,' said Corrigan encouragingly.

'I don't remember much about it.'

The duty solicitor looked at Watts, his face resigned. 'I think this interview is too demanding for this witness.'

Hearing this, Myers sent him an offended look.

Hanson leant to the microphone and spoke directly into the small device in Corrigan's ear. 'Set the scene for him on the night Watts and I were at the field. It might give him some focus.'

He did so. Myers gave him a gracious nod.

'Thank you for clarifying. I was some distance away but I'd noticed the police there. I didn't want to get personally involved. I legged it. I was stopped by two young constables who manhandled me across the field—' Myers raised a finger and pointed it at Watts – 'to him.'

Myers rolled on. 'I expected him to ask about my Secret Service background but he didn't. He asked if I was at the field a year before. I said yes. Like I said, A1 memory. At that time I'd had a particularly nasty operation . . .' Ellen touched his arm. Myers looked at her then back to Corrigan.

'No. That was another time. The time you're asking about, I was moving residences. That's why I remembered it. I told him.' He pointed to Watts again. 'And a woman who reminded me of a Rossetti painting, *Proserpine*.' Hanson's lips twitched. 'That I heard a voice, male, calling for his mother to come and find him. Want me to do it?'

Watts gave an abrupt nod as Myers leant his head back and swayed, his voice a croon, arms spread. '"Oh, come to me. Look at me. Look into my eyes".' He straightened. 'That's it. Can I go?'

He got a long look from the duty solicitor who turned to Watts. 'I've given you my opinion of the witness.'

Watts' eyes were fixed on Myers. 'What did you think when you were in that field and heard those words, Mr Myers?'

Hanson closed her eyes. *Don't ask him for ideas, impressions. Stick to facts.*

Myers lifted his head and squinted upwards and to the right. 'He was after something.'

'Can you say anything else about that?' asked Watts.

'Yes. I've thought about it.'

Hanson waited, scarcely breathing. *Come on, Michael.*

'He wanted her to do something for him. Give him something.'

In the silence Myers looked at each face then shrugged. 'He was asking the wrong person.'

Watts' eyes were all over Myers' face. 'What do you mean?'

Myers shrugged again. 'It's obvious. His mother wasn't there. He was talking to that young girl the papers are full of, the one the police have dug up and she never said anything.'

Hanson listened as Watts asked Myers about the vehicle he'd told them he heard.

Myers nodded, looking scholarly. 'In my opinion it was extremely powerful. A Lamborghini I once owned sounded very similar.'

Nuttall turned to her and shook his head. 'He's all over the place. We need a better witness than him.'

Hanson quelled a snappy offer to knit him one, her eyes on the duty solicitor who was speaking.

'You know why the police were at that field that night. You know that the body of a young woman was found there. If you know anything about that you need to tell these officers.'

Myers' next words rooted all of them where they were sitting.

'I knew her.'

No one moved inside the interview room. Ellen looked horrified. Hanson stared, stunned. Nuttall looked from her to Myers and back.

'Who?' demanded Watts.

'That girl. The one in the field.'

'What do you mean, you knew her?'

'I know she was a really nice girl.' Seconds ticked by. Hanson guessed that Watts was pondering the next question and how best to deliver it. When he did, his tone was quiet and deliberate.

'How do you know that, Mr Myers?'

'It's obvious,' said Myers. 'It said so in the newspapers.'

Adrift, Watt searched for words. 'You're saying you read about her in the newspapers?'

'I was more interested in her photos,' said Myers, getting Hanson's full attention.

'I've got her photos at my house,' he continued chattily. 'From when she was little and then bigger.'

Watts stared. 'What do you mean, you've got her photos?'

'I rang them up.'

Watts reddened. 'Rang *who* up?' he asked.

'The newspapers.'

Hanson knew the questions in her colleagues' minds right now because they were also in hers. If Myers' knowledge of Elizabeth Williams had come from newspapers, what was his motivation for trying to obtain photographs of her? She went over all that they knew about him: he spent time in the area where Elizabeth had been found, seemingly moving around it at will during the day and often in darkness. Was it possible that Myers had seen Elizabeth whilst she was still alive? That he'd had some level of contact with her which had developed into an obsession?

'Where are we going with this?' whispered Hanson, aware of Nuttall's eyes on her.

Watts's hands were raised, palms up. 'OK, OK. Let's slow this down. Get it straight. You phoned the newspapers and got copies of photographs of Elizabeth Williams, the girl who was murdered, yes?'

'No, I didn't.'

Hanson saw Watts's shoulder muscles tighten. He pointed to the PACE machine, emphasizing his next words.

'That's what you just told us, Mr Myers. We've got it on record.'

Myers regarded the machine with interest. Hanson glanced at Ellen.
She was looking worried.

Watts's eyes were fastened on Myers. He took a deep breath.
'Did you have photographs of the murdered girl?'

'Yes.'

'Where did you get them?' asked Watts.

'From the newspapers.'

His eyes were fixed on Myers' face. 'Did you buy those
newspapers?'

Myers grinned. 'Didn't have to. The Sanctuary has them
delivered.'

Hanson closed her eyes and released a long, slow breath. Myers
had not obtained photographs of Elizabeth Williams from any
newspaper offices. They would have given him short shrift as a
non-relative, particularly if he had failed to provide a lucid account
of himself. What he'd done was remove photographs from the
newspapers available at The Sanctuary. It made a kind of sense.
She frowned. That still left the possibility that Myers had seen
Elizabeth in life and had taken more than a passing interest in her.

Watts wasn't finished. 'Why did you want photos of Elizabeth
Williams?'

'Somebody told me that she looked after her mother. That means
she was a nice girl, like I said. I lost my mother, you know.'

Preoccupied, Hanson left the observation room as Watts brought
the interview to a close. Michael Myers' loss of his mother, his
general presentation suggested that there had been no one else to
care for him after she was gone. Or if there had been, they were
unable or unwilling to meet his needs. Not every family is a refuge.
What they had learned so far was that Michael Myers had obtained
some fragmentary, reinforcing memory of his own mother from
Elizabeth's photographs.

Hanson came into UCU and stood before the board, looking at
the two large photographs there.

What had your killer wanted from you, Elizabeth?

Myers had left headquarters. Corrigan had gone to armed response
duties. Back inside UCU, Watts looked worn.

'Face it, doc. Myers is one on his own. With him, words mean
what he wants them to mean and it changes every five minutes. Yes,
he has got photos, then no, he hasn't.'

'His thinking does tend to be chaotic,' she acknowledged.

'You can say that again.'

'If we'd had the kind of early life experiences Myers probably had, it's very likely we'd be chaotic.'

He gave his face a brisk rub. 'Is it possible he's cleverer than he's letting on? Trying to confuse us?'

Hanson thought about it. 'I haven't observed anything about him which suggests he has a capacity for manipulation.'

Watts gave her a sharp look. 'If you ask me, he's got staff at that Sanctuary place looking out for him.' He caught her facial expression. 'Yeah, yeah, I know. He's vulnerable. But look at how he turned up today. Now he's told us he took an interest in Elizabeth Williams. He never mentioned that before. You've said it often enough, doc: we need to keep an open mind. We can't rule Myers out.'

Hanson leant against the table, running her fingers through her hair. She and Watts were sometimes at odds, despite working for the same goal. Their professional ways of operating were very different. She'd heard him summarise it once in typical fashion: 'I call a spade a spade when I see one, whereas the doc wants to ask it what it's thinking, how it's feeling and why.'

She gave him a tired look. 'Solicitors smarten up their clients when they think it'll aid their case. Michael Myers needs somebody on his side, which makes him lucky that he's got The Sanctuary looking out for him. He doesn't have anybody else.'

'I hear you, doc and I can see he's a sympathetic figure but you just heard him throw a big cat among our pigeons. We have to ask what the chances are that he clapped eyes on Elizabeth Williams prior to her being murdered.' Hanson had no argument as she watched him go to the board. He added a single line beneath a name then turned to her.

'Michael Myers, a witness, is also a person of interest, along with Chris Turner the boyfriend and Vickers the tutor.'

Hanson pulled her diary from her bag. 'When are you seeing Vickers again?'

'He's agreed five thirty this afternoon.' He watched Hanson churn her bag for her phone. 'He reckons he's too busy before that. I want to leave Turner alone for a couple of days, then approach him on little cat feet. Corrigan thinks the same as me: if Turner gets so much as a hint we're interested in him, he'll start shouting "harassment" and we'll have a fight on our hands to get anything from him.'

Hanson dropped her phone into her bag. 'I've texted Maisie to get the bus with Chelsey and stay at her house until I get home.'

She thought of the many times Chelsey's mother helped her out. Candice didn't appear to keep a tally but Hanson did, the kindnesses often causing small jabs of maternal guilt because she couldn't return them so easily.

She turned towards the door. 'See you at the college.'

'Hang on.' He pushed a cellophane wrapped packet across the table towards her. 'Take this with you. I can survive on my fat. Make sure you have a break and eat it, yeah?' She took it.

'Thank you.'

ELEVEN

Hanson arrived at the college to find Watts among a throng of waiting students outside a door bearing the nameplate: Dr Lawrence Vickers. Senior Lecturer.

He glanced at his watch, voice low. 'A student went in there about fifteen minutes ago. I'm hoping she'll be out soon.'

As if on cue the door swung open and a young woman appeared, followed by a man who looked to Hanson to be in his mid-thirties with collar-length hair and low-fit jeans. He was smiling.

'Now, just remember what I said: head down, other parts of the anatomy up and stick at it till it's finished.' He watched her walk away then turned. Catching sight of Watts, his face sobered.

'Is it that time already? Come on in.'

They followed Vickers inside his office which was littered with folders, papers and textbooks. He moved some off the seats of a couple of chairs and dropped them onto the carpet.

Watts introduced Hanson and she saw Vickers' double take as he heard her job title and where she worked. 'There's no need to tell you about students' universal resistance to work, particularly at this end of the year.'

'I wouldn't put it that strongly but I know what you mean.'

He dropped onto the chair behind the desk. 'What can I do for the West Midlands Police?'

'Tell us all you know about Elizabeth Williams,' said Watts.

Hanson watched Vickers lean back on his chair, eyes raised to the ceiling. 'Terrible business. A really nice girl. Hardworking. Keen to learn. Here against all the odds.' He looked across at them. 'You're aware of her background?'

Watts nodded. 'When did you last see her?'

Vickers stared at him. 'You asked me that last time. I told you she attended my Friday afternoon lecture. That was the last time I saw her.'

Watts kept his tone even. 'We've got reason to believe she had a tutorial with you on the Saturday morning, around ten thirty.' They waited. Vickers shook his head.

'Your information is wrong.'

Making a show of note-taking, Watts let the silence in the room lengthen, then looked up. 'You never saw Elizabeth Williams on that Saturday?'

Vickers' eyes moved from him to Hanson and back. 'No. I didn't.'

Watts adjusted his tie, not looking at him. 'Two people have informed us that she had a tutorial that Saturday morning. With you.'

Vickers shrugged, looking calm. 'Whoever said that is mistaken.'

Watts slow-nodded. 'Where were you that morning, Dr Vickers?'

'Here in my office.'

'On a Saturday?'

'I often come into college to catch up on paperwork.' He looked at Hanson. 'I'm sure your colleague's experience is the same as mine. There isn't enough time in the five-day week to lecture *and* do administrative tasks.'

Hanson kept her face neutral.

'How was Elizabeth when she was in your lecture on the Friday?' Watts asked.

Watching him, Hanson got the impression that he relaxed at the reference to another day. 'She seemed fine. Upbeat.'

Watts gave a slow nod. 'Sounds like you spoke to her.'

A few seconds went by. 'I'm not sure that I did. It was just an impression I gained. Elizabeth was very . . . expressive. One knew her mood from her face, her demeanour.' He fell silent, his face bland. He gave a quick nod. 'Actually, now that I think about it, she did speak to me. Very briefly. She said something about going shopping the next morning, which was the Saturday. She had plans for that morning so clearly there was no tutorial.'

'How was it that she came to mention this shopping trip to you?' asked Watts.

'She passed me on her way out after the lecture.'

'Why would she tell you she was going shopping?'

'I can't tell you why. She just did.'

Watts was on his feet.

Vickers looked up at him. 'Have we finished?'

'For now.'

Watts headed for the door, his face set. Hanson followed with a head full of questions.

'Why did he look relieved when the questions turned from the Saturday to the Friday? Why would a student mention a shopping trip on her way out of a lecture? I can't recall that happening to me. And, why did you tell him we had information that he had a tutorial with Elizabeth Williams that Saturday morning? You've criticised me in the past for "cutting corners".'

In the relative early evening quiet of headquarters, Watts leant against the big work table in UCU, arms folded. 'Simmer down, doc. He wasn't about to tell us anything so I cut it short. Something I've learned: leave them hanging and worried.'

Hanson turned her attention to the note she'd made. They included Vickers' comment to the young female student as she left his office: 'Head down, other parts of the anatomy up.' She recalled Vickers' hairstyle, the low jeans, wondering how agreeable he found his job, surrounded by young females. Maybe very agreeable?

She stood. 'In your eagerness to leave, we didn't ask him what he knows about Elizabeth having an internship.'

'He's not going anywhere and he knows we'll be seeing him again.' He glanced up at her. 'I've seen that look on a terrier with a rat.'

'Not one of your more flattering observations but I am interested in Vickers.'

'Any particular reason?'

She thought about it. 'He appeared relaxed but as I watched him I thought of how ducks sit on water, all the time furiously paddling beneath it.' She reached for her bag and her keys.

'By the way, I've arranged to see Chris Turner tomorrow morning. He didn't sound thrilled at the prospect but he agreed.'

'On your own, why?'

'I want to see how he interacts with a female to whom he has no emotional connection and doesn't regard as a possession.'

Inside her study at home, Hanson's eyes drifted over the words Jess Simmonds had spoken, then at the questions she planned to ask Turner. Based on what Simmonds had told her, she'd seeded them with key words: 'quality', 'casual', confide', 'problem-solving'. Questioning Turner about his relationships posed a potential problem. Aware of the possible risk of repercussions she could not reveal to him that Jess Simmonds was her informant.

Hearing feet bypassing her study door, pounding the stairs, then returning, she added a final question and closed the notebook.

Heading for the kitchen she found Maisie sorting clothes.

'Why all the rush of activity?'

Maisie gave her an impatient look. 'You're always on at me to get my stuff ready when I'm going to Daddy's so that's what I'm doing – but these need washing.'

Hanson took several items from her. 'I'll put them in now. They'll be dry by the morning.' She gave the clothes a quick glance.

'Have you left some things at your father's?'

Thick curls tumbled as Maisie reached down to retrieve underwear which had fallen to the floor. 'I'll bring them back if I remember.'

'Try, or you'll find all the ones you like aren't here when you want them.'

'You and Daddy are *so* different.' Maisie observed with a slow headshake.

Hanson said nothing, not wanting to encourage further comment. Maisie required none.

'When I can't find something or I forget something, Daddy's like, "Don't worry, Mouse. It'll get sorted." But not you, Mum. No, sir-ee.'

'Probably because I'm generally the one who does the sorting.'

Maisie gave an emphatic nod. 'Daddy says you're "over-responsible".'

Hanson went into the laundry to put the clothes into the machine. She returned to the kitchen to find the conversation still open.

'He says you're a "dominant female". Stella looked really narky when he said it the other day and I heard them arguing in their bedroom and he said something about having "picked another". I don't think grown-ups make a lot of sense.'

Hanson stopped what she was doing. 'That's because you were eavesdropping. I've told you not to do that.'

Maisie widened her eyes. 'It's not *my* fault if Daddy's apartment is small and I just, like, hear stuff and anyway he says stuff when I'm *there*. He calls Stella his "Spice" and you his "ex-Spice". Why don't grown-ups say what they mean?'

Hanson went back to her study, shoved what she needed for the following day into her briefcase, then switched off the light.

Right, Kevin. Tomorrow, you'll be hearing just how dominant I can be.

She knew he'd regard anything she said as proving his point. She didn't care. He had to start watching what he said when Maisie was around. She had no reason to doubt what Maisie had told her. When it came to adults and their behaviour, Maisie was a sponge. That was something else he needed to know.

TWELVE

anson's eyes were fixed on sun-bright red brick beyond the leaded window of her university room, Kevin's words rushing into her ear. He sounded stroppy. He generally did when he felt at a disadvantage.

'I don't know why you're obsessing about it,' he snapped. 'She doesn't pick up on half she hears.'

She felt a rush of irritation. Why did he find it so hard to get? She knew the answer. He didn't really understand Maisie because he didn't actually know her that well. His agreed weekly contacts with her in the past had often been sporadic, depending on what was happening in his life at the time. This usually meant whichever woman he was or wasn't dating. His current rate of contact was more regular but his understanding of what was appropriate to say around Maisie remained limited. Added to that, Maisie's academic prowess skewed his view of their daughter: he tended to view her as a short adult. Hanson was about to put him straight.

'She shouldn't be hearing adult conversations which feature me or Stella. She's only just turned thirteen but she's quick to latch on to anything she hears. She might not understand all of it but she's not above using what she does to play us against each other.' She took a breath. 'All I'm saying is that you need to be careful when she's around. I don't discuss you or your situation with Maisie. I don't encourage her to talk about you. I want the same from you when she's at your place.'

A heavy sigh drifted into her ear. 'You always want something.'

She frowned, annoyance spiralling. 'Meaning what?'

'*Meaning,* it's always your way or no way. I'm due in court in an hour. I haven't got time for this.' She closed her eyes. She should have known. Her ex-husband's job was far more important than anyone else's.

'Neither have I. Just bear in mind what I've said.'

'So now I've got to keep schtum in my own home?'

She lowered the phone, breathed deeply then put it to her ear again. 'I'm saying be careful what you say on the days she's with you. Maisie isn't a young child and she may appear to know everything, but she doesn't.'

'Right. Anything else?'

'Yes. When she leaves your place to come home, make sure she has all of her clothes with her. Better still; ask Stella if she wouldn't mind doing it.'

She ended the phone call, small scenes from years before inside her head, one of Kevin jiggling plump, one-year-old Maisie over the breakfast table. 'OK, Tink. Let's shake some of that fairy dust over your cereal', and Maisie squealing with laughter.

Good times. Just not enough of them.

With a quick glance at her watch she reached for her keys.

Chris Turner led Hanson inside the common room she'd seen on her previous visit. It was deserted.

'Thank you for agreeing to see me, Mr Turner.'

'No problem. My pleasure,' he said, waving her to a seat. She'd decided to begin by asking him about himself, suspecting he would like that.

'What stage have you reached in your studies here?'

A satisfied look appeared on his face. 'I've finished my degree.

I'm anticipating a first and I've fixed up a really good job down south. I'm ready to leave here and get on with my life.'

She smiled. 'You sound happy at the prospect.'

He glanced at her. His face turned sombre. He shook his head. 'Actually, I'm not. This terrible news about Elizabeth has taken the edge off everything. We were very close.'

She gazed at him, knowing that he'd probably reflected on her previous visit here. Watts had a term for someone like Turner: 'cool customer'.

'The internships that students here are expected to take up, did Elizabeth find one prior to her disappearance?'

'I already answered that. No.'

'Tell me about her. What was she like?'

His facial expression was unchanged but she saw cheek muscles move beneath his skin. 'She was a nice girl, a good student.' He fell silent, his eyes roaming. *He sounds like he's talking about somebody he knew merely in passing.*

'How would you describe Elizabeth as a girlfriend?'

He folded his arms. 'She's been gone a long time ago but it's still upsetting for me, so I'd really rather not.'

She put down her pen and leant forward. 'Mr Turner, as the boyfriend of a young woman who we now know has been murdered, it shouldn't take too much intellectualising to appreciate that the police want information from you as to the quality of your relationship with her. If you don't tell me, my police colleagues will be back to get it.'

Turner's brows met. 'What do you mean by quality?'

Mindful of Jess Simmonds, Hanson chose her words. Murderer or not, she knew that Turner was a bully within his personal relationships. Simmonds was free of him now and Hanson wouldn't utter a single word to jeopardise that.

'I've got a few questions to help get you thinking about that.' She suspected he understood very well what she was asking of him but she reeled them off. 'For example, did you and Elizabeth anticipate that the relationship would last or was it more a casual, short-term arrangement?' He didn't reply, his face stone. 'Did you and she have a lot in common? Did you confide in each other?'

He fixed her with a look and Hanson was glad that the room was spacious and the door was behind her not him.

'I'm not "casual" about relationships. They're important or I don't get involved.'

She looked into his eyes. 'What do you expect from an important, close relationship, Mr Turner?'

He sat back, his eyes locked on hers. 'All the usual things. Commitment. Respect. Absolute truth.'

She raised her brows. '"Absolute truth"? That's a tall order. I'd say impossible.'

'I don't happen to agree.'

Hanson gave a slow nod. 'In my opinion, relationships are about problem-solving. What do you think?'

'Again, I don't know what you mean.'

The silence between them lengthened.

She regarded him with interest. 'I'm getting the impression that you don't want to answer reasonable questions which anyone who's been in a reciprocal relationship would understand. This feels like pushing water uphill, Mr Turner. Why is that?'

'You seem to have all the answers. You tell me.'

Hanson was happy to oblige. 'OK. One possibility is that you don't have reciprocal relationships. Perhaps your high demands around commitment, respect and absolute truth impact on the relationships you do have?'

Self-centred he might be but he wasn't stupid. She saw his eyes narrow.

'You know nothing about me.'

'Which is why you need to talk to me, Mr Turner. Tell me if you think I'm wrong.'

He didn't answer.

'How did you and Elizabeth resolve differences of opinion?'

His eyes darkened. 'There weren't any. We were mature about things. We were very compatible.'

It felt like talking to a wall but she wasn't about to give up. 'When people tell me that their relationships are totally free of dissent I usually don't believe them.'

The thin smile didn't reach the eyes. 'Maybe that says more about you than them? All I expect from partners is respect and honesty. If you asked most people they'd say the same.'

'How did you get respect and honesty in your relationship with Elizabeth?'

He lounged on his chair, eyes sharp. 'By putting my case as to why those things are important. Why they must be a part of the relationship. It's not rocket science.'

She gazed at him. 'That doesn't sound like you got what you wanted by agreement.'

'What is there to "agree"? They're universal values.'

'What if a partner doesn't see it quite like you do?'

He regarded her for some seconds. 'Then something has to change. Her. Or the situation.'

She knew what he was. Jess Simmonds had told her. Her own training, her psychological evaluations of males like him enabled her to picture his behaviour, his manner, his attitude when he made his demands. She could anticipate how they were received because she'd talked to many women who'd had somebody just like him as a partner. For many of them the experience had been one of extreme psychological or physical abuse. Sometimes both.

Yet, for all her theoretical knowledge and experience there was still a tiny part of her conscious mind which struggled to fully accept that this man sitting in front of her had done such things. She believed what Simmonds had told her but still she struggled. It wasn't about Turner. She knew he was a bully, its shadow evident in this exchange. She recognised him for what he was, yet she still struggled with the actuality. Her usual response to the violent and the cruel sitting opposite her in interviews as they smiled and drank coffee was often, 'surely not?' Her friend Celia had been succinct about it. 'That's no surprise. You're trained to recognise the worst but you're also normal, like most of us. Normal people find it hard to believe the worst. It doesn't stop you doing your job.'

Hearing the door open and the sound of voices, she leant forward, keeping her own voice low. 'I've listened really closely to all you've said. You're wrong when you say I know nothing about you. I've met you a hundred times and more, and each of you is depressingly similar. You are a bully, Mr Turner. Any partner you have won't be entitled to views of her own. You demand deference because you regard relationships as a one-way street. It's the only way you know to control the threat you see in opening yourself up to another person.'

His face was frozen, unreadable.

One of the students who'd just come in called across the room. 'Hey, Chris. You ready for that return match and a thrashing?'

Turner's face changed in an instant to affable. 'Give me a minute to get my stuff together.'

Hanson walked to the door and turned. He was lifting a heavy sports bag, laughing as he did so. He looked beyond his fellow student to Hanson, his face ice. He sauntered towards her and stopped close to her. Too close.

'You know your way out.'

She looked up at him. 'You'll be getting another visit very soon, Mr Turner.' She saw something deep within his eyes.

'Sorry, I'm planning to spend a few days with friends in Berkshire.'

'Dates?'

'Not yet decided.' He went past her to the door then turned. 'Ask Laurence Vickers what he thinks of relationships, casual or otherwise.'

Inside her car Hanson considered Turner in the role of Elizabeth Williams' killer.

The aunt's impression had been that Elizabeth left her house to go and see him. But given his anger, his personality, if he had killed her I would have expected gross signs of injury on her remains. Facial injury. Broken bones. Signs of his rage. Chong didn't find any.

She wrote down Turner's comment about Vickers.

THIRTEEN

After spending the remainder of the morning at the university, ending it with a basic crash course on statistics to a panicky student, plus a promise of practical help, Hanson walked into UCU. Watts passed her with a 'drink?' motion. She nodded, aware of Corrigan's amused look. She sent him a quick frown.

'What?'

'You're looking pent.'

'I am.' She pulled her notebook from her bag. 'I've been to see Chris Turner.'

'What did he have to say?' asked Watts.

'Quite a lot he probably didn't plan on revealing.'

Lifting the laptop she talked them through their conversation. 'He was all aggression cloaked in arrogant resistance. It was like questioning Vesuvius about to start an active phase.'

Watts brought tea to the table with a slow wink for Corrigan. 'Who?'

She continued, eyes on the board as her fingers raced across laptop keys. 'Under the good looks there's a massive anger. As a partner he's a jealous, demanding controller.'

Watts stared at her. 'You think he might have killed Elizabeth Williams?'

'I'm saying that for me he's the most compelling person of interest in this case so far, but with a possible reservation.'

Corrigan searched her face. 'I'm guessing you're not one hundred percent sold on him as the killer because you think if he had lost it with Elizabeth he'd have done her some serious physical damage.'

'Exactly.'

Watts mused at the notes appearing on the board. 'We don't know how she died. What if he overpowered and smothered her? That wouldn't leave many signs.'

She considered this. 'Elizabeth was athletic. Strong. Fit. Surely she would have put up some resistance? I suspect if Turner killed her, even mild resistance would have triggered his temper and Chong would have found evidence of it.'

'I still think he could have waited until Elizabeth was asleep.'

Hanson reconsidered it. 'I can't see her putting up zero resistance and there was no indication of drugs or alcohol to render her even marginally compliant.'

She finished with the laptop and pushed it away, pointing to the board. 'See what he said about Lawrence Vickers, the tutor? "Ask Vickers what he thinks of relationships, casual or otherwise." Maybe Turner has some issue with Vickers or maybe he said it to deflect attention from himself. Or, he knows something we don't. We need to see Vickers again.'

'We will,' said Watts, giving her a quick once-over. 'You could do with a break. Got any plans after work?'

Hanson stretched both arms upwards, then ran her hands through her hair. 'At around nine o'clock this evening I've got a date with a very comfortable sofa and a television set. I haven't seen much of either in what seems like a month.'

'Watts and I are thinking of take-out food later at my place. How about it?' said Corrigan.

She considered it. 'Maisie's at Kevin's so that's really tempting.'

He smiled. 'So give in to temptation. You have to eat.'

Before she could reply the phone rang. Watts spoke into it then hung up.

'Our mother had a saying: "Talk of the devil and he'll turn up." She was right. That was reception. Guess who's just walked in?'

Lawrence Vickers was pacing as they came into reception. He turned to them, his fleshy face pale. Watts ushered him into the informal meeting room.

Looking at Vickers, Hanson couldn't decide whether he was fuddled from a few drinks or disoriented from some other cause. She breathed in. Alcohol. He was staring at the floor. A man with a lot on his mind. They waited.

Corrigan broke the silence. 'It was your choice to come here, sir. You have something to say to us?'

Vickers opened his mouth then closed it again, making no eye contact.

Watts gave an exasperated grunt. 'You're here, Mr Vickers. You might as well tell us.'

Vickers spoke, his voice strained. 'I don't want you to get the wrong idea about me.'

Watts's eyes were on him. 'I'm getting one already because you're not telling us anything.'

Vickers' upper body slumped forward. He rubbed his eyes. 'I saw her. That Saturday morning.'

Tension spiked. Nobody moved. They knew who Vickers was talking about but he had to say it.

'Who?' asked Corrigan.

'Elizabeth Williams. We had a tutorial that Saturday morning.' The small room felt charged.

'So, where's the problem in acknowledging it?'

Vickers stared down at his hands. 'None as far as I'm concerned. But when you came to the college I thought that if I mentioned it you'd suspect I had something to do with what happened to her. So I was . . . less than forthcoming.'

Watts looked deeply unimpressed. 'Lied, you mean.' Hanson saw Vickers flinch.

'Why didn't you tell us?' Watts demanded. Vickers remained silent. Watts glared at him. 'Why lie about something that's part of your job? Unless you know something about that tutorial. Did something happen inside your office?'

Vickers' gaze stayed resolutely on the floor, Watts' impatience growing. 'Come on, Dr Vickers. We could have you for obstruction. Start being forthcoming now or I'll consider it.'

Vickers began a halting account. As Elizabeth left his Friday afternoon lecture, he'd reminded her that they had a tutorial the following morning. She'd arrived at his office about five minutes late that Saturday morning.

He continued, his face now grey, 'She arrived in a rush and I noticed that she looked, I don't know . . . excited. I told her to sit and calm down. I gave her a drink.'

Watts looked like a Pointer who'd just spotted a rabbit. 'What kind of drink?'

'Juice.'

Vickers looked down at his hands again. Hanson saw they were shaking. 'We talked about her college work and then . . . I did something stupid.'

Hanson felt Watts's eyes on her. 'What did you do, Mr Vickers?' she asked.

'I told her I found her very attractive.' He covered his face with his hands. 'I don't know what came over me. I invited her to have dinner with me.'

'And?'

Vickers looked up at her. 'That was it. She said she'd think about it. As soon as she left the room, I realised how stupid I'd been. The college frowns on that kind of thing. You'll understand what I'm saying.'

Vickers looked increasingly rattled in the silence that followed his outburst. 'This is exactly what I expected,' he finally said, filling the silence. 'The reason I didn't mention it. You're thinking I did something to her. I *didn't*.'

Head propped on one hand, Watts fixed him with a look. 'I'll tell you what I'm thinking. After you saw us the other day, you thought about it and realised you were in a hole. We'd been told Elizabeth Williams had a tutorial that Saturday morning and being smart you realised we wouldn't leave it alone, that we'd follow it up.' He leant towards Vickers. 'What wasn't smart was not admitting it when you had the chance!'

Vickers looked contrite. 'I know. After you left my office I started thinking. I thought of the way she'd looked at me when I invited her out.' He covered his face with his hands again, speaking through them. 'It was embarrassing. As though she felt sorry for me. She said she'd think about what I'd said but I could see she wasn't interested. I started to worry that maybe she'd tell some of the other students and the faculty would get to hear about it.' He removed his hands from his face, looking worn.

'It was a spur-of-the-moment thing. It had been an exhausting week, the academic year was winding down and that Saturday, for the first time in days, I was able to breathe. She arrived and she looked really nice.' He paused. 'I like tutorials.' He glanced up; saw Watts's eyes on him.

'What I mean is, they're enjoyable because they're one-on-one . . .' He stopped, releasing a shaky breath.

'Did you get as far as arranging a time and place with her for dinner?' asked Corrigan.

Vickers gave a vehement headshake. 'No! Of course not.'

Corrigan studied him. 'You didn't volunteer any of this to the original investigation.'

Vickers gave a mirthless laugh. 'No way! When I heard that nobody had seen her after that weekend, I was shocked then worried in case she'd mentioned the invitation to somebody. I didn't think she was the kind of girl to joke about something like that but there was no way I could be sure. I couldn't very well ask anybody, could I? Those few days were the longest I remember in my whole life.'

'What did you tell the police at the time?' said Watts.

'I told them I last saw her on the Friday. Then I waited for them to come back and question me again. Arrest me, even.'

'And?'

'They never did. I thought that was it and for a whole year, it was. Until last week when you phoned.'

Watts looked unimpressed. 'You should have gone to them. Told them what you knew.'

Vickers stared at him. 'I *couldn't*. I would have put myself under suspicion when I hadn't done anything, plus people, the faculty, would have found out what I'd said to her.'

Hanson glanced at his wedding ring.

'Does "people" include your wife?' asked Corrigan.

Vickers stared at the floor.

'So why are you here now?'

Vickers bowed his head. 'Because it's like the last time. Waiting for the axe to drop. I'm exhausted from thinking and worrying about it.'

Watts's eyes were still on him. 'Just because you say you didn't see her again doesn't mean you didn't.'

Vickers looked up, horrified. 'I didn't! I didn't lay a hand on her! For God's *sake*, it wasn't that serious an invitation. It was out of my mouth before I knew what I was saying and almost straight away I knew it was a bad idea. I thought of texting or emailing her to say, "Sorry let's forget it", but that would have got me in deeper still.' He looked at them. 'After you came to see me, I knew what I had to do. That's why I'm here. I'd hardly come here and tell you all this if I'd killed her, would I?'

Hanson took in the jeans, the longish hair, a tutor's take on the trendy. *You might.*

'Why was Elizabeth excited?' she asked.

Vickers looked confused. 'What?'

'You said that Elizabeth arrived in a rush and that she was excited. What was she excited about?'

He shrugged. 'I don't know. I didn't ask and she didn't say.'

She glanced at Watts, then: 'Do you know if Elizabeth had arranged an internship?'

He frowned, running a hand through his hair. 'I don't get involved with that stuff. All I know is, the students take what the college has on offer or they find their own.'

Watts stood. Corrigan and Hanson did the same. 'All right, Mr Vickers. Thanks for the information.'

Vickers got up, glanced at each of them then back to Watts, his voice subdued. 'Does what I've told you have to go any further?'

Watts walked to the door and held it open. 'I'll arrange for somebody to take a witness statement from you. We'll be in touch. On your way home you might think about whether to tell all this to your wife.'

Hanson watched Vickers go. He looked like a condemned man.

Hanson glanced around the high-ceilinged room with its subtly painted walls and bookshelves, wood shutters half-closed on falling darkness. Earlier in the evening, Corrigan had shown her around the rest of his home. She'd admired the maple cabinets in the kitchen, then gone upstairs to do the same for the grey slate walk-in shower and the master bedroom. The spare rooms were empty except for the one providing storage for Corrigan's mountain bike. Everywhere there were hardwood floors in the American style.

Rupe, the basset hound had followed them from room to room, with adoring looks for Corrigan. She thought back to how he'd acquired the hound during UCU's previous case, one which had involved fine art and low duplicity, culminating in Corrigan being injured and Hanson fearful for his life.

Downstairs again, she counted the dining table's place settings as her two colleagues brought food to the table. 'Who else is coming?'

She heard the doorbell and found herself wondering if the caller was a woman, a friend of Corrigan's.

'I'll get that,' he said. She watched as he left the room, Rupe on his feet and following.

Watts handed her a container of rice. 'Relax, doc. Here you go.'

She took it, ears straining. Recognising the visitor's voice, she felt relief mixed with irritation. What was it to her who Corrigan might be seeing or inviting to his house?

Julian came into the room. 'This looks good. I'm starving.'

Watts pointed at what was on the table. 'I ordered for you, Devenish. I didn't want to be bothered with cooking tonight.'

Hanson recalled her doubts when Julian first began renting one of Watts's spare rooms. They were so different: middle-aged cynic and academic youth. Against all the odds it was working. Spirits lifting, she spooned more rice onto her plate.

Corrigan placed a drink on the table next to her. 'One weak G & T, ice n' slice.'

For the next few minutes there was comparative silence as they ate, broken eventually by Hanson.

'Can we talk shop for one minute? Where are we with Vickers?'

'He's a person of interest and depending on what he says when we see him next, he could be on his way to suspect,' said Watts.

'Because he lied about the Saturday morning?'

'Because he admits he was trying to get off with a student almost young enough to be his daughter, a young woman who disappeared very soon after and was then murdered. He had motive. He had opportunity. I'd have expected you to have plenty to say about his inviting Williams out, given his age, that he's married, plus you having a similar job and being a feminist.'

Hanson eye-rolled. 'I'm not any kind of "ist". Women have the right not to be harassed. Liaisons like that are discouraged because of the power differential between tutor and student, but they happen.'

She thought of Vickers and what he'd told them. 'We only have his word that he and Elizabeth didn't have that date. That field where she was left is no more than a couple of miles down the lane from the college.'

'Anybody remember the colour of his office carpet?' asked Corrigan.

'Green cord, hardwearing,' said Hanson promptly. 'Question is, is there any cream wool carpet or rug in his life?'

Watts reached for the naan bread. 'That field's off the beaten track. Remember the lane leading up to it? From the start of this case it occurred to me that whoever killed her was local. Somebody who knew that field. Look where Vickers is working: the college on Genners Lane. The same applies to Turner. I'm starting to see some light in this case.'

Watts and Julian had left almost an hour before.

'I should go,' she said.

Corrigan shook his head. 'Have some more coffee.' He poured it then sat with his hand on Rupe's head.

'We haven't shared a meal in a while. I was reminded tonight of what a rewarding eater you are.'

'A what?'

'You make these little sounds of appreciation when you eat.'

'I don't!' she protested. 'Do I?'

'Yep. Sounds like this.' She watched as he closed his eyes '"Mmm . . . oohh."'

She laughed. 'You're making it up.'

'It's cute and barely audible. The sound of someone who's passionate about food and eating. It's real nice.'

'Pity it doesn't translate to my cooking.' She drank her coffee then glanced at her watch.

'I have to go.'

He fetched her jacket and held it for her as she put it on. She pointed to a nearby straight sided glass vase filled with flat white disks, each with a hole at its centre from which radiated petal-like markings.

'What are those?'

'They're sand dollars. From a beach in California.'

He reached inside the vase, lifted out two of them and placed them on her palm.

'They're beautiful,' she said as she handed them back to him.

'Take them.'

She looked up at him, uncertain. 'No. I couldn't.'

'Sure you can.' He walked her to the door. 'It was a nice evening.'

'Yes. It was.'

Hanson was home and feeling unsettled. Something had changed this evening although she wasn't sure what. She and Corrigan had gone out as colleagues several times in the past to eat or for drinks. He'd come here with Watts and Julian for the kind of meal they'd had this evening. Maybe it was being inside Corrigan's home which had made the difference? Whatever it was, she had a sense of some kind of line being crossed. One she hadn't realised existed.

That's ridiculous. Corrigan comes here, you went there. So what? The thought stayed, resolute.

She went up to her bedroom and took off her jacket. Reaching inside one of the pockets, she drew out the sand dollars and put them inside her bag. About to draw the curtains, she looked out of the window, recalling what she knew about him. Divorced, one daughter now adult. Traditional Boston-Irish Catholic upbringing, its emphasis on family. She sensed he was someone who valued commitment. She heard her own thoughts, delivered in her friend Celia's voice.

In which case, he's not going to like the way you operate in relationships is he?

The sky was patched with cloud. It looked like it was going to rain. She pulled the curtains closed and blocked it out.

FOURTEEN

Hanson came into UCU in the early afternoon.

'What's happened?' she asked, picking up the downbeat atmosphere as she brushed raindrops from her hair.

'Nothing,' said Watts.

Julian swivelled on his chair. 'He's got Michael Myers, Chris

Turner and Lawrence Vickers as persons of interest and now he's wondering how to work up a case against one or other of them.'

'Thanks, Devenish. I can do my own talking. Switch the kettle on.'

'Corrigan not here?' she asked.

'He's with Armed Response giving taser training. Should be back soon.'

She reflected on the persons of interest in the case and who she'd elevate to suspect, if any, starting with Chris Turner. Jess Simmonds had described him as abusive and controlling towards her. Hanson believed it. She also believed he had been much the same towards Elizabeth Williams. Belief wasn't proof.

She continued down the list: Lawrence Vickers, college tutor, married, attracted to Elizabeth to the point where he invited her out shortly prior to her disappearance, then kept it to himself for a whole year despite being questioned by the police at the time and now. They had only his word that things hadn't progressed between him and Elizabeth.

Michael Myers. A witness, as far as they knew. Yes, she was sympathetic towards him but she'd learned never to make assumptions about anybody. She glanced at Watts, wondering how receptive he might be to what she had in mind. His heavy face wasn't encouraging.

'What about coming at the case from a different angle?' she suggested as the door opened and Corrigan came in.

Watts looked at her, his face all downward lines. 'That angle being?'

She pointed at the photographs on the board. 'Elizabeth Williams herself.'

She stood as Julian reached for the laptop. 'Let's start with the kind of person Elizabeth was. What were her strengths?'

'Given her history, I'd say she was caring, loyal and responsible,' offered Corrigan. 'Intelligent. Independent-minded.'

Watts raised his head. 'Why independent?'

'She wouldn't settle for an internship provided by the college,' said Julian. 'She had her own ideas.'

Watts frowned. 'She sounded like an upbeat type to me. Energetic. Always on the go.'

Julian typed and Hanson studied the words tracking their way across the board. 'That's Elizabeth's upside. What about her vulnerabilities?' They looked at each other.

'Too trusting, according to her friend Jess,' said Julian.

'How about a bit too independent?' suggested Watts. 'If she'd stayed living with her aunt she might have been OK.' He finger-pointed the screen.

'Hang on, though. She was in a relationship with Turner, the boyfriend from hell. What does that say about this independence of hers?'

Hanson thought about it. 'From what we've been told, I think Elizabeth was independent but I also think she was naïve. Both characteristics could well be the result of her childhood experience.' She looked at each of them.

'I don't know about you, but it's hard for me to imagine what it feels like to be a child whose parent depends on you for daily care. I've tried to imagine Maisie in that role.' She shook her head.

'I can't, yet she's four years older than Elizabeth was when she became her mother's carer. I'm not suggesting that that kind of situation is bad for a child. I can see a lot of gains, for example the independence we've identified, plus the chance to develop empathy and take responsibility.' Hanson came to the table. 'But remember what her aunt said about her? That Elizabeth soaked up whatever she did for her "like blotting paper". And then there's Jess Simmonds' view that Elizabeth was taken advantage of at times. I think that despite Elizabeth's strengths she could have been highly vulnerable to someone, a male who presented himself as caring and interested in her.'

Watts was scouring the list of POIs. 'I'm struggling to see Myers being able to do that but if you think about it, he's got the workers at that Sanctuary place putting themselves out to help him. That tells me he might be capable of a bit of manipulation when it suits him. From what he said here in interview, we can't rule out his and Elizabeth's paths crossing when they were both out and about in the area around the college. I think she was the type to feel sorry for somebody like him. If he struck up a conversation with her I don't see her as the kind who'd ignore him or complain about him.' He glanced at Hanson.

'I like this outside-the-box approach.'

Corrigan was watching information appear on the board. 'Turner's not the caring type but I'd say he's capable of acting it to suit his purposes. And then there's Vickers. According to him, Elizabeth didn't reject him outright. Could be he's another who's able to persuade to get what he wants. All three are in the frame.'

His index finger against his mouth, his eyes went from the board to Hanson. 'I'm only just seeing how much of this case is to do with relationships.'

She looked at the information and saw the point he was making. He took the laptop from Julian and added three words to the board.

Hanson read them. 'Locard's Exchange Principle.'

'We're all familiar with it,' he said. 'Criminals leave traces behind at scenes and take stuff away with them. Apply that same principle to relationships: we all give to them and we all get something back, right? From what we've been told, Turner is selfish and demanding. Why would Elizabeth stay with him?'

Myers' words drifted around Hanson's head: *He wanted her to do something for him. Give him something.* Corrigan looked at her.

'Any ideas as to what Elizabeth might have been getting?'

'Kudos? Affirmation?' She had another thought. 'Didn't Jess Simmonds tell you that when she was in a relationship with Turner the other students viewed them as this good looking "golden couple"? If my impression of Turner is accurate, it was probably a similar situation with Elizabeth. They made a very attractive couple. Along with the kudos and the affirmation, maybe it gave her a sense of being valued by her peers. I'm guessing she hadn't had much experience of that kind of belonging when she was younger.'

'Sounds reasonable,' said Watts.

'OK. What have we got?' Hanson read words aloud. 'Elizabeth Williams was a kind, caring, intelligent and responsible young woman, independent but also a little naïve, a little too trusting and with a need to belong.' It made sense. It also introduced another possibility.

'I can see how this links to one or other of the three POIs. But what if her killer isn't one of them? Maybe her naivety led her to accept someone she didn't know at all?'

Watts's eyebrows shot upwards. 'Hang on! I'm just starting to get optimistic.'

She looked at him. 'You don't need me to tell you we have to consider that the killer might be somebody Elizabeth didn't know.'

He let his head fall back. 'Just when it was starting to make sense.' He got up from the table, went to the board and added a large question mark beneath the list of persons of interest. 'If he's faceless, we're nowhere.'

Hanson quickly tapped laptop keys. 'So what we do is we create the next best thing.'

He watched as the words raced across the board: Silhouette of a Killer.

She looked at him. 'Elizabeth is going to help us.' She pointed to the descriptive words they'd generated.

'She's already begun by telling us about herself. Now she's going to tell us what kind of person her killer is. No one else has mentioned the existence of any such person. Maybe she'd only just met him, or maybe she was keeping him secret? Either way, if she was regarding him as a potential partner, psychological research has something to say about sexual attraction and partner selection.'

'I thought it might,' grumped Watts.

Ignoring him, she continued, 'Research on the "Matching Phenomenon" suggests that we're drawn to those we perceive as like us on various levels such as intellect, education, physical attributes, social background and so forth.' She saw Watts rummaging in his pockets.

She waited. 'You're not buying this?'

'I'm hanging on every word while I find my paracetamol. Carry on.'

She sat on the edge of the table. 'If Elizabeth had an arrangement to meet someone that weekend and she was attracted to him, he's likely to have been pretty much like her. Not necessarily the same age but the same social presentation.'

'I hear what you're saying,' said Watts. 'She would want somebody presentable like herself. No scruff. On the ball. Strike Myers from the list.'

Hanson stopped at a place in her notes. 'Both her aunt and Vickers had the impression that Elizabeth was upbeat about something.' She frowned. 'We know she had her suit cleaned. Not the usual student garb, in my experience. Which suggests what?'

'She had a date, an arrangement with somebody which she regarded as important,' said Corrigan.

Hanson paced, hands together at her mouth. 'She wanted to present as sophisticated.'

'How about she and Faceless had a secret arrangement to go off somewhere that weekend?' said Watts.

She sat on the table next to him. 'Possible, but what do we actually know? Elizabeth Williams was looking for something.'

'An internship,' he said.

'Exactly. How about she made contact with someone she thought might offer her work experience? The suit could indicate a formal arrangement she had to meet somebody to talk about that.'

Watts looked doubtful. 'On a weekend?'

'Leave out the detail for now. She dressed in her smart suit. She wanted to impress. She'd identified him, even superficially as similar to herself and therefore not a threat, which would have lowered her defences. He was someone she could trust. *He* would have made judgements about her: her strengths and her vulnerabilities. If that person was her killer, whenever and wherever she went to meet him, he had Elizabeth Williams where he wanted her.' Hanson stopped. 'Which means he wasn't a stranger to her.' She looked at each of her colleagues. 'They'd already met.'

Watts broke the silence. 'How sure are you about this?'

'I'm hypothesising, which is all we can do, but it gets us considering the possibilities, given what we know about Elizabeth's character and her plans as suggested by her behaviour that weekend.'

'It could as easily have been someone who merely saw her and attacked her,' suggested Corrigan.

Watts caught Hanson's nod of agreement. 'Bloody hell. This just got worse again.'

Hanson created space on the board, then reached for the laptop. 'What else are you going to do right now? Keep after one or other of the persons of interest?'

'Why not?' he said.

She glanced up at him as she started to type. 'Because while you're doing that, there's somebody out there believing he's got away with murder. We need to consider all possibilities.'

He propped his hands either side of his wide middle. 'All this theory is just that. *Theory*. It could have nothing to do with what happened to her.'

She went to the board and tapped an icon. 'We know something which did happen. I want another look at that field.'

The 3D image appeared, first of the lane, narrow, shadowed, lined with trees on either side, their branches joined and overhanging in parts, the robust hedge separating it from the field. Watts came and stood next to her.

She waited, studying his face lit by the screen, his eyes absorbing the detail. 'Say what's on your mind, Watts.'

'OK: Elizabeth Williams was buried in that field in the dark. It was black as the ace of spades when we got there, the lane hardly wide enough for one car and the gap in the hedge not easy to find. The first time I drove to it that night, I had the location details, I was looking for it and I still missed it. He had to have been local to take her there and bury her. Turner and Vickers are just up the road.'

She asked the question she knew he wouldn't like. 'If he was local, how is it he didn't know that this seemingly lonely location wasn't that lonely in reality?'

He stared at the image on the board. 'You're asking how come he didn't know that local kids use that field for games. How come he hadn't picked up local knowledge that types came to the pavilion?'

'He's not on the fringes of local criminality or he'd have known about the pavilion drug dealing,' said Corrigan.

Hanson pointed at names on the board. 'I'm starting to question how local this killer was. He didn't realise he might attract attention but he did: Endo, the cannabis dealer and Michael Myers.'

Watts folded his thick forearms, looking dismissive.

'They're all we've got,' said Hanson, flicking pages of notes. 'We need to take seriously what Myers told us. I'm confident as to when he heard those words because his memory of them is linked to a traumatic life event he was experiencing at the time: he was losing his home. Imagine how that would have felt for somebody like Myers who has so little.' She closed the notebook and dropped it on the desk.

'I agree with you about Endo's limitations but there's no indication that he and Michael Myers have ever met. Yet both described experiences which fit together logically.'

He ran a hand over his hair. 'I hear you but "Myers" and "logically" in the same sentence doesn't increase my confidence.'

He walked from her. 'We're saying whoever Elizabeth went to meet would have been somebody presentable and quick-witted like her. But how quick was he, given that he didn't check out that field and its surroundings?'

Corrigan was at the board, pointing to a photograph. 'Both Turner and Vickers were at the college last year. It's some distance from that field. They know that field's location but maybe they haven't been close to it that often.'

'Exactly,' said Hanson. 'Local, but not local enough.'

'What does the file say about where both those guys lived last year?'

Watts pulled the case file, bristling with post-its towards him and opened it. 'Turner had a rented place a few miles away in Selly Oak. He's still there. Vickers lived just off the Bristol Road. Still does.'

He thumbed pages. 'Those cream wool carpet fibres under Williams's nails. It says "expensive" to me. It's saying "Turner". He looks as though he's got an eye for stylish stuff.'

Hanson did a slow headshake. 'You just said he rents. In my direct experience and those of my students, student rental accommodation is very basic.'

'Then how about Vickers? As a lecturer he'll be on a good wage with a "lifestyle" to go with it.'

She and Watts didn't see eye to eye on a lot of things, one being the financial largesse he fancied academics enjoyed. She looked doubtful.

'Chong's evidence is that Elizabeth got the fibres under her nails by gripping the carpet they were attached to, the inference being that it happened during the attack on her. Vickers is married.'

'So what?' he asked. 'Wives go out.'

She knew he was buoyed up by a return to their persons of interest. 'Still risky.'

'Maybe she was away for a few days.' He looked at Corrigan. 'We'll drop in on him at home. He's already rattled so we'll be subtle about it but we'll check out his domestic setup.'

Hanson had had the discussion mostly her own way for the last hour and she wasn't about to second-guess basic policing decisions. At this stage none of them was able to judge which actions were relevant and which weren't.

'Take a look at his garden while you're about it. See if it's full of trees, dead wood.'

'And massive stag beetles,' murmured Julian.

Corrigan turned to Hanson. 'You've still got it?'

'Yes. I called in at the environmental science department yesterday but there was a meeting going on and no one around who I could leave it with. I'll drop it off the next chance I get.'

Later that afternoon, Hanson opened her front door in response to the bell, her mind on the case. She stopped at the sight of the statuesque blonde woman with a wide smile standing there. Friends from childhood, a staunch mutual support system still, they didn't see each other nearly enough.

'Cee! I don't believe it. Come *in*.'

They hugged, then arms linked headed for the kitchen. 'This is great. Coffee? How about some walnut bread Maisie's made?'

Celia laughed, patting her waist. 'What are you trying to do to me? Coffee's fine. I've got a hair appointment in the High Street in an hour but I decided to drive down the avenue in case you were here. I hope you're truanting and idling.'

'I wish.'

Celia raised her head and listened. 'Ah. All alone. No tryst?'

'No and that's fine by me,' said Hanson, starting on the coffee, not wanting to encourage further comment about the way she chose to live her life.

Celia sat at the kitchen table, eyes skimming a number of photographs lying there. 'Right now, I envy you. My house is a wellspring of teenage hormones. When I finally got all three out of the house this morning I closed their bedroom doors on the anarchy they'd left behind. Then I realised I was a free agent and within ten minutes I was on my way to Birmingham. I've spent the day in town, didn't buy anything except lunch, booked the hair appointment and came here. Oh, thanks.' She took the coffee.

'Stay the night,' said Hanson on impulse, knowing that Celia's husband would take it in his stride. 'You could do your own thing here tomorrow morning then come to the university and have lunch with me at Staff House.'

Celia brightened. 'I fancy a pudding involving custard . . . Damn! I can't. I've got to be home for when the engineer comes in the morning to fix the washing machine. I daren't cancel. I've waited nearly a week as it is.'

She watched Hanson gather up the photographs, one or two of them of Hanson's parents and put them inside their folders. 'Taking a ramble down Memory Lane?'

Hanson shook her head, feeling Celia's eyes on her. 'Maisie had them out.'

'She still does that?'

'Yes.' She knew the topic wasn't about to go away. Celia's next words confirmed it.

'Surely Maisie can't still believe that you single-handedly

introduced red hair into your family? If she does, it won't be
long before she learns that her red hair gene was passed down to
her by her father, aided and abetted by your mother who had reddish
hair.' Hanson said nothing, the words reinforcing her own worry.

'You still haven't told her, have you?'

'No.'

'When are you going to tell her, Kate?'

'Soon.'

Celia regarded her across the table. 'Better make it very soon.'
After a small silence she said, 'It would have been easy to do it
when she was, say, four years old. She'd have accepted just a few
words from you. Any questions she had, you could have answered
later, as and when . . . What am I saying? You know all of this.'

It was true. Hanson did know it. But as the years had gone on
it never seemed quite the right time to raise it. First there had been
Maisie's demanding behaviour at nursery and in reception class,
then the testing which established her high IQ, followed by the
extra maths lessons to challenge her so that she wasn't bored.
Running through all of that had been Hanson's worry that Maisie's
gift would set her apart from her peers. Amid such anxiety the
information Hanson was withholding became less pressing. Time
passed, Maisie flourished, as she continued to do at the King Edward
High School across the road from the university campus where she
now attended twice weekly maths lectures with students half a
decade her senior.

Hanson felt something squeeze inside her chest. Maisie was
clever, full of curiosity and queries. In this last year she'd been
asking increasingly direct questions about Hanson's own family.
Hanson knew that the borrowed time she was on was fast running
out.

'I am going to tell her. I just need to sort out how I do it.'

After Celia left, Hanson returned to headquarters and an empty
UCU. It was hushed and lifeless. The task she'd decided on nudged
her. She raised her hand and moved it across the board, her finger
circling and dragging words and dates.

She stepped back, looking at the time line she'd constructed of
last sightings of Elizabeth Williams based on information from all
of those who had acknowledged seeing her on that last weekend,
including the reluctant Vickers. She stood back to examine the

progression of events as told to them, finding no contradictions or anomalies.

So far as it's possible to establish from what we know, Elizabeth walked or was taken away from her life sometime after six p.m. on that Sunday evening. She never contacted anyone and wasn't seen again.

She looked up on hearing the door open. It was Corrigan.

'Hey, Red. Thought you'd quit for the day.'

'I had. Has Watts left?'

'He's with the chief, putting a case for a re-enactment of Elizabeth Williams' disappearance. Nuttall is arguing against, on the basis that we can't be certain what she was wearing at the time, where she was when she disappeared or the location where she was killed. What happened to her after Sunday afternoon is a black hole. We can't offer potential witnesses anything to relate to and get them thinking, "Hey, I saw her" or "I was at that location". I kind of see Nuttall's argument.'

He came to stand next to her at the board. 'What's this?' he asked.

She looked up. 'It's a timeline of the weekend Elizabeth disappeared. It shows that the information we've obtained from various people so far appears to be consistent. She disappeared sometime after leaving her aunt's house late that Sunday afternoon.'

She leant against the table, eyes on the board. 'I've been thinking about the discussion we had earlier about the killer's choice of the field as a burial location for Elizabeth. If he was some stranger, how did he know about it? Like Watts said it's not that obvious a location.'

He pointed at names. 'All the more reason to stay focused on Turner and Vickers.' She sighed. 'True.'

Feeling at odds with the case, unsure where she was with it, she reached for her notebook and opened it. In the easy silence she read every note she'd made over several days: descriptions of places, people, their words verbatim, details of the bits of paper which had once belonged to Elizabeth: the two receipts, the indented marks on the internship form. Ren. Bill.

She glanced up at the screen a few times to check the accuracy of what she'd written, once or twice going to it to bring up information and check it, hearing the deep cadences of Corrigan's voice as he spoke on the phone, then Watts coming through the door.

Corrigan replaced the phone. 'I got to thinking about that field and who might own it. I just talked to a guy at the city planning authority.'

'Don't tell me. Some investment company doing nothing with it, hoping it'll triple in value?' said Watts.

'No. It's still in local authority ownership.'

'And?'

'A few companies have lodged development plans over the last decade or so. He's sending us the details.'

Hearing a signal he said, 'We've got mail.'

They watched the names and details appear on the board, all of them building companies except for one.

They read the single word, exchanged glances, read it again. Renfrew.

Corrigan googled the name. 'It's a conservation set-up with offices in Calthorpe Road. Been there around twelve years. There's a phone number.'

Hanson waited, cautioning herself against reading anything into so small an amount of information. She looked up as Corrigan finished the call.

'I just spoke to an Aiden Malahide. He's one of two partners who own the business. He's agreed to a visit tomorrow afternoon at four. They've got a big meeting there until that time.'

He glanced at Watts. 'Can you go? I'm giving taser training.'

Watts nodded. 'How about you, doc?'

'I'll see you there.'

FIFTEEN

Watts was already there, parked half on the pavement as Hanson slid to a halt behind the Range Rover, her eyes on the white, late-Georgian house. Like so many in this area it was now converted into offices, a garage with double doors to one side. Originally a coach house, judging by its height. The parking area immediately in front of the building was filled with cars and 4x4 vehicles. Watts lowered himself into her car with his usual grunts of discomfort.

'Looks like the meeting Corrigan mentioned is still going on. Conservation's big business. These firms are springing up like mushrooms.'

Hanson grinned. 'Conserved mushrooms?'

'Smart Alec. When we see this Malahide we keep it simple. We say nothing about the reference to "Ren" in Elizabeth Williams's papers, right?'

She nodded. 'You're the boss.'

He looked across at the building and reached for the door handle. She followed his gaze. The glossy black front door was now open and people were streaming down the steps, all male and of mixed appearance, some in suits, most in work clothes and boots. The flow gradually dwindled.

'Let's go,' said Watts.

Inside the building's cool-tiled reception hall Watts introduced himself and Hanson to a woman seated at a desk.

'Mr Malahide's expecting us.'

She smiled at him as she stood. 'Wait here. I'll tell Aiden you're—'

A heavyset, fiftyish man had suddenly materialised behind her in the hallway.

'Oh, Aiden, your four o'clock has arrived.'

'Thank you, Dee.' He gave Watts and Hanson a cheerful smile. 'Would you follow me?'

Watts and Hanson followed him into a sparsely furnished room, its windows looking out over the building's extensive rear grounds. Hanson gave them a brief glance then turned her attention to the room and its hardwood flooring. What there was of furniture was functional. She looked at Malahide who was round-faced and plump at his middle, dressed in a loose-fitting cream linen suit and soft brown suede shoes. He looked like someone who might favour comfort, rather than this hard-surfaced interior. Right now he was looking warm.

He talked as he shook their hands. Hanson noted that his was soft. 'Apologies for the lateness but we've had a big meeting here.'

Watts gave a genial nod. 'I didn't get the impression Renfrew is such a big concern.'

Malahide looked rueful. 'It isn't. Most of the people who attended are our subcontractors. We don't employ workers on a permanent basis. It would be too expensive and demand for our services varies

depending on how many projects we have up and running. We
employ them on a contract basis as and when required.' He waved
them to a couple of chairs then crossed to a sash window which
slid easily upwards.

'Coffee? Tea?'

They declined and Malahide sat and gazed good-naturedly
across the glass top table which appeared to serve as a desk, judging
by the files and writing implements on it.

'We don't get many detectives here. To be honest, I don't recall
any. I'm curious to know what this is about. I wasn't told during
the phone call but if it's to do with any problems relating to our
projects you really need to speak with Hugh, my business partner.'

Watts regarded him steadily. 'What kind of problems might
they be?'

Malahide looked uncertain. 'Well, I can't actually think of any
which would interest the police but whatever you do these days if
it involves land use or change, somebody has a view on it and
probably won't like it.'

Watts slow nodded. 'We're investigating the murder of a young
woman.'

Malahide's eyes widened in his plump face. 'Good heavens!'

Hanson's attention was on him as Watts gave him Elizabeth
Williams' name. She saw no hint of recognition.

'Maybe you've seen recent reports about her in the papers or on
television?' Watts suggested.

Malahide looked from him to Hanson. 'Actually, no. I work fairly
long hours here.'

She listened as Watts gave a purposely meagre outline of their
case.

'Elizabeth Williams was a student at a college in Bartley Green.
At the time she was killed she was looking for an internship with
a local firm.' Getting no response, he gave a verbal prod. 'We were
hoping your firm might know something about that.'

'I'm sorry?' said Malahide, his smooth brow creasing.

Hanson said, 'We thought you might be able to clarify if Miss
Williams ever approached Renfrew for an internship – a work
experience placement.'

Malahide's face cleared. 'Oh, I *see*. If the American officer who
rang had mentioned this on the phone I could have saved you a
wasted journey.' He shook his head. 'We don't offer them.'

Hanson and Watts exchanged a quick glance. 'At all?' Watts asked.

'No.'

'Has Renfrew ever made exceptions?' asked Hanson.

Malahide gave a vehement head shake. 'Impossible. The sort of work our contractors do involves heavy plant, excavation, reclamation which could place a young person at risk of serious injury. The insurance implications for us would be massive.' He shook his head again. 'Out of the question.'

Watts slid a photograph across the glass. 'This is Elizabeth Williams. Does she look familiar at all?'

Malahide looked at it briefly then shook his head. 'No. I'm sorry. I've never seen her.'

Watts tapped the photograph. 'The place where her body was found is about a mile or so from the Bartley Green Reservoir. She was buried in a field.'

'I see,' said Malahide politely.

'Your company has some kind of involvement or interest in that field.'

Malahide's brows shot up. 'Where did you say this field was?'

'Bartley Green. Off Genners Lane.'

Looking mystified he stood and went to a series of Ordnance Survey maps on a nearby wall, running his hand over a couple of them. It stopped and he returned to his seat.

'I know the location you're referring to. We were never involved in any real sense. We'd seen its geographical location and surroundings from maps. We expressed an interest to the local council about conserving it then turning it over to local people to protect and maintain. There was some initial interest, but by then the economic downturn had started. We're a charity. We rely on grants and the support of people who think long-term and believe in what we do here. When we learned later that several building companies were keen on developing the land we knew our proposal didn't stand a chance. We didn't pursue it further.'

Hanson watched Watts absorb this, wondering how he was going to move the conversation on.

'Elizabeth Williams was aware of your company prior to her disappearance,' he said, tapping the photograph.

Malahide frowned and pursed his full lips. 'Really? Well – I don't know what I can say about that. Are you sure it's us? There are other conservation firms in the city you know.'

Watts eyed him. 'In the year since she went missing Elizabeth Williams' body has been in that field which we've established your firm had a link to. That's why we're here.'

Malahide's genial face looked troubled. He glanced at the photograph again. 'I'm sorry, I hear what you're saying but I've explained our minimal involvement with that land and I don't recognise her.'

'What about your business partner?' suggested Watts. 'Maybe he can help us.'

'I don't see how. He only knows what I know about the land you've mentioned.'

'We'd still like a word with him if he's around. What's his full name?'

'Hugh Downey. But he's not here. This is our busiest time and Hugh's been working ten to twelve hour days so he's taken a couple of days off.'

'When will he be back?'

'Tomorrow possibly. He has a lot of claims on his time.'

'So have we,' said Watts. 'Give me his contact number, please.' He wrote it down then turned his attention to the maps on the wall.

'Can you give us some idea of what your company does?'

'Of course. As a conservation company we improve and protect areas of vacant land. We also advise on management to landowners or voluntary groups. We promote environmental issues relating to specific areas.'

Watts made notes. 'How, exactly?'

Malahide stood. 'If you follow me I can show you.'

He led them out of the room, down a long central corridor to the back of the house, his suede shoes almost soundless. Emerging through a door Hanson and Watts found themselves in the extensive grounds she had seen through the office window. Malahide waved his hands across the verdant space, traffic noise from the distant Hagley Road muffled by the surrounding trees.

'We initiate all kinds of projects but they all have conservation at their heart. Some of them generate a lot of income, others very little. We regard all of them as of equal importance. These grounds are a micro-example of our work. Most of our clients know exactly what they want but on those occasions when they don't we show them out here. It can help generate more or larger-scale ideas. We waste nothing. See the hives way over there? We've made this whole area bee-friendly. Each plant and shrub has been selected to encourage them.'

'What about that?' asked Hanson, pointing to a small wooden building with a tiled roof, its windows blank, what looked like a stockpile of timber beyond it.

'The summer house belongs to Hugh. He bought it for his wife to use as a studio but she found it too hot to work in so he brought it here. Dee, our secretary, fancied working out here during the summer but she had the same problem. Now it sits there looking attractive but we don't mind that. No harm in things looking nice even if they aren't productive.' He gestured to them to follow.

'Come and have a look at this.'

He led them a few metres away to a small natural-looking pond concealed by tall grasses of various types.

He pointed out various features, his face intent. 'All these plants attract life. We get newts and frogs in the breeding season and those plants over there were selected to attract butterflies. The world is teeming with life. If that's going to continue, we have to protect it.'

'You're very enthusiastic about what you do,' observed Hanson.

Smiling faintly he looked around the grounds. 'That would amuse Hugh if he was here. I'm the accountant. I organise the labour side and leave all the physical work to him. But I know about conservation. It's how we met. We both worked for the Forestry Commission.'

They followed him back inside the cool building.

'I'm sorry I can't tell you anything about this girl,' he said, frowning as he brushed bits of grass from his trousers, tutting at others on his shoes. He looked up as the faint sound of a car's remote being activated drifted into the hallway.

'You're in luck. That's Hugh.'

Following his gaze through a window to one side of the front door, Hanson caught a glimpse of a slim-built man. He disappeared from view momentarily then the front door swung open and he came inside.

'How did the meeting go?' he asked Malahide, giving them a brief nod.

'No problems. This is Detective Sergeant Watts and Dr Kate Hanson.'

Downey extended his hand. Hanson guessed he was in his mid-to-late forties. She glanced at his clothes: leather sandals on bare feet, worn jeans, and a long-sleeved sweatshirt unravelling slightly at the neck.

Picking up Hanson's glance he raised his hands either side. 'Excuse my appearance. I'm having a couple of days at home. This is unexpected. We don't attract much police interest here.'

Malahide nodded. 'That's what I said. They're asking questions about a woman whose body has been found.'

Downey's face lost its smile. 'Oh?'

Watts repeated what he'd said to Malahide about Elizabeth Williams's awareness of Renfrew, her disappearance the previous year and the discovery of her body. Downey looked mystified as he walked with them into the office they'd been in earlier. Malahide passed Elizabeth's photograph to Downey who looked at it.

'You say she was a student?'

'Yes. Sports science, at the college in Bartley Green.'

Downey looked at the photograph again then at Malahide. 'I've never seen her. She's not been here, has she, Aiden?' Malahide shook his head.

'She was looking for an internship,' said Watts.

Hanson saw sudden comprehension arrive on Downey's face. 'We don't offer anything like that.'

Malahide nodded again. 'I've explained our position on work experience.'

Downey handed the photograph back to Watts. 'Sorry.'

Watts took it. 'You know the area of land where she was found.'

Downey went to the wall maps as Malahide had done and ran his hand over one of them, pointing. 'This is it but we had no actual involvement with the land. We learned of its existence from maps like this one and approached the local authority with a proposal, one that would benefit the land and give the local people a stake in it.' He shook his head. 'The need for housing won out.'

'There's still nothing on that land,' said Hanson

Downey raised his shoulders. 'What can I say? It demonstrates what we're often up against. People need homes and everybody has plans and then there's an economic downturn or a change at the council and the land stays as it is and we get frustrated.'

The sound of the doorbell echoed through the nearby hall. Malahide was on his feet.

'Our secretary will have gone now so I need to get that. It's our five o'clock.' He glanced at Downey.

'Are you staying, Hugh?' He got a nod. 'How's Nan?'
'Not now, Aiden,' said Downey, his tone brusque.
'I'll get the door.' Malahide went silently from the room.
Hanson's attention was back on Downey, recalling what they'd
been told about his recent hard work. He did look tired.
'I'm sorry I wasn't here earlier,' he said, holding out a business
card to Watts. 'If you need to see us again just ring me on that
mobile number and we'll sort something out. If you'll excuse me,
I need to be at this meeting.'

They left Renfrew and stood together at the roadside.
'What do you think?' asked Hanson.
Watts gazed at the building's façade then turned away. 'Not a
lot. How about you?'
She pushed her fingers through her hair. 'I thought we were onto
something but it looks like I was wrong.'
'This is a first.'
'What is?' she snapped.
'You accepting what people say.'
She gave him a weary look. 'I don't distrust every single person
I meet.' She got into her car.
He leant down to look at her. 'You look like your tail's dragging,
doc.'
'I'm fine.'
'Don't let this setback worry you.'
'I'm not worried.'

Washing potatoes ready for baking, Hanson cast fleeting glances at
Maisie who was at the table eating ice cream. Preoccupied with
what Celia had said earlier, she hadn't made an issue of the pre-
dinner snack. Celia was right. She should have told Maisie the truth
years ago. That the man Maisie believed was her grandfather,
Hanson's father, was not a blood-relative of either of them.
Hanson gave one of the potatoes a vigorous scrub. Maisie had
rarely met him and it was unlikely she remembered him, but she
regarded him as a significant figure in her life. How might it affect
her, just into her teens to learn that he wasn't actually related to
her? Hanson didn't need any psychological theory to answer that.
Like everyone else she had direct knowledge of the importance of
identity during the teenage years. Was this really the time to tell

her? She dropped the potato into water and stared out at Mugger performing a perfect balancing act on the distant back fence. *Here you go again. Talking yourself into putting it off.*

She glanced towards the table. She knew why Maisie got out the photographs. She was curious about her extended family, such as it was. People she'd rarely seen or never met, including Kate's mother who'd died a short time before Maisie was born. Hanson knew there was a reason beyond curiosity for Maisie's search.

She's looking for something. She doesn't know it, but that's what she's doing. She wants to know about the people she came from. The people who made her.

This meant that Hanson herself would have to become involved with at least one of them, despite the existing situation suiting her just fine. She thought of the questions about genetics that Maisie had begun asking over recent months. *Celia's right. I must tell her.*

She stared out of the window again. Inside this house there was a photograph. One which Maisie had never seen. Only Hanson knew its whereabouts. She visualised the four people in it, standing in their somewhat outdated clothes at the side of a dusty road in bright sun: her mother and the man Hanson had believed was her father either side of a plump, fair-haired woman she didn't recognise. A small distance to one side of them stood another man, his hand shading his eyes, his thick, dark red hair ruffled by a breeze as he gazed at their photographer.

'Wha'?'

She started at Maisie's voice. 'Sorry. What did you say?'

'Nothing. You're looking at me funny.'

Hanson abandoned the potatoes and dried her hands. 'Come on.'

Taking a last, quick spoonful of ice cream, Maisie jumped up. 'Where are we going?'

'Out. For dinner.'

'Mum, have I ever told you you're seriously weird sometimes?'

'Yes, you have. Too weird to be seen with at Pizza Express?'

Maisie darted from the kitchen. 'Five minutes. I want to wear my new maxi-dress that Daddy bought me.'

Hanson watched her go, recalling the first time she herself had seen the photograph. She'd been twenty-three or thereabouts, Maisie on the floor in her car seat, plump fists waving as Hanson went through her mother's personal effects at the family home. She'd picked up the photograph, dropping whatever else she was holding. She still remembered the rush of recognition as she'd stared at the man with the sun in his eyes. It was there in the colour of his hair, the detail of his face. It had made sudden, blinding sense. It had felt like a homecoming. Maisie deserved that same resolution. Hanson knew she had to get it right when she started the process which would give it to her.

SIXTEEN

A casual observer of the dark haired young woman wandering through the milling crowds at the Bewdley Country Fair might not have guessed that she was distracted or unhappy. But there was one person within the throng who knew. Because there was nothing casual about his observations of her. Over the last couple of hours he'd picked up on her low mood and a lot else besides. She'd come here alone. He'd seen her arrive in the car park, watched her get out of her car, distracted, not noticing that the seatbelt was dangling, the car not properly secured. He'd changed his plans to leave. She was too full of promise.

He remained where he was, watching her as he dealt with the voice inside his head. He was going into alien territory again. He could put a stop to it, right here, right now. Easy to think. Hard to do. It had always been a private thing but now he didn't have that luxury. His eyes were fixed on her as she moved past the bright, noisy stalls and slowly out of sight among the throng. Quickening his pace he caught up, then overtook her.

He arrived at her car, unconcerned that the press of people might notice anything. They were tired, searching for their vehicles, many of them with fractious children in tow. He lifted the bonnet. A few minutes later he dropped it back into place, wiping the metal he'd touched with a tissue, doing a swift calculation. From a conversation he'd overheard her have with an older couple and another young woman, he'd learned which area of Birmingham she was from and that she was intending to leave for home soon. He estimated that she'd get about halfway into her journey before the car began giving her trouble. He had a plan for that eventuality. He knew of an ideal place to wait for a person needing to pull off the road. And if she didn't stop there it didn't matter. He had all night. He'd follow her into the darkness until she did. Eyes scanning, he walked casually away from the car.

Within five minutes he had her in his sights again, talking to the same people. He wandered in their direction, close enough to listen. Her parents and her sister. Right now, the mother was looking concerned, the father frustrated as they exchanged perfunctory hugs. He knew now that her name was Amy and that the fair had been a regular attraction for her and her family for the last four years. But not this year. Amy was upset. She'd argued with somebody called Eddie who had refused to come to the fair with her so she'd come alone. Now she was on the move again.

He maintained his distance behind her then pulled ahead to take a brief glance at her. She was looking hot and tired, a little defeated. He felt sad for her. His eyes swept the milling crowd bent on care-free enjoyment, eating hotdogs, drinking colas and beer. He glanced back to her again. She was heading into the car park. He followed then passed her and strode on ahead.

For Amy Bennett this whole day had been a terrible mistake. She shouldn't have come. Without Eddie the whole thing had fallen flat. The argument they'd had had been her fault. Eddie had made a harmless comment about her moods and she'd rounded on him. Even worse, her mother had kept asking about him today, until her father told her to stop. Her boyfriend-less sister had listened to it all, looking like the cat that'd got the cream.

Amy felt hot and sluggish and the smell of the hotdogs wafting towards her made her want to heave. She reached her car. Dusk wasn't too far off. Opening all the doors she waited for the hot air to roll out of it then sat sideways in the driver's seat, her feet on the grass. They felt like hot coals. She thought of slipping off her shoes then decided against it. The drive home was daunting but when she got there she'd tell Eddie she was sorry for how she was acting. In fact, she'd tell him right now.

She reached inside her bag for her phone, berating herself for her quick temper. She swiped the little screen, getting a 'Low Battery' signal. She tried to text him. It failed. On the verge of tears she threw it across the car. It landed with a sharp thump and disap-peared. Turning awkwardly, she pushed the key into the ignition.

The engine puttered a little, appeared to gather itself, puttered some more and died. She stared at the dashboard in disbelief.

'*No,* please. Don't do this. Come *on.*'

She tried again. It puttered then died. She pressed both hands to her mouth as hot tears spilled down her face.

'Can I help?'

Without looking up for the source of the voice, she brushed the tears away, shook her head. 'No. I'm fine.'

She tried again. The engine started. She listened to the puttering as she pushed the accelerator, heard the brief lull followed by the engine roaring into life. She closed her eyes.

'Thank you, thank you.'

Heaving herself from the car to close the doors, she glanced around. Several other cars were leaving. She got back into the driver's seat, looped her seat belt over one arm, reversed out of the line of parked cars and headed for the exit.

It was getting dark as she joined the Kidderminster Road, heading for Birmingham, the black ribbon of road illuminated by her headlights. The car rolled steadily onwards, its engine humming. She would have completely lost it earlier if she'd had to abandon the car and get her father to drive her home. Taking a couple of deep breaths, breathing out steadily through her mouth, she pressed her back against the seat, her eyes on the road ahead. In an hour, maybe less, she'd be home. They needed to talk, she and Eddie.

Sudden, full headlights flooded her car from behind, reflecting off her rear-view mirror, dazzling her. She narrowed her eyes, adjusted the mirror, trying to make out the vehicle.

'Idiot,' she murmured. 'Just *pass.*'

She checked her speed and decreased the pressure on the accelerator. The vehicle stayed with her. She increased her speed. It did the same. They continued on into the darkness and she felt a first, small flicker of unease. The road was empty. There was loads of room. Why didn't it overtake? She took more deep breaths, checked her speed and focused on the unlit road ahead. The vehicle stayed close behind her, matching her speed. She gave a quick glance in her wing mirror. Was it going to stay on her tail all the way to . . .?

The sudden engine roar sent her heart pounding against her chest wall. Lights veered and the vehicle swung out from behind her, zoomed past and into the darkness. She watched its tail lights disappear. Weak with relief but still rattled, she shouted after it.

'Thank you, you *bastard*!'

Remembering her resolve to stay calm, knowing that her temper was the reason she was alone right now, she reduced her grip on the steering wheel, took more deep breaths, aware now of pressure in her abdomen. She continued on for a few minutes, the pressure growing steadily more demanding. She still had miles to go. Glancing at the scene beyond her window she saw one or two houses rushing past in the darkness.

The sound of a couple of subtle hiccups from the engine made her catch her breath. She gripped the steering wheel, listened. There it was again! A lump came into her throat. She stared at both sides of the road. There was nowhere safe to pull over. No houses. No lanes off.

Panicked now, ears attuned, picking up more hiccups, she saw a sign. It told her exactly where she was. She was approaching the garden centre she and Eddie had visited several times recently to buy plants, followed by tea and cake. She'd pull in there. The abdominal pressure was insistent now. Once she had the car off the road and she'd visited the outside restroom she'd consider what to do.

Reducing her speed she scanned the scene flashing past, not wanting to miss the turn-off. She saw it just ahead on the right. Slowing, signalling despite there being no other cars, she turned into the wide entrance, tyres crunching gravel, engine stuttering as she pulled into the deserted parking area.

The garden centre itself was in darkness, the only illumination coming from a soft drinks machine against its pale blue wooden wall. She brought the car to a halt then took a few shaky breaths. Pushing open her door, she stopped. There was another vehicle here, parked in heavy shadow beneath trees on the opposite side of the wide gravelled area. She couldn't make out anyone inside it. Maybe someone else had had car trouble and left it there?

She pushed her door further open, eyes scanning the side of the garden centre's wooden structure. She was desperate now for that restroom. If she turned off her ignition, her car might recover in a few minutes from whatever problem it had and she'd be on her way. She frowned. But it might not start again. She sat; hand on the keys, irresolute.

As she listened to the sound of the still-running engine the light from the drinks machine was momentarily blocked. She raised her head.

'Excuse me; do you have change for the machine?'

At the sound of his voice her heart leapt into her throat. He was standing at her open door. He'd come from nowhere. He was pointing at the vending machine.

'No, I haven't—'

With a single, smooth movement he seized hold of her by the front of her cotton top and started pulling her out of her car. Incapable of making a sound, she grabbed at the handbrake then the steering wheel, anything to keep herself inside the car. She wasn't quick enough. His hands were tight on her upper arms now. Shocked, disoriented, she felt one of his hands grip the back of her neck. Her leg jerked and the engine roared. Her breath rasping her throat, she kicked and felt one of her shoes make contact with him then fall from her foot. The ignition was turned off, the engine died and the driver's seat slid away from her. Panic claimed her brain.

He had her out of the car now, her back turned to him, his arm across her chest, his hand clamped tight over her mouth, his other arm tight around her abdomen. They stood together in the dark and the quiet; the only sounds their laboured breathing and the clamour of fear inside her head. She squeezed her eyes shut on a surge of dizziness. He spoke.

'Do exactly as I tell you and everything will be fine. You shouldn't be alone out here. You need somebody like me to keep you safe.'

She stood there, incapable of moving. He shook her.

'Did you hear me?'

Feeling his warm breath against her ear, she nodded, opened her eyes to gaze over his hand, seeing and hearing nothing that made sense, pulling air into her chest, incapable of constructive thought. She felt his breath against her ear again.

'I'm going to turn you round to face me.' She started to cry. He shook her again.

'Stop it. Calm down and everything will be fine.' Another shake. 'Yes?'

She nodded and he slowly released her mouth. She felt his hands grip her shoulders. She had the sensation of being turned. A wave of dizziness hit. She closed her eyes and stood numb, her head bowed, feeling the weight of him against her, his warm hands at her neck. She tensed as one of them slid slowly upwards then down – and up again. Her eyes widened, hysteria bubbling in her throat. He was touching her neck like Eddie sometimes did when they . . . Beyond terrified, she felt wet warmth gush and flow between her legs.

He was talking. She heard the words but couldn't make sense of any of them.

'Do you feel that on your neck? That's all it is. But you have to look at me. Open your eyes. *Open* them!'

She turned her face away. He gripped it hard, pulled it back to him. 'I said *open* them. Watch me. *Watch.* I want to see your eyes blaze.'

His hand continued to move. She was lightheaded now. Drifting. Gasping for air, she scrabbled for his hand. He punched her in the side of the head, leaving her queasy and more disoriented.

'You're *ruining* it.'

He lessened his grip on her body, but his hand, his fingers remained on her neck. 'Keep your eyes on mine, mother.'

The word jolted her to the direness of her situation. She was in the worst trouble of her whole life. She thought of Eddie and she thought of Pickle. They were hers and she loved them. She would not give them up. All of the frustrations and upset of the day melded into cold fury. She made herself relax, felt him do the same. The pressure on her neck was there again, his upper body pressed against hers. She felt light-headed now. This was it. Her last chance. She moved her lower body, slowly raised one leg and drove her knee upwards as hard as she could into what she hoped was his groin.

He wasn't expecting it. His hands flew from her. He doubled, sank to the gravel, harsh noises coming from deep inside his throat.

Scrabbling away from him she pushed herself inside the car, the steering wheel striking her belly. Gasping, nauseated, she turned the key. Nothing. She burst into hot, desperate tears.

'*Start!*' she screamed.

He was on his feet. He was coming for her. She had no choice. She felt her anger soar. She had to fight.

'You sick *bastard!* You keep away from me, you mad bastard!' she screamed.

Sobbing, she turned the ignition again, pushing her foot down, seeing only his face, big as the moon, twisted and raging as he closed in, one hand raised towards her. Hysterical now, she stamped on the accelerator. The engine roared into life. Scrabbling at her door as he reached for it, she heaved it shut. Fighting dizziness, she hit the lock, gasping at the searing pain in her abdomen and side, hearing her own words over and over, 'Thank-God-thank-God-thank—' He was at the window, his face contorted. 'You'll never *know*. We could have *shared* it, you stupid, *stupid*—' Throwing the car into reverse she swung it away from him towards the exit and onto the road, his howling voice following her.

SEVENTEEN

T he woman who opened the door of the small, modern, semi-detached looked to be in her late thirties. She was holding a plump infant on one hip. Another child peered from the folds of her long skirt.

'Mrs Vickers?'

'Yes?'

'Is your husband in?'

Watts knew he wasn't. He'd phoned the college earlier that morning and learned that Vickers was there until two o'clock today, after which he would be working from home. He'd hung up, made a swift calculation of travel time between the college and the Vickers' address. It would take him about thirty minutes to reach home. Which was why they were here now.

She shook her head, her face bemused as she studied the identification he was holding out to her. 'I'm sorry, he's at work but I'm expecting him home soon.' The infant on her hip grizzled. She looked suddenly worried. 'There isn't a problem, is there?'

'No, no,' soothed Watts, with a nod at Corrigan. 'My colleague and I just wanted to have a quick chat with him about an incident that happened near the college recently. Did he mention it at all?'

'I don't think so.' She gave the infant gentle little bounces. 'Can I get him to ring you?'

'How would you feel about us waiting for him?' He pointed to Corrigan's Volvo parked at the kerb. 'We can wait out here.'

Having picked up its sibling's low grizzle, the child hanging on her skirt was starting its own version. She shook her head and stepped back from the door.

'No, come in. Laurie won't be long. I'm late feeding these two so I have to get on.'

They walked inside the house, most of what was visible of its ground floor taken up by a sitting room, filled with the paraphernalia of small children. Watts gave the elder child a grin. It hid its face.

He and Corrigan looked casually around the large room as she took the children into the adjoining kitchen, leaving the door open. The expanse of floor was laminated. No carpet. No rug. Watts went to the window and peered out at the rear garden. Picking up encouraging words from Mrs Vickers to the children, he went to the doorway, saw her pushing something mashed into their mouths.

'Your garden's a good size.'

She looked up at him. 'It's the reason we bought the house. Laurie likes gardening.'

'Mind if we take a look at it?'

If she was surprised at police officers taking an interest in a suburban garden it didn't show.

'Go ahead. The door isn't locked,' she said.

They stepped out onto a small patio, their eyes on the far fence lined with trees as Watts closed the door behind them. He recognised an oak and a willow.

'I don't recognise half of these,' he said to Corrigan.

Corrigan pointed to a couple near the side fence. 'Those two with white flowers are dogwoods. They're popular in the States. That one over there is a sycamore. That's all I know.'

Watts headed for the small greenhouse to one side of the garden and shaded his eyes to squint through the glass at empty plant trays, a coiled hose and a large, heavy duty plastic bag, its top slashed open, its label indicating the contents to be bark chippings. Nearby, a car door slammed and the children inside started up a cacophony of excited squeals and shouts.

'Sounds like Vickers is home,' murmured Corrigan looking through the glass, pointing out another bag: wood chippings.

Heading back inside, they found Lawrence Vickers in the large sitting room, his attention seemingly on his children as he smiled and nodded at what his wife was telling him about her and the children's day. It was convincing if you didn't look at his eyes. They waited as his wife took both children into the kitchen.

Vickers turned to them, pretence gone, eyes skittering between them and the kitchen door. 'Why are you here?' he demanded, his voice low. 'I expected you'd come to the college if you wanted to talk to me again.'

Watts kept his words and his tone casual. 'Take it easy. We were in the area and decided to drop in.'

Only now did Vickers make very brief eye contact with them. 'My wife said something about an incident near the college,' he said, his voice loud enough to reach the kitchen.

Watts gazed into his face. It was rigid. A mask. It was evident that Vickers hadn't told his wife about Elizabeth Williams and was now envisaging the possibility of an axe about to fall on all that he had here. He chose his words, mindful of Mrs Vickers' proximity.

'That's right. We're speaking to people who work in that area such as yourself. I think most people at your college know about the finding of Elizabeth Williams' remains.'

Vickers' face blanched.

Watts lowered his voice. 'Tell us exactly what happened on that Saturday morning.'

Vickers shot a quick look in the direction of the kitchen. 'I already did,' he hissed.

Watts stared down at his open notebook then up. 'You gave us the bare bones.' He saw colour rush Vickers' face.

'OK, OK. She was late. She came into the office and she looked – upset, excited, I told you, I don't know what it was about. She drank the juice I gave her—'

'Where'd the juice come from?'

'What? I took it with me from here. Part of my lunch.' He stared at Watt. 'If you're thinking I put anything into—'

'Carry on,' murmured Watts. 'She's got her juice.'

Vickers ran a hand through his hair. 'I talked her through the assignment I'd marked, pointed out the good bits and others I thought she could have improved on and that was it.'

'Not quite. What about your invitation?'

Vickers' hand went to his mouth and his eyes went to the kitchen door. They heard the children's voices, Mrs Vickers making placatory noises. 'I told you what I said.'

They waited. Vickers' voice dropped further. 'I told her I thought she looked very nice. She smiled. I said that I thought she was . . .

attractive.' His word was scarcely audible. 'I asked her if she'd meet
me for dinner.'

'Where?' demanded Watts.

'I don't know! We didn't get that far.'

'Did she tell you where she was going after she left you?'

There was a tremor in Vickers' fingers as he passed his hand across
his forehead. 'I was distracted by what I'd said to her, like I told you.
She said something about a dry cleaner but to be honest I wasn't
listening.' He looked from Watts to Corrigan. 'As she left I think she
said something about meeting somebody.'

'Who?'

'She didn't say.'

It was Watts' turn to frown. 'Did she say where and when?'

'No. I don't know. I don't remember what she said.' He lowered
his voice. 'Like I told you, my mind was taken up with what I'd said
to her—'

Mrs Vickers was standing in the kitchen doorway, looking at her
husband, her face bemused. 'Is everything all right, Laurie?'

Vickers went to her, his eyes still on the two officers. 'Darling,
I forgot to tell you about something that happened near the college
a couple of days ago.'

She looked at him, then at Watts and Corrigan. 'It isn't anything
to do with the awful news on the radio? About that woman who
was found?'

'It's a long way from the college. Nothing for us to worry about.'

Her eyes on his face, she turned away as shrill squeals took her
back to the kitchen.

Watts tucked his notebook into an inside pocket. 'Family life,
eh? Keeps you on the go, I bet. Tell you what, Mr Vickers. We
don't want to intrude on your home life so if we need to follow
anything up, we'll do it when you're at work. We know where to
find you.'

Vickers' face was wooden. 'I'll show you out.'

They followed him into the hall. At the door Corrigan turned.
'I have a question, Dr Vickers.'

Vickers waited, his face empty, shoulders slumped.

'I just moved into a new place and the garden's real wild. It
needs some care. I noticed you've got bark and wood chips in your
greenhouse. You think I might need some of that stuff?'

Vickers said nothing for a few seconds, looking thrown by the conversational change of direction. 'Probably. It improves the soil. Encourages worms. It also cuts down on watering.'

Corrigan raised his hand. 'Thanks for that.'

They felt Vickers' eyes on them as they walked the path to Corrigan's car.

Inside it, Watts made speedy notes. 'Don't know what you think, Corrigan, but Vickers strikes me as a man who's able to lie himself out of a deep hole without too much trouble.'

Inside a low-lit UCU Julian checked the board for messages and any requests for his expertise. Finding none he went to the desktop computer. The screen's glow on his face, he scrolled through the incident log which he did most days he came in here. He loved data. It had caused him a load of trouble a couple of years back. That affinity mixed with curiosity had taken him into the university's financial records database. That was all in the past. No way would he hack again. Ever. Hanson had defended him when the VC was ready to pull the plug. He wouldn't let her down. He wanted his doctorate. Headquarters' demands on his time were less since he'd started it, but he called in often, liking the relative quiet here when everyone was out. Better than trying to read at uni. He drank tea, realising he was hungry.

Information appeared on the screen and he began reading. No more than half a dozen words in and he'd forgotten about food. He reread them, excitement rising. He scrolled downwards, reading the whole of the Incident Log. The door opened. He glanced up. It was Watts.

'You need to see this.'

Watts leant over the youthful shoulder, lips moving as he absorbed the first few words. 'Where's this from?'

'It was picked up by Hagley police who responded to a call from a couple of residents about a hysterical woman banging on their door late last night saying she'd been attacked. Look at what she told them.'

Watts read it. He read it again, more slowly. 'Good lad. Pass us the phone.'

Hanson reached for her phone. It was Watts. 'Glad you called. We didn't get much opportunity to speak to Downey at Renfrew yesterday so—'

'Can you drop whatever you're doing and meet me at Corbett Hospital near Hagley, soon as you can? I'll give you the address and postcode.' She wrote it down and was on her feet.

'I'll be with you in— Watts?'

Forty minutes later she walked past several police cars, into the hospital and on to the inquiry desk.

'Hello, my name's Kate Hanson. I'm meeting a colleague here, Detective Sergeant Watts.'

Following directions she headed down a long corridor then took the stairs to the first floor. She didn't need to be told which room. There were two uniformed constables, one either side of the door. They examined her identification and allowed her inside.

She and Watts exchanged glances in the hush, broken at regular intervals by subtle, repetitive bleeps. Hanson looked towards the bed. Whoever was lying there was scarcely visible, hooked up to drips, surrounded by machines and nurses.

He came quietly to her side, keeping his voice low. 'I persuaded them to allow us in by promising not to get in the way and to leave when told.'

She stared up at him. 'What's going on? What's happened?'

He nodded at the bed. 'Amy Bennett, aged twenty-six. She was driving along the A456 last night sometime between half nine and ten. She pulled off the road and into a garden centre where she was attacked. She managed to get away from him.'

Hanson absorbed the few details. 'So, why are we involved?'

He took an A4 sheet from an inside pocket. 'Read this and you'll see why. These are notes one of the householders made after she arrived at their door.'

She took the page, her eyes flying along the words: '. . . He said to me, "I'm going to turn you to face me." He did and he hit my head and said, "I want to see your eyes blaze. Keep your eyes on me." I was terrified. I couldn't understand what he meant about my eyes. He was stroking my neck and then he pressed and I felt faint. He said the word "mother" so he knew exactly what he was doing to me.'

Hanson's head snapped up. 'These words—'

Watts took the sheet from her and looked at it for probably the sixth time. 'Maybe Myers isn't as out of it as he seems.'

She pointed at specific words. 'I don't understand this: "He said the word 'mother' so he knew what he was doing . . ."?'

'Amy Bennett is seven months pregnant.'

Hanson stared up at him aghast, looked back to the woman surrounded by equipment and nurses. 'How is she?'

'Nobody's saying,' he said, his voice gruff. He looked down at her.

'Come on, doc. Buck up. We've got a lot to do. The local station is expecting us.'

They left the hospital. She got into her car and followed Watts' vehicle for a short distance then parked.

'Who have we come to see?' she asked as they approached the building.

'Al Jones used to be part of the Birmingham force years ago. The Bennett case has just landed on his desk now he's part of the Hagley local police force, but he doesn't know what we know: that it's linked to the Williams murder. It's ours. I want it. What I don't want is for it to look like the big city headquarters is muscling in. We haven't got time for resistance and delay.'

Inside Hagley Police Station it was a scene of high activity, phones ringing and officers moving at speed, emails and other information in their hands. Hanson was willing to bet it far exceeded what happened here on any normal day.

They were shown into an office where an officer a few years Watts's junior was sitting. His black epaulettes and insignia told Hanson he was an inspector.

He stood. 'Bernard. Good to see you again.'

Watts took the outstretched hand and nodded. 'Al.' He introduced Hanson.

'How's Goosey?' Jones asked of Chief Superintendent Gander.

'Big as ever.'

Jones fixed him with a direct look. 'I've heard about this cold case unit of yours.' He glanced at Hanson. 'Read about it in the press as well. I'm guessing there's a connection between it and your interest in the Amy Bennett attack.'

'Spot on.' said Watts. He reached into an inside pocket and took out two A4 sheets, one of them Hanson had read at the hospital. He laid it flat on the table and pointed at the lines of writing.

'See where Amy Bennett quotes what her attacker said to her?' Jones read it then looked up to see Watts handing him the second sheet.

'Now have a read of this. It's a statement from a witness in our case. Read what he says where it's highlighted.'

Hanson watched Jones' eyes move over the words. He stopped reading, looked up at them.

Watts nodded. 'I want to investigate the Bennett attack alongside our cold case.'

Jones paused then lifted the phone and asked for someone to join them. When a constable came inside he handed a thin file to him. 'Copy everything in this, quick as you can.' As the constable left, Jones gave both of them a steady look.

'That's everything we've got on Bennett. It's not much. I'll ring Gander and suggest we do the transfer with a minimum of paperwork. This attack is bad. The doctors aren't telling us yet if she'll be OK. Even if she is, will she remember anything?'

The door opened and the constable came inside with the slim file and some photocopied sheets. Hanson thought how meagre they looked. She reminded herself that the Amy Bennett case was only hours old.

EIGHTEEN

A t eight the next morning, Hanson came into her study and gazed down at the information from the Bennett case she'd left there late the previous night. She'd read it all, such as it was. She touched the handwritten sheet of words spoken by Amy Bennett. Next to it were formal statements given by the householders from whom she'd sought help.

Both witnesses described someone beating on their front door and a woman screaming. Alarmed, they'd looked through a window to see a car abandoned haphazardly at the side of the road, its driver's door open and a heavily pregnant woman they now knew to be Amy Bennett swaying and crying on their porch. They had helped her inside as she implored them to lock the door.

Hanson read on, skimming the words with her finger. The householders had called the police and comforted Miss Bennett, who'd repeatedly referred to her attacker's focus on her neck. Both described Miss Bennett as extremely upset and agitated. Police and paramedics had arrived, performed a swift physical examination then removed her from the house to the nearby hospital. They had observed a bruised area to one side of her face but no other visible injury to her head, neck or elsewhere.

According to the female householder, 'The woman who came to my door who I now know to be Amy Bennett told us that she had been approached by a male at the garden centre off the main Kidderminster Road about a mile from my house. She said a large vehicle, similar to a Jeep, was parked there when she arrived. A man had appeared suddenly, dragged her from her car then subjected her to further assault, holding her so she could not move. He forced her to face him and look into his eyes as he held her and stroked her neck. Miss Bennett said that he kept insisting she look him in the eye. She described him playing with her neck. She told me that he used the word "mother", which she found particularly disturbing and upsetting, given her condition.' The witness had ended the statement with a reference to Amy Bennett managing to escape her attacker by kicking him.

Knowing she had a full morning at the university, followed by a second visit to Renfrew, Hanson quickly pushed the statements inside her briefcase. She wanted to read them again at the first opportunity. They had raised a number of questions in her mind, not the least of which was, 'Why would any man intent on attacking a woman insist that she look at him?' In Hanson's experience of violent offenders who attacked women the reverse was the norm. They insisted that their victims not look at them and were willing to use violence or cover the victims' eyes to ensure they didn't.

She doesn't say he had a mask or other covering on his face so why wasn't he concerned about being described later, possibly identified?

She shrugged into her jacket then reached for her keys.

Was it his intention at the outset to kill Amy Bennett but he was deflected from doing so because he hadn't anticipated that she would fight him?

NINETEEN

At Renfrew Hanson was greeted by the secretary she and Watts had met on their first visit.

'Good afternoon, Dr Hanson. Hugh's on his way. He's asked me to apologise for his lateness. We've got some really good coffee. Can I offer you one while you're waiting?'

'That would be nice, thank you.'

The secretary went to the coffee maker in the corner and Hanson searched her memory for her name. Something short. Alphabetic. A-B-C-*Dee*. She glanced at her watch, wondering how long Hugh Downey was going to be. She'd left work unfinished at the university and on the journey here she'd questioned the value of a further visit to the consultancy. The only link had been the imprints of three letters: 'REN', and Renfrew's historically distant connection to where Elizabeth Williams' remains had been found. It wasn't much, even if considered in the light of Elizabeth's passion to save the planet.

Hanson frowned. *If it comes to that, we don't even know for sure it was a passion.* Whether it was or not, it was perfectly possible that Elizabeth had approached one of the other conservation consultancies in the city which Aiden Malahide had mentioned in passing. So far, they had persons of interest known to Elizabeth but the Amy Bennett attack suggested the likelihood that it was a faceless killer they were looking for. Hanson bit her lip, wondering how the young woman was. She'd heard nothing from her colleagues. Dee was speaking.

'He doesn't have far to come. He's been working since seven thirty this morning in Hall Green. At Sarehole Mill. You've probably heard of it?'

Hanson had. It was a well-known place of local interest. She tried to recall what Maisie had said about it. 'My daughter went on a school visit there a few months ago.'

Dee handed her the coffee. 'He's not at the actual mill. There's a large area of open land next to it. Our subcontractors are preparing part of it to create a habitat for herons. People tend not to like herons because they steal fish from garden ponds.'

She laughed. 'The way I see it, it's what herons do. It's their job.' Sipping her coffee, Hanson asked, 'Have you worked here long?'

'About seven years.'

'It sounds like you enjoy it.'

Dee sat at her desk, waving Hanson to a chair. 'I do. Aiden's easy to work for. He does his own few letters as long as they're straightforward, keeps track of Renfrew's financial side, prepares all the business accounts. He's mostly in the office which suits him, although he does get out occasionally.'

Seeing that Dee was pleased to have someone to talk to, Hanson asked, 'What about Mr Downey?'

'It's chalk and cheese with those two. Hugh oversees the actual projects and negotiates and plans new ones. I more or less have to stand over him to get him to sign time sheets and return people's calls but his work is very physical and he's often overstretched so I haven't the heart to be cross with him.'

Hanson glanced around the spacious hall with its black and white tiled floor and large palms in planters. 'You don't have any other administrative help here?' she asked conversationally.

'No. Just me. Hugh's wife used to do a couple of days a week but that was before she got ill.'

Hanson recalled her last visit here and Malahide's question to his business partner. 'Is that Nan?'

Dee's face registered surprise. 'He talked about her, did he? He doesn't usually.'

'A little,' said Hanson. *True. Sort of.*

'She's not doing too badly now but it was a shock when it happened, I can tell you.'

Dee lowered her voice, although as far as Hanson was aware they were the only people in the building.

'A stroke. At forty-five. Can you believe that? A year ago this May just gone. Makes you think, doesn't it?' She gave a deep sigh. 'Do you ever feel that some people have really bad luck?' She didn't wait for a response. 'Take Aiden, for example. He sails through life, cool, calm and collected, as they say, everything organised and nothing ever seems to happen to him.' She laughed. 'Not that I want it to, of course. I'm saying his life goes calmly on, like Mrs Malahide's. Fit as a fiddle, she is.'

Seeing Hanson's confusion, she said, 'His mother.'

Hanson sipped coffee. 'It is bad luck to have a stroke so young.'

'Hugh was off for weeks when it happened and Aiden had to shoulder all of Hugh's work responsibilities the whole time he was off.' She looked pensive. 'I never thought Aiden would cope with being on site and having to instruct the subcontractors. He's a bit on the fussy side, not one of the boys, if you know what I mean, but he managed it although he looked half-dead. It's Hugh and Nan I feel sorry for.'

She gave Hanson a conspiratorial glance. 'Nan mentioned that one or other of his parents had poor health and he had to help out when he was young. I think she feels bad that he's in that position again. He has to help her quite a bit.'

'How is Mrs Downey now?' asked Hanson.

'She's pretty much OK but Hugh never stops worrying about her. Whenever he has a minute in the working day he's on the phone to see how she is and if he can't reach her he's off home. I tell him to relax but I understand his worry. I think he's afraid she might feel unwell and have a fall or something.'

Hanson decided to raise the reason for her visit. 'Do you recall anyone, a student, requesting an internship here last year?'

'A what?'

'It's like work experience.'

Dee shook her head. 'No. Nothing like that's ever happened since I've been here.'

The sound of a car door closing filtered in from outside.

'That's probably Hugh,' she said.

She gave Hanson a hesitant glance. 'Look, I'd rather you didn't mention what I've just said about Nan. I wouldn't want him to know I was talking about him.' She grinned. 'Aiden says I talk too much.'

She began tapping her keyboard as Hugh Downey came through the front door.

'Dr Hanson, I hope you haven't been waiting long? Dee, be an angel and put some coffee on.'

'A few minutes at most,' said Hanson.

'Good. Follow me.' He turned to the secretary. 'Forget the coffee. I'll chat to Dr Hanson then pop back home for five minutes on my way back to Sarehole.'

Getting a look from Dee, Hanson followed him. He was dressed for heavy work today in a blue cotton shirt, black cargo-style trousers and boots. He led her into a huge, front-facing room with a high ceiling, draped curtains and comfortable sofas. Just this side of sumptuous. She glanced down at a large, soft cream rug.

Downey sat at the ornate desk, indicating a chair for her. 'I've been at Sarehole since early this morning.' He stopped and smiled. 'Never tell a busy person how hard you're working, right? OK, Dr Hanson, what do you want to know?'

She reached into her bag. 'We showed you a photograph last time.' She placed it on the desk. 'I hope you don't mind but I've brought it again. It can be difficult sometimes to recall someone from a brief look, particularly if the memory is fairly old. Would you mind taking another look?'

He reached for it. 'No problem.' Hanson watched as he ran his eyes over it, taking his time.

'You said she was a student?'

'Yes. Nineteen years old. We know she disappeared sometime after six on Sunday the twenty-third of June last year.'

He shook his head and handed the photograph back. 'How terrible. Sorry, but I've never seen her.'

It seemed there was little else to say but Hanson wanted to explore every possibility, rather than return here. 'Did Renfrew have any casual staff here around that time? Is it possible the office was open at weekends?'

'Casual staff, no. The work our subcontractors do is hard, very physical.' He grinned. 'If I so much as suggested weekend working of any description, I'd have anarchy on my hands.'

A shadow passed over his face. 'I guard my weekends as much as the next person. It's family time. I'm afraid I can't help you, anyway. I was hardly in the office between the sixth of May and the end of June.' He looked away from her. Hanson glanced at the ring on his left hand.

'You took some leave,' she said.

He gathered papers on the desk, not looking at her. 'Not of the holiday kind. My wife was ill.'

She recognised the same brusque tone she'd heard on their first visit when Malahide had enquired after Nan. He looked across the desk at her and she could see he was uncomfortable.

'This is something I don't tend to talk about but given the reason you're here, I know this isn't a social conversation. I wasn't in the office at all during that time. My wife had a stroke last year. She was in hospital for several weeks. The hospital let me stay with her at night because she was very frightened. There's a lot of criticism about hospitals these days but they were excellent.'

'Which hospital?'

'The Queen Elizabeth not far from here. After that she went to a rehabilitation unit close to where we live in Moseley. They were excellent too.' He studied his hands. 'She found it hard to do things for herself. That whole episode was a shock for both of us and an additional cruelty for Nan. She's an accomplished artist yet there she was, struggling to hold a spoon.' He stopped, looked away, then back to Hanson.

'I don't know where all that came from. All you wanted to know is what I was doing back then.' He glanced around the elegant room. 'This place is our livelihood but I can tell you that that kind of sudden, unexpected event shows you your priorities. As far as I was concerned, Renfrew had to take care of itself while she was so ill. Aiden kept the projects ticking over that whole time.' He looked away again.

'I owe Aiden a lot because I knew he would find it stressful. Aiden's the idealist in this setup but typically he doesn't get his hands dirty. I'm no idealist. I see conservation as *the* thing now and I'm lucky to have the skills for it. It's me who gets the dirty hands.'

'Mr Malahide stepped up when you needed him,' she said.

'Yes. Twelve-hour working days, sometimes in the office, mostly on site, was a complete departure for him, although it helped that he lives here. Not far to go home.' He smiled, looking suddenly younger than the mid-forties he had to be.

'Mr Malahide lives here?' repeated Hanson.

He nodded. 'When we first got this place Aiden liked the look of the self-contained flat on the third floor so we agreed he'd have it.'

Hanson brought the conversation back. 'The last time I was here with my colleague we asked about internships and Renfrew's involvement in such schemes. I was wondering if you'd had any more thoughts about it?'

He gave a slow headshake. 'Sorry. Like we said, we don't offer anything like that. We're just too small an outfit to bear the insurance costs and the kinds of projects we undertake wouldn't be suitable for young people. Was the firm whose details I gave you any help?'

She shook her head. 'Afraid not, for very similar reasons to yours, but thank you anyway.'

Sliding Elizabeth's photograph into her bag she glanced around the room then down to the thick, pale rug. There had to be thousands like it in this city.

Reaching for her bag she said, 'I wish my office was as luxurious as this.'

He shook his head. 'It isn't mine. It's Aiden's. He's a sucker for comfort. He spends a lot of time behind this desk so I don't begrudge it. Mine's a cell by comparison.'

They walked into the hall. Dee, the secretary, was nowhere in sight. At the front door he turned to Hanson.

'I'm really sorry we can't help. Good luck with your case. She looked like a nice girl, the one in the photograph.'

'Yes. I think she was. Nineteen is too young to suffer that kind of end.'

Downey looked subdued. 'I can hardly remember being that age. *Media vita in morte sumus.*'

She gazed up at him. '"In the midst of life we're in death".'

He smoothed his hair, suddenly uncomfortable. 'It's a realisation that hit me like a train last year. One minute everything in your life is going along just fine. You've got everything you want and the next, it's hanging by a thread. Well – that's how it felt.'

He opened the door for her. 'I've got a reputation now among friends and colleagues for giving unsolicited advice, mostly of the "enjoy and appreciate what you've got while you've got it" variety.' He gave a fleeting smile. 'I try to keep a lid on it.'

They shook hands. 'Thank you for your time, Mr Downey.'

He gave a brief wave then slowly closed the door.

TWENTY

Back at the university, Hanson dropped her phone into her bag. She'd spent several minutes following up similar setups to Renfrew, including two on the outskirts of the city. Like the one whose details Hugh Downey had supplied, none of them offered work experience placements.

The phone on her desk rang and she snatched it up. 'Yes!'

Silence. It was of the same quality as a silent call she'd had earlier. It had been followed immediately by one from a third-year student so Hanson hadn't had a chance to retrieve the number. Now she sat with the phone pressed to her ear, listening.

'Who is this?'

Maybe it was the effort of trying to hear something, anything, but she thought she detected something faint, the muted ripple of a low laugh. Gripping the phone she waited, saying nothing, hardly breathing. It went dead.

Uneasy, she replaced it, her hand still on it, one name inside her head. Chris Turner. She leapt as it rang again.

'What!' she demanded, robbed of yet another chance to obtain the number.

'Who's snapped your garters?' It was Watts.

'Is this the first time you've called me this afternoon?' she demanded.

'Yeah, and just as well by the sound of it.'

'I've had two silent phone calls.'

'Ring one-four—'

'I know *that*. This phone doesn't have a number calling indicator so it was my first thought, but before I could do it somebody else rang. And now, you.'

'Probably one of them end-of-year student pranks. How about something else to think about?' Without waiting for a response, he said, 'Forensics are at the garden centre where Amy Bennett was attacked. Fancy a ride there?'

'If it's soon. Have you heard how she is?'

'According to the hospital this morning, mother and unborn baby stable was all they'd say.'

Mother.

'Something else you might like to know. I've been in with the chief this morning. Nuttall tried to block it but the Bennett case is now officially ours. I'll pick you up in ten minutes.'

Arms folded, Hanson contemplated the garden centre bathed in bright sunlight. It was certainly an attractive place, surely a magnet for visitors in weather like this. Her gaze moved slowly over the front aspect of the main building. It was constructed of wood painted a delicate eggshell blue, a tall, humming soft drinks dispenser against it. Multiple pots of flowers stood on the ground either side of the main doors. But there were no plant-seeking visitors today. The whole area was cordoned off, officers at the roadside waving would-be customers away.

Keeping to the perimeter of the thickly gravelled parking area, Hanson's eyes drifted across to the other side and the heavy tree cover along it. She gazed up at the fresh green foliage and tried to imagine how the place looked in darkness. She came up with two words. Lonely. Secluded. She shook her head. It wasn't somewhere she would have chosen to stop at night if she were alone. Apparently, Amy Bennett had had no choice. Watts had told her that Amy was having car trouble.

Glancing to the left of the building she saw a sign pointing to a narrow pathway and a twenty-four-hour restroom. Amy was seven months pregnant. Yet another reason to stop at what must have felt like a desolate location at that late hour.

Watts was at the other side of the parking area talking to Adam and a couple of his forensics team, their heads close as they looked down at a picnic table which Adam had pressed into service. Others of his team were on kneeling pads examining the outer edges of the area beneath the trees.

Watts looked up, hooking a finger in her direction as an officer headed towards her with shoe covers. Putting them on, she joined Watts and the forensic officers at the table. Heavy duty white paper had been spread on it. She looked down at the several clear plastic trays containing numerous items: buttons, coins, several discarded admission tickets and a glove which looked far too small to have belonged to an adult and had probably been here a while. Hanson knew from experience that most if not all of these items would eventually prove to be irrelevant. Two small items of thick paper printed with a series of squares in various shades from light to dark green caught her attention.

'What are these?'

'They're sheets for identifying the type of soil in your garden,' said Adam. 'They sell them inside but we're bagging everything that doesn't look like it's been here since Domesday.'

Hanson looked to where Watts was now standing at the edge of the parking area, almost within the trees. Nearby, a forensics officer was on his knees pouring what she knew to be distilled water into a plastic bag of white powder, squeezing the bag to mix water and powder together.

She went to him. 'You've found some impression evidence?'
'Come and see.'

She followed and he pointed beyond the gravel, to where the earth looked soft. 'There, see? A section of tyre track. According to our information Amy Bennett said that there was a vehicle already parked, almost within the trees when she arrived.' He pointed to the thick gravel surface on which they were standing.

'This generates a lot of dust in dry weather so on and off during the day employees mist it with water. The surface around the trees is more soil than gravel. It gets any run-off and stays damp. We might get a cast good enough to identify the tyre make and type.' He looked up.

'Here comes the other print.'

Hanson followed his gaze to an officer holding out a light coloured item to Adam who took it from him and brought it over. It looked to Hanson to be the impression of some kind of heavy soled shoe.

'One of the first things we found here,' said Adam. 'Made by a man's boot, judging by the size. It was in the same area as the tyre impression. I'll let you know when we've examined it if there's any more to say about it.'

The bright sun, the passing traffic noise, the voices of the forensic workers dimmed around Hanson as she turned her back to the road and again faced the pale blue building. She was thinking of Amy Bennett driving in here, heavy in body, tired and distracted, wanting only the safety and comfort of home. Her car had delivered her into mayhem.

Hearing shrillness she saw Watts bring his phone from his pocket and speak into it. He looked at her, cut the call and walked towards her, his face closed.

'Amy Bennett's gone into labour. I'll keep you posted as and when I get anything else.'

Hanson looked at her watch as the sun slipped behind cloud, taking some of the day's brightness. 'I need to get back to work.'

'I'll drop you and go on to headquarters.'

They returned to the city in silence, Hanson's thoughts on Amy Bennett in darkness and chaos, held, immobilised as her attacker spoke to her, repeating words which sounded to Hanson like they were a deliberate choice. How did that fit with the way he'd attacked her? From what they knew he'd seized her before she knew what was happening. A blitz attack. She gazed out of the window at rolling fields rushing past. The intention behind blitz was immediate incapacitation. The attacker had achieved that. He could have made whatever plan he had in mind easier by rendering her unconscious. He hadn't.

Her eyes were on the road ahead, brows drawn together. He didn't want her unconscious. He wanted her under his control but fully alert and aware. Why? Why the insistence on her looking at his face? *Controlled. Orchestrated. He wanted Amy complicit. Engaged. For what?*

The last of Hanson's student group brought his presentation to a close, shuffled his notes and sat down amid a smattering of applause, some good-natured comments and ruffling of his spiky hair.

Hanson looked along the semicircle. 'Well done, all of you. Good work on case linkage. Remember that as an investigative tool, linkage requires that offending behaviour between cases demonstrates evidence of consistency.'

Hanson knew by heart the words Michael Myers claimed he heard in the field where Elizabeth Williams was concealed. Now they had the words said to a live victim, Amy Bennett. It wasn't much but together they suggested a very distinctive way of thinking and speaking. They had linkage.

She looked at the keen faces of her students. 'What's the link all investigators hope to find between cases?'

'DNA every time,' responded one.

'Does the presence of DNA inevitably lead to arrest?'

'No,' said another. 'The DNA has to be on the system already.'

'And if it isn't?'

An earnest-looking student spoke. 'If you have nothing which points to the offender, you might DNA test specific populations in an area, say males between certain age limits, but it's expensive and there's no guarantee of a result. A guilty person could move away, avoid being tested, which means more money and delay in tracing them.'

Hanson gave her a nod. 'Well put. Physical markers left by offenders don't always provide a solution. If we have a fingerprint with no match on file then we have nothing until a strong suspect is identified or an arrest is made. The same applies to other trace evidence, which is why we need psychological tools such as offence linkage. They help narrow the field of search.'

She paused. 'As criminologists should we feel discouraged as we search for offenders who've left nothing to immediately identify them?'

It was a question she'd posed to them several times in the early weeks of the academic year when they'd arrived here to start their degrees, expectations honed by smooth-running television crime, anticipating instant Holmes-like solutions. They knew the words of the response she had provided for them during those early weeks. She saw several grins as they recited it.

'No, just get used to it!'

'Too right.' She said.

With the students gone, Hanson was fully occupied by UCU's two cases. Corrigan had checked Elizabeth Williams's background information and run similar checks on Amy Bennett. The result had shown zero links between the young women as individuals and zero connection between either of the women and a known, violent offender. Hanson was back to the only link they had: the words spoken by the person preparing Elizabeth Williams' grave, according to Myers, and those spoken to Amy Bennett when she was in fear for her life. How long would it be before they could speak to her?

She read through all of the words supplied by Myers, knowing that any defence barrister would make short work of him as an unreliable witness, but it was still there: that uncanny consistency in what he'd said he heard and the words Amy Bennett had recalled mere hours ago. It couldn't be coincidence. There was too much similarity. It was compelling.

Hanson felt her frustration climb. She wanted to analyse all of those words now, but there was no point. She needed to wait until Amy Bennett was well enough to talk. She was a live witness and she might remember more. If that happened Hanson would talk to Myers again and see if he could do the same. In which case she would need to obtain whatever else he might know without provoking the exaggeration or misrepresentation caused by his low self-esteem and anxiety. On the plus side his naivety made his exaggerations relatively easy to discount but they were a distraction when she needed him focused. She frowned. There was no saying when Amy Bennett might be sufficiently recovered. A sudden, sickening thought occurred. Surely she would recover? And the baby?

She raked her fingers through her hair then rubbed her hands over her face. Maybe she'd call in to see the forensics team later? She decided against it. There was no point. Tyre print search and evaluation took time. It might point to a particular type of vehicle such as the Jeep which Amy Bennett had suggested or the powerful vehicle Myers had described, but until they had a suspect it was of little value.

Optimism reasserted itself. No matter. They had two cases separated by a year involving similar words and similar vehicles. She pushed files into her briefcase. She'd work at home for the rest of the day and later she'd give more thought to the attack on Amy. But first, she'd call in at headquarters to check on any progress.

Hanson stopped when she caught sight of her two UCU colleagues inside the informal interview room just off reception at headquarters. They were facing a young woman who was looking at them with an anxious facial expression. Corrigan saw Hanson and beckoned. She opened the door and walked inside.

'This is our colleague, Dr Hanson,' said Watts to the young woman. He turned to Hanson with a meaningful look. 'This is Chloe Jacobs. She's come here voluntarily to give us some information.' He turned back to her. 'Miss Jacobs, would you tell Dr Hanson what you've just told us?' Jacobs gazed at Hanson as she took a seat.

Hanson gave Jacobs an encouraging look as she quickly evaluated her appearance. *Early to mid-twenties. Athletic looking.*

'OK. I finished my sports degree at the sports college a couple of years ago. Somebody who was there at the same time messaged me on Facebook about the police investigation into Elizabeth Williams. I didn't know Elizabeth although I remember her. Anyway, the message I got was that the police working on the investigation had found out something about one of the lecturers.' Watts' lips compressed as Jacobs continued. 'She didn't give me a name but she said he was coming on to Elizabeth.' She stopped, looked at Corrigan.

'That's pretty much where we're at,' he said to Hanson.

Jacobs gave each of them an anxious look. 'I don't want to cause trouble for anybody.'

'We understand that, Miss Jacobs,' said Watts. 'How about you tell us what you know?'

She still looked strained. 'During my third year at the college one of my tutors there who was always very friendly, a bit of a laugh actually, well, the first thing I noticed was that he changed my tutorial day. He asked me if I minded. I said no.'

Hanson broke the short silence. 'What change did he request?'

'From Friday morning to late Friday afternoon.'

'What time on the Friday afternoon?'

'Six o'clock.'

Jacobs caught the brief glance which passed between Hanson and her colleagues.

'It didn't bother me. If I was going out it was never before about nine so . . .' She shrugged. They waited.

'Anyway, this one Friday I had a tutorial with him and everything was OK. I was getting my books and stuff together and . . . he asked me out.'

'What exactly did he say?' asked Hanson.

'He said, "How about we grab a coffee sometime? How about later?"' Jacobs shook her head. 'He was going on about some out-of-the-way restaurant he knew. I was embarrassed. He wasn't one of the young lecturers. He was in his thirties at least.' She looked across at Watts and Corrigan and bit her lip.

'And he was married. I didn't know what to say so I ignored it. Pretended I hadn't heard. He asked me again. I said no. I picked up my stuff and went to the door. He followed me.'

'Did he make any direct contact with you?'

Jacobs frowned. 'No, not really.' Her hand went to her shirt and she pointed to the gold heart-shaped locket suspended by a fine chain at her neck. 'I always wear this. My mum and dad bought it for me when I passed my A levels.' She looked down at it.

'It's a bit old fashioned but I like it.' She looked up. 'He stood really close to me at the door and said how lovely it looked around my neck.'

Jacobs' eyes went from Watts and Corrigan to Hanson. 'Have I said something?'

'Did he make any *physical* contact with you?' pressed Hanson.

'No. If he had, I would have reported him. What I just told you is all that happened. Just words.'

'Did he do anything at all to stop you leaving?'

'No. He stood back and I opened the door. I think he said something like, "Take care. See you, next tutorial."'

'We need his name,' said Watts.

Hanson saw a brief struggle play itself out across Jacobs' face. 'Dr Vickers.'

Inside UCU Watts was looking out of the window, his back to them. 'He's a sex pest. He likes them young.'

Hanson rhythmically tapped the table with her pen, Maisie inside her head. She straightened. 'You're getting him in?' She already knew the answer.

'Count on it.'

Corrigan slow-walked his way to the window, his gaze on the floor, arms folded high at his chest. 'We need to keep it low-key. There's nothing to link him directly to the Williams murder or to Amy Bennett.'

Watts frowned. 'I agree. He's a quiet operator, a cautious type who tests out situations before he acts. I want to know everything about him, including his shoe size and what he was driving last year.'

Hanson walked to the board and summoned up the photographs of Elizabeth Williams and a fairly recent one of Amy Bennett her family had just released to them. She studied each of them: Elizabeth was tall and slender, dark-haired. Amy's hair was also dark. The photograph suggested she was of average height and build. She recalled Chloe Jacobs: fair-haired, shapely without being plump. Around five foot five.

She turned from the board. 'So far there's no clear indication that this offender has a type.' She knew her next words would be a red rag to Watts but they needed to be said. 'I agree Vickers needs interviewing again, but I agree with Corrigan. It has to be low key.' She looked up. Watts' facial expression was what she'd anticipated.

'You're always going on about "inappropriate behaviour", male to female. That's what we've got here with Vickers.'

'Yes and he needs to be talked to. What I'm also saying is that we can do without getting tunnel vision in this investigation – or at all.'

'After thirty-plus years policing, which started when you were still in your pram, I'm telling you that I've learned to keep a wide view, all right?'

She nodded. 'If you say so.'

He looked at his watch. 'I'll ring him at the college first thing and tell him we need his assistance. That should get him in here. Academics like that kind of approach.'

'You don't say.' She went across the room and sat down at a spare desktop PC and jiggled the mouse to wake up the screen. Corrigan was on his feet, car keys in hand, his eyes on her.

'Busy?'

She started typing into the Google toolbar. 'I need a tree surgeon. There's a branch that keeps tapping against the house and waking me.' She looked up. 'Where are you going?'

'To see Amy Bennett at the hospital,' said Corrigan.

She looked at Watts and back. 'How is she? What about the baby?'

'Both are OK as far as we know,' said Corrigan. 'Her medics say she's insisting on talking to us. On balance they've decided to allow it. The facial compositor guy from upstairs is coming as well.'

Hanson stood, reaching for her bag. 'I want to hear whatever Amy Bennett can tell us about her attacker.'

'Bear Vickers in mind when she does!' Was Watts' parting shot.

Hanson opted for the rear seat of Corrigan's Volvo. She gazed out of the window at the rushing scenery on this side of the dual carriageway. 'Venus and Mars' definitely applied to her and Watts.

She tuned into the conversation between Corrigan and the technician. They were talking about the EFIT-V technology the technician had brought along in the black case she'd seen him stow in the boot of the car.

'What your witness gets is groups of computer-generated faces. All she has to do is look at them and select one from each group on the basis of the image of the face she's got inside her head. The software gradually draws together the key characteristics of that stored face to produce the final product. It's a purposely slow process. There's a good chance we'll get a likeness without putting too much stress on her.'

Corrigan glanced in his rear-view mirror, changed lanes. 'Hope so. She's been through a lot. She's still going through it.'

The technician nodded. 'So I heard.'

'You're saying the process could take a while?' said Corrigan. 'Any idea as to how long?'

He shrugged. 'Let's see how it goes.'

*　*　*

One of Amy Bennett's doctors came to talk to them, addressing his comments to Corrigan as the police officer.

'My clinical opinion is that she's not up to this but she's adamant she wants to talk to you so we've decided on balance that it's best she does. She's still very fragile. I'm assuming I don't need to tell you how to proceed with her in light of that?'

'No. We'll take it as it comes. There'll be no pressure.' Corrigan turned to Hanson. 'This is Dr Hanson. She's a forensic psychologist. She has expertise and a lot of experience in talking to traumatised witnesses.' He gestured towards the technician holding the black case. 'This is Ricky Ahmed who'll assist Miss Bennett to construct the face-fit.'

Corrigan waited as the doctor acknowledged each of them. 'Amy Bennett is your patient. Do you have any advice, any preference as to how we approach her?'

The doctor nodded. 'Yes. I suggest Dr Hanson goes in first to prepare the ground and the technician last.'

'We'll do that, sir.'

Amy Bennett was watchful as Hanson came inside the room. Hanson thought how small she looked, propped up in the large bed, her arm still connected to the drip delivering its slow, steady infusion into her arm. She looked drained of life. Hanson's attention moved to the Perspex cot nearby. It was empty. Amy gave a weak smile, her voice soft.

'They're giving Pickle some tests. That's what we called him while he was a bump.' She paused and Hanson saw the rapid rise and fall of her chest. 'Are you with the police?'

Hanson took a chair to the bedside. 'Yes. My name's Kate and I'm a psychologist. I'm not expecting you to talk to me right now. It might help if you stay as quiet as you can. We've agreed with your doctor to take this slowly. Lieutenant Joe Corrigan is waiting outside. He's a police officer, one of my colleagues investigating what happened to you. He has some questions for you. Ricky Ahmed is also here. He's a facial construction technician and he's going to help you create a likeness of the man.' She left it there.

Faint colour appeared on Amy's face. 'I want to talk. I have to tell you all about him. Show you what he looks like.'

Hanson nodded. 'That's good, Amy, but if you get tired and need

a break, that's also fine. We don't even have to finish today. We can
come back if you need us to.'

Amy's eyes were on Hanson's face. 'When can we start?'

Touching the woman's cool arm, Hanson stood. 'In a couple of
minutes.'

'How's it looking?' asked Corrigan as Hanson emerged from the
room.

'She's very keen but I'm not sure how aware she is that it could
be difficult. We need to take our lead from her.'

They followed Hanson into the room and she hung back with
Ricky as Corrigan introduced himself, thinking that his deep,
soothing voice was ideal for reassuring anyone who was anxious
or fearful. The technician gave Amy a brief nod and went and sat
unobtrusively in a corner, taking the laptop from its case and
powering it up.

Hanson watched Corrigan place his hand on the chair near to
Amy. 'Is it OK if I sit here to ask you some questions or would
you prefer me to be over there?' Hanson caught Amy's 'nice man'
glance at her.

'Here's fine.'

'OK, Amy. We'll take this at your pace. Are you ready?'

She nodded, her eyes wide.

'You arrived at the garden centre. Tell us about that.' Hanson
saw her hesitate.

'. . . OK. I thought it was deserted when I pulled in but suddenly,
he was just there.' She stopped, her brows coming together.

'No. That's not right. I didn't see him straight away. I saw a
vehicle, a Jeep, I think parked some distance away to one side.
Almost within the trees. I think it was his but I'm not sure.'

'A Jeep,' repeated Corrigan.

'That's what I thought it was.' Her hand went to her forehead.
'It was big, square-looking. I don't remember the colour but it had
those rails on either side of its roof so you can tie things to them.
I described it to Eddie my boyfriend. He said it sounded more like
a Shogun.' She bit her lip. 'I don't know much about cars.'

'That's OK, Amy. Tell us why you decided to stop there.'

'My car started playing up so I had to get off the road.'

Quick colour coming onto her face, she glanced at Hanson. 'I
needed a restroom really badly. That's one of the things about being

pregnant. I'd been to that garden centre before and I knew there was one there.'

'Where were you when the car trouble started?'

'Halfway along the Kidderminster Road . . . No, wait. I've just remembered. It actually started in the car park at the fair.'

'What happened?'

Amy's face was intent. 'I was leaving. I started the car and then the engine kept fading and dying.' She pressed her lips together.

Corrigan gave a brief nod. 'What happened next?'

'I was desperate to get home. Somebody asked if I needed help but I pushed on the accelerator and suddenly it was OK.'

Hanson registered Corrigan's pause before he spoke again. 'Tell us about the person who offered you help.'

Amy gave a small shrug. 'I didn't see him. He was somewhere behind the car when I was trying to start it and by the time I managed to get it running he was gone.'

Corrigan asked, 'When you first got back to your car did you notice anyone near it?'

Amy shook her head. 'I don't think so. There were people milling around, arriving and leaving but nobody I particularly noticed.' She gave a heavy sigh.

'I just felt lucky that it was still there.' She looked up at him. 'I hadn't locked it. That's what it's been like these last few months. My midwife says it's pregnancy amnesia.'

'Can you recall what the man in the car park said to you?'

She looked uncertain. 'Not much. Something like, "Do you need help?".'

'But you didn't see him.'

'No. I just heard his voice. But that was at the fair. That was ages before anything happened.'

'Can you say anything about his voice?'

Amy shook her head. 'No. It was nothing unusual, just ordinary. He didn't sound local.'

Corrigan paused. 'Tell us all you can about the drive from the fair to the garden centre.'

'I took the A456 which runs past it and all I could think about was the car and whether it would make it and . . .' Annoyance appeared on her face. 'I've just remembered something. There was a car. It drove up behind me and just sat on my tail for what seemed like miles. He could have passed me easily but he didn't. He just sat there, his lights full on, dazzling me. I was trying to stay calm but I was getting really edgy and then he zoomed out, overtook me and disappeared.'

'You're doing well, Amy. Can you describe that car?'

She shook her head. 'No. It was really dark and his lights were too bright. I just got an impression as it passed that it was a man driving.'

Amy's face was flushed now. Hanson looked at Corrigan, trying to gauge what he was thinking.

His voice low and calm, he said, 'This is a safe place you're in now, Amy.' Amy lay back against the pillows, her hands clutching the bedcover.

'When you were at the fair, were you aware of anyone who was giving you any kind of undue attention?'

She frowned. 'What do you mean?'

'A stranger who maybe tried to strike up a conversation? Anyone you thought was hanging around too much?'

Amy shook her head. 'No, nothing at all, apart from the man who offered to help. When you're the size of a house you don't tend to attract much attention like I think you mean.'

Hanson smiled faintly.

Corrigan slow-nodded. 'So you arrived at the garden centre.'

Seeing the colour ebb from Amy's face, Hanson folded her arms tight against herself. *We might have to stop this soon. But if we do, she'll probably be upset even more than she is now.*

Amy swallowed. 'I'd opened my door to get out and he just appeared. He said something like, "Have you got change?" She looked up at them. 'There's a Coke machine at that place. Then he grabbed me.'

She lifted both hands to the neck of her hospital gown. 'It's all mixed up inside my head. He grabbed me and pulled me out of the car. He said, "Come on. You have to turn round. I'm going to turn you round to look at me." And he did and he had his arms around my shoulders and then across Pickle . . .' Her lips trembled. 'The pressure made me feel sick.'

'Nice and slow, Amy. Take as long as you want,' said Corrigan.

Hanson's pen sped, turning Amy's words into shorthand strokes. Looking up she saw bright tears. *We'll need to make a decision very soon. Right now, we're better placed than Amy to decide what's best.*

Amy wiped her face. 'This is all mixed up . . . He told me to do what he said. He moved his arm from Pickle and put his hand against my neck and I knew he was going to hurt me, like strangle me or something but . . . he didn't. He just kept running his hand over my neck and . . . staring at me.' She stopped, looked up at Hanson. 'This might sound weird but the way he touched me – it felt like the way Eddie does sometimes, you know.'

Hanson wrote down Amy's words, already trying to wring some sense out of what she was hearing.

'How about we take a break?' said Corrigan quietly.

'No, *please*. I've got to get this out of my head.'

She looked up at him, eyes welling. 'All I could hear was pounding in my ears, my head. I couldn't breathe. I was passing out and he hit me on the side of my head – that might have been earlier, and then he said, "I have to see your eyes blaze".' Tears were running freely now, falling onto the bedcover.

'He said, "Keep your eyes on me." He went on and on, insisting I look into his eyes, which frightened me because if I knew what he looked like and was able to identify him . . .' She stopped, pressing her fingers against her lips. 'That's when I knew,' she whispered. 'He wasn't going to let me go.' She looked across at Hanson. 'He told me I shouldn't be there on my own. He said I needed somebody like him . . .' She began to sob, her hand against her mouth. 'To keep me safe.' Nobody moved. Hanson was scarcely breathing.

'It made me so angry, that he was doing this to me and saying I was safe with him.'

The atmosphere in the low-lit room was taut. The technician's gaze was on Amy, the laptop forgotten.

'But it was when he said the word "mother", I knew I had to do something. He could see I was pregnant. He didn't care. I *had* to get away from him for Pickle's sake. If I didn't I knew he'd finish us both.'

She leant back, tears sliding into her hair. Hanson caught Corrigan's look, saw the almost imperceptive shake of his head.

Amy covered her face with her hands. 'Sorry.' She sobbed.

'You've given us a lot of really vital details, Amy,' he said. 'We'll leave it there for today.'

'No.'

Wincing, she pushed herself upright. 'I want to make the picture of him while he's still in my mind. I want him caught. *Please*.'

Hanson went and placed her hand lightly on Amy's shoulder, hearing the subtle click of laptop keys. Amy took some deep breaths.

'Please let me try.'

Hanson looked to Corrigan. He nodded and the technician carried the laptop, placed it in front of Amy and explained in basic terms how the process worked. She listened, gave a quick nod, her face revealing nothing.

Hanson looked at the pale young woman. She understood the ambivalence of the doctors to what they were doing here. Whichever decision was made, to proceed or stop, Amy would be distressed. She gazed towards the window, listening as the process unfolded, hearing Amy's rhythmic responses as she viewed the faces displayed on the screen. They had to see what Amy had seen.

The quiet, steady responses continued for a couple of minutes.

'That one. Number five.'

'Number four.'

'Number . . . three.'

'. . . Five. No . . . I can't . . .'

Picking up increasing hesitancy, Hanson turned to Amy. There was a round spot of colour on each of her cheeks. The technician looked up at them with a quick headshake. Corrigan came to Hanson, keeping his voice low.

'As each of her choices adjusts the main composite it's upping her tension.'

'Let's end it,' she said.

Corrigan returned to the bedside and put his hand on the technician's shoulder. 'Stop now.'

Amy's eyes, huge and shadowed, were turned from the screen. 'I'm really sorry. I can't do it.'

She sank against the pillows. Hanson lightly squeezed her hand. 'It's OK, Amy,' she said, knowing that for the young woman it really wasn't.

After they'd left Amy's hospital room, Hanson made a call. Her phone to her ear, she waited for Julian's voicemail message to end. She glanced at her notebook which she'd left on a chair. She wanted a data search but was unsure of the details and what Amy had told them wasn't any obvious help.

'Hi, Julian. When you get this, run a search on all sexually-motivated attacks on females between the ages of . . . sixteen and thirty in the Kidderminster area during the last twelve months.' She cut the call.

Back in UCU the technician started up the EFIT-V programme as Julian handed a print-out to Hanson. 'Got the search results you requested, Kate.' He pointed at them. 'There are a lot of hits for sixteen-to-thirty age range in the area, from exhibitionism to rape.'

'Sorry, Julian. I should have set some search limits.'

'No problem. I thought about the Williams and Bennett cases and had a go at refining it. I added "athletic" because of the Williams case, plus Amy Bennett's attack occurring in a fairly rural area got me thinking about the kinds of females who tend to use the open countryside, such as dog walkers, so I upped the age range.'

He passed her another print out. 'One MISPER. Female, active, sexual attack suspected. She's not what I'd describe as young. I've put all the details on the board.'

Hanson looked up and saw details of a disappearance in 2010. Jean Phillips. Age forty-five. Unmarried schoolteacher. Enthusiastic hiker. Failed to return from a planned ten-mile hike in the Wolverley area, near Kidderminster.

Julian had also found a data entry for the Phillips disappearance. She read it. The only witnesses who came forward at the time were a hiking trio of retirees, two women and a man. They described Phillips as well-built, dressed in black shorts, white T-shirt, hiking boots, a bright red sweatshirt tied around her waist. She was carrying a small black backpack. One of the witnesses stated that Phillips was walking in a way which suggested she'd sustained some kind of minor injury. The other two hadn't noticed this. All three described her demeanour as cheerful.

Hanson took the sheet to the table. The area in which Jean Phillips disappeared was in the same general location as that in which Amy Bennett was attacked. Beyond the 'athletic' descriptor there was nothing to link her disappearance to the murder of Elizabeth Williams.

'There aren't enough similarities to our two cases. We have zero information about what happened to Phillips after she was seen by those three people.'

He took the sheet from her. 'File it?'

Hanson nodded and got out the notes she'd made at the hospital, flicked pages and looked at Corrigan.

'You heard what Amy said about the man in the car park.'

'Sure did.'

'What do you think?'

'I know what *you* think,' he said. 'He might have caused her car problems.'

'You don't think so?'

'Maybe,' said Corrigan. 'And maybe he followed her along the road.'

Doubts edged inside Hanson's head. 'But how would he have known she'd stop at that garden centre?'

Corrigan considered it. 'If he knows enough about cars to disable them, maybe he had an idea how far she'd get before she had to find somewhere to pull over. He was prepared to wait for her to reach that garden centre. If she'd passed by he could easily have resumed his tracking of her. Cat and mouse.'

'Is that what you think happened?' Hanson pressed, knowing Watts's deep dislike of maybes.

'I know as much as you, Red.' He turned to the technician. 'Let's take a look at what Amy did.'

They studied the unfinished composite. Hanson looked up from the unfamiliar face to the technician.

'Would you try again if the witness is willing?'

He gave her a quick headshake. 'Doubt it. She more or less froze as we progressed through it.' He closed the laptop. 'But you know where to find me if things change.'

They watched him pass Nuttall who was on his way inside UCU. Nuttall inspected the board, instructing Julian to summon up all the information gathered. He read through it, then frowned at Corrigan.

'You're giving a lot of time to the Kidderminster Road attack on this pregnant woman.' He turned as the door opened and Watts came inside. 'The chief agrees that the attack on Amy Bennett is linked to the Williams murder,' he said. Nuttall's gaze swept over each of them. 'Three of you taking on two cases simultaneously means you're spreading yourselves too thin.' He looked at Hanson and shook his head.

'I know what you're about to say. "Get us some extra help." I've tried. The chief says no. Williams is *the* designated cold case as far as UCU is concerned so that's your priority. I want it off the books or back to "cold" before I leave at the end of the month.'

Hanson's view of Nuttall was not wholly negative but he was going a step too far with this. 'We've got verbal evidence which links the attack on Amy Bennett to the murder of Elizabeth Williams.'

He gave her a direct look. 'In that case it's a matter of finding Williams's killer and you'll have the Kidderminster attacker as well.'

Annoyed at what she considered a lack of logic, she aimed her words at the closing door as he left. 'And if we investigate *both* simultaneously, it gives us *two* chances of identifying him!'

Pushing Nuttall from her mind, she fetched her notebook, went quickly through the notes she'd made of Amy's words as uttered by her attacker. It was unlikely they'd get more from her. Those words were all they had to help them identify the shadow man who'd said them. He'd assigned Amy a role in a terrifying, two-character scene of his own creation. A role and a scene which Hanson didn't understand.

TWENTY-ONE

Ellen, the worker at The Sanctuary was giving Hanson an uncertain look. 'You want to ask him to tell you again what he saw?'

Hanson shook her head. 'What he heard. We need him to try to remember all of it.' She chose her words. 'The thing is we both know Michael's tendency to say things which aren't strictly true.'

Ellen nodded. 'You mean his exaggerations. The trouble with him is that we think there's a bit of truth in a lot of what he says. Like when he goes on about being in the SAS. He showed me a photo of himself once in army uniform. But that's how he is. What do you want me to do?'

'Let Michael know I'm here and say that I need to talk to him again. Afterwards, I'd appreciate your telling me if there was anything unusual about his demeanour when he arrived today.'

'Like what?' asked Ellen, bemused.

'Anything which you think might have impacted on his ability to remember. For example, did he seem his usual self when he arrived? Did he appear unusually tired, troubled or distracted? Was his mood low? Did he appear to have had alcohol? You're more likely to pick up on those things because you know Michael really well.'

Ellen's eyes stretched. 'Alcohol? Michael? He doesn't drink. I've never known it in the five years I've been here and nobody else has mentioned it.'

Hearing this, Hanson wondered how many other people like Michael Myers might benefit from having someone like Ellen supporting them. 'OK but I need you to tell me about anything else you notice about him. I need to get as much as I can from him about what he remembers of his visit to that field by the reservoir last year and I need it as soon as possible. If he is distracted in any way today, I'll have to come back another time and I don't want to do that. Time is something we don't have a lot of.'

Hanson didn't add the other reason for her reluctance to return. If UCU identified Elizabeth Williams's killer, there would be a court case and a defence team ready to pounce on anything they might construe as undue pressure on a witness, particularly one as vulnerable as Myers.

Ellen stared at her. 'You're a psychologist. Can't you make him remember?'

Hanson shook her head. 'No, and anyway it has to be up to Michael to tell me whatever he can. He's a valuable witness. It has to be his recall of what happened.'

'I didn't realise it's so complicated.' The implication behind Hanson's words dawned on Ellen. 'Witness? You're saying Michael could be made to go to court? I don't think he'd be very good at that.'

Hanson silently agreed. The criminal justice system was not renowned for its positive handling of people like Myers.

'If he does have more information, if he gives it to me in a straightforward way without exaggeration it could help us stop whoever killed that young student from doing the same to someone else.'

Ellen looked doubtful. 'That sounds like a lot of "ifs".'

'When do you expect him?' asked Hanson.

She looked at her watch. 'Any time now. It's tea and biscuit day.' Her smile faded. 'I'd help if I could.'

Hanson studied her open face. 'Actually, you can, Ellen. After he arrives and you show him in, could you stay? You won't have to do anything but I'll know that you're listening to what I'm saying. It will keep me focused so that I don't encourage or lead him. It's an easy trap to fall into.'

Ellen hesitated. 'I hope I don't get mixed up in any trial.' She sighed. 'OK. I'll stay.'

The doorbell rang and she stood. 'That's probably him. I told you we can set the clocks by him.'

Hanson watched her leave the room. She picked up the sound of the door opening and Myers's voice, followed by Ellen telling him that Hanson was here and would like to talk to him again. He came into the room. The improvements made to smarten him up for his headquarters interview were gone.

He gave Hanson a wide grin. 'Back again? People will start talking, you know.'

She smiled. 'Sit down please, Mr Myers.'

He took a nearby chair, watching as Ellen chose one in a corner. 'See? Ellen thinks we need a chaperone.' His face changed. 'I can only spare a few minutes. They'll be making the tea soon and there's some right greedy so-and-sos in this place. If I'm not in there pronto I can wave the biscuits ta-ta.'

'I'm sure they'll save you some,' said Hanson.

She chose her words, keeping it brief. 'Tell me again what you heard at the field last year.'

'Why? Have you forgotten?'

Hanson shook her head. 'No. We haven't forgotten. I wrote it all down.' She stopped. She wouldn't convey how important it was and risk him embellishing his recall.

Her notebook in plain sight on her knee, her pen ready, she said, 'I need you to say it again. Everything you remember.'

He gave an exaggerated wink. 'I get you. You're not into interrogation methods, right? I've been interrogated many times and revealed nothing.' His head came up, he squared his shoulders. Any optimism Hanson had hit the floor.

'Just tell me everything you heard.'

She watched him lean his head back. 'He said, "Oohh, I'm right here and I know you're here and I said we'd always be together so look into my eyes again, mother."'

Hanson shot a quick glance at Ellen who was looking unnerved. 'How was that?' he asked. 'I might have missed the odd word because he wasn't talking that loud.' He tapped his fleshy nose. 'Sounded like he was on about something a bit personal. I've just remembered something else.'

Hanson paused, her face and her voice relaxed. 'Tell me.'

'He said, "You could have been safe but you didn't stay."'

She knew this was the first time he'd said this. She fought a strong urge to fix him with a look and demand that he focus.

'Did he say anything after that?' she asked, her voice even.

Myers shook his head. 'No. It sounded like he ran out of breath. Probably all that digging he was doing.'

Digging.

Hanson stared at him as he pointed at the wall clock and stood. 'I'd better get off to the tea room now.'

Knowing that she was diverting from her plan to merely listen, she said, 'Wait! You're saying he was digging?'

Myers gave a quick nod. 'Yeah. I heard it, plain as anything.'

'What about his voice,' she asked. 'Did he have a local accent?'

'You mean, like Birmingham?' He gave it some thought. 'No.'

She watched as he went, followed by Ellen. The door drifted closed.

The words Myers had heard were spoken by a man digging Elizabeth Williams' grave. Twelve months later that man attacked Amy Bennett.

Hanson was at home, examining the words supplied by Myers and those provided by Amy Bennett, now printed on side-by-side sheets, her eyes moving from one to the other then back. Each contained certain recurring words although few of the utterances matched completely. She saw again the insistence that the victim look directly into his eyes. What exactly had this man wanted from Elizabeth Williams? She was already dead when he said those words. What had he wanted from Amy Bennett? Her life? Two lives? She shook her head. All of it meant something to him. Myers had described it as 'something a bit personal'.

Hanson's eyes narrowed on specific words from Myers' recollection: 'You could have been safe but you wouldn't stay.'

What did that mean? It made no sense. Elizabeth *had* 'stayed'. He'd killed her. Was he blaming Elizabeth for her own death?

Hanson pressed her fingers against her eyes, blinked, read the words again. 'You could have been safe.' It sounded as though he was rebuking Elizabeth – but why? Had his expectations of Elizabeth not been met? It wasn't unusual for men who sexually attack women to demand certain verbal behaviours from them. Complimentary words about their attacker's power, his prowess, his skills. Others tried to shape the attack into something else, transform it into a date, a relationship even, by demanding that the victim say how attractive she found him or that she loved him and wanted to be with him. In fear of their lives, wanting to get away, victims often complied with those demands. Hanson knew of one offender who'd arranged a date with his victim as he left her, bruised and bloodied. He'd duly arrived two days later at the appointed place and time his victim had 'agreed' to meet him. He had been shocked to find the police waiting to arrest him.

She shook her head, out of ideas and answers. Neither of these young women had been safe with him. He'd killed Elizabeth Williams and traumatised Amy Bennett.

Hanson's spirits dipped further. Beyond the emphasis on the neck, there was little to no confirmation of any clear sexual interest in either of their cases. She looked down at the words used by a man focused on his victims' faces, their eyes. As far as it was possible to know, Elizabeth Williams had not been strangled. Hanson reached inside an envelope lying on her desk and drew out copies of police photographs taken of Amy soon after she arrived at the hospital. She examined them for several seconds, angled her desk lamp and examined them again. Amy had told them she feared he might strangle her yet the photographs showed no physical signs of violence to her neck. Had something occurred which stopped him carrying through with that behaviour?

She read all of the words again for what had to be the eighth or ninth time. What did they say about the man who'd uttered them? That, rather than wanting to create some kind of relationship with Amy Bennett, he was controlling and directive? 'I want to see your eyes blaze.' She frowned at the last word. An unusual choice. Not one she recalled ever being used by any offender in the cases in which she'd been involved. Did he want Amy angry? Did he want her to fight him? Does this man fear women? Does he resent what he perceives as his dependence on them? Does he loathe what he regards as his own vulnerability where they're concerned? Had he killed Elizabeth Williams and attacked Amy Bennett as a way of showing that the power was his?

Hanson thought of the men whose names they had so far. Michael Myers who pined for his mother and struggled to act appropriately towards women he didn't know. Chris Turner, a young man who related to women by bullying and controlling them. Lawrence Vickers, who saw Elizabeth Williams and Chloe Jacobs as sexual opportunities. She thought of two other names: Hugh Downey traumatised by the near death of his wife. Aiden Malahide who visited his elderly mother and had no wife.

Hanson's thoughts drifted to the men she knew: Kevin and his chafing at the demands of a long-term relationship and his serial romancing, Watts, still mourning the loss of his years-dead wife although he would never admit it. And Corrigan, whom she knew had a close relationship with his mother.

She pushed away from the desk. So much for theory. There seemed to be as many different ways for men to relate to women as there were different men. She scribbled a reminder in her diary: they had to see Amy Bennett again.

She started at the slam of the front door and looked through the window as the headlights of Candice's car swept the drive.

'Hi, Mum!' called Maisie.

Hanson came into the hall and gave her a hug. 'Did you have a nice time at Chelsey's?'

'Yeah. Candice took us to see Chelsey's grandpa. He's been ill but he's fine now. He made pound coins drop out of our ears.' Seeing her mother's grin she said, 'He *did*. I know it was like a trick but you couldn't tell.'

'Have you eaten?'

'We went to the High Street and had Chinese food which was yummy.'

They walked into the kitchen together, Hanson listening as Maisie chattered. She knew what she had to do later this evening. It didn't require planning or analysing or any other kind of over-thinking. It was something she'd been avoiding for far too long because it left her feeling open and vulnerable.

But this wasn't about her. It was about Maisie.

They were in Hanson's bedroom, Maisie grinning at the screen action of the film she'd chosen.

'I love this, even though it's ancient. Just imagine, Mum, if it like, *really* happened and every day for me it was a lesson on

Citizenship that I had to do over and over, and for you it was Bernie Watts ringing you on your mobile and saying "Is that you, doc?" every, *single* morning.'

'I get the horrific drift,' murmured Hanson, getting out of the bed. Opening her wardrobe door she reached inside then returned with a small envelope which she placed on the bedside table. The film ended and she aimed the remote.

'Go on, Mum. What's your idea of a terrible repeat day? Don't tell me, I can guess: Daddy coming here and complaining about his work–life stress.'

'Your father's fine,' she said quietly.

Maisie's head was all that was visible above the duvet, curls spread on the pillow, face earnest. 'Do you think it's wrong to talk about people? I don't. It's fun because people are interesting.' She squirmed to look up at Hanson. 'You must agree 'cos people are your job.'

Hanson looked down at her. It was as good an intro as she was likely to get. 'I want to talk to you about something interesting and important about people.'

Maisie wriggled her feet under the duvet. 'Fire away. Is it about boys? Daddy says next time you bring it up, looking all serious like now, I should say "What's up, Mum? If there's something you don't understand, ask me." Daddy's funny.' She laughed up at Hanson, then stopped. 'Wha'?'

Hanson took a breath. 'OK. This is about my family. My mother and father.'

'My grandmother as was and my grandpa who still is.'

'Exactly.' She paused, the cornflower blue eyes on hers. 'You'd like to see him, wouldn't you?'

In a single movement Maisie was on her knees facing her. 'When?' she demanded.

Hanson raised both hands. 'Wait, Maisie. Before that happens, there's something I need to tell you.'

The blue eyes still on hers, she hesitated, feeling her way forward.

'My parents didn't get on very well while they were married.'

'Just like you and Daddy,' said Maisie.

'Yes, maybe . . . Anyway, what happened was . . . my mother met someone. Another man. They liked each other a lot and . . . she got pregnant with me.'

Maisie absorbed the words then frowned. 'So what was Grandpa doing at the time?'

'He was . . . around. Anyway, the point is that my father, your grandpa, isn't actually a blood relative of either of us.'

'Right,' said Maisie, frowning. 'So, he's not anybody?'

Having got this far and wanting to avoid getting diverted, Hanson reached for the envelope, took out the photograph and passed it to Maisie, the one which showed both of Hanson's fathers, one of them biological, the other not.

Maisie took it, stared at it, then up at Hanson. She held it up, pointing to the man off to one side of the photograph. 'This is your father?'

Hanson nodded, relieved at her quick reasoning. 'Yes.'

Maisie leapt to her feet and started bouncing on the bed.

'Red hair! He's got the red hair!' Small fists punched the air. '*Look* at it, Mum. Dark red and thick, like mine and yours.'

She dropped onto the bed, still staring at the photograph. 'Holy moly, he looks like you.'

Hanson watched her daughter, searched the heart-shaped face for signs of upset. There were none. All she could see was pure delight.

'I should have told you sooner but I didn't know when or how to do it.'

Maisie wasn't listening. She was on her knees, looking down at the photograph now lying on the duvet's white cover. 'He's got the red hair! Yay!'

In all the scenarios Hanson had run inside her head for this moment, this wasn't like any of them. 'You do understand what I've told you, don't you, Maisie?'

Clutching the photograph, Maisie lay down and squeezed herself against Hanson. ''Course I do. My grandmother, who was your mother, had, you know, a thingy with the red-haired man in the picture and got pregnant with you. That's cool. I didn't think people did that kind of stuff in the olden days.' Hanson watched the possible ramifications cross Maisie's face.

'Did Grandpa know about it?'

'Maisie, you do understand what we're talking about?'

Maisie looked impatient. 'Mum, I'm thirteen. I'm not a child.' Her eyes rounded. 'What did Grandma do? Did she tell Grandpa and her friends about you or were you hushed up? Like, kept behind a veil of secrecy?'

'I'm thirty-five!' protested Hanson. 'This didn't happen in Queen Victoria's reign.'

'Soz. So did Grandpa know or not?'

'Maybe.' Hanson shook her head. 'I don't know for sure. All I do know is that when I was about fifteen he left.'

'Didn't he ever mention it when you saw each other later?'

'I haven't seen him that often, have I? But no, he didn't. I never said anything to him because I didn't know about it until after your grandmother died and then, well, it seemed like history.' She looked down at Maisie. '*Recent* history.'

Lying on her back, arms folded behind her head, Maisie looked up at her. 'He probably wanted to get away from the past. Start again. You'll never be in my past, Mum, 'cos I'm the one with the future and you'll be in it.'

'Thanks for that. I think.'

'What's his name? The red-haired man?'

Hanson took the photograph from her and gave it a wistful look. 'I don't know.'

Maisie got out of bed with a wide yawn. 'Daddy's right, you know. You shouldn't take everything so seriously. What you've just told me is cool. Take my word for it, Mum, when Grandpa left, it was a case of, OK, YOLO.'

Hanson looked up. 'What?'

'You only live once.' She padded to the door. 'G'night.'

Hanson watched her go, YOLO reverberating inside her head. Maisie was most definitely Kevin's daughter. Why had she never noticed how alike they were?

She called after her. 'Maisie? Can I have the photograph?'

She brought it back. After a few more seconds of studying it, she looked up at Hanson, eyes shining. '*Red* hair! What happened to him?'

'I don't know that, either.'

She took Maisie by the shoulders. 'The thing is you have a grandpa.' She pointed to the tall man in the photograph. 'The man you've always known about and sometimes met.'

Maisie nodded. 'My grandpa. Your sort-of father. When do we get to see him again?'

Hanson heard the inclusiveness behind Maisie's words. She wasn't about to tell her that it wasn't that simple. That this man whom she'd known as her father for the first fifteen years of her life, who had left, had only rarely contacted her since.

'Leave it with me.'

'Cool. Can we go to the Thinktank museum tomorrow?'

*   *   *

Hanson lay staring at the blank television screen. It had gone much better than she'd dared hope. Maybe she had worried too much about it? She frowned. Had it gone too well? Was Maisie too worldly for her age? That was ridiculous. Maisie was in many ways quite young for her age. Kevin's voice came into her head.

Oh, zip it.

She thought of the impact of early relationships and how they influence later ones. *My father left because he was cheated on by my mother and I chose Kevin who was and is a serial cheat. And now I have to contact the man who was my father until he decided or knew that he wasn't and left. And what about the man who really is my father?*

She did some deep breathing. She was no longer keeping a secret from Maisie. Maisie was happy. It was enough.

'Zip it.'

TWENTY-TWO

Watts and Corrigan exchanged glances then looked back at the tall, well-built man with a faint twang in his voice sitting across from them inside the small interview room.

Watts gave him a close look. 'Let's get this straight, Mr Hollis. You were a student at the college at the same time as Elizabeth Williams?'

'Yes,' said Hollis. 'But not in the same year. She was a second year. I'd just finished my fourth, a post-grad master's degree.'

'Right. Carry on.'

'Like I said, I didn't know any of the second year students very well but I knew Elizabeth because she often used the track when we were there.'

'We being?'

'The guys I did football training with outside of lectures. It was that Sunday, the twenty-third of June when I saw her at around two thirty in the afternoon.'

'How come you're so sure of that?' asked Corrigan.

Hollis looked at him. 'I'd dropped in at the college to check I hadn't left anything. I had a taxi waiting to take me to the station.

I was staying overnight at Heathrow then flying out next day to Austin, Texas. I'd been offered a one-year contract to play with a soccer team there. I saw Elizabeth as I was coming out of the college. She was heading out too.'

'Did you speak?'

'Yeah. I told her I was leaving. She wished me luck and said she was looking for an internship which was worthwhile rather than just career-related. So I wished her luck with that.'

The two officers exchanged glances. 'You've got a good memory Mr Hollis,' said Watts.

He gave an easy grin. 'I remember what she said about the internship because she was doing the opposite of what I was doing back then. I kept my focus totally on sport. It got me to Texas.'

'Did she give you any details about this internship?' asked Corrigan.

'If she did I don't recall, except that she had an interview somewhere around Five Ways that day, which I thought was kind of odd, it being a Sunday.'

Hollis appeared unaware of a sudden rise in tension.

Corrigan regarded the tall, open-faced man. 'Did she say anything else?'

Hollis frowned. 'I remember I offered her a lift in my taxi but she said she didn't need one. That she was on her way to visit a relative and then she had to change her clothes for her interview. I remember thinking that her interview had to be pretty late.'

Watts studied him for a few seconds without speaking, then 'What else did you make of what she said?'

Hollis shrugged. 'Nothing much, except like I said, I thought Sunday was a strange day for it.'

Watts leant on his forearms, eyes on Hollis. 'How come you're here now telling us this?'

'I came back to Birmingham a few days ago, picked up with some friends who used to be at the college and they told me what happened to her. It was a real shock. I knew nothing about it.' He met Watts' eyes.

'When they said that her case was open again I phoned you straight away.'

'Anything you wish to add, Mr Hollis?' asked Corrigan.

He shook his head. 'No. That's it. We spoke for about five minutes, if that.'

The two officers stood and Hollis did the same. 'We appreciate you coming in,' said Watts. 'Got a contact number? We'll need to get back to you for a statement.'

Hollis took the notepad from him and wrote down the details. 'This is my parents' place but I'm flying back to Austin next week.'

'In that case we'll take your statement now.'

'How's the soccer going?' asked Corrigan.

He grinned. 'Great. I'm on a five-year contract.'

Corrigan nodded. 'Good man. How are you finding the Texan summers?'

Hollis shook his head. 'Jeez, they're murder.'

They watched him leave, then returned to UCU.

'What do you think of him, Corrigan?'

'Straight arrow.'

Watts pointed to the board. 'Five Ways. Renfrew's near there but it isn't the only conservation set up. The doc's checked out some but got nothing. I want to spread the net wider but you know what'll happen if we do.'

Corrigan nodded. 'A lot of yelling by the chief and Nuttall about costs.'

Watts read the notes he'd made from Hollis's visit. 'This soccer business. Is it the one with the shoulder pads where they move a yard every half hour?'

He laughed. 'No. US soccer is English football. What you've described is American football.'

'Sorry I asked.'

Watts transferred his attention to the board. 'Hollis's information is a help because it confirms what we already know. According to him, he saw her at around two thirty and she was planning to visit a relative and we know that's what she did. The aunt confirmed that she stayed until around six. Thanks to Hollis we now know that after that she had an appointment connected to this internship she was looking for. Which fits with what Hanson has said about her getting her suit cleaned.'

He turned from the board, his face grim. 'And sometime after six o'clock on that Sunday she dropped off the radar. Until a few local kids found what was left of her.' He turned to Corrigan.

'Before we move on to any net-spreading, we give some more

attention to what we already know.' He circled a name on the screen.

Renfrew.

Watts gave Hanson the information they'd gained from Hollis. 'Renfrew needs a further look before we go any further,' he said. She gazed at the name circled on the board. 'I saw Hugh Downey very recently. I didn't pick up any more than we got from the other visit.'

Corrigan's eyes were also fixed on the board. 'We can't ignore the other conservation setups in the city. How about we focus on the one or two in the Five Ways area? What do you say, Red?'

She thought about it. 'Renfrew's name was imprinted on Elizabeth's application form and her body was hidden on land Renfrew once took an interest in. Tenuous links, but we need to be sure we've fully explored them.'

'Very tenuous. Possibly coincidental. I don't like coincidences.' Watts glanced at Corrigan. 'You won't know about a case down south around ten years ago. A nurse was arrested on suspicion of killing three infants because those deaths and several emergencies happened when she was on duty. She was jailed. Three years later her conviction was overturned for lack of evidence. A year after that another hospital employee was arrested and sent to prison for the deaths.' He looked at Hanson. 'You remember it.'

She nodded, searching information on the board. 'I reference it when I lecture on confirmation bias: coincidental factors pointing to guilt. What we have on Renfrew isn't much and it may be co-incidental. We have nothing which confirms that either Hugh Downey or Aiden Malahide has any knowledge of Elizabeth Williams.'

She turned from the board. 'I've just realised something. Downey and Malahide aren't the whole company.'

'Who else is there?' asked Watts.

She pointed at the board. 'Remember our first visit? The meeting they were having? Renfrew subcontracts its manual work. How many people did we see leaving that day after the meeting? A dozen? More? All male. We need to talk to all of them, show them Elizabeth's photograph. See if anyone recognises her.'

Watts reached for the phone. 'I'll get on to Renfrew. I want the subcontractors' details.'

As Watts's spoke into the phone, Hanson went to the board and added a couple of words. She turned to Corrigan. 'Talking of coincidences, I wouldn't want to estimate how many pale cream rugs there are there in a city of this size, but I saw one recently. In Aiden Malahide's office.'

Watts ended the call. 'The secretary's told me that both Downey and Malahide are out of the office now and not in tomorrow either. Chatty sort, isn't she? I've told her I'll pop in there in the morning. I haven't mentioned the subcontractors details to her. I don't want her phoning either of them to square it. The sooner we get that information, the sooner we start talking to these contractors and checking them out.'

Hanson stood and gathered her belongings with a glance at Corrigan. 'You look tired.'

He stretched his long arms. 'I was here at six a.m. Taser training.'

She caught herself wishing he was just a detective. But if he was, it was unlikely he would be in the UK at all.

And what exactly is it to do with you what he does?

At close to midnight Hanson was on her way to bed when she heard the familiar creak of her study door. She detoured, knowing it was a fatal move. Once inside she got drawn into work.

Going to her desk she switched on the lamp, trying to recall exactly what Hugh Downey had said about the contractors Renfrew used. She went through her notes, finding very little, flinching at a series of soft but insistent nudges against the side of the house and scribbled a quick note in her office diary: find tree surgeon.

She stopped at a place in her notebook and what Dee, Renfrew's secretary, had said about a current project the company had next to Sarehole Mill. She tried to remember what Maisie had told her about her school visit there. Something about the writer Tolkien. Switching on the desktop she entered the mill's name. Chin on fist, she read the search result. It was the last surviving watermill in Birmingham. Built in the sixteenth century, now restored. J.R.R. Tolkien had lived in the area at one time, knew the mill and was said to have gained inspiration from it and the surrounding area for 'Middle Earth'.

She looked at the picture but couldn't see the open land on which Dee had said the contractors were working. She'd take a look tomorrow after her morning lecture.

TWENTY-THREE

'**N**ice coffee, this,' said Watts.

Dee gave him a warm smile. 'You're welcome. If it wasn't for you coming in I'd have been on my own.' He drank more coffee, thinking about women. He didn't know many. His wife's friends had gradually drifted away, which was all right by him. He thought of work. Chong and Hanson were two of a kind in some ways: all work. He gave a mental headshake. That wasn't all they were about. Both were conscientious and exacting and headquarters was lucky to have them but neither had time for socialising. He was the same. Except for when it looked like it might pay off work wise. He glanced at the secretary.

'Does it get lonely here?'

'No. There's always people in and out and Aiden's here most days. He's booked a couple of days off to take his mother out.'

He nodded. From what Myers and Amy Bennett had said, the man UCU was looking for had had a lot to say on the subject of 'mother'. His own? Somebody else's? Watts still wasn't setting too much store by anything Myers said.

'These people who are in and out. Are they the subcontractors?'

She nodded. 'A lot of them have worked for Renfrew for a while.'

'What are they like?' Watts asked. 'A rough lot?'

'Actually, some of them are really nice. Polite. Easy to talk to. But there's quite a few of them, so I'd say they're a mixed bunch.' She sighed, shook her head. 'I generally finish here at around four. I used to leave pens in my desk drawer, the occasional packet of biscuits. The next morning they'd be gone. I gave them a ticking off, told them to keep out of my desk but they all pleaded innocence. I told Aiden about it but he didn't do anything. Too laid back, you see.'

Watts nodded. 'People taking your stuff is annoying. There wouldn't be any more of that coffee?' She took his cup.

'Tell you what,' he said. 'How about you run me off a list of these subcontractors? It might be a big help to us in our investigation.'

She came back with the coffee and a hesitant look. 'Oh, go on then. If we can't trust the police, who can we trust?'

He grinned at her and raised his cup. 'Very nice.'

Watts was on the phone inside his vehicle, working his way down an alphabetical list of twenty-five names. He'd reached 'G'.

In the absence of Julian, he'd had Whittaker make a data search. Whittaker's voice was back in his ear. 'Found something for you, sarge.'

'Good lad. Read it to me.'

'Sean Gill. The full name and the date of birth is the same as you've got.'

'Go on.'

'Grievous Bodily Harm with Intent.'

'Date?'

'2001.'

Watts's eyes narrowed. 'Give me the victim details.'

'Female. Age: twenty-three. After he was arrested for attacking her, he claimed she was his girlfriend and that they'd had a bit of a domestic. According to her, she wasn't. She said he tried to start a conversation with her late one night in the area where she lived and wouldn't leave her alone.'

'Where was this?'

'Bristol. He beat her up. He claimed she came on to him.'

'What did he get?'

'Six years, reduced to four-point-five on appeal on the basis of his previous good character. This looks like his only offence.'

'The only one we know about, more likely. We'll be seeing Mr Sean Gill.'

Shielding her eyes against the sun, Hanson gazed at the area beyond Sarehole Mill. It looked deserted. She checked her watch. Maybe they were having an early lunch? She removed her jacket, threw it into her car and started in its direction, hoping to find at least one or two subcontractors at work.

She found the wide access path in the perimeter hedge and followed it onto the sweep of undulating land, hearing the low rumble of voices. Some way off a digger started up. She watched its jaws rise, slowly lower and bite into tough-looking grass, scraping it from the chestnut coloured earth. Looking beyond it she counted seven or eight male figures moving to and fro, all wearing yellow hard hats. She walked several metres to the nearest one.

'Hello?' He turned to her.

'I need to speak to whoever's in charge here. I think a Mr Downey?'

The man gazed at her, his face flushed and slick with sweat. 'I've not seen Downey today. You want Sean. Hang on.'

He turned from her, placing his hands either side of his mouth. 'Sean! *Sean!*'

A man appeared in the doorway of a wooden hut some distance away.

'The lady here wants to talk to you!'

The man covered the wooden steps in a single stride, moving purposefully towards her, hard hat in hand. Watching him move, Hanson's impression was of a man with a large physique. As he neared she revised that impression. He was solidly built but of barely average height. He neared, his amiable face creased into a smile.

'Sean Gill. What can I do for you?'

She picked up the slight West Country accent. She would start with him. 'I'd like to talk to you about your work for Renfrew.'

He was now standing next to her. Close enough for her to feel his heat. 'What about it?'

'Were you working for the company this time last year?'

He gave an easy nod. 'Possibly. Who wants to know?'

'I'm part of a West Midlands Police investigation.'

In the harsh sunlight she got a fleeting impression of a change in his face then decided she was mistaken. He was still smiling.

'Bright out here isn't it? Come into the site hut. We can talk there.'

Hanson walked with him, aware of the eyes of the other men on her as she passed. One of them called to him. 'Hey, Sean! We're still having trouble with the digger.'

Gill turned to her. 'Hang on here a minute.'

She watched him retrace the few steps to the large machine, throw the engine cover open and look inside it. After a short interval she heard him shout. 'Try that!'

The digger's engine restarted and its jaws rose again.

He walked back to Hanson and they continued on to the hut. He raised a hand, indicating for her to go inside. She felt the wooden floor vibrate as he followed her inside then turned to pull the door closed after him.

'Can't hear yourself think out there,' he said.

Her vision adjusting to the dim interior, she looked around. There was a table covered in heavily-stained mugs, used plates and what Hanson thought were probably rolls of plans. Around it were several canvas chairs, a sagging sofa along one wall, newspapers abandoned on the floor near it. The hut appeared to function as a combination site office, eating area and a place for workers to relax. It smelled of wood, stale smoke and sweat. Gill quickly cleared a space at the table and pulled out a chair for her.

'Here. Have a seat. It's nearly lunchtime. The lads will be in for their break soon.'

She sat, looking up at him. He was still standing. Still smiling.

'Were you working for Renfrew in June last year?'

'Yes I was. Why?'

'Do you recall any mention of plans around that time for Renfrew to create a work experience placement for a young woman?'

The smile disappeared. 'Can't say that I do.'

'Or, maybe a young woman who phoned or visited a site you were working on with a similar request?'

He folded his arms. Beyond the door the site had fallen quiet. Hanson waited.

'A young woman, you say?' He stroked his chin, looking thoughtful but saying nothing.

'Were you or any of the other workers approached like that?' she prompted.

'Last year, you said? I've got to think about this. Got any details on her?'

'Tall, dark-haired, late teens.' She watched his head turn slowly towards the door then back again.

'I'll have to give this some thought. I'll ask my lads. I've worked with them on and off for the last eighteen months. Like I said, they should be in soon.'

She listened, hearing nothing from the land beyond the door.

'Do you remember which sites you worked on during that time?'

He drew in a breath through his teeth. 'Now that's *really* hard to say without looking at our records and they're all at the office. Next time I drop in, I'll check. How do I contact you?'

Hanson reached into her trouser pocket, took out a card and held it towards him. 'I'd like to speak to the other workers while I'm here. They might recall something relevant.'

He was studying the details she'd given him. He looked up at her, his gaze steady. 'How does a doctor come to get mixed up with the police?'

'I'm a forensic psychologist.'

Again she got a fleeting impression of something changing within his face.

'You don't say?' he whispered. 'That must be interesting.'

'It is.'

'I thought they worked in prisons.'

'Some do.'

'A mate of mine had a bit of legal bother and he met one of them.'

'I see,' said Hanson for want of something to say. Deciding that he wasn't about to give her anything useful, she stood and took a few steps towards the door.

'I've taken up enough of your time, Mr Gill. If you do recall anything, perhaps you'd ring me.'

'Hang on. What's the rush? Tell me more about this young woman you're looking for.'

Hanson was now weighing his limited responses, the tone of his questions, the smile which wasn't reaching his eyes. She had a sudden need to be outside.

'I don't think you have the information I'm looking for, Mr Gill.'

He raised his brows. 'Come on. Give us a chance. A young woman you said?' He grew silent, his eyes on hers. 'No. You're probably right. I don't remember the bosses at Renfrew ever mentioning anybody like that.' He smiled. 'I can't see a young woman fitting in here with this hairy-arsed lot I've got working for me. Can you?'

She met his gaze. 'Probably not.'

Gill was studying her. 'And that makes me wonder if Downey and that creep, Malahide sent you here to check up on things.'

Hanson was moving to the door. 'I already told you I'm with the police.'

'That's right! You *did*. Thanks for reminding me because now I can tell *you* something. I follow the news. I read the papers from front to back. Not like the rest of them here: straight to the sport.'

Inside this makeshift building, in the middle of a prosaic

Birmingham suburb in daylight, with its houses and pub close by, Hanson knew that her situation was all wrong. She glanced at the door's latch. A single pull to the left would release it.

'This is my newspaper here. See?'

She looked back at him. His flat eyes were fixed on her face. He was holding the newspaper open at a whole-page report of the Elizabeth Williams murder investigation, including a photograph.

'That's her, isn't it? The woman you're talking about? She doesn't look nineteen to me. More like twenty-five, but you'll never get a straight answer from any of them. You think I was mixed up in that?' There was no smile now and his eyes were fixed on her face. 'You think I had something to do with that?'

Hanson turned to the door, legs in sudden tension. She sensed him move closer, his voice dropping.

'Don't turn your back when I ask a reasonable question. *Look* at me.'

Her back to him, her eyes on the door, those last few words hit Hanson's ears. She realised that no one at headquarters or the university knew she was here. She felt the tremor of his footsteps approaching across the wooden floor. In an eye blink he was in front of her. Between her and the door. Now his voice was as flat as his eyes.

'You think I had something to do with what happened to that woman in the paper?'

Hanson didn't respond.

'You think I'm the type that attacks women?'

Aware of his heat, the odour of his sweat, her body in tension, Hanson was weighing up her options: dart around him? Hit and kick before he did? Shout? Her gaze was fixed on his, her peripheral vision assessing the space each side of him and the distance beyond him to the door.

He took a step towards her. 'Why would you think that? You don't know anything about me. Do you?' He took another step. 'You've had plenty to say up to now. Why so quiet?'

A sudden, loud thump on the door threw Hanson's heart against her ribs and sent her hands flying to her mouth. She and Gill stood, eyes locked, as a voice filtered inside. One she recognised but couldn't place.

'Gill? Open up!'

Gill's eyes moved from her face and Hanson lunged for the door as it swung open, crashing into Hugh Downey who was coming inside. He steadied her, his face quizzical.

'Dr Hanson . . .?'

'I was just leaving,' she whispered.

Downey's eyes were fixed on Gill. 'That's fine. You do that.' She went quickly down the steps, stumbling onto the rough ground, her eyes on her distant car. She crossed the deserted open space, reached it, got inside and engaged central locking then sat, eyes on the windscreen, getting control of her breathing. Hanson pulled out her phone and rang UCU. No reply. She rang Watts's phone, heard his voice.

'What's up, doc?'

She pictured his grin as he said the words, the little joke pulling her back to familiarity and safety.

'I'm at one of Renfrew's projects next to Sarehole Mill. I've just had what I wouldn't call a conversation with a man named Sean Gill, who's a kind of foreman here at the site.'

'We know him. He's got previous for GBH.'

She closed her eyes. 'I want him questioned in connection with our cases.'

She ended the call, Gill's three small words filling her head.

Look at me.

The bronze coloured Range Rover arrived, followed by a patrol car. Seeing her colleagues heading towards her, she got out of her car. The labourers who'd probably returned from a pub lunch were going about their work with intermittent glances towards the patrol car.

As Watts and Corrigan neared she pointed to the site hut then walked with them and the two uniformed officers they'd requested to where Hugh Downey was standing.

'Where's Sean Gill, Mr Downey?' asked Watts.

Downey nodded towards the hut. 'Getting his belongings together.'

Watts pointed at the constables. 'You two get over there and fetch him. Tell him we want a word with him.'

He turned to Downey. 'You're working here today?'

Downey shook his head. 'No. I came here to talk to Gill about . . .' He turned towards the hut, frowning. 'What's that?'

Hearing the commotion Watts and Corrigan headed towards it. After a couple of minutes they emerged with Gill, his wrists joined together, followed by the two uniformed officers. As Gill was led

past, he stared at Hanson. She and Downey watched in silence as
he was escorted to the patrol car, Corrigan placing a hand on Gill's
head as he lowered himself inside.

'What happened?' she asked Watts as they returned.

'He resisted, and hit one of the officers so I've arrested him for
assault.'

TWENTY-FOUR

Hanson was against the far wall of the observation room
away from the two-way glass, watching and listening to
Sean Gill speaking to her colleagues. His face was calm
and engaged, his hand movements expressive, the West Country
burr drifting across the room to her. He was no longer a veiled
threat. Now he was one of the boys.

'OK, you're right. I shouldn't have kicked off like I did but I've
had a crap day. First this woman arrived and I did my level best to
help her, even though she had a bit of an attitude and then the boss
comes to tell me I'm finished.'

'Tell us about your conversation with Dr Hanson,' said Watts.

Gill looked from Watts to Corrigan and back. 'I can't tell you
anything about it because I don't get what the hell happened. Whether
she got upset because she misunderstood something or she didn't
get what she wanted, I don't know. You'll have to ask her.' The duty
solicitor nodded at this seeming reasonableness.

Watts studied him. 'I'm asking you.'

Gill shifted on his chair and sighed. 'All I can tell you is she's
asking about some teenager who's gone missing, I tell her I know
nothing about it and she starts giving me funny looks. *Next* thing I
know, one of the bosses is at the door, telling me to get my stuff
together and *then* you lot arrive.'

He lowered his head onto his folded arms then looked up at
Watts. 'How long are you keeping me here?'

'Until we're satisfied we're hearing the truth. You're attitude to
Dr Hanson was threatening.'

Gill straightened. 'Oh, yeah? Has she said how I did that? Did
I raise my voice? No. Lay a hand on her? No. Stop her leaving?

No. If she said I did any of that, she's a liar. She's the one with the problem, not me. You ask my lads if they heard anything. They'll tell you they didn't.'

Corrigan hadn't taken his eyes off Gill's face since the interview began. 'You meet many women who have problems with you, Mr Gill?'

Gill's eyes narrowed. They went to the duty solicitor and back to Corrigan. 'Meaning?'

Hanson watched Corrigan pick up an A4 sheet. She knew what it was: Gill's police record.

'According to our information, another woman had a problem with you. In 2001.'

Gill's face was dismissive. 'You don't want to take any notice of *that*. That was years ago. That bitch was a liar but the police and the judge bought every word she said.'

Hanson came to the glass. Gill's face was getting increasingly red and he was becoming loud and fidgety. The duty solicitor's eyes were on her colleagues.

'This is the exact same situation! That woman shows up. I'm pleasant towards her, helpful. I don't lay a hand on her! I don't raise my voice!'

'Which you are doing now, Mr Gill,' advised the solicitor quietly.

Gill turned on him, his face congested. 'What!'

Pressed to the glass, Hanson watched horrified as Gill lunged at the solicitor who shrank away, arms raised to protect his head. Corrigan seized hold of Gill who began aiming punches and kicks at anyone and anything. A distant alarm shrilled, followed by feet rushing past the observation room. She saw the door of the interview room fly open and hit the wall as four officers piled inside, took hold of Gill, still fighting, cuffed him and hustled him out.

They passed the door of the observation room, Gill raving as he went, 'She turned her back on me! I don't take that from anybody, let alone a woman!'

Hanson had provided a formal statement about her experience of Gill at the site. Hugh Downey had done the same although she hadn't seen him at headquarters. She wanted to thank him. He'd arrived at that site office with no awareness of the scene playing itself out inside. She preferred not to think of the possible outcomes if he hadn't. She and her colleagues were inside UCU, Watts looking more upbeat than she'd seen in a while.

'What happens to Gill now?' she asked.

'We hold him until he gets a court hearing, maybe tomorrow and hopefully he'll get remanded, which gives us a chance to take a closer look at him,' said Corrigan. 'He's got another problem. According to Hugh Downey's statement, Gill is suspected of theft of building supplies from Renfrew. That's why Downey was at the site: to fire him.'

Watts gave her an intent look. 'Gill's got something else to worry about as far as I'm concerned. His possible involvement in Elizabeth Williams' abduction and murder. He told you to turn round and look at him. What do you think about him as a potential suspect?'

Hanson was reviewing the whole scene and her responses inside the site hut. 'His threatening attitude was so covert I didn't pick up the cues when I should have done. Which makes me think that young women such as Elizabeth might not have seen them at all. On the other hand, yes he said those words but in such a charged situation I'm reluctant to give them a significance they might not have. They're fairly commonplace words.'

Watts's eyes were on her. 'Doc, this is no time to be even-handed. Gill's got form for violence against a woman. You've said you felt threatened by him. He doesn't like women. Commonplace or not, he said those words. We have to consider him for Williams.'

Seeing the frustration on his face she understood. She'd already considered Gill as a potential suspect for the Williams murder but her experiences of him suggested another possible explanation.

'I think there may be more to it.'

He looked at her. 'There usually is with you. What's your objection to considering the most obvious line?'

She returned his look, recognising his frustration with their two cases. He didn't like the message she was giving. He still had to hear it.

'When Gill said those words to me, yes I felt threatened. I thought exactly the same as you but isn't it possible he said them because he believed I was being dismissive of him. Look at his 2001 conviction. Statements from the time indicate that he made a nuisance of himself around the woman he attacked and that she rebuffed him. Gill's problem is that he becomes impulsive and aggressive when he believes women are dismissing him.'

'We don't know that that didn't happen with Elizabeth Williams or Amy Bennett for that matter,' he said.

'I see a difference where those few words are concerned,' she said. 'When Amy Bennett's attacker used them I think they were part of a situation he was trying to create with her, rather than borne out of anger. He had a situation already inside his head which is why he was so insistent that she had to be facing him. "I'm going to turn you round to look at me." There's a difference between that and what Gill said to me.'

She'd worked with Watts long enough to know how irritated he was.

He spoke slowly. 'We've all had cases involving sex attackers driven by fantasy, doc. I say we do some digging where Gill's concerned.'

Suddenly weary, she rubbed her eyes. Watts was right. They didn't know nearly enough about Sean Gill. A glance in Corrigan's direction told her that he agreed with Watts.

She learnt towards them. 'OK, I hear what you're saying. But what I'm saying is we need to consider that Elizabeth Williams' murder and the attack on Amy Bennett happened because the man who did both had a picture inside his head of something other than physical violence.'

Watts got up from the table. 'If you want my advice you won't say that to Amy Bennett. He punched her in the head.' He turned to her. 'Chong couldn't find evidence of sex in the Williams case and Amy Bennett hasn't confirmed it. We don't know what those two cases are about. But Gill is a thug with a GBH conviction against a woman. That does it for me where he's concerned even if it doesn't work for you.'

Hanson searched for words. 'I just have this idea that our two cases are something very different from Sean Gill's crude, antisocial response to what he perceives as female rejection. Yes, the man who killed Elizabeth Williams and attacked Amy Bennett is controlling, yes he's capable of violence but he's also . . . creative.'

She saw the surprise on Corrigan's face. Watts turned to her, his hands propped either side of his waist. 'What's that supposed to mean?'

She thought of Myers' crooned words at the field. 'I'm not sure. Maybe it's to do with loss or regret. Something he's trying to recapture.' She was aware of a heavy silence. 'Right now, that's the best I can do.'

Corrigan's focus was on the table as Watts stared at her. 'Let's hope you're right about Gill having no involvement in our cases. His threats towards you, plus the scam he was pulling at Renfrew if he's charged won't bring him much custody.'

Hanson thought of Gill's voice, his accent. Amy Bennett had told them that her attacker wasn't local to the Midlands. She gathered her belongings. This wasn't the first time her thinking was at odds with that of her colleagues.

Which is why I'm here. To think.

She started as the phone shrilled. Watts answered it then hung up.

'That was reception. Lawrence Vickers has arrived.'

He stood as they appeared in reception.

'I've had to cancel one of my lectures to come here. I really do think that—'

'Take it easy, Dr Vickers,' said Watts. 'We need to sort something out with you. Are you OK to talk with us or would you prefer your solicitor here?'

Vickers stared at him. 'My solicitor? Why would I need *her*?'

'It's your choice. We don't mind waiting until she gets here.'

Hanson watched as Vickers took some deep breaths. 'I want to get on with whatever it is you want clarified so I can get back to college.'

They walked with him into the informal interview room where he dropped onto a chair, looking irritated.

'OK, Dr Vickers. We've talked to you already about what happened between you and Elizabeth Williams—'

'Nothing happened with her. All I did was ask her out to dinner. It had been a tough year and I was tired. There was nothing to it.'

Watts slow-nodded, his eyes on Vickers' face. 'That's what you told us. Have you ever propositioned another of your students?'

Vickers looked up at the ceiling. 'I don't like the word "propositioned" but no, I haven't.'

'Sir, we'd like you to tell us about a student named Chloe Jacobs.'

At Corrigan's words Vickers folded his arms but said nothing. Hanson studied him. *Why isn't he bothered by what he's just heard?*

'Have you anything to tell us, Dr Vickers?' asked Corrigan.

'This is idiotic. I'd forgotten all about this Chloe, whatever her name is.'

'Jacobs,' said Corrigan. 'We understand you invited her out to dinner.'

'What if I did? Which, by the way I don't recall doing.' He narrowed his eyes at Watts. 'Somebody has evidently said something to you. Well, let me tell you, colleges are a hotbed of gossip and—'

'A lot else besides, by the sound of it,' said Watts. 'Why did you ask her to have dinner?'

'*If* I did, it would have been a casual thing. I probably wanted to discuss her work, her progress.'

Watts grunted. 'Course you did.'

'I'm tiring of your attitude,' said Vickers.

'I'm not mad about yours so we both know where we stand.' Watts gave him a slow once-over. 'When we spoke to you about inviting Elizabeth Williams out, you were worried. You don't seem worried about Chloe Jacobs. I'm wondering why not.'

Vickers stared at him. '*Because* Elizabeth Williams was murdered, that's why. I know about how the police operate, how they get it wrong. I didn't want to get mixed up in that. Chloe Jacobs is different. For a start, she's still alive as far as I know!' He folded his arms and stared down at the table.

'You admired something about Chloe Jacobs' appearance on the day you suggested taking her to dinner.'

'Did I?' Vickers let his head fall back. 'You obviously know all about it so you'll have to enlighten me because I can't remember.'

'OK,' said Watts easily. 'She was wearing an item of jewellery.'

Vickers straightened, regarding him with what looked like dislike. 'I don't even remember inviting her to dinner so why would I remember what she was wearing?'

Watts stood. 'OK, Dr Vickers. We don't seem to be getting anywhere so we'll be seeing you again. How about at your house if that's all right with you?'

Vickers looked up with an expression on his face which Hanson read as smugly triumphant. Now she got it. *He's told his wife about Elizabeth Williams.*

'Perfectly. My wife knows about what happened with Elizabeth Williams. She knows it's nothing. That it wasn't important. She understands.'

Watts went to the door and opened it. 'Let's hope she's as understanding about Chloe Jacobs if she gets to hear about her.'

Vickers sauntered out. 'She will be. She knows the strain of the work I do. She knows I do it for her and the children.'

'In that case, we'll be seeing you at the college.'
Vickers gave him an angry look as he headed out of reception.

Hanson walked inside her silent house. Kevin had taken Maisie to the Midlands Arts Centre to make up for his missed contact. She felt nauseous and shaky, probably because she hadn't eaten for hours. The memory of Sean Gill was back inside her head.

Going into the kitchen, she fetched chicken from the refrigerator, rolls from the breadbin, set them down on the table and stared at them.

If I feel like this because of how Gill was towards me earlier, how must it have felt for Amy Bennett on that lonely, dark road?

Closing down her thinking on Elizabeth Williams' experience at her killer's hands, she went to the glass doors. Mugger was sitting on the grass looking plump, kittenish even, in his black and white 'dress suit', his eyes half-closed. He looked a cat's version of relaxed. She needed to do the same. What had happened to her today had been disturbing. She'd taken pride in her ability to read situations, avoid danger. It was one of the upsides of the work she did. Yet, she'd walked into the situation with Gill with zero awareness of his potential threat. So unaware that she'd doubted the shadows crossing Gill's face, the tiny cues around his behaviour. Until it was almost too late.

She saw a small bird swoop down onto the lawn. In a split-second Mugger's chest hit the grass, his forelegs splayed, tail high and wafting, eyes drilling. Within another two seconds he had the bird. It hadn't stood a chance.

Leaning her forehead against the glass, she felt the slight headache which had begun earlier that afternoon roll like thunder inside her head. She closed her eyes.

TWENTY-FIVE

Crystal's voice came from the adjoining room as Hanson walked inside her office the following morning.

'Got a message for you, Kate. Can you ring Lieutenant Corrigan as soon as you can? He called fifteen minutes ago. I told him you had a lecture until eleven.'

'Doing it now.'

Hanson listened to her call ring out then Corrigan's voice in her ear. 'Hi, Red. Sean Gill has been remanded to Birmingham prison. We wanted you to know that he's out of circulation for now.' He paused. 'We got a call earlier from the hospital. According to Amy Bennett's medics, she's fretting about the EFIT-V. She wants to give it another shot. They're OK with us going back so I guess I am too. What do you think?'

'Having seen how upset she was before, I'm not sure it's such a good idea.'

'Know how you feel, but we're between a rock and something as hard. If we don't offer her the opportunity, she'll still be upset and we could be passing up a chance to get some idea of what the guy who attacked her looks like. I think we should give it a try. The tech and I are on our way in half an hour. I think Amy would appreciate you being there and so would I. What do you say?'

As the call ended, Hanson saw a mug of coffee being placed in front of her. She hadn't slept much, her mind racing after formless shapes, and half-understood ideas, her headache of the previous evening still flexing its muscles.

She stood, grabbed her belongings and headed for the door. 'I'm going out, Crystal.'

They walked the hospital corridor, the technician following with his laptop, a large flat bag slung across his chest. The constable guarding the door acknowledged them with a nod, tapped the door, then opened it. Inside they found Amy sitting on a chair beside the bed. She was wearing a robe and looking frail. A man in his early thirties paused in the act of taking a plastic cup from her to look at them.

'These are the people I told you about, Eddie.'

Hanson watched him go to the cot and carefully lift the small infant from it, then sit with him against his bare chest where his shirt was open, its tiny back covered with a soft piece of cloth.

'How's baby?' Hanson asked Amy.

'He's doing really well. He's out of the incubator and in the heated cot all the time now and we've been shown how to hold him, skin-to-skin, see?' Corrigan looked across the room to Eddie and the baby.

'Shall we give you a few minutes?' asked Hanson

Amy shook her head. 'It's the baby's cuddle time and Eddie can do that as well as I can.' She hesitated. 'Thanks for coming back. Eddie finds it hard to listen to what happened but I've told him I have to do it. This probably sounds mad but I'm remembering small things all the time.'

'It's not mad,' said Hanson. 'It's often like that after trauma.'

'What I'm remembering is a bit like what I already told you but I think there's more detail. I can see it in my head now without getting too upset. He was so insistent I look at him. He made me face him. I couldn't look into his eyes even though he kept saying, "Look at me, look at me. Keep your eyes on mine." And it sounded . . . stupid. I mean, why would he want me to do that?' She stroked one of her temples, distracted.

'I think there's a lot I can't remember still. He hit me on the side of my head so I probably didn't take everything in.'

Hanson followed her glance to her partner who was gently rocking the baby. She could tell he didn't like what he was hearing.

'When I came to, he was stroking my face then my neck, up and down. Pressing it but not hard.' She looked across the room again. 'I have to tell them, Eddie. The police have to know.' She looked back at Hanson and Corrigan.

'He wasn't a big man but he was strong. Wiry.'

'What about his hands?' asked Hanson. 'What were they like?'

She thought about it. 'They were clean. He wasn't wearing a ring.'

Hanson recalled Sean Gill inside the site hut. He hadn't been wearing a ring either but his were the hands of someone used to regular manual work.

'I keep thinking about what he said, about being "safe". Where was the sense in that? When he said, "You need somebody like me to keep you safe." I remember thinking, That's rich, coming from you! How dare you say that to me? Then he was back to the "look at me" business. "I want to see your eyes blaze." I wanted to shout at him, "Take a look and you'll see it all right!" but I couldn't. I was too frightened.'

Hanson felt a quick rush of admiration for this spirited young woman who'd been through such a terrible ordeal.

Amy bit her lip. 'What he said, it doesn't make sense.'

She looked beyond them to where the technician was patiently waiting with Corrigan. 'I want to try again. Now.'

At a signal from Corrigan, the technician approached. Hanson watched him open the laptop and caught Amy's wary look as he started up the programme. When the initial screen display for the EFIT-V appeared her face filled with apprehension. The technician quietly reminded her of the procedure and she nodded. They were two minutes into it when the technician paused then turned to look at Corrigan. Hanson caught the almost indiscernible headshake.

A series of small bleats and snuffles drifted across the room. Corrigan came to Amy. 'How about we take a break while you enjoy your baby for a while?'

They stood together outside the room.

'It's not going to work,' said the technician. 'She's too tense. I'm worried that if I carry on with it, it'll be like the last time. She'll get upset.'

Arms folded high at his chest, Corrigan glanced inside the room then at Hanson. 'How about we call it a day?'

Hanson turned to the technician. 'I'm wondering if she's afraid that if she continues her attacker's face will suddenly rise up from the screen.'

'I was thinking the same. Which is why I brought these with me.'

They watched as he reached for the large, flat bag. They looked at the box of fine pencils and the sketch pad he was lifting out.

'There's always a place for old technology. What do you think?'

The baby was back inside the Perspex cot, the room quiet.

'Can you describe the shape of his face?' asked the technician, his voice low.

Amy gave a slow headshake. 'I'm not sure. It wasn't round. More oval I'd say.'

'What's your best memory of him?'

She thought for a few seconds. Her face changed. 'There was one look on his face I won't forget.'

'Describe it to me.'

'His face was above mine.' She put her hand to her forehead, swallowed. 'Maybe he was shouting but I couldn't hear him. He had his mouth open really wide and he was . . . just glaring down at me, his mouth stretched and his lips sort of disappearing. I remember his teeth.' She looked up at the busily sketching technician.

'Tell me about his teeth,' he said.

'White. Even. Looked after.'

'What about his mouth?'

Amy paused. 'I'm not sure. Whatever his lips were like, ordinary, thin, thick, I can't say. I didn't notice. But when he shouted that time and his mouth stretched open like I said, he looked like . . . an animal. He raised his arm, his hand up here, the fingers like this.' She spread her own fingers, her voice barely a whisper.

'That was the worst part of all. The most frightening. Funny, how I hadn't thought about it until now.'

'What about his eyes?'

Amy's forehead creased. 'I'm not sure of the colour. Possibly blue. They went really narrow when he got angry like that.' She bowed her head. 'He was so angry.'

There wasn't a sound in the room other than the technician's pencil whispering across the paper as he constructed Amy's words into a visual representation with quick, deft strokes.

Hanson asked, 'Can you remember anything which might have led him to look like that?'

'I think it was after I pushed my knee into him. Up until then he hadn't been like that. He'd said what he wanted, what was going to happen. He was calm. Like he was in charge.' She looked down at her hands. 'Which he was. But after I did that to him he was raging.'

'I think I'm getting a general idea of him,' said the technician.

After a couple of minutes or so of silence, of feathering lines and shading, he took out his phone, photographed the sketch then gently removed the sheet from the pad and placed it face down near Amy on the bedside table.

'I'll leave it with you for a day or so until you feel ready to look at it.'

'I'm ready now,' she said.

The technician slowly turned the sheet over. Amy's partner came and laid his hands on her shoulders. They looked at the sketch and her eyes filled.

'It's *him*,' she whispered.

* * *

Hanson was in her kitchen, feeling the warmth of the late afternoon, her thoughts on Amy Bennett's words. Watts was right. The man who'd attacked her was angry. They couldn't discount Gill. 'Let me have another look at it.' She took the sheet from Corrigan and looked at the face the technician had created. The skin on her shoulders crept and something squeezed at her diaphragm as she stared at Amy Bennett's attacker, the man they believed also killed Elizabeth Williams. His hand was raised above his head, fingers splayed, face distorted, mouth stretched into an elongated hole from which she could almost hear his rage. Eyes fixed, his hand raised he was a slasher-movie madman, a silverback asserting his dominance, a child-man tantrumming his demands for a look or a word. A feral killer whose face in repose probably looked like that of any other man. Husband. Father. Brother. Friend.

She saw some echo in it, perhaps a semblance of the angry, violent, incarcerated individuals she'd met in the course of her work. Could Sean Gill be the doer in both their cases? She stared down at the pencilled face. She couldn't see a resemblance. She placed it on the table.

Please. Don't let that be the last face that Elizabeth saw.

The front door banged shut and Corrigan slid the sketch into its envelope.

'Hi, Mum!'

'In here.'

Maisie came into the kitchen, looking overheated, hair a mass of springs. 'Hi, Joe.'

He grinned at her. 'Hey, Catswhiskers. How's it going?'

'Really well. I've got the hang of that chord you showed me. Don't move. Wait there.'

'Sorry,' said Hanson as Maisie rushed for the stairs. 'She doesn't have the concept of a hard day.'

'And neither should she. It's not a problem.'

Maisie returned, guitar in hand and settled onto a chair. 'Watch and listen.'

She played, her small fingers nimble, stretching to make the chords, face intent. Hanson glanced at Corrigan. He was listening, absorbed. As Maisie finished, he applauded. 'That was first-rate.'

Flushed, she stood and headed for the door. 'I have to Skype Chel before Daddy gets here.'

'There's not much I can teach her about the guitar,' he said as she went. 'In fact, how do I book a lesson?' He stood and they went to the hall.

'Tell me what you think of the sketch, Corrigan. What does it convey to you?'

He thought about it. 'It's the essence of evil.'

The Volvo pulled away, Hanson returned to the kitchen. *Evil.* She couldn't agree with Corrigan's choice of word although she understood it. He was Boston Irish Catholic. It was part of the vocabulary of his faith. But a word like 'evil' didn't work for her. How could it? It implied a belief in the existence of holiness. She shook her head. She preferred theoretical concepts: 'aggressive ideation', 'chronic hostility' and others relating to the developmental process and early influences. Concepts which could be measured: low-medium-high. She thought of Watts. Over the two-plus years they'd worked together his knee-jerk negativity to the theory she brought to UCU had lessened. Still not keen on it, he now accepted that it offered explanation. 'Evil' didn't attempt to explain. As a concept it just . . . was.

Listening to thumps and squeals from the first floor she stared out of the tall windows. Twice as many men died through violence than did females but the nature of the violence perpetrated against females was different. Often fantasy-driven. In consequence, much of it was gratuitous and shocking.

And we're right back to early experiences. Add some societal attitudes into the mix and we get Sean Gill. Had the man who killed Elizabeth Williams wanted to do the same to Amy Bennett and her unborn child?

She had no answer.

TWENTY-SIX

After seeing Maisie leave with Kevin, Hanson also left the house. By seven fifteen she was inside headquarters, picking up the steady hum of work continuing well into the evening. Switching on just a couple of lights inside UCU she went to the board and drew her hand across its cool smooth surface to reveal information. Tapping and sliding a finger, she circled words and phrases as she went, searching for a theme. When she could find no more words she tapped again. The words morphed into a list. Sitting on the table she read it. 'Fury, rage in your eyes, look at me, into my eyes.' On it went. She read them a second then a third time. These words were all they had to provide insight into the nature of the violence perpetrated against two young women. Hanson stared at them, seeing the control within them but foundering as she searched for anything more.

She looked at the trace evidence list. Pale fibres. At some point in the progression of events leading to Elizabeth Williams' death, she was in close proximity to a wool rug. Close enough to dig her fingers into it, grip its soft surface. In a paroxysm of fear? Hanson frowned.

You don't know that. What if this was prior to any violence? What if this was a situation which morphed into sex? What if Elizabeth Williams had gripped that rug during sexual ecstasy?

Hanson closed her eyes, running her hands through her hair as Chong's words resounded in her head: no evidence to support sexual activity.

She went back to the emotions: fury, rage. Were her earlier ideas about loss and regret wrong? Was rage a truer reflection of what drove Elizabeth's killer? Gill's face came into her head. She got up from the table and closed down the board. The more they learned the less sense it made.

She left headquarters and drove the short distance home through darkness, feeling itchy and on edge. She brushed at her hair and her neck. She'd take a quick bath, rather than a shower. She frowned, running a hand over her hair as she came onto her drive. Glad to be home, all she needed was that bath to dispel her tension.

Almost an hour later she climbed out of the tepid water. She'd fallen asleep in it when it was hot. *How do I manage that, yet wait for sleep when I'm in bed?*

Feeling chilled, Hanson tugged the soft blue towel from the heated rail, clutched it, warm and soft to her face, neck and chest. She was back thirteen years in a brightly lit hospital room, in the aftershock of giving birth, wrapped in a warm, soft blanket, her job done.

Dried and in pyjamas she went to her bedroom. Within half an hour she was drifting. A series of taps on the side of the house brought her back. *Damn branch.* She sat up, staring at nothing. She didn't know where she was going with these cases. Somewhere in the words and phrases she'd looked at earlier there had to be a theme, a motive. A man.

She couldn't see any of them.

She was already inside headquarters when Julian arrived.

'Hi, Kate.'

She looked up at the wall clock: 8 a.m. 'What's brought you in so early?'

'I wanted to check on any progress, see if there was a job for me before I go into uni to do some stuff of my own.'

'I don't have anything right now and there's no request from Watts or Corrigan for you.'

She told him what had happened at Sarehole Mill the previous day, reminding herself that she hadn't yet thanked Downey for his timely arrival.

'What do you think about this Gill for the murder and the attack?' asked Julian.

She smiled. 'That depends on when you ask me. Right now, it's a "don't know". I'm going into the university in a few minutes if you want a lift.'

Hanson slid the key into the ignition as Julian squeezed into the passenger seat. Maisie wasn't the only young person who was growing apace. The early-morning sun in her eyes, she started the car. Looking for sunglasses and not finding them she pulled down the sun visor and checked her mirror, ready to reverse.

A quick movement very close to her head snagged her attention. Immobilised, she watched the steady, determined movement along the top edge of the visor. Halfway along, the steadiness faltered. One of its legs rose, as if testing the air. Julian was speaking but she couldn't absorb what he was saying. Couldn't breathe. Daren't breathe. The slightest movement could dislodge it.

Heart racing, she pressed against the seat. It had been in her car last night. It had been *on* her. The horror of that realisation made her skin prickle and crawl. She had an overwhelming need to thrash her arms, scream and throw herself from the car. She didn't dare. It would bring it down on her.

'Kate . . .?'

Eyes fixed on it, dimly aware of Julian's voice, she watched it, her lips curled in disgust. It was on the move again. Keeping her own movements minimal, she reached slowly for the door handle. She pulled at it, lips pressing together at the sharp '*dnk!*' of the door's mechanism. She pushed the door away from her, slid slowly across the driver's seat then hurled herself out of the car.

Pain shooting through her knee, she leapt up, brushing at her legs, her arms, her hair, breath coming in ragged gasps.

Julian was out of the car, staring at her. 'Kate? What is it? What's wrong?'

She stopped, looked at him in disbelief. 'Don't tell me you didn't *see* it?'

'See what?'

'You must have seen it! How could you not?'

She ran past him to the passenger door still standing open. She stopped. She couldn't look. When she was a student here her beloved elderly PhD supervisor had offered to help her address the fear. She'd declined on the basis that it was rarely a problem. She stood, her eyes fastened on the interior of her car. Right now it was a big problem. She could not get inside whilst 'it' was still there.

She gestured to Julian. 'Come and see.'

Uncertain, he came to her then turned to the little car. Head bowed, he leant inside.

After a few seconds he said 'There's nothing here, Kate. Whatever you saw . . .' He stepped away from the car, his face set. 'OK. I've seen it.'

She stared at the car then at him. 'It has to come out. It can't be in there. *Wait.*'

Aiming her key fob at the boot, cringing at its sharp '*thunk!*' she went to open it and eyed its contents, senses keening for any signs of movement, all logic gone. She reached for one of Maisie's plastic snack boxes, picked up a plastic carrier bag between thumb and forefinger, the whole of her car now tainted. She returned to Julian, handed the box to him and saw the expression on his face as he looked at it, then at her.

'I never saw one that big, Kate.'

She turned towards headquarters main entrance. 'It's OK. Stay here and – keep an eye on it. I'll get an officer to sort it out.'

'*No.* I'll do it. Just – give me a minute.'

Box in hand, he approached the car and slowly leant inside. Nothing happened for what seemed like an age. She started at a sudden thump from inside. Julian was out of the car, the plastic lid on the box, a large, dark shape huddled in one corner, unmoving. Flushed, he looked at her, 'Shall I let it go?'

'No. Put the box in here.'

She held out the plastic bag, arms extended, grimacing as he placed the box inside. Even this proximity was too much. 'It's not going anywhere until I know it's not dangerous. I'm taking it to someone who can tell me.' She looked up at him. 'Julian, can you go into UCU and fetch the stag beetle? I'll wait here.'

Inside the School of Geography, Earth and Environmental Sciences, Dr Adrienne Capaldi greeted Hanson. 'You've brought your stag beetle. Sorry I wasn't here when you came the other day.'

'There's something else.'

'OK. Show me the stag first.'

Using fine tweezers, she removed it from its small plastic evidence box and placed it gently on the stage of the microscope.

'This was found near a body, you say?'

'Yes. Within a tarpaulin covering.' Hanson watched as she peered at it through the microscope.

After several seconds, Capaldi spoke, eyes still fixed on the stag beetle. 'There's remnants of a lot of soil and dead wood inside her. Given that and her size, I'd say that she'd mated and was preparing for the arrival of eggs.'

'When would that occur?' asked Hanson.

'Between May and early August.'

Hanson nodded. 'That fits. What kind of habitat would you expect to find it in?'

'As it was around the mating season, it had to be somewhere where she had access to dead wood.'

Hanson frowned. Adam had referred to remnants of dead wood on Elizabeth Williams' body. She didn't recall seeing any at the field but she hadn't been looking for it.

Adrienne removed the remains of the stag and placed it carefully inside its box. She pointed to the lunchbox Hanson had left at the far end of the table.

'Is that the "something else"?'

Seeing Hanson make no move towards it she smiled and went to fetch it.

Hanson retreated to a distant lab stool. 'It looks dangerous to me. I got Julian, my PhD student, to trap it.' She swallowed, her eyes skimming the box's dark, squat occupant.

Adrienne grinned across at her. 'Phobic?' Hanson nodded. As the box lid came off, Adrienne lost the grin. 'Where on earth did you find *her*?'

Hanson shuddered. 'Spare me the pronoun. Is it dangerous?' Adrienne took a strong lens and tweezers and began a close examination. 'She's a big girl, beautifully coloured and – *wow!* – aggressive. You're missing a real treat here.' Hanson remained where she was, eyes averted.

'*Got* it!'

Hanson jerked on the lab stool. Capaldi was looking pleased.

'I've identified her. Green iridescent jaws and no obvious epigyne – that's female genitalia. I can't see them, which is what I would expect. It confirms my earlier gender identification, plus she's got six eyes.'

Hanson was reaching the edge of her endurance. Description was almost as bad as seeing. Adrienne put down the lens with a sharp click, causing another involuntary start.

'Your spider has a name: *Segestria Fiorentina*. She's feisty and capable of delivering a good bite. I'll give her a home here if you don't want her.'

'Where did it come from? Somewhere hot inside a box of bananas?'

Adrienne laughed. 'I think much of that is probably urban myth. No. She is a long way from home but not that far.' She went to a shelf, took down a manila folder and withdrew a single sheet which she handed to Hanson.

'Take this. It's "101" info for our undergrads. It'll tell you all you need to know, plus there's a very nice photograph.' With a grimace, Hanson took the sheet.

'She's a native of Berkshire,' said Adrienne.

Hanson stared at her.

Berkshire.

Hanson returned to headquarters and went straight to UCU. Her colleagues looked up as she came inside. Watts did a double-take.

'What's snapping your garters?'

'I'll show you.'

She pushed Capaldi's information sheet across the table to them, watching as they got the gist.

Watts looked at the illustration with distaste. 'Nasty.'

'How's this relevant to you, Red?' asked Corrigan.

'One just like it was inside my car last night.'

Watts pushed the sheet back to her. 'Like I said, nasty, but let's face it, these things get around.'

'Not from *Berkshire* to Birmingham without a lot of help they don't.'

He frowned at her. 'Meaning?'

She went to the board, hit an icon and pointed. 'The day I spoke to Chris Turner at the college he told me he was going to Berkshire for a few days. See? I made a note of it in case we needed to see him again.'

Her two colleagues exchanged looks. Corrigan pointed at the sheet on the table. 'You suspect Turner of planting that in your car?'

She nodded. 'His attitude to me that day was extremely challenging, so yes, I do.' She had another thought and glanced at Watts. 'I've also had a couple of silent phone calls, remember?'

She brought up the three-dimensional image of the field. 'I've got some information about the stag beetle. Capaldi found soil and dead wood inside it which apparently indicates that it had mated and was preparing for egg-laying. Mating season is May to early August which fits with Elizabeth Williams' disappearance. Whether the stag was in the field would depend on there being a source of rotting wood.'

They came and stood before the screen, examining the field's surface detail. Hanson shook her head. 'There's no rotting wood there that I can see.' She saw Corrigan reach for his keys.

'Where are you going?' she asked.

'To see Chris Turner.'

'I'm coming with you.

Turner lounged in his chair inside the common room, his full attention on Corrigan. So far he hadn't spoken directly to Hanson and barely looked at her.

'For all I know, she's got a downer on men.'

Corrigan pointed at him. 'That's disrespectful.'

Turner yawned widely then stretched, with a brief glance in Hanson's direction. 'You tell me how I'm supposed to have done whatever it is that's happened to her car which frightened her. I don't even know what she drives.'

She looked at him. 'You told me several days ago that you were going to Berkshire.'

'Yes? So?'

Hanson held onto her temper. 'It's relevant to what happened to my car.'

He folded his arms and rested his head back, his half-closed eyes on her. 'I take off for a couple of days and suddenly, somehow, I'm responsible for something I know nothing about. Is that what you're saying?'

She and Corrigan exchanged a glance then stood. They had no proof and Turner knew it. She looked down at him. 'Why would you think it was something which "frightened" me, Mr Turner?'

He looked away. 'Call it a lucky guess.'

They came into UCU. 'He did it. He put that . . . *thing* inside my car. I don't care what he says about not knowing what I drive or how he managed it but he did. For me, he's a suspect in the Elizabeth Williams murder.'

'You might be right, but it's not something we can prove. He's not the only person of interest.' Watts handed her a written sheet of A4. 'Hugh Downey's statement relating to Sean Gill.'

She read it. It tallied with her own experience of the incident near Sarehole Mill. Downey had confirmed that he'd visited the site to dismiss Gill because of suspicions that he was involved in defrauding Renfrew. She thought of their earlier decision to open up the investigation to include Renfrew subcontractors.

'We have to see Aiden Malahide and ask him about Gill's and other workers' access to the offices. If Elizabeth Williams was ever inside them it might have been where she was first seen by whoever killed her.'

'The secretary told me they drop in as and when,' said Watts.

'Malahide has to give us the names of any whom he knows go there most regularly.'

Watts's bulldog features were downturned. 'If we don't get a lead from the subcontractors that will be it for me as far as Renfrew is concerned. I'll want to focus on the persons of interest who actually knew Elizabeth Williams, which means Turner and Vickers.'

Hanson copied Downey's address from his statement. 'I'm going to see Downey's wife. She did some secretarial work at Renfrew last year. I want to know if she recalls a student ringing or calling into the office to ask about work experience. She might also have something to say about the subcontractors.'

'Wouldn't Downey have told her about our investigation into the Williams murder and relayed anything she had to say?' said Corrigan. Hanson looked doubtful. 'He might not have done, you know. My strong impression is that he's very protective of her because of her health.'

'I'd come with you but I've got armed response in half an hour until six thirty this evening.'

Hanson shook her head. 'I can't see either of them today. I'll go and see Nan Downey tomorrow morning. How about we both see Malahide? We'll get the names of the subcontractors who regularly frequented the office last year and follow them up.' She glanced at her open diary. Closing it she put it into her bag. 'I still need a tree surgeon.'

At six forty-five Hanson was tidying the kitchen when the doorbell rang.

She went towards the door and the dark shadow beyond it. She wasn't expecting anybody. *Always on alert. Always the fear. Except when it came to Sean Gill.* Taking a deep breath, she opened it. It was Corrigan.

'Bad timing? I was on my way home and thought I'd look in.'

'No, come in.'

He turned to his car. 'I've brought something with me.'

She watched him open the Volvo's boot and lift out a chainsaw. He brought it inside.

'Look, Corrigan. You don't have to do this. I can take care of it.'

'I know you can but it makes sense. I've got the chainsaw and I don't need hiring.' He waited, seeing her indecision. 'Want to show me this darned tree?'

She led him out of the kitchen doors and around the side of the house. 'It's this one, here.'

He nodded. 'I got it.'

She watched him climb, sure-footed in black work boots, position himself on a low fork to examine the problematic branch, tugging at it, his voice low and pleasant. She followed the lyrics: 'I drove all night to get to you.' He grinned down at her. 'I drove a mile across Harborne, doesn't scan nearly so good.'

TWENTY-SEVEN

Next morning Hanson drove to the Downey's Moseley address, her mind closed to what had been inside her car the previous day. She had a life. She had to get on with it. Something she wouldn't do was give Chris Turner any further satisfaction that his escapade had affected her.

She found the Downey house number and pulled into a space on the opposite side of the road from the large double-fronted Victorian villa. There were close-parked vehicles all along that side, at least two of them 4x4 vehicles, one a Shogun. It could belong to anybody around here or shopping in Moseley Village.

She headed for the house, rang the bell and waited. She reached for it again but stopped at small signs of movement some distance beyond the door. A figure was slowly approaching it. Still unnerved by the incident the previous day, Hanson squared her shoulders, chin up.

The woman who opened the door was pale, almost ethereal and looked to be suffering from a head cold although when she spoke her voice was clear and pleasant.

'Yes? Can I help?'

'Mrs Downey?' She showed her identification. 'My name is Kate Hanson.'

The woman's face broke into a smile. 'Dr Hanson!' She opened the door wide. 'Hugh's told me all about you. Come in!'

Hanson stepped inside the warm house, chiding herself for not taking what she'd learnt about Nan Downey's health into account when she decided to call here.

'Mrs Downey, I'm sorry. I should have phoned first. If you don't feel well enough to talk—'

Nan Downey's quick laughter transformed her face. 'I'm *fine*. It's lovely to see someone and after listening to Hugh I was really curious to meet you. What an exciting job you have. Listen to me chattering and leaving you standing. Come through to the kitchen.'

Hanson followed her along the hall, listening to the light, bubbly voice, noting that she walked with a pronounced limp.

'Hugh has told me a bit about the police investigation you're working on. It's dreadful but your part in it sounds so interesting.' She looked at Kate, her face suddenly serious. 'He also told me about what happened at Sarehole the other day. What an awful experience. He never liked Gill. He wanted rid of him. He's made a statement about him at the big police station in Harborne.'

Hanson nodded. 'I was very grateful that your husband arrived when he did.'

'Hugh was glad he could help.'

Nan led her into a bright kitchen, gesturing towards a room off it. 'I'm painting. When I'm really engrossed I don't hear a thing but today . . .' She shrugged. 'It isn't going so well. Tea? Coffee?' She saw that Hanson was about to refuse and shook her head.

'*Please*. Don't say no. I so rarely get visitors these days.'

Seeing Hanson's smiled nod, she lifted a large tortoiseshell cat from one of the chairs. 'Sit down. I'll get some coffee going.'

Hanson took in the loose smock over a roll-neck sweater and trousers. She glanced up at Nan. Her eyes did look bleary. She watched the hesitant turn, followed by slow progress across the kitchen. She decided not to offer help. She'd gained the impression from Hugh Downey that Nan took pride in the independence she still had. Gazing around the bright, yellow-painted kitchen she looked towards the room Nan had indicated, a decorative metal doorstop propping open the door. Just visible was the splayed leg of what looked like an easel.

Nan brought coffee and a plate of shortbread to the table. 'I like to bake, especially biscuits.' She smiled. 'Hugh loves them yet he still manages to stay slim. Being so active, I suppose.' She sat opposite Hanson. 'That's what he's doing today. Rushing from one site to another, checking progress because he's taken a couple of days off. Ever since I was ill a lot has fallen on his shoulders but he manages to do everything with a cheerful will. He helped his father take care of his mother when she was ill, so he's sensitive to what I need.' She looked away and Hanson thought she saw tears in her eyes.

'He works so hard. Sometimes, he's naughty because he won't slow down, won't stop.' She blinked. 'But I'm grateful to him every day for all that he does do for me.' She looked up with a quick, bright smile. 'Sorry to chatter on. It's because I don't see many people. You've come here for a reason.' She looked at Hanson expectantly.

'Yes. I thought you might be able to help with our investigation,' said Hanson.

Nan clasped her hands together. 'How exciting. I will if I can.'

'You worked at Renfrew as a secretary for a while?'

Nan gave a brief nod. 'Yes. Only on a casual basis when they needed extra help. I enjoyed it but then I had to stop. That was in May of last year.'

Seeing that no more details were forthcoming Hanson asked, 'When you worked there, do you recall any kind of inquiry from anyone, a student maybe, about work experience?'

Nan was silent for a few seconds, her brow furrowed. She shook her head. 'No, sorry. I don't recall anything like that.'

Hanson pressed on. 'This inquiry could have come in a letter or an email or even an unannounced visit to the office. The person making the inquiry might have referred to it as an "internship".'

Nan put a hand to her forehead. 'Let me think about it. It sometimes takes me a while to remember things.' After a few more seconds she looked at Hanson with a headshake. 'Sorry. Tell me about the kind of person who would have been asking.'

'It would have been a student. She's likely to have been around nineteen years old.'

'She?' asked Nan.

'Yes, if it was the person we're interested in.'

Seeing Nan still frowning, Hanson changed tack. 'Can you tell me about the subcontractors employed by Renfrew when you worked there?'

'That's something I can help you with. There were always quite a few of those. I didn't meet them all.' She leant towards Hanson. 'Gill was one of them. He'd pop in to bring timesheets, that kind of thing. There were a few others as well. Nice, cheerful men, mostly.' She smiled. 'A bit loud.'

'Did you feel uncomfortable with any of them being around?'

Nan shook her head. 'No. Not even Gill. Actually, I did mention to Aiden once that I thought one or two of them dropped into the office to scrounge coffee or help themselves to things. Dee, the full-time secretary, didn't like it but Aiden, Hugh's partner, didn't do anything about it. It wasn't a big problem anyway.'

They both heard the sound of a key in the door. Nan got slowly to her feet.

'That's Hugh. He drops in whenever he can to check that I'm OK.'

Hanson recognised Hugh Downey's voice coming from the direction of the hall.

'Nancy Louise Downey, I know your boyfriend's here and you can get rid of him right now, do you hear?'

She saw Nan's face light up as the kitchen door opened and he came in. He stopped when he saw Hanson.

'What's all this?' He smiled at Nan and kissed her cheek. 'You've been painting and now you're socialising. I've warned you about holding soirées.'

The small scene was full of the gentle affection between two people who'd been together a long time. Hanson felt out of place. As if he'd picked up on her thoughts, Hugh Downey turned to her with a wry grin.

'Don't rush off and don't mind us. I haven't seen this woman for a whole three hours. Has she looked after you?'

Hanson smiled. 'Yes, she has.'

He sat next to Nan, his eyes on her face. 'Memo to social butterfly wife: the doctor told you that a daily nap is a must and you were up very early this morning.' Now Hanson really did feel like an interloper as he took his wife's hand and she rested her head against his shoulder.

He softened his voice. 'How can I trust you to do as you're told while I'm away?'

'I will, Hugh. I promise.'

He stood. 'Come on.'

He walked her to the door, looking down at her, his face mock-stern. 'Half an hour's rest and then I'll bring you some tea.'

She turned to Hanson. 'Bye, Dr Hanson. Please come again.' She turned slowly away.

Hugh Downey grinned. 'Go on. Skedaddle!' He watched her go then closed the kitchen door, his face sombre. 'She tires very quickly but it's the devil's own job to get her to take it easy.'

He took a chair opposite Hanson. 'Anything I can do to help?'

'I want to thank you for yesterday.'

He looked surprised. 'You mean Gill? Forget it. I'm glad I was around. We have something in common where he's concerned. He's furious with both of us.'

'You've dismissed him for dishonesty?'

'And being an idle sod, if you'll excuse the expression. Gill is a con man. Aiden told me he'd found that Gill has been raising fake invoices for goods in Renfrew's name. Aiden was onto it before it had properly got going but it was an ingenious scheme. It might have cost us a lot if it had run on. We didn't know about his previous conviction although I was aware of a space in his CV. Not that a police record would mean we'd automatically rule anybody out of a job.' He looked at her. 'Is that why you're here or is it about the murder of the student?'

'Your secretary mentioned that Nan used to do secretarial work at Renfrew. I thought she might recall a casual approach by a young woman asking for an internship.'

He looked doubtful. 'Did she?'

'No.'

He sat back, his face serious. 'I'd have been surprised if she had. If anything like that had happened while Nan worked there, I doubt she'd remember it.' He hesitated and Hanson guessed he was wondering whether or how to proceed.

'I don't know if you've ever lost anyone who mattered.' He raised a quick hand. 'And I'm not asking, but when Nan had her stroke I honestly believed she was going to die.' He paused. 'We don't have children. Everything looked very bleak. But she rallied and I got her back.' He looked up at Hanson. 'Nan's still with me, we're still together but it's not the same. Before it happened, I suppose like most people I thought of life and death as two separate states. I've learned that that's not entirely true. There's such a lot she doesn't remember. Things we did together. We're close apart, if that makes any sense. Today is a good day. There are others when she isn't as mobile as you saw and she gets very frustrated.' He ran his hand through his short hair. 'And I'm ashamed to admit I get a bit grumpy because I'm tired.' He gazed across the table at Hanson.

'Maybe you'll understand when I say that I think it's possible to have a little death.'

Hanson chose her words. 'I'm sorry. I'm also sorry for intruding.'

He shook his head. 'Don't be. It was nice to see Nan looking so upbeat. Something else I've learned over the last year: friends don't always hang around when illness happens. I don't mean friends we share. I'm talking about the girlfriends Nan had. There weren't that many. Three or four at most but it's sad for her because they don't call or visit so much now. She's still as sociable as she ever was but she doesn't always have the energy for visitors.' He looked across at her.

'I took our life together for granted. Maybe we could all do with cherishing what we have a bit more.'

Hanson was thinking of those in her own life whom she cherished. 'Isn't that what we all do, though? Take people for granted because we're so busy with daily living? I don't think we should blame ourselves for that.'

He gave her a close look. 'Is that what you really think?' She nodded. 'Yes. I also think it's inevitable to feel some guilt whenever there's loss. It's not logical. It's what happens.'

They both stood. He walked her to the front door. 'Getting back to what you were asking Nan about this work experience, I'm sorry neither I nor Aiden were any help.'

'Is it at all possible that due to pressure of work either one of you might have forgotten something like that?'

He thought about it. 'I hear what you're saying. Aiden and I are like ships passing but I know I never had that kind of request. Feel free to speak to him again about it. I'm sure he won't mind. When Nan has rested I could try asking her for you? See if she recalls anything?'

Hanson shook her head. 'I don't want to cause her unnecessary stress. Actually, I'm hoping to see Mr Malahide this morning.'

'He's in the office. Drop in and see him.'

'One last thing. What level of access do Renfrew's subcontractors have to the office?'

He gave it some thought as they paused by the closed front door. 'They call there when they need to. To collect plans and other paperwork and to give Dee their timesheets. That's probably how Gill got hold of blank invoices for his scheme. It's shown us that we need to make the office less available. Be less trusting.'

He opened the door for her. 'Thanks for coming, Dr Hanson. I know it was a professional visit but I haven't seen Nan so buoyant in a long time.'

TWENTY-EIGHT

Corrigan rang the bell at Renfrew. Hanson was aware that the usual light-heartedness between them was missing. 'Something wrong?' she asked.

'Sean Gill got bail this morning.'

She stared up at him, open-mouthed. 'He *what*?'

'The magistrates decided against remand on the basis that his 2001 conviction was "old" and they took his subsequent lack of offending into account.'

Dee, Renfrew's secretary, opened the door to them. 'Come in. Hugh phoned to say you were coming. Aiden's expecting you.' She turned quickly to find him standing behind her.

'Here he is.' She laughed. 'I never hear him coming.' Malahide gestured for them to come inside.

'Dr Hanson, Lieutenant Corrigan. Hugh said you wanted to talk to me but he didn't say why. I'm assuming it's about Sean Gill and his dishonesty?'

They followed him into the comfortable sitting room-cum-office. Hanson glanced at the pale, soft looking rug, thinking that Corrigan was almost certainly doing the same.

Malahide went to the deep bay behind his desk, opened one of the windows and fussily pulled at one of the curtains. 'It's a little warm in here, don't you think?'

'What can you tell us about Sean Gill, sir?' asked Corrigan

Malahide turned to look at him, his plump face annoyed. 'He'd worked for us for quite a while but he was hardly more than satisfactory. He took occasional days off but we weren't aware of any dishonesty until now. We're a small company. Any theft by people who work for us is a threat to our viability, particularly if a scam such as Gill's had continued.'

'Has your secretary indicated any problems with him?'

Malahide nodded. 'She complained about one or two of the contractors going into her desk drawer but she didn't name him specifically.' He caught sight of Corrigan's face. 'Oh.' He looked suddenly prim, his face heating up. 'You mean something more . . . personal? No, nothing like that as far as I know.'

'How about the other subcontractors. Do they freely access the building?'

'I wouldn't say "freely",' he said. 'They need to come here to bring timesheets and so on, although Hugh is now talking about providing each team with a laptop or asking them to email that kind of thing from their phones. He tends to be less trusting than I am. I suppose we both need to be more vigilant.'

'I guess that's important in business: trust and a sharp eye.'

Malahide sighed. 'This business with Gill proves that they're both essential.'

'Does Renfrew network with other businesses to build trust and support?' asked Corrigan.

Malahide looked from him to Hanson and smiled. 'What I think of as the American business model. Yes, we do. Two or three times a year we host meetings here. We invite companies sympathetic to our ecological aims. It helps us build business links. It helps us judge which businesses are ethically and financially sound before we consider possible collaboration in projects. Hugh is the one for the ecology, of course. Business-wise, and he says it himself, he doesn't get involved. I take care of that side of things.'

Corrigan was looking thoughtful. 'You organise those business meetings?'

'The networking? Yes.'

Corrigan gazed around. 'This is a great room. Big enough for meetings like that?'

Malahide nodded. 'Yes. We open the doors so that people can circulate in the hall.'

Watching him, Hanson could see that he was uncertain where Corrigan was heading. She wasn't entirely sure herself although she had an idea.

'You also use this room for interviews,' he said.

Malahide looked bemused. 'We don't interview that often.'

'We asked you previously if you recalled a young woman coming here either spontaneously or by arrangement with a request for work experience.'

Malahide stared at him. 'Yes. I told you, no.'

Corrigan nodded. 'Have you considered that a forensic sweep of this room might yield evidence which indicates she was here?'

Hanson knew that such an action couldn't happen. There was no justification. She glanced at Malahide. He clearly didn't know this. The amiability had drained from him, like a plug being pulled. The plump face heated up again.

'I don't have to consider it. She didn't . . . She never came into . . .' He stopped, his mouth slack. The words were equivocal but the look on Malahide's face said it all. He faltered, his hand going to his mouth.

'If there's something on your mind, sir, you need to tell us,' said Corrigan quietly. Malahide didn't speak. 'Here or headquarters. What's your choice?'

Malahide's face looked pallid, doughy. 'It's not what you think,' he whispered. 'I didn't do anything to her.'

'Who?' asked Corrigan.

'That student you're asking about. Elizabeth Williams.'

Corrigan's eyes were fixed on him. 'What exactly are you telling us?'

A sheen of perspiration had appeared on Malahide's fleshy face. 'She was here,' he whispered. 'I don't know how it's come to this. It's not what you think.'

Corrigan stood and fixed him with a direct look. 'Aiden Malahide I'm arresting you on suspicion—'

Hanson looked down at the soft cream rug as Malahide was informed of his rights, then back to him. He looked as though he was about to pass out.

'Do you want us to inform Mr Downey?' she asked.

He looked at her, horrified. 'No! I don't want anyone to know about this. It's all a mistake. A misunderstanding.' His head dropped forward onto his hands.

They were inside UCU, Nuttall wearing a jubilant expression. 'Good work.'

'He hasn't been questioned yet,' said Corrigan.

'You've arrested him so make it stick. Forensics are getting samples from the rug in his office to compare with what was on the girl.' He looked at Corrigan. 'Hope you're well up on UK law because you need to get a move on. You've got twenty-four hours to charge him.'

'Thirty-six if it's a serious case,' responded Corrigan easily.

Nuttall looked rattled. 'Malahide's been informed of his rights?'

'Yep, and he's not asked for a lawyer yet but he will. As soon as the shock of arrest wears off.'

Hanson was inside the observation room, searching Malahide's face as he waited in the room next door. He looked stunned. She watched her colleagues take seats opposite him, listened as Watts delivered the caution. Malahide stared down at the table.

'Tell us about Elizabeth Williams,' said Watts.

Malahide's voice sounded as though he hadn't used it in days. 'She came to the office.'

'When?'

He cleared his throat, looking fuddled. 'It was the Wednesday. The secretary had gone and Hugh was taking time off because Nan was ill.' He looked down at his hands.

Watts gazed at him. 'Why didn't you tell us this when we first saw you?'

Malahide shrugged his plump shoulders. 'I don't know.'

'Come on, Mr Malahide. If you don't, who does?'

Hanson's eyes were on Malahide's hands. They were gripped together, shaking.

'That first day you came I wasn't expecting it. I'd hardly given her a thought since she came to the office that day. She was there five minutes, if that.'

Hanson's eyes were fixed on the plump face. *Hardly a thought since.*

Watts glanced at Corrigan then back. 'When you say "hardly", that suggests to me you did think about her.'

Malahide looked up at him, unfocused. 'What? No, but I did just wonder why she hadn't contacted me.'

Hanson guessed that her colleagues' thinking was similar to hers: if what Malahide had said so far was the truth, that he'd first met Elizabeth Williams on a Wednesday, he would have had to see her again if he'd murdered her.

'When did you see her again?'

'I didn't,' said Malahide.

'You didn't see her later that week?' asked Watts.

Malahide was getting agitated. 'I just *told* you, I didn't see her again. That was it. As I said, I didn't give her another thought.'

Watts's eyes were fastened on his face. 'Her disappearance was on the news.'

Malahide shook his head. 'I don't have a television. I listen to music.'

'Why were you expecting to hear from her?'

Malahide's face was flushed. He looked at the floor, the walls, the glass beyond which Hanson was standing. Anywhere but at the two officers.

Watts sat forward. 'Come on, Mr Malahide. You just said you wondered why she never got back in touch.'

'Please. Let me get this straight in my head.' His voice a monotone, he said, 'She seemed a nice girl. Keen on what Renfrew is about. Strong, athletic. Ideal for the physical work involved in conservation, but I knew Hugh wouldn't allow it. I'd told him often enough about the insurance implications. But there are other firms like ours, larger set ups which I thought might be more flexible. I wanted to help her. I told her I'd contact a couple of them for her. I suggested she give me a couple of days.' He looked down at his hands.

'Actually, it was a good job she didn't ring back because I forgot. I was under unbelievable pressure at the time. I was doing Hugh's job as well as my own. It was very difficult for me with the long hours and being on site in all weathers.' He looked agitated at the memory.

Watts frowned. 'What was causing you all that stress exactly?'

Malahide looked away, saying nothing.

Watts slow-nodded. 'OK, Mr Malahide. Let's get back to the brass tacks of the day Elizabeth Williams arrived at your office. What time was it?'

'I finished early that day. It was five thirty.'

'You sound very certain.'

'I am. My mother was expecting me.'

'Where?'

'At her care home.'

'Where?'

'Solihull.'

Hanson looked up as the observation room door opened and Nuttall came inside. He nodded to her then looked intently at Malahide through the glass as Watts spoke.

'Why was she expecting you that day?'

'I visit her regularly, two, three times a week.'

Watts sat back, his eyes riveted on Malahide. 'That's commendable. Very dutiful.'

Hanson saw the first indication of annoyance on Malahide's face.

'It is *not* duty. My mother is very important to me.'

'Got anyone else in your life, Mr Malahide? A partner?'

'No.'

'Come on, Mr Malahide,' encouraged Watts, his eyes searching his face. 'You need to be straight with us.'

'There is somebody, although I don't see what it has to do with this.' Hanson saw that the shock of arrest was wearing off. 'It's a casual arrangement. No. That sounds wrong. We're good friends. Occasionally, a little more.'

'What's this person's name?'

Malahide was silent. Hanson watched as the clock in the observation room ticked away the time.

'Marjorie.'

'Surname?'

He shook his head. All he would say was that Marjorie was the forty-eight-year-old head of a primary school who sometimes accompanied him to business functions and the occasional concert and had done so for the last ten years. At those times she often stayed overnight at his flat.

'Is she a single woman?' demanded Watts.

There was a brief pause. 'Married.'

Watts regarded him across folded arms. 'Right. You're highly stressed, it's five thirty, possibly a Wednesday, you're just leaving your office to visit your mother and Elizabeth Williams arrives. Carry on.'

'I asked her inside.'

Hanson saw her two colleagues exchange a quick glance. Nuttall raised his fist in the air.

'She only came as far as the hall. She told me she wanted one of those internships you hear about these days. I said our company couldn't provide it but that I might be able to help and to give me a couple of days, then ring me. She never did. I never heard from her again.'

Watts's eyes drifted over Malahide's sweating face. 'Why didn't you tell us this when we first came to see you?'

'I just thought it would cause unnecessary complications. I hadn't done anything wrong. I didn't intend to deceive you.'

'Obviously,' said Watts, heavy on the irony.

Malahide rallied. 'Look, I'm here without a solicitor. Surely that shows you I've got nothing to do with your investigation?'

Watts gave him a level look. 'The sorts of people we meet often do the same. They just stick with their story, no matter how unconvincing.' He sat back on his chair with a glance at Corrigan.

'Sir, would you confirm that you live on the top floor of the Renfrew building?' he asked.

'Yes. Why?' Hanson watched Malahide get the implication behind the question. His whole body tensed.

'She never went up to my flat! Never.'

'We hear you, sir, and we have officers there right now, verifying it or otherwise.'

To Hanson, Malahide looked like a marathon runner who has just realised he cannot go on. His body sagged.

'I don't need a solicitor because I haven't done anything wrong but I want to call mine. Now.'

Hearing this and without a word, Nuttall turned on his heel and headed for the door.

They walked Renfrew's sweeping staircase to the second floor, Watts was looking jubilant but trying to suppress it.

'There's something dodgy about him that's as obvious to me as a cracked bell,' he said as they reached the door of Malahide's flat.

Corrigan knocked and a white-suited SOCO opened the door to them. Within five minutes they were similarly covered and moving around the flat.

Hanson's first impression was of opulence, an echo of the office on the ground floor. She moved around the large, ultra-neat sitting room, its colours predominantly honey-toned, her feet sinking into soft, camel-coloured carpeting.

The kitchen confirmed her second impression. Despite the presence of several SOCO's and their equipment, it was immaculate. She opened a wall cupboard to stare at rows of neat tins and packets. Regimented. Facing outwards. Arranged by content and size. She closed it, went on to the refrigerator. Inside it was the same spotless, regimented story. Bottles on one side. Jars on the other. She reached inside to examine the fresh food, all of it shrouded in plastic, neat with handwritten labels showing date of purchase. Nothing out of date.

She heard Corrigan's soft call of her name. Closing the refrigerator she left the kitchen and found him in what looked to be the main bedroom. Watts was crouched at the open doors of the wardrobe. He looked up as Hanson stared at what was probably twenty-plus white cotton shirts, each on a beige plastic hanger, each facing to the right. The several linen suits were similarly hung, all of the same style, each varying slightly in colour from cream to camel. The footwear below formed a pristine line, each item containing a shoetree, each pair similar to its neighbour: beige, suede, laced.

Watts was still looking at her. 'No wonder he was stressed doing Downey's site job. Out in all weathers, mud, dust, you name it. So stressed that when he saw Elizabeth Williams he completely lost it.'

They had to wait over two hours for the forensic results on the rug in Malahide's office. Comparison of the fibres from the rug in the ground floor was inconclusive. Adam had told them that although the fibres 'were of similar construction' they were insufficiently distinctive to be regarded as a match. There was nothing to indicate that Elizabeth Williams had lain on it. Malahide had already admitted that during the last year he'd had the rug professionally cleaned. The forensic sweep of his flat had produced no indication that Elizabeth Williams had ever been inside it. It was the same story for the ground floor office. Malahide was released without charge due to insufficient evidence.

Watts was wearing a determined look. 'I don't give a damn what the evidence does or doesn't say. He's iffy and he's staying at the top of my list. He lied through his teeth about never having seen Williams and now we've seen another side of him. Nobody has a wardrobe like that, a kitchen like that.'

'You might do if you needed the comfort of feeling totally in control of your life,' said Hanson.

'Why would feeling in control be such a big deal for him?'

'I don't know,' said Hanson evenly. 'We know hardly anything about him so far.'

Watts frowned at her. 'No, but we will. He had that office rug cleaned. That's another strike against him, if you ask me.' He looked at Corrigan. 'What do you think about him for the Williams murder?'

'What we know so far is he's a guy who has to have cleanliness and order. My jury's still out. He's a wait-and-see.'

Watts was thinking, lips pursed. 'What he said about this woman friend. We've only got his word that she was anything more than somebody he took out occasionally. I'm not convinced he's in a relationship with a woman of any age. If I'm right what does that tell you?' Hanson gave a slow headshake. 'On its own it wouldn't tell me that he's a stressed-out, sexually repressed killer, which is where you're heading.'

'Have it your way. It still says to me that he could be a mass of sexual frustration – and Elizabeth Williams just happened along at the wrong time.'

Hanson gave him a weary look. 'Chong hasn't confirmed a sexual element to the murder. Plus, if we suspect Malahide of killing Elizabeth Williams we have to consider that he attacked Amy Bennett. So far there's nothing in what she told us to link him to that, including the sketch.'

Watts stood before the board. 'Maybe the two cases are separate after all.'

She stared at him. 'What about the verbal evidence we've got? The words, the phrasing which links them?'

He turned to her. 'Yes, and look who gave us some of it. Myers!'

Corrigan looked across at her. 'Amy didn't provide much physical description of her attacker.'

'No, she didn't but the sketch suggests a thin face whereas Malahide's is plump, soft.' She cast around the table.

'Where is it? The sketch.'

Watts pulled it from a pile of papers and passed it to her. 'The Bennett case is a stumbling block where Malahide's concerned. He's the type who's clueless about what happens under the bonnet of any vehicle.'

Hanson looked up. 'But we know somebody who isn't. Sean Gill.'

Watts took the sketch from her. 'We'll interview him again in the next few hours, this time about the Bennett attack.' He studied it. 'Corrigan says this is "powerful". I see what he's saying but I'll tell you right now, for identification it's a non-starter. Inside Amy Bennett's head is a bloke in a right state, his face distorted by how he's feeling and she's terrified. It's possible he looks nothing like this.'

Hanson glanced at the sketch again. He had a point. A few hours before, they'd believed they had a breakthrough. Both cases were now in disarray.

*   *   *

At home in her study Hanson listened to her call ringing out. She'd conducted the conversation several times inside her head over the last few days. She took a deep breath and squared her shoulders as her call was picked up. A deep voice she recognised came into her ear.

'Charlie Hanson.'

Every thought, every planned word deserted her. All that was in her head right now was that her mother had always called him Charles.

'Hello?'

She gripped the phone. 'It's Kate.'

The silence on the line lasted an age. She closed her eyes. How long was it since they'd last spoken? Four years? Longer. Maisie hadn't long started school and Hanson had phoned to tell him about the IQ test results. She recalled his delight and the subtle hints she'd picked up that he wanted to see her and Maisie. She'd chosen not to respond to them. Life was simpler that way. He'd chosen to leave her life. She accepted it. Right now, she didn't want this conversation. She didn't want or need him back in her life. But Maisie did.

The deep voice was inside her ear again, warm but tentative. '*Kate?* What a lovely surprise. How are you?'

She got straight to the reason for the call. 'Maisie is asking to see you.'

She picked up genuine pleasure in his response. '*Really?* That's great news.' There was a brief silence. 'How do you feel about it?'

She gripped the phone. 'You and I need to discuss it.'

'I could come to the house—'

'No. I prefer somewhere neutral.' There was a short pause.

'It's your choice.'

'Yes, it is. We need to discuss the practicalities of any meeting you have with Maisie.'

'I understand that.'

His voice had sent Hanson back to the day he'd left. She'd come home from school to find that the first man she'd ever loved was gone and her mother angry and silent, refusing to give any explanation. It was two years before Hanson saw him again and only sporadically after that. She had to ensure that Charlie Hanson understood her concerns about his meeting Maisie. She needed a promise from him, but she wasn't about to discuss it now. When she did raise it, she had to see his face, look into his eyes.

'Good. Let's agree a date, time and place.'

'You wouldn't consider coming to my home?' he said.

My home.

She'd never been there although he'd once shown her a photograph of a wide-fronted house near Worcester. Maybe he'd moved since but wherever he was living she wouldn't go there. She didn't want to meet anyone he might be living with. She didn't need tangible evidence that he'd moved on.

'I prefer to meet here in the city.'

They agreed a date and time. She ended the call then tidied her desk, ignoring the ache inside her throat. She was doing this for Maisie. She would set the rules. One thing had to be clear between them: if Charlie Hanson wanted to be involved in Maisie's life he had to assure Hanson he understood that he could not leave it when it suited him.

TWENTY-NINE

I t was midday when Hanson came into UCU, stopped momentarily by the casts of the tyre and boot impressions from the garden centre lying on the table. Her colleagues were examining them. She went and ran her fingers over the rough surface of the boot impression. Adam picked it up and pointed out features.

'It's a Timberland Pro Pitboss. A work boot with a steel toecap. The print was found near the spot where Amy Bennett says the vehicle was parked. We preserved it with hair spray before we made the cast. Take a close look at the detail.' He pointed at the grooves in the sole then picked up an enlarged photograph of it.

'You can see on this and the cast itself how sharp the detail is. See these wood fibres caught in the cast?'

Hanson studied cast and photograph. *Such a lot of wood in this case. Including a site hut with a wooden floor.*

'This was the only boot print we found so I can't tell you anything about the wearer in terms of stature or gait. The boot itself is a size nine so I doubt he's six feet tall. We examined the boots worn by Sean Gill when he was arrested. He takes a seven-and-a-half and the make and soles were different. We didn't find any other boots in his possession. Which doesn't mean he's never had any. We know that Malahide takes a nine.' They were silent as he put down the cast and reached for the one of the tyre.

'The tyre track is from the same area. Here're the photographs we took of it. It's a Goodyear Wrangler. The track width indicates a large vehicle. Amy Bennett thought the one she saw at the garden centre was a Jeep, possibly a Shogun?' They nodded. 'We've compared this track with a database of tyre designs and measurements. It's consistent with tyres suitable for both vehicles. Gill doesn't have his own transport. He gets lifts in a van owned by one of his co-workers.' He gathered the evidence together.

'None of this helps you right now. Once you have a suspect, let us know and we'll examine his footwear and vehicle. Assuming he's still got them.'

Adam had gone. Watts was not happy.

'All Malahide's got in his wardrobe is around a dozen pairs of near-identical suede boots and shoes.' He glanced at Hanson. 'Which I think is more than odd, even if you don't.'

'Do we know what car he drives?' she asked.

Corrigan nodded. 'A silver Lexus. We watched him secure it before we brought him in.'

Watts was reluctant to let it go. 'None of which means he never wore heavy work boots when he was working all hours to fill in for Downey and never got access to a 4x4.'

The phone rang and Watts reached for it. Corrigan stood.

'Coffee, Red?'

'No thanks. I'm going. I need to be back at the university in an hour or so.'

She glanced at Watts talking into the phone, saw the look on his face.

'What?' she mouthed.

He held up a hand. 'Yes. OK. Leave it with us, Dee. We'll check it out. Yes. We'll let you know.' He replaced the phone.

'That was the secretary at Renfrew. She's in a state. She's been trying to speak to Nan Downey for most of the morning but getting no reply. She's worried because Mrs Downey doesn't go out much.'

'Where's Hugh Downey?'

'At some conference in Edinburgh. When he's away he gets the secretary to phone his house on a daily basis in case he can't. I said I'd go over with Corrigan and take a look.'

Hanson checked her watch. 'She knows me. If she's ill, it might help if I was there. I'll come with you.'

They walked the path to the house. Watts rang the bell. Hanson listened to it drift and fade into silence. He raised his hand again. 'Wait,' said Hanson. 'She moves fairly slowly. Give her a chance to reach the door.'

After a pause of several seconds, the sound of Watts's fist pounding the door reverberated inside the house. It also died. He pounded again. Beyond the door, the house sounded empty, lifeless. Watts peered through the narrow glazed window to one side.

'Maybe she has gone out,' he said.

Hanson recalled what she'd learned on her last visit here. 'I think she's able to manage a short walk but didn't the secretary say she'd been trying to make contact for several hours?'

'Does she drive?'

'I don't know.'

'I'll take a look around back,' said Corrigan, heading for the side of the house. He was back in less than a minute.

'There's a ground-floor window open but no sign of forced entry. It leads into what looks like a storeroom off the hall. Given what we know about her health, I'm going inside.'

As Corrigan disappeared down the side of the house again, Hanson gazed up at the house, all its windows closed. They waited, hearing sounds from inside. A quick movement inside the hall, a shadow on glass and Corrigan swung open the door.

They entered. It felt chill.

'Hello! Mrs Downey? Nan?' called Hanson.

Getting nothing but silence they moved along the hall.

She headed for the door directly ahead which she knew led into the kitchen. It wasn't closed, just pulled to. She raised her hand to it. Watts arrived at her side.

'Easy, doc. We're first in.'

The door swung slowly open. The kitchen was cold, empty, orderly.

She followed her colleagues inside, saw them look around it then walk to the back door. She heard a key turn in the lock.

'She could be outside,' said Watts. 'If she is, we'll give you a shout.'

Hanson nodded, her eyes drifted around the kitchen. It was just as she remembered it except for the warmth. Nan Downey's warmth. She saw the glass cookie jar, the cafetière half full. She placed her hand against it. Cold. Turning, she saw the door leading to Nan's studio. It was closed.

She went to it, reached for the handle then pulled back at the faintest of sounds from inside. Heart rate soaring, she looked in the direction of the back door. Neither of her colleagues was visible. If it was Nan inside, she needed help. Grasping the handle, she pushed it down and threw open the door.

A screeching, formless shape rushed her and shot past. Hanson spun, gasping as the large tortoiseshell cat halted and cowered in the corner of the kitchen, puffed-up and hissing. Getting control of her breathing, she slowly approached it, keeping her voice low.

'Shhh . . . It's OK. Don't be frightened.' It spat and cowered.

With more shushing noises she went to it, crouched beside it, reaching out a tentative hand to rub the top of its head between its ears. The cat lifted its head to her hand, weaving to one side then the other.

'There. You see? You're fine. Where's Nan, mmm? How about some milk?'

Standing, she looked down at multiple paw prints on pale tiles. Prints of varying colour and clarity. Some the richest, darkest red, others with a mere hint of colour. Too startled, too focused on the cat to notice them before, she turned. They led back to the studio.

Paint. Has to be paint. Please. Make it paint.

She pushed the door wide. Paint came in tubes. It squeezed out thick and held its shape. It didn't form pools. Hanson's hands rose to her mouth. Nan Downey was on her back, her head surrounded by a halo of pooled blood, the metal doorstop close by, her neck a mess of gore and blood, her eyes turned to the ceiling. She looked surprised.

Hanson found herself at the back door. '*Here!*'

Minutes passed like seconds, her head filled with noise. Her colleagues' quick footsteps, a siren clamour, the doorbell shrilling, the door knocker's *bang!-bang!-bang!* More footsteps and the voices of paramedics as they entered the hall and headed for the kitchen and the studio.

'No need to rush,' she whispered. 'We're hours too late.'

THIRTY

Hanson was bringing her afternoon lecture to a close. She'd come here directly from the Downey's house and was glad now that she had. She'd filled her head with work until she was able to think about Nan Downey. She pointed up at the change of screen. 'This is the best way I know to convey the importance of early case linkage. These six cases each feature four plus murders.' She aimed the laser at one then another. 'If linkage had been identified earlier in these two it would probably have saved a further eight lives . . .'

Sensing movement at the back of the auditorium she looked up. Her two colleagues had come into the lecture hall and were standing discretely to one side.

'OK. Anyone who wants the references, please see Crystal. You know where to find her.'

Watts and Corrigan came down the stairs towards her as students streamed either side of them.

'We've just finished at the Downey's house and we're on our way to headquarters,' said Watts. 'We're expecting Hugh Downey in the next hour. You free now?'

She closed down images inside her head of kindly, lonely Nan and her cat's blood-mired paws.

'I'll see you there.'

Hanson listened as Watts read Chong's initial report on Nan Downey. It was short.

'All we know so far is that somebody caved her head in with the doorstop then struck her in the neck for good measure.'

She bit her lip. 'Do we have an idea when?'

'Not yet.'

'Does Hugh Downey know what's happened?' she asked.

'No. We've stifled the news until he gets here and we can tell him. I've sent a couple of officers to the airport to meet him.' He checked the time. 'He should be on his way here now and he'll be guessing it's more than a problem at his office.'

The phone rang. Corrigan reached for it then hung up. 'He's here.'

They went to reception. Hugh Downey was gazing out of the window, a small carry-on by his side. He turned to them, looking tired and worried.

'Is this about Aiden? Dee rang to tell me you'd arrested him. Look, I want to help but I need to get home. I haven't managed to speak to my wife in a while—'

'Come in here for a minute please, Mr Downey,' said Corrigan, his hand on his arm as he opened the door of the small informal interview room.

Downey hesitated then went inside. Hanson retrieved the forgotten carry-on and brought it in with her. He looked at each of them in turn.

'My phone's flat. May I call home from here?'

Watts indicated a chair. 'Have a seat, please, Mr Downey.'

Hanson's gaze was on the floor. She enjoyed her work with the police. She enjoyed the challenge, the pressure to understand and explain human deviant behaviour which it brought. The downside was what she'd seen at the Downey house. Another downside was the situation they were now in. Hugh Downey was about to be given the worst possible news. The atmosphere was charged, her colleagues' faces grave. She watched as Downey looked from one to the other.

'What's wrong?' His eyes darkened. 'Something's happened to Nan, hasn't it? Somebody's hurt her.'

Watts told him that his wife was dead.

Hanson made herself look at Downey. The mix of emotions on his face was indescribable. She thought she could see disbelief. He tried to speak, failed, tried again. He stared at them then covered his face with his hands. She dropped her gaze as the dry, racking sobs came. After what felt like an age, Watts spoke again.

'We're very sorry, Mr Downey.'

'I don't understand,' whispered Downey. 'Why would anybody want to hurt Nan?' He covered his face and wept. Hanson thought that she'd never heard such a desolate sound.

'We don't know,' said Watts.

'Where was she?'

'At home.'

Downey's head came up. '*What?*'

He stared at them, aghast. 'That's not possible . . . I assumed she'd gone for a walk and been knocked down. Mugged or something.'

'Somebody got inside the house, possibly through a side window.'

Downey clamped his hands over his mouth. They waited again. After a couple of minutes he got a semblance of control.

'What happened?'

'She was struck on the head.'

'This can't be. It's impossible. Where is she? I have to see her.' He looked up at Hanson, his eyes red, unfocused.

She asked, 'Is there anyone we can call to be with you?'

He shook his head. 'I . . . Can't think.'

Watts gave a slow nod. 'You got any relatives living in Birmingham, Mr Downey?'

'What?' Downey shook his head. 'No. Can you phone Aiden?'

'We will. You've been in Edinburgh this last couple of days?'

Downey looked up, his face a blank. 'Edinburgh?'

'When did you leave Birmingham for Edinburgh, sir?' asked Corrigan.

'Yesterday. No. The day before . . . I think.'

'Were you with people who know you?'

He nodded. 'Some of them. An ecology conference. I did a presentation. You tend to see the same faces at those things. We were all staying at the same hotel.'

'Which one, sir?'

Downey looked at Corrigan, his eyes empty. There was no indi-cation that he was seeing the relevance of the questions he was being asked. Hanson had never seen anyone look so exhausted.

'Radisson.'

'When did you last speak to your wife?' asked Watts.

Downey ran his hand over his forehead. 'Have to think. It was yesterday. The evening. Around nine.'

'How was your wife when you spoke, sir?'

Downey stared straight ahead, bereft. 'Fine,' he whispered. 'She told me she'd had a good day.' His head dropped down.

'OK, sir. We'll contact Mr Malahide to let him know you're on your way. We'll provide transport.'

Downey rallied. He shook his head. 'No. I've changed my mind. I just want to go home, please.'

Hanson and her colleagues exchanged looks. Downey had just

been told his wife had been murdered at their home. He hadn't fully absorbed it.

'I'm sorry but we can't let you do that, sir,' said Corrigan.

Downey looked at him then bowed his head.

Downey had left headquarters looking totally disconnected. Hanson and Corrigan looked up as the door opened and Watts came into UCU.

'I've spoken to the Edinburgh hotel and the airline. What Downey told us checks out.'

She searched Watts's face. 'I couldn't do what you do. Give bad news.'

He shrugged. 'You just have to hope you get it right. Trouble is, it's never clear what's right.'

Hands in his pockets he peered out of the window. 'Years ago I got it wrong. A man died in an accident and I broke the news to his wife. By phone. I've not forgotten that.' He turned from the window. 'I don't suppose she has either.'

Chong arrived in UCU an hour later.

'I've just heard that the chief has given the Nan Downey murder investigation to Upstairs.'

She glanced at Watts. 'Where are you going?'

'I'm on my way up there now to tell them that Sean Gill's got a couple of good motives for murdering Hugh Downey's wife. Downey sacked him a couple of days ago. Gill was ripping off Downey's business.'

Chong's face below the pixie-cut hair regarded him patiently. 'If you've got two minutes to listen to my post-mortem findings you can report them to Upstairs and say there'll be a fuller report in a day or so.' She looked at each of them. 'Nan Downey's cause of death: blunt force trauma to the back of the head from one strike with a cast iron doorstop. There was a second strike to the front of the neck. When you found her she'd been dead for over twelve hours. No defensive injuries.'

Hanson looked up. 'None?'

Chong shook her head. 'She was hit from behind. She never saw it coming. Which was a mercy, if you ask me.'

Hanson absorbed this. 'You're saying she sustained a blow to the back of the head and was then struck again? From the front?'

'That's my opinion so far. I agree with Adam's initial analysis of the blood evidence at the scene. She was already down, lying on her back when that second blow arrived.'

'But the cause of death was the blow to the head?' asked Hanson.

'Definitely. She couldn't have lived for long after it. The wound to her neck was post-mortem. There was no blood loss from it.'

Hanson imagined the scene. Why would somebody inflict a lethal blow, then add a second? 'How much later?'

Chong considered this. 'My guestimate is several minutes.'

Hanson recalled her first visit to the Downey's home. 'I met her a few days ago.'

'So I heard,' said Chong.

'She was a really nice woman, cheerful and happy in spite of the health problems she had. You probably know that she had a stroke last year.'

Chong gazed at them. 'I found another problem. She was heading for heart failure in the next few months. I'll let you have my report as soon as it's done.'

They watched her leave.

In the silence Hanson asked, 'Do we know if anything was stolen from the house?'

Corrigan responded. 'We'll check that out with Hugh Downey but her bag, her wallet with credit cards and money appeared intact.'

Watts had reached the door when he stopped and came back to the table. 'I've just remembered. Joy Williams, Elizabeth's aunt, called to ask if one of us can show her the field where Elizabeth was buried. I agreed to take her over there tomorrow at two but it's very likely I'll be briefing Upstairs on Gill and getting him in for interview.'

He held out the pink phone message slip to Corrigan. 'How about it?'

Corrigan took it. 'Sure.' He glanced at Kate. 'The aunt might appreciate another woman there.'

'I'll see you there. I want another look at the field.'

In the subdued light inside her kitchen Kate pored over the available information in the Williams and Bennett cases. She glanced up at the clock. Eleven thirty. She spoke her thoughts, needing to hear them.

'OK, focus on Williams for now. What do we know? What do we know for certain?' She flicked pages of notes then pulled the Smart Notebook closer. It would send her thoughts to the board in UCU.

'Facts relating to the Williams case: number one: body shallow-buried in field, wrapped in tarpaulin. Two: no clothing present. Belongings: one scarf, one gold ring. Three: No known cause of death.' She stopped. 'Which I suppose is an absent fact, like the clothes. Four, wool fibres caught in her fingernails.' She reread the words on the small screen.

'What does all of this tell us? That her killer is forward-looking, a careful type who plans. He wrapped the body to avoid any smell from the remains attracting the attention of animals. That suggests he's forensically aware.' *Who isn't these days?*

'If she was killed in a domestic setting he either lives alone or he can rely on significant periods of time when he has full possession of his living space. If he's got someone in his life, it suggests a girlfriend, rather than a wife.' Watts's words drifted inside her head: 'Wives go out.'

She rested her head on one hand. 'Absence of clothing. What might that suggest?' She gazed at the kitchen doors, unseeing.

'Concerns about DNA? That would confirm his forensic savviness. Or were they souvenirs, mementos of what he'd done which he could use afterwards, say to reinforce and build on his fantasies?' She sighed. 'Very possible. Almost de rigueur for the types I search for.' She stopped.

'My God, I just said "types". I sound like Watts.'

She read the information on the small screen again. 'But why take all of her clothes and where exactly is this leading me? Another fact: Elizabeth Williams was actually killed in some kind of domestic environment but Amy Bennett was attacked outside.'

She reached for her notebook, leafed through it and stopped. Here were the quick notes she'd made relating to the disappearance of Jean Phillips the forty-five-year-old schoolteacher-hiker Julian had discovered in his data search.

'Killed outside. A killer who isn't too concerned where he actually kills.' She frowned. 'But there's nothing specific to link our cases to the Phillips disappearance.' She went back to the small screen, fingers flying over keys.

'Stick with the basics. He's careful, forward-thinking and he plans.' She thought again about the Williams burial location details and sat back.

'It doesn't fit.'

THIRTY-ONE

The previous evening still in her head, Hanson made a detour to headquarters to stare at the board's 3D representation of the field, her eyes drifting over its features: the area of thick dark trees from which Myers had appeared, the dilapidated pavilion, the hummocky grass over which local children had run during their ball game, one of them falling, tripped up by chewed tarpaulin and a dead girl's hand.

She shook her head. It made no sense at all.

At one forty she parked her car and stepped from it into hush, the only sounds bird calls and a barely audible traffic hum from the direction of Genners Lane. She walked towards the dense hedge and through the gap, blue-white police tape hanging limp on each side.

Coming onto the deserted field she stood, and looked around. This was the first time she'd seen it in daylight. She walked its perimeter then criss-crossed the field itself. No dead wood.

The area where Elizabeth's remains had been discovered was still easy to identify. The grass had been replaced but it was evident that it had been recently disturbed. She headed towards it. Everything procedural and scientific had been done here, the whole field searched quadrant by quadrant, fully documented, measured, photographed and sketched, all of its physical evidence gathered. Before she left headquarters, she'd read the forensic report looking for any reference to dead wood. As Adam had told them, there was none. There was nothing here. Only a disturbed rectangle of grass.

Hanson stood beside Elizabeth Williams' makeshift grave then looked to her left at the old pavilion just a few metres away. She looked back to the field's uneven grassy surface where an innocent game had revealed death. In daylight, it still made no sense.

Attracted by movement from the direction of the road, she looked up to see Corrigan walking with Joy Williams across the field towards her. She waited as they approached. Miss Williams was wearing a black coat and carrying a spray of white, pink and blue flowers tied with pink ribbon. They reached her and Hanson picked up the sweet scent of freesias and carnations among the lilacs Elizabeth's aunt was holding.

'I've brought these to leave here,' said Miss Williams. 'I think they'll last a little while if we don't get rain. Do you think anyone will object?'

Hanson shook her head. 'No. Where would you like them to go?'

She watched as Miss Williams approached the disturbed area of grass, wondering if it was any comfort for her to know the exact place where her niece had lain for the last year.

'I'll put them just here.'

She placed the flowers at the centre of the grassy area. Hanson looked down at them, fragile and vulnerable, one or two of the freesia petals fluttering. She hoped if local children or visitors to the nearby pavilion saw the flowers they'd understand and leave them in peace. Giving Miss Williams a few minutes alone she and Corrigan walked some metres away.

She turned to him. 'When Watts and I first came here, it seemed reasonable to suppose that Elizabeth's killer chose this place because he was local and he knew it. We revised that theory a little: he knew it but not directly because he hadn't taken account of the risks attached to it from visitors to the pavilion, plus the local children. But this man is a planner. He's very careful. He killed Elizabeth in a domestic environment then moved her somewhere else. Somewhere accessible. Hc must have perceived it as safe but perhaps he decided it was too close. He finally disposed of her body by bringing it here. I don't think he'd ever been here but he knew of it. Maybe it gave him what he wanted: distance between himself and Elizabeth.'

Corrigan gazed across the field. 'How about he saw this location on the plans at Renfrew?'

She glanced in the general direction of the college. 'That sounds reasonable.' She looked over to Miss Williams who was still standing where they'd left her. 'I'll say goodbye to her then I have to go.'

'Where?' he asked.

'I'm meeting someone. He's nothing to do with work.'

*   *   *

Hanson sipped water, her eyes on the door of the café inside the Mailbox complex. *Calm down.* She looked away, sipped more water, her eyes dragged back to the door as it opened. A woman came inside pushing a smart baby buggy.

Hanson was tense. She wished she hadn't had to come. She wasn't clear what she'd say to Charlie Hanson when he arrived, which was adding to her tension. But this was about Maisie and what she needed. She knew exactly what she wanted to say about that. The door opened again. She looked up.

He was here.

She watched as Charlie Hanson – tall, upright, a little broader than she remembered, his hair still mostly dark – came towards her.

'Hello, Kate,' he said warmly.

She saw his hands reach out towards her. Not having anticipated direct contact she gave one of them a quick shake and slid a menu across the table.

'I've decided on just coffee but you choose whatever you want and I'll call the waitress.'

He sat, looking directly into her eyes. 'It's lovely to see you. You look wonderful. It's been a long time.'

'Yes. It has.' She couldn't think of anything else to say. The waitress came, took their order and went away. His eyes were still on Hanson.

'I wanted to contact you so many times but I was never sure of the reception I'd get. I didn't think you'd welcome it.'

Her eyes were focused on a point slightly to the left of his face. She didn't say anything.

'I was thinking about you the whole time I drove here. It's twenty years since I left.' *Left me.* 'Yes. I know.'

He gazed at her. 'I wish you'd responded to my letter all those years ago.'

She gave him a direct look. 'What letter?'

His brows came together. 'The one I left for you that day.'

It felt like she was drowning. 'I didn't get a letter.'

Silence stretched between them. Hanson had no reason to disbelieve the letter's existence. The fact that she hadn't ever seen it could mean only one thing. Her mother had acted to make sure she didn't. She looked across at Charlie, guessing he was thinking much the same. He looked at his hands.

'I should have phoned you when I heard nothing but your mother made clear that I wasn't welcome to contact you or call at the house. I didn't want to add to her anger in case it impacted on you.'

She swallowed. 'It doesn't matter. It was all a long time ago.'

His eyes drifted over her face. 'I'm sorry. I did what I felt I had to do. Don't blame your mother.'

'Why not?'

He looked into her eyes. 'Because she's dead, Kate, and it's a waste of energy.'

After a short silence he said, 'We had something in common, you and me. She didn't understand you and she didn't approve of me.'

Hanson thought of the times her mother had either mocked or berated her for 'wasting time reading, reading, always damn' well reading!'

'I don't think she approved of me, either.' She watched him choose his words.

'Your mother and I were mismatched. Me, a stuffy lawyer who liked a quiet life, your mother the social one who loved parties, the theatre, holidaying with friends.' The old photograph she'd shown Maisie flashed inside Hanson's head. She wanted to know who her biological father was. His name. She couldn't ask Charlie Hanson. It was still unspoken between them that Charlie wasn't her father. He was still talking.

'She was very easily bored by the domestic life but I know there were times when she enjoyed having you and young Celia in the house, running around the garden.'

Hanson sipped water. 'Yes. I remember. Celia was athletic. She admired that.'

A memory surfaced of Celia, thirteen years old, already five feet seven, sailing effortlessly over the school high jump.

You always set the bar too high, mother. Mother.

'Kate?'

'Sorry?'

'I said I would love to see Maisie. How do you feel about that?' She gave a firm nod.

'I'm fine with it. Because it's what Maisie wants.' She paused. 'You have to understand something. There has to be an agreement between us. You can't come into Maisie's life and then leave it, no matter what the reason. I won't allow it. If you have the slightest doubt about having long-term contact with her you need to tell me now.'

'I understand what you're saying. I want to be part of Maisie's life. And yours. I give you my word.'

She looked at him directly. She'd had a child's implicit trust in him once. Could she trust him to do the right thing by Maisie? Right now, control of the situation was in her hands. She took a deep breath.

'I haven't decided yet about the best place for you to meet Maisie for the first time. I'll think about it and let you know and we can agree on a date and time.' She stood, offered him her hand.

He took it, drew her gently towards him and kissed her lightly on the cheek.

She reached for her bag, turned, walked out of the coffee shop staring directly ahead, back and shoulders rigid, lips pressed together.

She set the plate down in front of Maisie. 'Your favourite. Spag bol with a side dish of chunky chips.'

Maisie peered at them. 'Six to be precise.'

'Stop counting your food and eat. Take some salad as well.'

Hanson ate, her thoughts roaming over her meeting with Charlie Hanson. It had laid a few ghosts. Well, one or two. Now she had to decide where the meeting between Maisie and Charlie Hanson would take place. Until she did she wouldn't mention today's meeting to Maisie. It would send her high as a kite.

'Mum?'

'Mmm . . .?'

'Have you spoken to my grandpa?'

The forkful of salad stopped on its way to her mouth. Hanson looked at her. 'You are *uncanny*, do you know that?'

Maisie widened her eyes, mock-shocked. 'What a thing to say to your best girl.'

Best girl. It had been one of Hanson's names for Maisie when she was small: *You're the best girl I've got.* It wasn't long before Maisie had worked out that being her mother's best girl put her in a very select group of one.

Maisie waited. '*Mum?* Have you spoken to him?'

'Yes. He's really looking forward to seeing you.'

Maisie's eyes danced. 'When he comes here, guess what I'm going to do? I'm going to show him the teddy bear he sent me when I was born.'

Hanson nodded. 'That's a great idea.'

So, that's the place decided. I'll ring him tomorrow and agree a date and time.

THIRTY-TWO

I nside her room at the university Hanson rang the hospital where Amy Bennett was still a patient. After a short conversation she put down the phone. A few questions to Amy had confirmed what police inquiries had already established, but she'd had to be sure: there was no link between Amy Bennett and Elizabeth Williams. Their personal interests, educational experience and a seven-year age difference provided no common ground.

She read the names of the Persons of Interest in her notebook: Chris Turner. Lawrence Vickers. Michael Myers. Aiden Malahide. She talked herself through the process.

'Elizabeth knew Turner and Vickers.' She added lines linking the names, seeing another link. 'Aiden Malahide, he met Elizabeth on one occasion.' She went through her notes. Hollis, one time student at the same college, now resident of Texas was another. He'd spoken to Elizabeth on the day she disappeared. She added another line, connecting him to Elizabeth.

Hanson knew that Hollis's passport had been examined. It confirmed that it had been twelve months since he was last in England. She couldn't see how he might have killed Elizabeth. But he was here when Amy was attacked. They'd also checked with Elizabeth's aunt. She hadn't recognised the name Myers and neither had Amy just now.

'So nobody knows Michael Myers and all of this means . . . what?' She wrote quickly then gave the words a decisive underscore. 'All of our POIs were somehow part of Elizabeth's world or experience. None of them appear to have had any connection to Amy Bennett's life.'

She went to the heading Physical Evidence. Fibres for Elizabeth. Boot and tyre prints for Amy. Without a suspect, they couldn't move forward with any of it.

She moved to Similarities of Modus Operandi. The words

overheard by Myers, the words recalled by Amy Bennett. MO was still all they had.

'Whoever he was, those words are important to us because they were supremely important to him. He felt compelled to say them. They're all we have to link the two cases.'

Hanson knew that spoken words weren't a known signature in repeat homicides. How could they be? Anyone who heard them would be in mortal fear of his or her life, then deceased shortly afterwards. She had no doubt that Amy had been destined for a similar fate as Elizabeth.

'We got lucky because of Myers' nocturnal activities and also because of Amy's determination to survive for her baby's sake. We have his signature, his fantasy-based, ritual behaviour.'

She reread all she'd written and saw the size of the task facing them. If none of their POIs could be elevated to position of suspect for both cases they would be looking for someone who was a stranger to both victims. She understood Watts's sentiments. They were staring at failure because all they had were a few spoken words, limited physical evidence and precious little time.

'I have to know exactly what this fantasy of his is about.'

She collected her things and headed for the door, her mind on clothes.

Elizabeth Williams' clothes.

The brown boxes filled UCU's big worktable. Two were small and labelled: 'Elizabeth Williams. Effects.' The much larger boxes were marked 'Elizabeth Williams. Clothing.' There were ten of them.

'Has Adam's team finished with all of this?'

Corrigan nodded. 'Everything the original investigators removed from where Elizabeth was living at the time she went missing. The boxes of effects contain mostly small items like cosmetics. Her phone was never found. Adam's team has gone over her laptop. This is their report.'

He handed it to her. 'I didn't find anything that grabbed my attention but you might.'

She took it. The laptop had revealed very little in the way of personal information. Email and Facebook messages were innocuous, confined to a small circle of individuals, all female. Her eyes roamed over them a second time. She knew what she was seeing.

'These are the communications of a young woman who was in

a relationship with Chris Turner and knew she had to be guarded. She must have suspected he would search through them.' She put down the report and turned her attention to the boxes of clothing.

'Tell me what's on your mind and I'll help,' said Corrigan.

'Elizabeth's killer removed all of her clothes and took them away with him. The only things he left were the scarf and the small ring which was probably still on her finger at the time he buried her.'

'He wanted the clothes as souvenirs?' he suggested.

'In which case, why not take the scarf or the ring? Easy to remove. Easy to hide until he wants to look at them, relive the experience. Why take everything else? I don't think it was souvenirs he was after.'

She began searching through Elizabeth Williams' clothes. 'Hollis said Elizabeth told him that she was planning to change her clothes that Sunday afternoon. We know she had a suit cleaned. We have to establish if we can what she was wearing when she disappeared. If that suit is here, we have a problem. I'm hoping it isn't because of what it tells us about where she was going.'

They searched the boxes in silence. There was no suit.

Hanson took a deep breath. 'I'm confident now that Elizabeth had an interview on that Sunday evening. Malahide denies seeing her again after she called into his office the previous Wednesday. Right now there's no indication that he did, but we don't know that for certain.' She began repacking the boxes, glancing up at him. 'I'll pack this away if you need to leave.'

He shook his head. 'I don't need to be anywhere else. I'll help you finish up.' Not looking at her, his tone light, he said, 'How'd your date go yesterday?'

'It wasn't a date, Corrigan.'

'Not someone who's romancing you?'

She grinned at the quaint phrase. 'Definitely not.'

He gave her an intense, blue look. 'So tell me the kind of romancing you go for, Red. The kind that works for you.'

She didn't want to get into this. She wanted to keep it light between them, like it always had been.

'Oh, you know. Being with the person, laughing, talking and enjoying the moment. All the usual bells and banjos.'

He looked at her. The silence lengthened. 'You know how I feel about you.'

She didn't look at him. It had been said. It was out there. It couldn't be unsaid.

'Yes.'

'Is that a problem for you?'

'Yes. It is.'

'Why?'

She could feel his warmth. 'Because I don't do "romance".'

He looked down at her, brows raised. 'What's wrong with romance?' She looked at the dark hair, his face, his mouth. 'It carries an expectation.'

He frowned. 'People usually expect a relationship.'

'I don't. I don't want or need one'

'Is this about me in particular or all men in general?'

She thought of how much she liked Corrigan. She recalled Celia months ago, expounding on the attractions of his mouth. 'Have a look at his lips if you don't believe me. They're lovely. He's got these little tucks, one at each corner of his mouth which sort of lifts them, even when he's not smiling. They make his mouth look kissy.' She recalled her own hoot of derision. 'For God's sake, Cee! You're making every romance writer despair or gag.'

She studied his mouth. Edible. 'It's about me.'

Seeing his eyes darken, knowing he was a good friend she knew she had to offer him more. 'My father left when I was fifteen. Kevin left Maisie and me after two years.' She shook her head. 'I don't need more of that kind of hurt.'

'You don't know that that's going to happen.'

'Exactly. Over the last ten or so years I've learned to organise my life so that I don't get into situations which might lead to that kind of risk. Plus, it could cause other difficulties for us because we work together.'

The blue eyes searched her face. 'You can't close down your life because of what might happen. You're missing out on so much.'

She looked up at him. 'What makes you think I'm missing out, Corrigan?'

He looked confused.

She took a breath. 'I live my life exactly as I want. I don't miss out on anything, except what I don't want.'

'Tell me what you mean.'

She looked directly at him. *He has to know.* 'Sex without commitment works for me. I doubt it fits with what you're looking for.'

He frowned. 'I get it. Two men hurt you. That doesn't mean you have to organise your whole life like that.'

'It's my choice. It feels safer.'

'Because you call the shots? That's no way to live, Kate. We all need emotional connection. Closeness.'

Listening to his words she realised that he understood her better than Kevin ever had or ever would. It didn't change anything. Should she tell him or should she wait? *Wait for what? We're at an impasse.*

'You're right. It's not without its problems. There was someone who didn't like me calling the shots. We met about three years ago at the university when he attended a conference I'd organised. He was attractive. I thought he was a nice person. I was wrong. I ended it and he wasn't nice any longer.' Hanson took a few steps, putting distance between them. 'I found out he's the kind who likes to finish things.'

'And?'

'He made my professional life difficult whenever he got the chance.' She gave him a direct look.

'You know him, Corrigan. Or you did.'

He looked mystified. 'Who?'

'Roger Furman.'

The name of the one-time manager of UCU hung in the air. The silence between them went on for ever. Finally, he nodded, not looking at her.

She waited. 'What are you thinking?'

'I'm thinking that now it makes sense. The conflict between you and Furman was toxic. Yes, he's a poor excuse for a human being but the way he was with you and your response to him – I could never really get what that was about. Now, I do.'

'I'm telling you what I think you need to know about me. I evaluate people as part of my job but when it comes to the personal, I'm not very good at it. I choose the wrong men. See Exhibit One: Kevin Osbourne.' She looked away from him then back. 'That was unfair. Kevin has his failings as we all do, but he's not a bad person. What I'm saying is that I don't want you to be a wrong choice. I like you too much for that and we have to continue working together.'

He hadn't moved his eyes from her face during the last minute.

She picked up her jacket and bag and headed for the door. 'We're very different people, aren't we Corrigan? Now you know more about me you may want to rethink what you want. I'll see you tomorrow.'

THIRTY-THREE

Watts read what Hanson had written on the board, then turned to her.

'It's still just your assumption that she was wearing that suit when she was killed.'

'No it isn't,' she snapped.

He sighed. 'OK, have it your way. I think it tells us why she wasn't wearing it after he killed her. He was iffy about DNA. Or, he took it for a souvenir.'

'No, he wasn't. He didn't.'

He dropped heavily onto his chair. 'You don't let anything alone, do you? Right. Let's hear it.'

She pointed at the board. 'Elizabeth routinely wore casual clothes, like most of her fellow-students. She was keen to find work experience in an area she believed had some value. We know she'd arranged an interview for that Sunday because she told Hollis. By the time she talked to him she'd decided what she would wear: she'd already had that suit cleaned. She'd collected it that Saturday. I think whoever killed her stripped her for one reason: if she was ever found, investigators might come up with an idea as to where she was going. He feared that that might lead investigators to his door.'

Watts eyed her. 'Which door's that then?' He pointed to the list of persons of interest. 'Vickers, Turner, Gill, Malahide. There's a few to choose from.'

'I'm working on it.'

'And if it's none of our POIs, there's around two million people in this city and sometimes it seems like as many businesses.'

He got up from the table. 'Police work's not like your world, doc, where there's time and money to delve about for months, years even, finding out how a gnat's kneecap works. The real world is *here*. I spent two hours in a meeting yesterday, helping Goosey fit a muzzle on the chief constable who's going barmy over costs. We've got media eyes on us and next to no money, which means we're fast approaching zero hour.'

Hanson looked at him, all of the stresses of the last few days flooding her head. She felt irritation rising. 'Don't you think that after two years here, I know that? Stop telling me the damned obvious. This isn't one cold murder case. It's linked to a current attack on a pregnant woman and we have to find—'

'Who did it? Now it's *you* telling *me* the obvious.'

She pushed back her hair. 'I was about to say we have to find out *why* he did it.'

He placed his hands on the table, mustering patience. 'If we don't turn up a real lead on the Bennett case it'll get stored in the basement sooner or later. If it's handed to Upstairs, I can't see them doing any better than we have and it's the same pot of money their investigation comes out of.'

'Why is it always about money? We have to get justice for Elizabeth and for Amy. We owe them that!' She bit her lip. 'Sorry.'

She watched him reach for the local newspaper, unfold it and push it across the table towards her.

She read the headline: Cold Case Unit Stalls. She looked away.

He picked it up again. 'The chief constable and Goosey wanted chapter and verse from me on what we've got on the two cases. I told them about the leads we're following up. The chief constable went on about "local goals" and value for money and I wish I could say he went away happy. He didn't. He left Goosey scrabbling through this year's budget. He's probably still at it.' He glanced at his watch. 'He's expecting me back. Let's hope he's found enough to keep us afloat for the next few days.'

She watched him leave then rested her head back on her chair, pressing the heels of her hands against her eyes. She looked up, catching sight of the words they'd had painted in black flowing script above the window at the end of their last case.

Let Justice Roll Down.

THIRTY-FOUR

Hanson stared across the campus beyond the window. She felt secure here. UCU felt as though it was changing. After more than two years of working at headquarters she still struggled with the concept of a cold case. As she saw it, every case deserved continuing oversight, ongoing action when something cruel and terrible had happened to somebody's family member or friend. She knew how naïve that was. She thought of Hugh Downey and wondered how he was coping. She'd been aware of much activity from Upstairs whilst she was at headquarters. They had arrested Sean Gill and were pursuing a case against him for Nan Downey's murder.

The door opened and Julian's head appeared around it. 'Sorry, Kate. I knocked but when I didn't hear anything I thought you were somewhere else.'

'I was. Come on in.'

'Can I work in here?'

'Of course.'

She waved him to the old armchair and watched him unload textbooks from his backpack.

'Want to know the latest at UCU?' she asked. He stopped and looked up at her.

'We're within days of our first failure. Make that failures.'

'Why? What's happened?'

She turned her chair towards the window. It was dull outside today, the bright sun of the last few days obscured by cloud. 'We're out of money and we're out of time. Or as good as.'

'But there are leads which haven't been followed up yet. What about the tyre and boot prints?'

She turned to him, shaking her head. 'We don't have the time to wait for them to become relevant.'

'But we've still got the POIs.'

'Yes. People we're "interested" in. Some more than others. My view is: Turner, definitely of interest; Vickers, maybe; Malahide another definite. And then there's Myers.' She leant towards Julian. 'How'd you rate each of them as Elizabeth Williams' killer and Amy Bennett's attacker?'

She watched him turn over the question. 'I agree Turner and Malahide as definite. Vickers as a possibility. Not Myers. He's too . . . flaky, to use Joe's word.' He looked at her. 'I'll tell you something I don't think is helping and that's the sketch Amy Bennett helped produce of her attacker. I know she's confident that it's what she's got in her head, but the face is so distorted he looks off the wall. Not like anybody.'

Hanson felt a surge of discouragement. 'I know what you mean. But we can't discount it. She was there. We weren't.'

Watching him organise his books and open his laptop, guilt joined discouragement inside her head. As his PhD supervisor it was her job to assist and support him. This was his time to do research. She tuned into what he was saying.

'Maybe we shouldn't discount Myers. He's got a minor sex offence record.' He shook his head. 'Which means I'm trying to make him fit the crime and we've got no evidence that our cases are about sex.'

Hanson sat back, turning her pen end over end. 'And Myers doesn't own a vehicle, although according to the worker at The Sanctuary he can drive.'

She stared at the floor between them. 'This is a mess at every turn but we can't strike Myers from the list. We still don't know enough about these cases to do that.'

'So, what are you going to do?'

Hanson paused, looked down at the notes covering her desk. 'Go through all of this again to make sure I haven't missed something.' She pushed her fingers through her hair, looked up at him. 'I'll tell you what's troubling me about these cases, Julian. I'm *still* trying to find the why. *Why* was Elizabeth killed? *Why* was Amy attacked? I can't seem to get to the motive.'

He closed the book on his lap. 'OK. What have we got? One murder. One serious assault. Commonalities: a focus on the neck because of what Amy told us and what Myers said. The most obvious answer is that this is somebody into strangling women.'

Hanson thought about it. 'But we don't have physical signs of that for Elizabeth. If he was intent on strangling Amy Bennett, he made a mess of it.' She put a hand over her eyes. 'Hope that doesn't sound as awful as I think it does. What I mean is, he failed.' She reached for her pen and wrote one word: necks.

She looked up. 'So, why the scarf around Elizabeth's neck? If there was no strangulation, did it have a function?'

'Decoration?' suggested Julian.

She dropped the pen on the desk, needing an alternative focus, even for just a few minutes. 'How's the research going?'

'I'm following up all the research angles you suggested and they've led to two or three which really appeal to me.'

She recalled Watts's recent take on life in academe. He had a point.

'That sounds like progress.'

She heard the Chamberlain tower clock strike and looked at her watch. 'I have a lecture but if you're still here in an hour we can discuss those angles.'

When Hanson returned to her room, Julian had gone. She dropped her lecture notes on the armchair and gazed down at those on UCU cases still waiting on her desk. Crystal appeared at the door of the adjoining room.

'Drink?'

'A G and T would do nicely,' she said absently.

Crystal nodded. 'I wish. Unfortunately, I can only offer you the usual.'

'Then I'll have that.'

'Which one?'

'Surprise me. I could do with some excitement in my life.'

Closing down a sudden thought of Corrigan before it had a chance to develop, she sat at her desk, hands against her forehead and scrutinized the case notes. After one minute she knew that forcing herself to find the why of these cases wasn't getting her anywhere. They had a fair amount of behavioural information from both. This man's behaviour had to be the key. What he'd said and what he'd done were closely intertwined. She'd concentrate on that.

Hanson reached for the four A4 sheets of data Crystal had word processed and arranged them side by side. They showed all of the utterances which UCU had amassed from Myers and Amy Bennett. She looked at those Myers had given them at the field: 'I'm here. Look me in the eye. Lo-ok at me-e.' She recalled his voice as he half-sang those words. Eerie. Haunting. Possibly the reason he'd struggled to identify the speaker's gender.

She looked at the words Myers had spoken when he was interviewed at headquarters: 'Oh, come to me. Look at me. Look me in the eyes.' She stared at the similarities, the stress on eyes, the demand that the victim look directly at him. She pored over the words, anxiety surfacing about the differences in Myers's two recalls, aware of his general unreliability in what he claimed about himself. Maybe they couldn't place a lot of faith in what he'd told them?

Hanson turned the sheets over and looked at those bearing the words recalled by Amy Bennett. These had to be the gold standard for analysis, even taking into account the shock and fear she was experiencing at the time she heard them. She scoured them, seeing that Amy's recall also varied, no doubt due to being in abject fear. Myers had his problems. Was she being unfair to him, too critical of what he'd offered them?

She studied the words Amy's attacker had said to her immediately following his request for change for the drinks machine: 'You have to turn round. I'm going to turn you round to look at me', followed later by 'I have to see your eyes blaze.'

Hanson stared ahead, unseeing. Was this man a sadist? Was he driven to see the fear, the suffering he was inflicting?

She looked at what Amy had told them during their second visit about her fear of her attacker, her difficulty in looking at him directly and again his insistence that she 'Look at me. Look at me. Keep your eyes on mine.' Later she'd also recalled him saying: 'You need somebody like me to keep you safe.'

Hanson frowned at the last word. Safe. How did that fit with sadism?

She turned back to what Myers had recalled when she last saw him at The Sanctuary: 'He said something like, "You could have been safe but you didn't stay."'

She sat back, her eyes on Myers' words and shook her head.

'Where's the sense in Elizabeth's murderer saying that she didn't stay? She *did* stay. He'd killed her and he had her body right there with him. When he said those words he was burying her.

Hanson closed her eyes. They felt like hot coals. But she'd achieved something. The analysis had removed her concerns about Myers' reliability. What he'd said he heard and what Amy Bennett had reported bore striking similarities, provided by two different people who had never met.

Coffee arrived on her desk and the one already grown cold removed. Murmuring a 'Thank you, Crystal', Hanson checked the time. Five forty-five. She needed to be at the school playing field at six thirty to collect Maisie and Chelsey from netball practice.

She scanned Amy's attacker's words. There was no suggestion that he viewed her as an object. He was controlling but there was little evidence of the extreme control and anger which had been part of many of the attacks on women she'd analysed for other forces. Myers' delivery of the killer's words had sounded heartfelt. Almost beseeching. Maybe because they were uttered in the presence of death?

Hanson stared at the words until they moved on the page. This man had wanted something very specific from both Elizabeth and Amy. He was trying to create a scene, or rather recreate some scene already captured inside his head. If she'd had even the smallest, lingering doubt about a link between the murder of Elizabeth Williams and the attack on Amy Bennett these last few minutes had vanquished it. Both were the work of the same man. But what *was* it that he'd wanted? What had he been looking for? She read slowly through all that Amy Bennett had said of the attack on her and the intense emphasis on her neck. She stopped reading, hands clasped at her mouth, brows together. Her speculation on sadism was now being overtaken by another, more specific theory.

Did this man have an intense focus on an object or body part which he had to incorporate into sexual activity for him to be aroused? She recalled evaluating a man who had a fixation on high-heeled boots. He'd attacked women in order to steal them. Another had been fixated on hair which led to his standing behind females in club and cinema queues, snipping off pieces and curls with tiny gold-plated scissors. Was that what these two cases were about? If so, he'd killed Elizabeth because she could identify him. Amy had survived only because she'd managed to fight, then drive away from him.

She stood, rubbed the back of her neck then gathered the notes and put them into her briefcase. Opening the Notebook she tapped a message to the UCU smartboard requesting a database search.

This man was still a silhouette. He had to be forced out of the shadows.

THIRTY-FIVE

Hanson arrived in a deserted UCU the following afternoon and checked the board. The database search she'd requested had been done. It had yielded nothing which was useful to their case. Of the three known neck fetish rapists in the greater West Midlands, one was deceased; the other two incarcerated and had been for some years.

She turned as the door opened and her colleagues came into the room, followed by the clamour of voices raised in what sounded like triumph.

'What's going on?'

Watts was looking gratified. 'What you just heard was an Upstairs celebration. Gill's been charged with Nan Downey's murder. Their case is that he did it because of his sacking by Hugh Downey. They're saying he went to the house in a rage, not realising that Downey wasn't there.'

'Has he admitted it?'

'Behave, doc. People like Gill never put their hands up for anything. You could watch them do something and they'd still deny it.'

She looked across at Corrigan. He smiled at her, as open as always.

She considered telling them about the analysis she'd done on their cases but decided against it. It was too incomplete. She had to do more. But not this evening. She wanted to spend all the available time with Maisie.

A sudden, loud commotion started up in the corridor outside UCU. They exchanged glances. It did not sound celebratory. Hanson followed Watts and Corrigan as they rushed from UCU.

In reception, she was stopped dead by the scene there. Hugh Downey was being restrained by Whitaker and another constable. She watched as her two colleagues took hold of Downey who was still shouting and moved him into the informal meeting room. She stood in the doorway, shocked. Downey was now slumped, his head on the table.

She went to where Whittaker was standing. 'What happened?'

Face flushed, he pointed at Downey. 'He came to see Dr Chong saying he wanted his wife's body released so he can arrange her funeral. He thought he could just ask for it to happen. She couldn't get through to him that it didn't work like that in a murder case. After a while he seemed to accept it but somehow he picked up that Gill's here and that he's been charged with his wife's murder. He tried to open the security door. When he couldn't, he completely lost it.'

Hanson looked up to see Corrigan at the door of the interview room, beckoning her. She went to him. He lowered his voice. 'We can't release him in this state without somebody who's willing to be responsible for him. Would you ring Malahide?'

Back in UCU she rang him and explained the situation.

'Poor Hugh. What will he do without Nan? I'll be there in ten minutes.'

Hanson returned to the interview room. Downey didn't appear to have moved.

Watts said, 'We've told Mr Downey he needs to leave things to us for now. That right, Mr Downey?' Downey didn't respond. She laid a hand on his arm. 'Mr Downey? Aiden is on his way.'

He looked up at her, adrift. 'Apologise to Dr Chong for me, would you? I wasn't thinking straight. I understand that I can't bury Nan until the police release her to me. It was when I realised that . . . that . . . animal was here.'

'Will you be staying with Mr Malahide over the next few days? In case we need to contact you?' asked Corrigan

Downey summoned concentration with an effort. 'I don't know. A cousin of mine has invited me to stay with him in Malvern.'

He straightened his jacket which had come off one shoulder in the struggle and stood, looking as though getting to the door was a significant effort.

Hanson glanced at Watts who was staring at the floor, arms folded. She knew he didn't like expressions of emotion, particularly around bereavement.

He watched Downey move slowly to the door. 'I want the Malvern address and contact details in case you do go, Mr Downey.'

Downey nodded, reached into his jacket pocket, took out a piece of paper and handed it to him. 'That's his address and phone number. He's not on the net. He leads a quiet life. Maybe it'll help. I know I can't carry on like this. If I do go, I'll probably leave sometime tomorrow.'

To Hanson, he was the husk of the vital, active man she'd first met days before. She caught a wave from the direction of the reception desk.

'Aiden Malahide is here,' she said.

In reception Malahide looked shocked at the sight of Downey. 'Come on, Hugh,' he said quietly.

Hanson watched them all the way to the car park, Malahide leading Downey to the car. She saw him patiently settle Downey into the passenger seat.

She and her colleagues returned to UCU.

'Have dinner with me tomorrow night,' said Corrigan quietly

as they walked together. 'Seems to me we have unfinished business.'

'Sorry, I can't.'

Wearing a red onesie with white hearts, her head resting on Hanson's lap, her iPad propped on her stomach, Maisie's eyes were fixed on the small screen. Hanson watched a hectic construction exploding across it.

'What are you building? Don't tell me. It's some kind of palace. Or a cathedral?'

Maisie tutted, finger-pointing at curved arches of yellow bricks. 'I'm changing the cash registers Chel put in. She's rubbish at Minecraft.'

Hanson's elevated notion evaporated. 'I don't get what it is.'

'A McDonalds.'

Hanson thought over her meeting with Charlie Hanson. 'I need to talk to you, Maisie.'

Maisie groaned. 'I *said* I'd tidy my room.'

'No, not that. Remember I said I was going to arrange to see your grandfather?' Maisie squirmed to look up her. 'Well, I have.'

The iPad tumbled as Maisie leapt up, hands flying to her mouth. 'What happened? What's he like? What did he say? Did he ask about me?'

'Of course he did. He wants to see you.'

Hanson smoothed the vibrant hair from Maisie's face. 'What's he like? Let me see. He's a big man. Tall. He's got a kind face and he's gentle. Just like I remember.' She paused. 'What else?'

'Come on, Mum!'

Hanson pulled her close. 'He's around sixty years old. I think he's handsome.' She looked down at Maisie. 'His hair is mostly dark brown but with a little grey.' She guessed Maisie's next question. 'I couldn't ask him about the red-haired man in the picture, Maisie. He and I have never talked about anything to do with that.'

She understood Maisie's need to know. She wanted to know about him too.

'So? What happens now?' demanded Maisie.

'He's going to come here to the house.' Maisie looked overjoyed. 'I said I'd ring him and fix the date,' she said, fighting to keep her voice even.

'Ask him to have dinner with us, Mum. Or tea. I could make cupcakes!'

THIRTY-SIX

Nuttall was inside UCU when Hanson arrived the following morning. She sat next to Julian, picking up the drift of Nuttall's discourse with her colleagues.
'You're about to lose the Williams case. It's heading down there again.' He pointed to the floor. The basement cold case store. He glanced at the board then gave each of them an intent look. 'But I've told the chief how hard you're working and he's agreed to fund three more days.'

Surprised, Hanson looked up at him. She'd revised her initial opinion of him. Watts was probably right when he'd described Nuttall as a time-server reaching his swansong but she suspected there was more to him than that.

Nuttall looked around the table at them. 'So, what's your problem with it?' He didn't wait for a response. 'There isn't one. Forget the attack on the Bennett woman. This is a cold case unit. Focus all your efforts on the Williams murder. Get that sorted. If the attack *is* connected you'll have sorted that as well. Job done.'

Hanson looked across at her colleagues. Watts' eyes were fixed on the table, his arms folded. It was Corrigan who responded. 'The Williams case is difficult because we don't have a cause of death and we haven't established a clear motive.'

Nuttall frowned. 'Work the physical evidence. Some cases are motiveless. I should know. I've come across a few.'

Hanson shook her head. 'There's no such thing as a motiveless crime. We might not be able to identify what it is or understand it, but it is there.'

He gave her a direct look. 'Then you'd better find it. Remember: three days.'

He stood, walked to the door and out.

The silence was broken by Watts, his hands linked behind his head, his eyes on the view beyond the window. 'Motive.' He let his arms drop and looked at Hanson. 'Any ideas?'

She felt all eyes on her. 'I had the idea it might be a neck fetish.' She pointed at the board. 'I asked Julian to do a search of neck fetish offenders in the West Midlands. It produced three hits: deceased or incarcerated for several years.'

Hearing Watts's heavy sigh she added, 'It's possible the man who killed Elizabeth and attacked Amy Bennett has a neck fetish and he's managed to meet that need without coming to police attention.'

Watts gave her a tired look. 'It's hard to pick up on that kind of thing. We had a spate of assaults on women a few years back. The bloke knocked them down and took their handbags. They were investigated as muggings. It took us months to realise that what he was after was their lipsticks. When we eventually tracked him down, he had them all lined up on a shelf. Very keen he was to tell us that he didn't approve of lip gloss. Had to be lipstick. What's the psychology say about fetish?'

She summarised. 'Fetish is a link an individual makes between sexual arousal and say, a part of the body, the foot, the neck, or an inanimate object such as a lipstick. It can be anything from the mundane to the really odd. The connection usually occurs early in an individual's development.' *Mother.* 'Over time it's reinforced by fantasy. It's not unknown to examine the early lives of such offenders and find that they showed those behaviours within their family setting.'

'Any of our POIs strike you as fetish types?' asked Corrigan.

She looked up at the names listed on the board and shook her head. 'I can't say. We don't have enough information about them. People guard their fetishes because it's intensely personal behaviour. It's not as unusual as you might think and it doesn't necessarily lead to lawbreaking but they can still fear censure from people who might not understand.'

Personal behaviour. Myers had suggested that Elizabeth's killer was talking about something personal.

'What about Malahide?' asked Watts. 'You saw his flat, the stuff in it.'

Hanson knew she was on uncertain ground. 'We don't know a lot about his personal life but what we saw suggests that Aiden Malahide is a highly anxious person, possibly somewhat depressed. The way he lives reflects his need for control.'

Watts asked, 'Why's he need the control?'

She shook her head. 'I don't know. You'll need to ask him. He might tell you.'

'Next chance we get, we'll do that. I've still got him in the frame.'
He went to the board and pointed. 'I've also been thinking about
Vickers, Elizabeth Williams' tutor. He said something which stuck
in my mind. See? "Head down, other parts of the anatomy up".' He
looked at Hanson. 'You tick me off for not being politically correct
but that's not something I'd say to a young female. We've only got
his word that he never acted on his initial advance to Williams and
he was at it before that, with Chloe Jacobs.'

Corrigan came to the board to encircle Vickers' name. 'And like
you just said, there's still Malahide. He's admitted face-to-face
contact with Elizabeth Williams at a time Renfrew was deserted.
Who knows what else he might not be telling us?'

Watts looked gratified. 'And he's the one with the creepy-looking
flat two floors up.'

Hanson rolled her eyes. 'Did you hear what I just said about
him?'

He sat on the edge of the table. 'The POIs are all we've got,
apart from the trace evidence, the foot and tyre prints which are no
use to us until we've got a suspect.'

He gave his face a brisk rub. 'Right. I'm off Upstairs to find out
what they've got on Gill and whether there's any possibility of a
link between him and our two cases.'

Hanson glanced at Corrigan who was getting ready to leave. He
had more taser training scheduled.

She watched as they left, reflecting on her dislike of all weapons.
She'd fired a gun once in her life, during a previous UCU case.
She'd done it to protect herself and Corrigan who was lying bleeding
on the floor in front of her, dying for all she knew at the time.

Alone but for Julian surrounded by his textbooks, she took the
printed sheets from her briefcase and spread them on the table in
front of her.

'What does all this give us?' she said to herself.

Julian looked up. 'Try talking it through, Kate.'

She realised that she'd said the words aloud. How could she
explain it when she could hardly verbalise it to herself? She gazed
at him, thinking how far he'd come in the last two years. He might
get it.

'You know how in our heads there are impressions, wisps of
ideas? We gather in loads of data and it sits there, imperfectly stored
because maybe it didn't mean anything when we captured it? And

then other stuff comes along but the wisps stay there, just wafting around.' She pointed to the sheets on the table in front of her. 'I'm hoping that by going through all of this I'll see some connections and it'll start making sense.' She looked across at him. 'I've already tried and so far I'm nowhere.'

'Anything I can do?'

She looked at him, thinking that whatever work he eventually chose, he'd succeed. Because he cared about what he did. He was as driven as she was.

'Thanks for the offer but you've got your own work.' She paused. 'You like analysis don't you, Julian?'

'Yeah. It makes my spirit fly,' he said with no trace of embarrassment.

'And what hypothesis have you formed from that?' she asked.

He grinned. 'That my future job is almost certainly as a statistical analyst in criminology.'

'Absolutely,' she said, knowing that he'd have the whole world in which to pursue it. She said so.

He shook his head. 'No. I leave that constant moving around to my dad.'

She knew a little about his father, none of it heart-warming. A wealthy man who lived his life in one or other of the three homes he owned on as many continents. He showed little interest in, or commitment to, Julian, his one child.

'I like stability. I need it,' he said.

Hanson recalled her twenty-one-year-old self.

No way was I as insightful as Julian is. I didn't have a clue who I was or where I was heading, even though I was working on my doctorate at the university, Kevin was already in my life and Maisie a not-so-distant promise.

She recalled her recent contact with the man she regarded as her father. It had been too long coming.

Julian stood. 'I'm going to get some food but I'll be back.'

Reaching into her bag for a ponytail band, she slipped it onto her hair. She looked down at the sheets and the words of a killer; an attacker who had spoken to his victims. Forget the similarities of the words and statements, she told herself. Look beyond them. Search for the underlying meaning.

'Come on. What kind of person are you? What are you about? *Tell* me.'

She studied the printed lines, noting how he'd flagged up his intentions: 'I'm going to turn you round . . .' Amy had described what he did as 'planned', a man with ringless hands who'd been gentle at times, reassuring her that everything would be OK. This man who'd attacked her had exhibited some capacity to care. She made a quick note, then ran her fingers across her forehead. On the other hand, Watts was right. That same man had also shown a capacity for violence in his pursuit of what he wanted. 'What was it you wanted? What was at the heart of all of this? If it was strangulation, why didn't you *do* it?'

She glanced at more lines. Myers had described Elizabeth's murderer as wanting her to do or give him something. According to Amy, he'd shouted at her for 'spoiling it'. She shook her head. She'd heard similar sentiments from murderers and rapists. They merely fitted the fantasy-based thinking she assumed was at the heart of these cases. They did not reveal the exact nature of the motivation.

Rotating her shoulders, she refocused, one line capturing her attention: 'I have to see your eyes blaze.' Amy had described her physical responses during the attack, the pounding in her ears, her difficulty in breathing, the feeling that she was passing out – yet, she'd also described his touch on her neck as gentle. She'd likened it to the touch of her partner.

Hanson stared at the words, drilling down to find their core. Were Amy's physical responses borne out of fear, rather than anything specific her attacker did?

She traced her finger along a line: '. . . knew he was going to hurt me . . . like strangle me . . . but he didn't.' Whatever his aim, it had been something he wanted to share with Amy. And to do that her eyes had to be open and on his. He'd told Amy that she needed somebody like him to keep her safe. She went forward a couple of pages, looking for Myers' words about safety. 'You could have been safe but you didn't stay.'

Hanson's eyes narrowed on the words. She turned back again, to what he'd said to Amy: '. . . see your eyes blaze'. She read the line aloud, adding her own emphasis. 'I *have* to *see* your eyes blaze.' Or maybe, 'I have to see your eyes *blaze*.'

Her heartbeat picked up tempo. She searched her notes, knowing now what she was looking for. She stopped at what Amy Bennett had said: 'It wasn't a hard pressure but I felt faint.' She gasped as half-formed ideas merged. She went back to what Myers had said: '. . . you didn't stay.' She placed both hands over her face, sudden realisation cutting through her thinking like a laser. She was on her feet.

'Myers misheard. It wasn't "stay". It was "say".'

She was at the board, the multiple fragmentary statements, questions, directives, ideas and assumptions she and her colleagues had heard, discussed and written down over many days sending her brain's neurones scrambling to transmit informational links across synapses via multiple electrical signals. She closed her eyes. It all came down to five words.

Look at me. Blaze. Say.

She had the motive.

She breathed deeply for what seemed like the first time in hours. Her eyes drifted over the board, halted by a single line.

'I should have seen the assumption. He went straight to murder.'

The final connections came on a crescendo of triggers and signals inside her head. Safe as a false promise. Clothes to conceal. It was about sex after all. Sex of a kind. The kind which links sex to a particular part of the body, in these two cases, the neck. Elizabeth Williams died because her killer had a compulsion. He expressed it through a rhythmic stopping of her breath, a calculated hold-and-release-hold-and-release. It was deadly because he was driven to witness the shadow of death in her eyes.

'For him, it's the ultimate experience,' she whispered.

Dazed by the speed of the realisations, she turned from the board then back. 'He as good as told me. He *said* it, loud and clear but I was too busy looking at the person, rather than listening to the words. Why did it take me so long to get it?'

She rested her head against the cool board. He was dangerous. He had to be stopped. *But I have to be sure.*

At the desktop computer she summoned a list of hire firms, her heart sinking. So many. Too many. She didn't have the time and couldn't see a way to obtain the details she needed. It didn't matter. She was sure. It's how it had to have been. He'd gambled on Elizabeth Williams remaining concealed long enough to obscure any signs of what he'd done. But UCU had the words he'd said to her in death. They had Amy Bennett's testimony in similar words. Would it be enough to stop him, send him for trial?

He has to tell me what he did.

She was on her feet. Watts and Corrigan weren't available. There wasn't time to look for Julian but his belongings were still here. He would be back. Going to the board she added words and a name in big letters. She trusted Julian. He was a nimble thinker. He would see it. He would understand.

Reaching for her keys she was out of the door and heading for her car.

THIRTY-SEVEN

There were no windows open on any floor. No sign of human activity anywhere. Was she too late? One of the garage doors was slightly open. Hanson went to it, pulled it open and peered inside. A Shogun. She left the door as she'd found it and walked on to the main entrance. She reached for the doorknob. One turn and the door swung slowly open. Someone had to be here. She stepped into the hall. The whole building was silent.

She paused at Aiden Malahide's sumptuous office, glanced inside then behind the door. It was empty. She thought of the pale wool rug now at headquarters. One person knew the significance of that rug gripped tight by a young woman as air left her chest and none replaced it.

One of the desk drawers was slightly open. She went to it. Inside was a passport and money. He couldn't be allowed to leave, to disappear because his compulsion would create future victims.

She walked the straight hall and through the rear door into sun, scents and heavy buzzing. Pollen-heavy bees were hovering over the lavender. She looked at the summer house, its windows blind, dead eyes. She knew what had happened to Elizabeth Williams and to Amy Bennett. She knew why. She knew his secret.

Despite the heat out here she felt cold. She'd seen his passport but was it possible that in a rush of remorse he'd used his compulsion to self-destruct? Had he created a kind of poetic justice in all of this?

Hardly breathing she approached the summer house and stood, listening. There was no sound from within. If he was inside, destroyed rather than fled, she had to know. She pushed the handle, paused then gave it a sharp tug. The door resisted. Another tug and it gave. The internal heat hit her face. She went inside.

There was a narrow bed covered by a large, woven quilt, its folds reaching the floor. She gazed down at vermillion splotches, the colour of paw prints on pale tiles. She felt perspiration ooze onto her face. She ran her finger over one of the splotches. Dry. Dust-laden. Paint.

If there was a self-destructive finale here, she knew it wouldn't be bloody. It would be corded, knotted, maybe swathed in plastic. Rising, she looked at the bed and the hanging folds of the quilt. If he was beneath it she had to know.

She grasped its folds and tore it away, letting it fall limp at her feet. She went to her knees, ready to confront whatever lay in the dark space. There was nothing. It was empty.

Closing the summer house door she continued on to where thick fingers of old wood jabbed the sky. She'd seen them when Malahide showed them the rear grounds an eternity ago. It wasn't a random wood store but a careful construction assembled from dead wood, stumps, trunks, old floorboards, the dark, strong lines of railway sleepers mixed with old grey-brown arthritic tree limbs, all united in a fantastical shape. She'd seen one once before. She knew what it was. A stumpery.

Standing among the vigorous ferns around its base she leant forward and looked down into its heart, bright sun on a flash of red, large webs festooning interior angles, stretched taut between pieces of bark. She recoiled. Dead wood. Bark. A specially crafted home for all manner of species.

Hanson felt an insistent tug of something almost forgotten, dismissed as irrelevant. Pulse rate soaring, she seized a branch lying on the ground, lifted it, carried it to the stumpery, leant forward, mind closed to what lurked there and thrust the branch down into its heart. It caught on something, lost it. She tried again, caught it again, soft and yielding. She raised it slowly from within the dead limbs then lowered it to the ground. Stained, ragged, in bad shape, a sweatshirt, its red colour still bright in places.

Listening for sounds of vehicles, hearing nothing she turned towards the house.

Hugh Downey was standing at the rear door of the house. He raised his hand to her. Seeing him she felt a rush of relief. She watched his slow approach. He looked drawn.

'I was resting. I didn't hear you come. Has Gill confessed?'

'I don't think so. I think it's unlikely. I'm glad you haven't left. I need your help.'

He gave a faint smile. 'I've got time. It would be good to do something useful with it.'

'Where is Aiden?' she asked.

'I don't know. I've been avoiding him to be honest. Yesterday, he told me I'll "get over" Nan. I don't think he understands relationships. I feel I no longer know him. Maybe I never did.'

'What do you think you'll do?'

'I'd thought of staying here but I'm exhausted. I just need to get away. I don't want to see Aiden so I think I will go to that relative I told you about in Malvern. It's not that long a drive.'

She'd come to like this intelligent, sensitive man who'd created the grounds here into a habitat for life to thrive. She looked at his pleasant, open face, seeing the shadow of grief on it.

'You're right, Hugh. It isn't. Not nearly as far as the drive from Edinburgh to Birmingham and back in a single night.'

He stared at her. 'I'm sorry?'

'The long drive you made from your Edinburgh conference back to Birmingham to kill Nan.'

He looked stricken. 'What are you saying to me?' he whispered.

She recalled his arrival at headquarters, direct from the airport, already knowing that Nan was dead. That knowledge had stopped him making the immediate, most logical assumption an innocent man whose wife had been disabled by a stroke would have made: that she'd been taken ill. He'd gone straight to murder. Because he knew what he'd done.

She shook her head. 'It's no use. I *know*. I know about Elizabeth Williams. I know about Amy Bennett.' She took a breath. 'And I know about the ritualistic words. I should have been quicker to see it.'

She saw the stark shock her words had caused. If she wasn't so confident in what she knew, the look on his face might have made her doubt herself.

'Dr Hanson, Kate? What are you saying to me? I've not harmed anyone.'

'You have, Hugh, and we both know how. Talk to me. Tell me about erotic asphyxiation.'

Despite the heat his face drained of colour. She saw the struggle behind his eyes. Would he deny it? He wasn't looking at her. After several seconds he spoke.

'I don't know how you know but that . . . thing which happened between Nan and me was a private, *mutual* expression of affection.' He looked at her. 'I didn't harm Elizabeth Williams. Aiden saw her here and you know he has some problems. You should be questioning him.' He stopped, frowned. 'Who is this other woman you just mentioned?'

She stood her ground. 'It isn't only Aiden who has problems is it? I heard what you just said about the private aspect of yours and Nan's relationship but you know that there is no "safe" with erotic asphyxiation. It disabled her. It killed Elizabeth Williams. It could have done the same to Amy Bennett and her unborn child.'

He looked at her, saying nothing. She had to get him talking.

'How did it start, Hugh? When did you first have that intensely erotic experience? I'm guessing you were young.'

He looked at her, his face ashen now. 'You are wrong. I care for life. I loved Nan. I do what's right.'

Denial and self-protection. She pushed on. 'Lie to yourself, Hugh but not to me. You saw Elizabeth when she came here that Wednesday afternoon. It would have been easy to persuade her to return on that Sunday because she believed she'd found the perfect work experience. Until you had her on the floor, the rug gripped in her hand as she fought for her breath and her life.' Hanson slowly shook her head.

'She wasn't "trained" like Nan, was she? She didn't understand your fixation, your need to see that transition between life and death within her eyes as you pressed her neck. She didn't understand that a word you'd given her might save her life.'

His face looked anguished. His legs had begun to shake. She watched him slump against the wall and slide slowly to the ground.

'No. I never saw her. You've got this so wrong but I'm not a vindictive person. I'm prepared to forget your accusations if you admit how wrong you are.'

His level of denial was immense, more than she'd anticipated. She looked at the verdant space around them. At the stumpery. Home for a murdered woman's sweatshirt. Her backpack was probably still inside it. As Elizabeth Williams' body had been. He would have looked out from Renfrew's rear windows and known she was there. But it was a risk. She had to be moved. Despite his conservationist's knowledge, he'd taken her to a place where the flora and fauna did not match the trace evidence already accumulated on her body. A field he knew of but had never seen.

Time had worked in his favour. Erotic asphyxia leaves temporary traces in the eyes, transient signs on the neck which fade or are easy to conceal with a scarf, a roll-neck sweater. A doorstop. She looked to the stumpery bathed in bright sun. They now had all the evidence needed to charge him. He needed to begin the journey of accepting what he'd done. His hands were clamped against his head. He had to talk to her.

'Where is Jean Phillips?'

He didn't respond, his hands still covering his head.

'Where is she, Hugh? You owe her that.'

His voice drifted to her, slow and muffled. 'It wasn't planned. I noticed her because of her red sweatshirt. I got into conversation with her, told her I had an ankle bandage in my car. I walked her along a narrow path then forced her into a copse.' He brought his hands together at his face.

'She was so strong. God, how she fought.' He paused. 'There are some really large stones near that copse. A natural feature. After . . . a while, I pushed her under the lowest stone. A long way back. Then I saw her sweatshirt and backpack still lying on the grass. Someone was coming so I picked them up and brought them back here with me. I thought that if I hid them here, I could dispose of them any time.'

She gazed at the lush grounds heaving with life, listening for sounds beyond the birdsong and the buzzing. They'd be coming for him. They'd put him away and those compartmental walls he'd constructed inside his head to protect himself would fall. Was he a monster? Were his actions evil, like Corrigan had said? She looked at Downey as he got to his feet, saw the guilt etched into his face. She knew he wasn't hobbled by a lack of conscience, nor crippled by an absence of empathy. She knew he was capable of genuine love and sensitivity. She'd seen it.

Their cases had been full of words uttered by different players. Hanson recalled another of them.

'I asked you how it started for you. Were you young at the time?'

He hung his head, all energy gone. His response was a long time coming.

'When I came home from school my father would ask me to read to my mother. It was summer. Hot. There was always a face-cloth in cold water by the side of the bed. She was drifting most of the time, but if I saw she was uncomfortable I'd wring out the facecloth and wipe her face, her neck . . .' Hanson caught the convulsive sob before his hands reached his mouth to stifle it.

Hanson saw the scene inside his mother's bedroom as it ran, frame by frame, through her head. He'd probably been around twelve or thirteen when he pressed the cold facecloth to his mother's neck and experienced a sexual high he'd been driven to recreate for the rest of his life with his wife, then with women who were strangers to him. She recalled her visit to his house, her first meeting with Nan and Nan's words: 'Sometimes, he's naughty because he won't slow down, won't stop . . . I'm grateful to him every day . . .'

It had all been said but she hadn't understood. He had to tell her now.

'Why Jean Phillips, why Elizabeth Williams and Amy Bennett?' He wouldn't look at her. 'Did Nan refuse to participate in breath play?'

'She would only agree if I kept it totally safe.'

'Which wasn't enough for you,' she said softly.

He looked away from her. 'I had to see that transition. I had to see it happen.'

'Is that what happened with your mother?'

His head came up. He stared at her. 'I didn't kill my mother! She died in hospital. I never hurt anybody.' He was back to denial.

She shook her head. 'You hurt Nan.'

'That was an accident. It went too far.'

'You *killed* her.'

'No. I didn't.'

She looked into his eyes. 'I know why you did it. When I came to your house that day, Nan asked me about the person who we thought had come to Renfrew requesting an internship. I remember her surprise when she learned it was a female. That's when she guessed that you might be going beyond your relationship with her to get what you wanted: breath play to the death.'

'No. You're wrong.'

'Did she ask you about Elizabeth? Did you deny it?' She stopped, her eyes on the ground between them. 'Nan was a very gentle person. She probably accepted what you said. But I'm guessing that from that moment you saw her as a potential threat.'

'I *loved* Nan. I loved my mother! I've hurt no one!'

He was on his feet, eyes ablaze. She stepped back at this sudden switch to total denial. He was coming towards her.

'You make judgements yet you know *nothing*. That transition is a privilege. To make it happen during breath play, to see it, is the ultimate control. The ultimate power over life. That's all I did. I never killed anyone. *Never.*'

His weight striking her with unexpected force, he grabbed her arms, pushing her backwards, his build belying the strength he'd acquired from physical work. Hanson was transfixed by his face, his mouth stretching on the last word, saliva flying. This was the face Amy Bennett had seen, the last face Elizabeth Williams had looked into.

Her back struck the stumpery hard, knocking the breath out of her. He pushed against her, forcing her upper body backwards, his hands fastening on her throat. There was no 'play' now.

Her heart hammered her chest and pulsed inside her head as the big, yellow-red sun grew and filled the sky, turning slowly dark to black. Through the darkness she heard a voice she knew.

'*Stop!*'

Released from Downey's grip, Hanson hit the ground, a puppet with her strings cut. Gasping, coughing, her hands at her throat, she heard feet coming towards her, felt hands at her waist, half-carrying her away.

Julian lowered her onto the grass. Breath labouring, eyes burning she looked up to see Corrigan, legs flexed, the yellow and black taser gripped in both hands, his eyes fixed on Hugh Downey. Behind him were Watts and four other officers. They'd heard it all.

'*Do not move.*'

Downey stood, head bowed as armed response officers came for him. Julian helped Hanson to her feet and they listened as Watts arrested Downey for the murders of Jean Phillips, Elizabeth Williams and Nan Downey and the attempted murder of Amy Bennett and her unborn child.

They watched as he was led away. His professional expertise had enabled him to give life a chance. He'd also destroyed it. She couldn't characterise him as evil simply because it made it easier to understand him and what he'd done. He was now on his way to his own hell once his psychological defences shattered and fell.

She watched Corrigan working calmly with his team. She'd started to heal her rift with Charlie Hanson. *Most of us are part of a family. We go beyond it to create our own lives. And if we're like Hugh Downey, we construct our own personal hells.*

She looked at Julian. 'I'm glad you're so smart,' she whispered, her hand still on her neck.

He shook his head. 'It didn't take smarts. As soon as I saw what you'd written on the board I got onto Armed Response. It reminded me of one of your first lectures I attended around four years ago. The one on sexual fetishes. That was the first time I heard of breath play.'

'In that case, I'm truly grateful for your recall ability. I would be heartened to know that all my students gave that much attention.'

He glanced down at her. 'With your subject matter, Kate, you can rely on it.'

THIRTY-EIGHT

The doors were pushed wide, opening the kitchen to the garden. Hanson in a sleeveless blue linen dress looked at the table laid under a wide parasol. Maisie had picked the tiny buttercups in their blue jug early that morning and had laid out every item of china and cutlery needed. She turned back to the kitchen where Mugger was circling one of the counters, sniffing the air. Hanson counted the little multi-coloured cupcakes and neat sandwiches, turning at a soft sound.

'What do you think?' asked Maisie, her hair in two thick plaits secured on top of her head.

Hanson surveyed the outfit: mint green short-sleeved playsuit patterned with roses, dark green tights and brown lace-up boots.

She put her arms around her. 'You look great and your grandpa will think you look wonderful.'

Maisie's pleased look was replaced by a frown. 'Do you think there's enough food?'

'Twenty cupcakes and almost as many sandwiches? I think so.'

'Will you make the tea or coffee, Mum?'

'I thought you wanted to do that?'

'No, I've changed my mind. I don't want to mess it up.'
'You won't.' The sound of the doorbell drifted to them.
'He's *here*,' squeaked Maisie.'

Smoothing her dress, running her hands through her hair, Hanson went to the door and was back almost immediately, Charlie Hanson following, his arms full of flowers.

'Maisie, this is your grandpa. Charlie, this is Maisie.'

Acknowledgements

My grateful thanks go to all at Severn House Publishers. I also wish to thank Camilla Wray, my agent at Darley Anderson for her belief and Naomi Perry for her early, positive editorial advice. Appreciation is due to two specialists in their respective fields who have yet again given generously of their time and professional advice, without which I would be 'winging-it': Chief Inspector Keith Fackrell, West Midlands Police (Retired) and Dr Adrian Young, Consultant Pathologist, Birmingham. My thanks and deep appreciation also go to Dr Geoff Oxford of the Department of Biology, University of York who shared with me a small part of his extensive professional expertise, including some glorious pictures which for many are the stuff of nightmare - many thanks, Geoff! These three experts gave freely of their time and knowledge. Any errors in transmission are, of course, entirely mine.

Finally, to my family and friends, all of them great supporters and true 'radiators' - thank you.